"This is a great mystery with exciting
twists and turns."
—*The Sunday Advocate Magazine*, Baton Rouge

AND THEN YOU DIE

"Iris Johansen keeps the reader intrigued with
complex characters and plenty of plot twists.
The story moves so fast, you'll be reading the
epilogue before you notice." —*People*

"Fans of Mary Higgins Clark will enjoy Iris
Johansen's latest, a supercharged thriller. There's
peril, romance, and suspense aplenty as the good
guys race the clock to stop the villains."
—*Alfred Hitchcock Mystery Magazine*

"A well-crafted romance thriller." —*Kirkus Reviews*

"From the first page, the reader is pulled into a
realm of danger, intrigue, and suspense with a touch
of romance and enough twists and turns to gladden
the hearts of all of her readers." —*Library Journal*

LONG AFTER MIDNIGHT

"Iris Johansen is incomparable."
—Tami Hoag, *New York Times* bestselling
author of *Ashes to Ashes*

"One of the most thrilling books I have curled
up with in a long time."
—Michael Palmer, *New York Times* bestselling
author of *Silent Treatment* and *Critical Judgment*

"You'll be racing through to the last page."
—Catherine Coulter, *New York Times* bestselling author of *The Maze*

"Flesh-and-blood characters, crackling dialogue and lean, suspenseful plotting." —*Publishers Weekly*

"A lively, engrossing ride by a strong new voice in the romantic suspense genre." —*Kirkus Reviews*

THE UGLY DUCKLING

"A real knockout...[an] intense thriller...bravo!"
—*The Atlanta Journal*

"[A] spectacular tale of revenge, betrayal, and survival." —*Publishers Weekly*

"Outstanding. A real page-turner. Many will add [Iris Johansen's] name to their list of favorite authors." —Associated Press

"A well-executed story that deftly provides chilling suspense." —*Library Journal*

"Iris Johansen keeps readers turning pages to the book's suspenseful conclusion."
—*San Antonio Express-News*

"A successful hardcover debut. As Johansen quick-cuts back and forth between the good guys and the bad, in tried-and-true Sheldonesque style, the plot eventually delivers just desserts to all—thanks to inventive surprises." —*Kirkus Reviews*

Reap the Wind

Iris Johansen

BANTAM BOOKS
New York Toronto London
Sydney Auckland

REAP THE WIND
A Bantam Book

PUBLISHING HISTORY
Bantam mass market edition published 1991
Bantam revised edition / September 2002

ISBN 0-553-58612-2

Published simultaneously in the United States and Canada

Bantam Books are published by Bantam Books, a division of Random
House, Inc. Its trademark, consisting of the words "Bantam Books"
and the portrayal of a rooster, is Registered in U.S. Patent and
Trademark Office and in other countries. Marca Registrada.
Bantam Books, 1540 Broadway, New York, New York 10036.

PRINTED IN THE UNITED STATES OF AMERICA

OPM 10 9 8 7 6 5 4 3 2 1

Reap
the Wind

Prologue

Vasaro, France
July 12, 1978

"I've been looking all over for you. What are you doing hiding here in the grove at night?" Jacques D'Abler knelt beside the girl. "You should be in bed, *ma petite*."

"It's gone too, Jacques," Caitlin whispered. "He took my necklace."

Jacques's callused hand was gentle as it stroked back her hair. "Perhaps it will come back to you someday, little one."

"No, I ran after him down the driveway but he never looked back. Mother said he doesn't love us anymore." She burrowed her face in his shoulder. "She says he'll never return to Vasaro."

"Come along to the house." He stood up and pulled her to her feet.

"Is it true?"

"Yes, I believe it is true. He will never return."

"But why did he have to take my Pegasus? I loved it so. He *gave* it to me, Jacques."

"I know he did."

"He hung it around my neck and said it made me look as pretty as my mother. I knew that wasn't the truth but—" She broke off as another sob choked her. "I'm sorry. I'm being a baby about this, aren't I?"

"Twelve isn't so old. You're entitled."

"He said that someday he'd take me to see the real Wind Dancer and we'd—"

"Shh, don't cry. The pain will go away. In the morning we'll go to the fields and you can pick the flowers. Would you like that?"

"I have to go to school tomorrow," she said dully.

"I'll make it all right with your mother."

"It was so beautiful, Jacques."

"The flowers are beautiful, too, and they'll always be here. No one can ever take them away from you."

"Never?"

"As long as you guard and nurture them, they'll be here for you." He gripped her hand. "Come. Let us get you home."

She fell into step with him. "He never really meant to take me to see the Wind Dancer, did he? It was a lie, all the others."

Jacques didn't answer.

She suddenly became aware of the sound of the cicadas and caught the heady scent of earth and the lavender growing in the north field. Jacques plodded steadily beside her, as strong and sturdy as the olive trees around them. Comfort flowed through her, soothing the raw pain and sorrow. Jacques was right, Vasaro was still there and would never betray her. She wiped her cheeks with the back of her hand. "May I really pick the lavender tomorrow?"

"We couldn't do without you." His hand tightened on her own. "Forget about that son of a—your father. Vasaro will get along better without him and so will you."

They would *have* to get along without him, for he would never return.

And neither would her beautiful golden Pegasus.

"When he gave it to me, he told me it was worth a lot of money, but I never cared about that," she whispered. "It looked just like the Wind Dancer and I thought it meant something, Jacques. When he gave it to me I hoped..."

"Hoped what?"

She had hoped it meant her father really loved her, that he would never leave her again, that things would change at Vasaro. "Never mind."

"The Wind Dancer isn't magic, Caitlin."

"I didn't say it was magic." But she believed it was. Everything had gone wrong for her, but it wasn't the Wind Dancer's fault.

With the Wind Dancer, anything was possible.

1

The jeweled eyes of the Wind Dancer, secret, enigmatic, inhumanly patient, gazed out of the black and white photograph at Alex Karazov.

The uncanny impression that a mysterious sentience exuded from the statue had to be a trick of light the lens had captured. Alex shook his head. Impossible. But now he could understand the statue's mystique and the stories that had grown up around it. The book he held was over sixty years old and the picture probably didn't even do the statue justice. He skimmed the caption beneath the picture.

"The Wind Dancer, recognized as one of the most valuable art objects in the world. The famous 'eyes of the Wind Dancer' are two perfectly matched almond-shaped emeralds 65.50 carats each. Four hundred and forty-seven diamonds encrust the base of the winged statue of Pegasus.

"In her book *Facts and Legends of the Wind Dancer*, published in 1923, Lily Andreas claimed there were historical references indicating the Wind Dancer had been in the possession of Alexander the Great during his first campaign in Persia in 323 B.C.; later, it was said to have passed to Charlemagne during his reign. Andreas's book was the subject of controversy. She claimed that a host of the most influential figures throughout the ages had not only possessed the Wind Dancer but asserted that it had contributed decisively to their success or failure. Both the antiquity of the statue and its history were challenged by the London and Cairo museums at the time."

Alex impatiently closed *Art Treasures of the World*, pushing it aside as Pavel set a stack of five more volumes on the desk. He already knew the contents of Lily Andreas's book. He remembered Ledford quoting it chapter and verse as if it were the Bible.

Pavel raised one bushy black brow. "No luck?"

Alex shook his head. "Too early. I need facts, not legends." He reached for the top book on the stack, flipped it open to the index, ran his finger down the chapter headings until he found the one labeled "Wind Dancer," then thumbed to the correct page. "For God's sake, you'd think the damn statue had disappeared from the planet." Speed-reading through the chapter, he muttered, "At least this book gets us out of the roaring twenties. It mentions the Wind Dancer's confiscation by the Germans in 1939 and its discovery in Hitler's mountain retreat after World War Two." He slammed the book shut. "But I'm wasting time. Call the curator of the Louvre and—"

"Ask where the Wind Dancer is now," Pavel finished for him. He shook his head, an amused grin creasing his weathered, heavily jowled face. "You know, of course, they'll probably try to trace the call and notify Interpol. I imagine the management of the Louvre is a bit touchy since they 'lost' the 'Mona Lisa' yesterday."

"Maybe," Alex said, abstracted. He stood up and

walked across the room to a long table on which a number of headlined newspaper articles had been cut out and arranged like pieces of a jigsaw puzzle.

MICHELANGELO'S "DAVID" DISAPPEARS FROM FLORENCE

TERRORIST GROUP BLACK MEDINA ASSASSINATES CARDINAL ON WAY TO VATICAN

POLICE BAFFLED AT REMBRANDT'S "NIGHT WATCH" THEFT FROM AMSTERDAM MUSEUM

TERRORIST GROUP BLACK MEDINA KILLS THREE IN BOMBING AT CHARLES DE GAULLE AIRPORT

"MONA LISA" STOLEN FROM LOUVRE

Several other articles lay under a jade paperweight, and Alex glanced at them as he tried to decide whether he was interested enough to commit to it. If he was right, that call would cause even more furor than Pavel believed.

Oh, what the hell. Why not? He couldn't just sit there on this damn mountaintop and let his brain grow barnacles.

"Phone anyway. Give my name and say I'm doing research for a novel. I need to know where the Wind Dancer is right now. The Andreas family lives in the U.S., but I recall an article a few years ago about French public opinion on the Wind Dancer: the average French citizen considers it a national treasure. Find out more about that if you can. Oh, the Louvre curator's name is Emile Desloge."

Pavel nodded, his black eyes twinkling as he studied Alex's intent face. "I call the Louvre and you get another piece for your puzzle." He gave a mock sigh. "And when the statue is stolen, at whose door will the police come knocking?" He lightly tapped the massive bulk of his gray-sweatered chest with one hand. "Pavel Rubanski's door. You bring me nothing but trouble. If I had any sense, I'd leave you and find a job with someone who offers less pay and greater job security."

"You'd be bored as hell." Alex grinned as he sat down at the table and drew the latest article toward him. "God knows I am."

Lumbering to the door, Pavel halted and looked back at Alex in surprise. "I'm glad you're finally admitting it. Now I can do something besides feed you information for your infernal puzzles. What's the use of being a rich man if you don't spend your money? Instead of calling the Louvre, I'll phone the travel agent and arrange a nice, sunny vacation in Martinique. You always enjoyed going to Martinique at this time of year." His tone became coaxing. "Or we'll send for Angela and one of her friends to come to the chalet for a pleasant little weekend orgy. Sex is as good as a vacation anytime."

Alex's lips twitched as he looked at the hopeful expression on Pavel's face. "And you're betting one or the other of those distractions will take my mind off the Wind Dancer."

Pavel nodded. "You may be under KGB and CIA blankets of protection, but I'm not so favored where Interpol is concerned. I'm a peaceful man who wants only a little sunshine, a little sex, maybe a fine gourmet meal now and then—"

"Now and then?" Alex smiled affectionately. "You haven't stepped on the scales lately."

"That's not fat, it's muscle. I'm a big man and I need fuel. Besides, what else can I do up here in the mountains but eat? Now, on Martinique I could just lie on the beach with a piña colada and not have to worry about snow or ice—or Interpol asking me uncomfortable questions."

"Interpol's too busy clutching at straws and chasing after every clue in sight to bother with you." Alex thought about those recent newspaper headlines and frowned. "I wonder if that's part of it. . . ."

"Part of what?"

Alex didn't answer, his mind busily sorting out information, drawing conclusions, discarding them, moving the information to new positions, drawing other conclusions, and fitting pieces together until they formed a picture with which he could be satisfied.

"Never mind," Pavel grumbled. "I might as well live on this blasted mountain by myself. No one can talk to you when you're working on one of your puzzles. It's not as if you had to do it for a living anymore. You're a damn addict." He swung the door shut behind him.

Was Pavel right? Alex wondered. Probably. He had worked at the task too long and knew too well the heady exhilaration of finally solving a puzzle. After Afghanistan he had thought he would never delve willingly into a project again, but he hadn't counted on the habits the years had formed. Since he had come to St. Basil he had drifted back into the pattern of gathering information and projecting events for his own amusement on subjects as widely varied as the rise and fall of the New York stockmarket to which countries would host future Olympic Games.

But this new puzzle was much more intriguing than any he had ever run across, and Alex could feel the adrenaline begin to flow through his veins as excitement gripped him. He felt *alive*, functioning at the top of his form once more.

One hour later Pavel entered the study and tossed a legal pad on the table in front of Alex.

"Here it is. The Wind Dancer is owned presently by Jonathan Andreas."

"Where is it?"

"At the Andreas compound in Port Andreas, South

Carolina. Andreas is one of the wealthiest men in America and the compound is bristling with bodyguards and security people. The house has a state-of-the-art security system."

"So did the Louvre," Alex said dryly. "It didn't prevent thieves from stealing the 'Mona Lisa.'" He looked down at the notes on the yellow legal pad. "What's this about Vasaro?"

"Vasaro, the estate, is located near Grasse in France and raises flowers for the perfume industry. The family Vasaro is distantly related to the Andreases; it was the French cousins who convinced Jonathan Andreas's father to lend the Wind Dancer to the Louvre in 1939 to earn money to ransom eleven Jewish artists held hostage by the Germans. Five years ago, while she was attending the Sorbonne, a Caitlin Vasaro did a research paper on the significance of the Wind Dancer in history that was used as the cornerstone for a doctorate study by Andre Beaujolis."

"Do the Vasaros have any claim to the Wind Dancer?"

Pavel shook his head. "But the French government challenged the Andreas family in 1876 on the grounds that Marie Antoinette's gift wasn't legal under the revolutionary assembly. They lost the suit." He paused. "You think the Wind Dancer is going to be heisted next?"

"Probably not."

"Then may I ask why I've spent almost an entire hour on the phone with an extremely suspicious French curator?"

"Every art object stolen has been of major cultural importance to the countries of Europe. The statue of David in Italy, the 'Night Watch' in Holland, now the 'Mona Lisa' in France. The Wind Dancer would be a prime candidate for theft if it was still in Europe." Alex shrugged. "But it's not likely to be a target while it's safe on U.S. soil. Too bad."

"I'm sure Jonathan Andreas doesn't think so."

Alex chuckled, his blue eyes suddenly sparkling in his tanned face. "Why the hell are you so glum?"

"Because you're not. You're excited as hell and operating on all cylinders. You're on the trail of something. I know you, Alex."

Alex gazed at him innocently.

"Why did you have me call the Louvre when I could have found out what you wanted to know by tapping Goldbaum or one of the usual newspaper sources?"

"Interpol won't bother you, Pavel."

"But you did want me to stir something up when I made the call."

Alex nodded. "I had a hunch and wanted to leap-frog a few obstacles. Don't worry, it won't put your neck on the line."

"I'm not worrying. My neck has been on the line before." Pavel smiled. "Remember that prisoner at Diranev? I thought I'd had it for sure before you stepped in and chopped him."

"You owed me money. I had to keep you alive to collect."

"And all this time you had me convinced you'd done it because of the nobility of your soul."

"How could that be when I don't even know the meaning of the word *nobility*?"

"But you know the meaning of the word *friendship*," Pavel said softly.

Alex quickly looked down. "Lord, you're getting maudlin in your old age."

"I'm merely playing cleverly on your sympathy to gain what I want from you."

"And what do you want?"

"Martinique. I can't stand all this snow. It reminds me of Diranev. Why you decided to buy a house in Switzerland baffles me."

"It's one of the few countries left on earth that permits a man to live with a minimum of red tape."

"I can stand a little red tape if it gets me out of the ice and snow." He stared pleadingly at Alex. "Martinique?"

Pavel looked like a wistful puppy gazing at a bone just out of reach, Alex thought with affection. "Okay. Martinique. After I finish with—"

"Dammit, the next ice age will be here by the time you get to the end of this one." Pavel turned away and strode toward the door. "I should have sent for Angela without asking you. You're much more open to suggestion when you're operating on a physical and not a cerebral level."

"Pavel."

"Yes?"

"I'm expecting a call. Put it through right away, will you?"

"Who?"

"Ledford."

Pavel's eyes widened in astonishment. "Christ," he whispered.

"Hardly." Alex's lips twisted sardonically. "Our friend Ledford is much closer to Lucifer."

"You think he's responsible for all this?" Pavel nodded at the news clippings.

"Some of it bears his stamp. Ledford's always displayed a certain flamboyance and he headed several of the Agency's operations involving art objects before they assigned him to me."

"I'd forgotten that." Pavel frowned, trying to remember

the details. "He stole back that Del Sarto used to ransom a Portuguese diplomat in Brazil, didn't he?"

"Among many others."

"It's a CIA operation?"

"At first I thought so. Not now."

"Then what?"

Alex shrugged. "Perhaps we'll find out when Ledford phones."

Pavel's eyes narrowed. "That's why you had me call the Louvre. You didn't really think the Wind Dancer was the next target. You were issuing an invitation."

"More in the nature of a summons." Alex grinned. "Ledford always has had a passion for the Wind Dancer. He used to rave about it. He'll understand what my inquiry about the statue means."

"You believe the curator is collaborating with Ledford?"

"He's probably in contact with Ledford or whoever stole the 'Mona Lisa.' Security was too tight at the Louvre for anyone but the curator to be able to bypass it."

"Bribery?"

"It would have to be extravagant bribery. I'd say in the multimillions."

"That doesn't make any sense. Why pay millions to steal a painting that can't be fenced? Even a closet collector wouldn't risk buying a painting as famous as the 'Mona Lisa.' "

"An interesting question." Alex leaned back in his chair. "We'll have to find out, won't we?"

"Ledford won't discuss this over the phone. He'll come here."

"Probably."

"It's a mistake, Alex. If it is Ledford, you shouldn't have let him know you're on to him."

"He'll be no problem. I've dealt with him before."

"But you were on the same side."

"He's a bastard but not capable of any major mischief."

"He could have changed." Pavel grimaced. "He was different with you, and I believe you're underestimating him." He left the study.

Alex stared down at the yellow pad, doodling absently with a pen, drawing circles around the word *Vasaro*, underlining *Wind Dancer*, scrawling four question marks after the name *Jonathan Andreas*. Maybe Pavel was right and Alex was taking a risk. When he had spotted the possibility that Ledford was involved in the puzzle, his interest had escalated. His past dealings with the man had left a sour taste in his mouth, and he had looked forward to pulling this particular devil's tail. But perhaps this god-awful boredom was clouding his judgment and leading him to take chances he wouldn't ordinarily take.

Well, it was done now. If Ledford was involved, he now knew Alex was interested. Alex could only wait for Ledford to react.

Impatiently, he threw the pen aside, rose to his feet, and moved across the room to stand looking out the window at the snow-capped peaks of the Alps. The leaden gray sky hovered over the mountains while blacker clouds roiled in from the north. A storm was coming. It was the middle of June, and the storms should be over, but this year the weather throughout Europe had been unusual. Freak ice storms and torrential rains had deluged Italy and southern France and a blizzard had smothered Germany and Switzerland in snow just last month. Evidently St. Basil was going to be buffeted by yet another storm within the next few hours. Not that it mattered. The chalet was well stocked, had its own generator, and Alex rather liked the feeling of isolation created by banks of snow. He could adjust to society when necessary but preferred a solitary state. Even after all these years Pavel couldn't understand why Alex didn't share his gregariousness, his love for the company of others.

Yes, Alex thought, the fact that another storm was definitely on the way was of little importance.

"No!"

The agonized cry tore from Caitlin Vasaro's throat as she looked in horror at the darkening sky to the north. She had prayed the weather report would be wrong. Dear Lord, how she had prayed. "Not now. Blast it, give me one more day."

"Caitlin? What is it, dear?" Her mother's concerned voice came from the breakfast table behind Caitlin. "Is something wrong?"

"Wrong? There's a storm coming. The roses..." Caitlin whirled away from the window and ran toward the kitchen door. "All I needed was one more day, dammit. Why the *hell* couldn't I have had one more day?"

"Can't you wait until you finish your lunch? I spent two hours preparing—what difference will thirty minutes make?" A tiny frown marred Katrine Vasaro's unlined face, and her expertly made-up lips pursed in disapproval. "You're too thin. You can't afford to miss another meal." Her expression brightened. "Maybe the storm will go around us."

Caitlin glanced at her mother in disbelief. "You're worried about me missing a meal? Don't you understand? It's the *roses*. They're not in full bloom yet and we'll have to pick them anyway before the damn storm ruins them. Can't you—"

Why couldn't her mother understand? Caitlin wondered, exasperated. The roses weren't their most expensive crop, but they were by far their most popular. After the other losses they had suffered earlier in the year, they were fortunate the bank hadn't foreclosed on Vasaro two months ago. Caitlin had counted on the rose harvest to stall them a little while longer. She opened her lips to spit out the bitter words and then closed them again. It wouldn't do any good. Vasaro had never meant much to her mother, who regarded it as a mere business and would be happier living in Cannes or Monte Carlo. As Caitlin flung open the door, she tried to control the unsteadiness of her voice. "No, I can't wait until after I eat lunch, Mother."

The next moment she was racing from the manor house and down the hill toward the road. Across the road the rose field stretched out before her as far as the eye could see, the half-open blossoms glowed deep crimson in the sunlight. The sheer velvet beauty of the rich crimson moved her greatly.

There is no love like that snatched from beneath the shadow of the sword.

Where had she read those words? Oh, God, and how she did love Vasaro! She was suddenly conscious of how much she cared for every inch of the rich rolling fields, the orange and the olive groves, the vineyards.... Usually, she scarcely noticed the scents, but now in the sultry air the fragrance was overwhelming.

Beneath the shadow of the sword...

The sun was shining brilliantly and the sky overhead was a clear blue, but on the horizon hovered those ominous clouds.

Jacques D'Abler, her overseer, already had the workers streaming down the rows of rosebushes deep into the fields. All morning he had been watching the weather with the same anxiety as had Caitlin and acted as soon as the clouds edged the horizon. As she reached the rose field, Jacques was standing with legs astride on the bed of the ancient pickup truck, tossing down a huge wicker basket to each worker, cracking orders like the captain at the helm of his ship.

"Too bad," Jacques said quietly.

"Don't *say* that. It's not going to beat us. We're going to do it." Caitlin's green-gray eyes glittered fiercely up at him. She whirled toward Jean Baptiste Dalmas, who was picking in the row closest to the road. "Take the sedan and go to the Meunier farm and tell them we need their pickers for two hours. Only two hours." She hurled the car keys to him. "Tell them we'll pay them double. Hurry!"

Jean Baptiste bolted up the hill toward the driveway.

Jacques shook his head. "The Meuniers won't release their people."

"They might. They don't grow roses and I *need* them. God, how I need them. We have forty-two workers. If they'll lend us twenty more, we might make it."

"How will you pay them?"

"I'll find the money somewhere. Did you send someone to the village school to get the children?"

"Of course." Jacques gestured at the children picking roses beside their parents in the field.

"I'm sorry." She shook her head wearily. "I know you've done your best."

"I hoped the weather report was wrong."

"Me too." She smiled tremulously. "Mother Nature seems to have it in for us this year." She glanced at the darkening sky. "How long do you think we have?"

Jacques shrugged. "It's moving slow. Maybe two hours . . . if we're lucky."

"We're not lucky. We'd better count on one hour."

She looked at the men, women, and children working in the fields. Their experienced fingers picked the crimson roses and threw them into the baskets with feverish speed. She felt a thrill of pride. "An hour may be enough the way they're working."

"They know what losing the rose crop would mean to you. They're your people, Caitlin."

"Yes, they're my people." Her glance roamed the field. Guilleme Poiren, Pierre Ledux, Renée Boisson, Marianne Juniet, and many of the rest were like her own family. She had grown up with them, played in their parents' cottages, chased after fireflies in secret nightly trysts in the orange groves. She had even acted as godmother to many of those children trailing after their mothers down the row of rosebushes. "I've got to get to work." Caitlin grabbed a wicker basket from the bed of the pickup. "When the Meunier workers get here, set eighteen of them picking and keep two workers to help you empty the baskets. Be sure to keep those baskets emptied." She strode down the row of rosebushes, set her basket down beside Renée Boisson's, and began to pick the blossoms.

Six-year-old Gaston came running past her with a basket, his small face alight with excitement. "Caitlin, we got out of school!"

"I know, Gaston. But now you must be very grown-up and help me for a little while. It's very important."

"*Oui*, I will pick more than anyone in the whole field." He raced on down the row to where his mother, Adrienne Kijoux, was picking.

"Maybe it's not so bad." Renée didn't look at Caitlin as she finished one more bush and moved down the row to start another. "What can one day matter?"

"The difference between a high yield of potent scent and a low yield of mediocre scent." Caitlin was tossing blossom after blossom into the basket. "You know that as well as I do, Renée. For God's sake, we're even picking in the afternoon instead of the morning, when the scent would be strongest. We'll be lucky if we—" She started to laugh. "Now I'm doing it. I told Jacques we couldn't count on luck." She cast an anxious glance at the sky. Were the clouds moving faster? She whispered, "But there doesn't seem to be anything else to count on."

Renée gave her a sympathetic look as she moved on.

Caitlin worked quickly, her heart pounding, her mouth dry, trying not to focus on anything but the next blossom to be picked. The air was becoming hotter, more humid, more difficult to breathe. The pickers on all sides of her were unusually quiet. Ordinarily, the harvesting was accompanied by chatter, gossip, the rare philosophical discussion, but now even the children were silent.

Where the hell were those Meunier workers?

Jacques moved through the rows, exchanging empty baskets for the full ones, carrying the brimming baskets of blossoms to the pickup truck, and emptying them into the huge tubs.

"Caitlin?"

Caitlin glanced up to see her mother standing beside her, a tentative smile on her lips. "I know you were upset with me, and I want to help. I realize I won't be very fast, but I want to do my part." Katrine moistened her lips. "May I share your basket?"

Caitlin's eyes widened in surprise, and for the first time since she had seen the storm clouds felt the urge to smile. Katrine stood there in her perfectly tailored white Dior slacks and silk blouse, every dark hair of her chignon in place, her carefully manicured fingernails painted the most fashionable shade of mocha, and her expression as earnest as that of a small child begging a treat.

By the saints, this was all she needed, Caitlin thought

desperately. Mother was having a guilt trip and Caitlin was expected to make everything all right. For an instant she was tempted to refuse Katrine and send her back to the house.

"I used to pick the flowers when I was a child." Katrine smiled uncertainly and said again, "I want to help."

Caitlin hesitated before smothering a resigned sigh. "Of course you can share my basket. We need all the help we can get."

Katrine's smile widened happily, and she began to pick the blossoms with precise movements. "It's really quite nice down here, isn't it? I remember when my father lifted me on his shoulders and carried me through the fields. You never knew your grandfather, Caitlin. He was a big man and he laughed a lot. I wish you . . ."

A gust of cool wind touched Caitlin's cheeks, and she lifted her head to gaze at the horizon, no longer hearing Katrine's chatter. The clouds were writhing and seething.

Jacques paused beside her, carrying an overflowing basket of rose blossoms. "Jean Baptiste is back."

Caitlin turned toward him, her heart leaping with hope.

Jacques shook his head. "The Meuniers wouldn't release the workers. Their lavender is in bloom and they need them."

"Damn!" Caitlin glanced anxiously at the sky again.

"Wind." Jacques's gaze followed her own. "Strong wind. It's going to be a mean one."

Caitlin's teeth sank into her lower lip. "Fifteen minutes?"

"Ten." Jacques strode down the row toward the truck.

Ten minutes. And so far they had barely managed to harvest a quarter of the field. Caitlin felt the panic begin to rise within her as she reached out blindly to the bush in front of her and began to pick again. The minutes were flying; her fingers couldn't keep pace.

The wind quickened, tugging at her short tan curls, bringing the scent of rain and roses to her nostrils.

The sun disappeared and the fields were bathed in that queer golden light that precedes the storm.

Caitlin could hear an uneasy murmur, like the rustle of dry leaves, from the pickers as they worked faster.

The first low rumble of thunder sounded.

Her fingers fumbled frantically, as if they had never before harvested a blossom.

Caitlin was conscious of her mother's voice speaking to her, but she could no longer distinguish the words.

Jacques shouted to the workers to bring in their baskets.

She kept on picking.

A large raindrop splattered on her cheek and tickled its way down her neck.

"Caitlin." Jacques's voice was very gentle beside her. "The storm has come. Let me take your basket to the truck."

Caitlin looked up at him in wild protest.

The golden haze had disappeared and the field was cloaked in shadow. The wind tore at Jacques's short gray-peppered hair and flattened his white chambray shirt against the powerful muscles of his chest. "Give it up, Caitlin. You know the workers won't stop until you leave the field."

She looked at the pickers standing silently, watching her. If she kept on working, they would stay in the field by her side even through a deluge and pick wind-ruined and water logged blossoms.

Their loyalty brought tears that were quickly slapped away by the stinging wind.

She straightened and wiped her hands on the front of her jeans. "Take the basket." Her voice was uneven, and she had to steady it before she raised it to ring out over the rumble of thunder. "It's over. We've done our best. My deepest thanks to each of you. Hurry and take shelter."

Men, women, and children ran down the rows, tossing the last of their loads of blossoms onto the bed of the truck before setting off at a trot for the village over the hill.

"I think we did very well, don't you?" Katrine asked complacently as she started toward the truck.

Not well enough, Caitlin thought numbly, moving slowly after her mother. Not nearly well enough.

"Hurry, Caitlin." Katrine's pace quickened as the rain began to fall in torrents. "I don't know why I didn't think to bring my umbrella. Now I'll have to go to Cannes to the hairdresser tomorrow."

Caitlin watched as Jacques tied the tarpaulin over the bed of the pickup truck. "You go on up to the house, Mother. I'll go with Jacques to the processing shed."

"If you're sure." Katrine shivered delicately. "I do hate to get wet. It must be the feline in me. I've always thought if I were reincarnated, I'd like to be a white Persian. I can see myself lolling on a huge satin pillow with a topaz collar to match my eyes. . . ." She glanced back over her shoulder. "Did I help a little, Caitlin?"

Caitlin smiled with an effort. "You helped a great deal, Mother. Now go on up to the house and change those clothes. We don't want you catching cold."

Katrine nodded. "I'll make you a nice hot meal. One of my lamb specialities." She set off toward the manor, picking her way as daintily as the Persian to which she had compared herself.

Jacques had finished tying down the tarp and jumped from the bed of the truck as Caitlin came up. "Not as bad as it could be."

Caitlin looked back at the field now being ravaged by wind, beaten unmercifully by the downpour. Her aching sense of loss had nothing to do with the devastation of the harvest itself. Something fragile and beautiful was being destroyed before her eyes, something that was part of her roots, heart, and memory.

"Coming?" Jacques climbed into the cab of the truck.

"You don't need me. I'll walk up to the shed in a little while."

He watched her standing in the rain, her jeans and T-shirt plastered to her tall, thin body, her eyes filled with pain. He didn't argue. He knew it would do no good. "You'll make up your loss when you market your perfume." His gentle smile was a flash of white, uneven teeth in his wrinkled brown face. "And there's always the new growth next season."

But they both knew that some of these bushes would not survive a storm of this ferocity after their roots had been weakened by earlier storms that had battered them. And, as for the perfume, how could they market it when every franc went toward just surviving? Still, Jacques would not give up hope, and neither must she. She had learned through bitter experience that if you wanted anything in this world, you had to hold on with bulldog tenacity until you got it. They had lost and won many battles over the years; this was only one more. Caitlin nodded. "When I sell my perfume."

She stepped back to the side of the road and waved him on. Jacques put the truck into gear and the vehicle lumbered down the gravel road curving up toward the long stone buildings that lay beyond the manor house.

Caitlin ran to a hillside shelter. She sat in wet grass

and drew up her legs, linking her arms around her knees. The storm was denuding the rosebushes with a cruelty the pickers would never have shown. Some bushes were being uprooted by the wind, and crimson blossoms were lying everywhere, beaten into the mud, carried by the rivers of water gushing down the rows toward the road.

The storm continued for another hour, and Caitlin sat it out watching the destruction, waiting for the end.

Late in the afternoon the rain finally stopped, and a weak, watery lemon-yellow sun came out from behind the clouds. Caitlin stood up and moved slowly down the hill. They had lost at least half the bushes in the field.

But Caitlin hadn't stayed to be a guest at the wake. She had remained because she needed the reassurance that no matter how tortured by circumstance or nature, Vasaro always survived. The earth was always waiting to be nourished and come alive again.

She knelt and gathered a handful of muddy earth, cool and damp and alive as Vasaro was alive. She felt a sense of comfort flow through her in a warm stream, a balm to the rawness of the pain. Everything would be all right. She could get through this. She just had to be as strong as Vasaro. She would have to work harder, be cleverer, find a way to convince those people at the bank that Vasaro was more than a mortgage or a deed.

Her hand closed tightly on the damp earth.

Life.

"He's here, Alex." Pavel threw open the door and stepped aside to allow Brian Ledford to enter Alex's study. "Will you need me?"

"Of course we won't need you." Brian Ledford shrugged

out of his beaver-collared overcoat as he strolled into the room.

Pavel ignored him. "Alex?"

Alex shook his head.

Pavel hesitated, frowning uneasily, his gaze on Ledford. Then he shrugged his massive shoulders and shut the door.

"Cautious bastard. I'd forgotten how protective Pavel was of you." Ledford tossed his overcoat on the brown leather couch. "Good God, it's cold out there. I hope you appreciate my sacrifice in coming out in this weather to see you."

Beneath his coat Ledford wore a Savile Row gray tweed suit; he pulled steel-gray Italian leather gloves from his hands and unwound a blue cashmere scarf from his strong, thick neck. Other than Ledford's sartorial elegance, he looked little different from the man Alex had last seen five years before. His short, kinky dark blond hair had a little more gray threading it, his tall, deep-chested frame carried a few more pounds, but the broad, rawboned features were exactly the same, and so was the expression of boundless good humor beaming from his ruddy face and bright hazel eyes.

His voice boomed out heartily. "Ah, Alex, my boy, how good it is to see you again. When I spoke to you on the phone last night, I admit I was a little irritated with you, but I realize now how foolish it is to let present conflicts interfere with our fondness for each other." He smiled as he dropped into the deeply cushioned chair across from where Alex was standing by the window. He laid the gray gloves he still held on his lap before stretching out his heavily muscled legs and crossing them at the ankle. "Sometimes I miss those days in Virginia. I even miss our chess games." He grimaced. "I suppose that makes me a masochist, because I never won. But I'm an optimistic man, and there was always hope even when pitting myself against the Company's superman."

For an instant Alex felt himself being swept away by Ledford's charisma as he had so many years before. Then memory returned and he could look at him with clear eyes. He warily shook his head. "I'm afraid I never missed either you or those days, Ledford."

Ledford tossed the light blue cashmere scarf aside. "I gather you're not in the mood for pleasantries? Well then, let's get down to business. How much do you know?"

"You're part of the group behind the art thefts. It's probably a well-organized, well-funded operation." Alex smiled faintly. "And the thefts are only part of something bigger in scope."

Ledford nodded approvingly. "Anything else?"

Alex kept his expression bland as he took a wild shot. "Black Medina."

Ledford threw back his head and laughed. "When we started the operation, I expected you to make the connection eventually and I warned my associate that you'd be a danger to us." He shook his head. "He wouldn't believe me. You do have to admit you're pretty unbelievable at times."

Alex felt a ripple of excitement. Jackpot. He'd been right about the connection. "Associate? We're not talking about the Company, are we?"

"I left the CIA after you pulled off your grand slam and bolted the fold. I'm involved in much more lucrative endeavors now." He looked around the study with appraising eyes. "Gorgeous place, Alex. Excellent taste. I particularly admire that van Gogh you have in the foyer. The entire chalet is just what I would have expected of you. Private, aesthetic, and yet a touch of the voluptuous in color and fabric. You always were some-thing of a Renaissance man." His glance shifted to the stack of books on the desk. "An excellent library?"

"Of course."

Ledford nodded. "A stupid question. That inquiring brain has to be fed. I remember how you devoured every book in sight when you defected to us. I had to keep running out to the libraries and bringing you more." He gazed directly into Alex's eyes. "We were good friends then, weren't we, Alex?"

"Tolerable."

"You liked me." Ledford grinned. "Admit it. You thought I was Uncle Sam and Mark Twain rolled into one."

"You shouldn't congratulate yourself too much. I was easy. I was at a stage where I needed to believe in some-thing or someone." He inclined his head in agreement. "But yes, you were very good, indeed."

Ledford nodded. "You bet I was. The best. And I've gotten better since we parted ways. I consider my time in the CIA as basic training. I'm now reaching my full potential."

"You wouldn't be here if you'd gotten better. You're still predictable, Ledford."

"Only to you. We all have our own nemesis, and you're mine." He paused. "And I'm yours, Alex." He smiled. "May I have a drink?"

"No."

Ledford snapped his fingers. "I knew you'd say that. You, too, are predictable. You won't serve an enemy in your own house. There's something positively medieval about you at times, Alex."

Alex shrugged. "First I'm a Renaissance man and now I'm medieval. Make up your mind."

"I was right both times. You're brilliant and ruthless as any Medici and yet you have a certain code." He shook his head. "Such codes limit an ambitious man. I wonder how you've climbed as high as you have with that albatross around your neck." His brow wrinkled as he gazed at Alex. "And you've never learned the cardinal rule."

"I'm sure you're going to enlighten me as to what that is."

Ledford made a clucking noise. "Sarcasm isn't necessary. I was counting on conducting a nice, friendly conversation." He sat up straighter in his chair. "The cardinal rule is adaptation. Change your coloration to suit your surroundings."

"Some people would call that hypocritical."

"Only the fools of the world. And you're no fool, even if you do make mistakes."

"What mistakes are you referring to?"

"Having Pavel make that call to Desloge. You might as well have blown a whistle and waved your arms. First I was steaming mad, but then I was almost glad you decided to put your hand in. My feelings about you have always been ambivalent." He tilted his head, studying Alex. "You know you're a beautiful specimen. I was quite mad about you at one time. It was hard as hell to keep myself from trying to seduce you when we were working so closely together." He burst out laughing and slapped his hand on his knee as he saw the astonishment on Alex's face. "That rocked you. God, you never knew, did you?"

"No."

Ledford shrugged. "They were a macho bunch at the Company. One false step and I would have been out. Adaptation."

"I see."

"But you were a real temptation to me. You frustrated me sexually and bested me mentally." Ledford's smile faded. "I think that's why I started to hate you."

Alex leaned back against the windowsill. "Not because I beat you at chess?"

"Well, that too. I hate to lose. It hurts my pride not to be the best at whatever I do. How could I compete against that damn talent of yours?" His index finger idly rubbed the leather on the arm of the chair. "But I adapted. I became your buddy."

"And my controller," Alex added without expression.

"Someone had to do it. All that wild talent just waiting to be used...." He shook his head regretfully. "You made me look damn good until that conscience of yours kicked into gear. You weren't intended to know about the results of the Afghanistan project." A glint of anger appeared on his face. "When you exploded you brought a good deal of humiliation down on my head. I suppose it was Pavel who told you?"

"Yes."

"I advised the Agency against accepting Pavel when you both came over. I knew it would be better to isolate you."

"I wouldn't have defected without him."

"Ah, friendship... What a wonderful thing it is." Ledford smiled. "You've been together for how many years?"

"Thirteen. We met when we were both in the Spetznez. As you well know." Alex turned away from the window and stared at Ledford. "And you didn't come here to praise the merits of friendship."

"No, I came here to tell you to back off. This is a bigger operation than anything you could dream." Ledford stood up in one lithe, leisurely movement. "Stay on your mountaintop and work your puzzles. Leave the real world to those who are prepared to deal with it."

"Is that what your 'associate' wants?"

Ledford's smile remained but became set in place. "I

should have known you'd guess we weren't in agreement. No, he wants you on the team. He regards you as a valuable asset." His voice lowered in silken softness. "I would find that intolerable. I won't take second place ever again."

"No?" Alex's tone was deliberately mocking. "Pity. You filled it so well."

"You don't understand, do you? When you left the Company, everything for which I'd worked for fifteen years came crashing down around me. In another two years I would have taken over McMillan's job and been able to launch myself to the top, where I belonged." A flush reddened Ledford's cheeks. "I didn't leave the Company; they jettisoned me because I wasn't clever enough to see you were going after McMillan. I was pretty frenzied for a while. I wanted to take everything away from you, as you'd taken it from me. I regard it as a triumph of self-discipline that I've managed to subdue my anger and ignore you all these years." Ledford's eyes narrowed on Alex's face. "You've never understood the real reason I developed such a passion for the Wind Dancer, have you?"

"It's a magnificent work of art."

"And the ultimate symbol of power. From the moment I saw it, I knew it would always be a beacon, showing me what I could be."

"Delusions of glory?"

"Not delusions. Truth. You've got everything you want now. Money, security, women. Why dabble when it won't benefit you?"

"Perhaps because it's an interesting problem. You should know how difficult I find it to resist solving problems. At one time you used that weakness of mine." Why was he goading Ledford? Alex wondered wearily. He had thought he had put his antagonism and disillusionment about Ledford behind him, yet he found he was experiencing a perverse pleasure in taunting the man. It was rather like teasing a rattlesnake just to hear it rattle. "And it gets a little boring at times on my mountaintop."

Ledford nodded with immediate understanding. "I remember boredom was always a problem for you. Boredom and curiosity. You really should remember that curiosity killed that proverbial cat." He glanced at his wristwatch and smiled. "Well, I must run along. It was good seeing you and reliving old times."

Alex stiffened at the abruptness of Ledford's departure. "You're leaving?"

"My driver and two of my subordinates are in the living room waiting. I have to get to the airport while the weather is still clear." Ledford picked up his coat and put it on. "I knew when I came here it would be useless. You're obviously not going to be influenced by words, and I'm a very busy man."

"Another 'Mona Lisa' to steal?"

"We both know there's only one 'Mona Lisa.'" He tugged on his leather gloves. "Just as there's only one Alex Karazov."

Alex inclined his head in a mocking bow. "I'm now waiting for the shaft."

"No shaft. I told you my feelings for you were ambivalent." Ledford flexed his big hands, obviously enjoying the feel of the soft leather against his palms. "But I won't compete with you in my own arena, so I'll just have to discourage you from entertaining any offers."

"Which means?"

"I'd rather have you as an enemy than on the same team. Oh, I know I can't touch you at the moment. What a clever lad you were to get both the CIA and the KGB in a stranglehold. We really don't want to involve them in our plans right now." Ledford's broad smile brimmed with goodwill as he added, "By the way, you did know that luscious Italian model you've been screwing is a KGB swallow?"

"I've suspected it. I wasn't sure if she belonged to them or to the CIA," Alex said without inflection. "Angela's affiliations don't really affect our relationship one way or the other."

Ledford nodded. "You always were a cynical bastard where women were concerned. I thought you were too savvy to form an attachment with even the most skilled whore they could produce." He picked up his cashmere scarf and moved toward the door. "Still, there was the faintest possibility you cared something for her. Why don't you give her a call?"

Alex stiffened. "Is that a threat?"

"No, just a suggestion." He stared at Alex. "You're still finding it hard to see me as I really am. You remember me only as the man you knew five years ago. I told you I'd graduated from basic training and I assure you that I don't hesitate to make examples these days. Sometimes I even enjoy it. Good-bye, Alex. Our little chat has been pleasant. I do hope you won't force me to look you up again."

Alex felt a chill along his spine as he watched the door close behind Ledford. Those last words *had* been a threat and his reference to Angela no coincidence. Pavel was right; Alex had made a mistake in underestimating Ledford.

Christ, he hoped it wasn't too late!

He moved quickly to the desk, picked up the receiver, and punched in Angela Di Marco's number at her apartment in Rome.

No answer.

Alex listened to the ringing at the other end of the

line, the panic rising in him. Nothing had to be wrong. It was only midnight. Angela could be out for the evening or indulging in one of her frequent sexual encounters and not bothering to answer the phone.

"Hello." Angela's voice was impatient.

Relief surged through him. "Angela, stay in your apartment. Lock the door. If you've got anyone with you, get rid of him."

"Alex?"

"Don't argue. Just do as I say." He paused. "It might be a good idea to call your contact in the KGB and tell him to reassign you somewhere out of Europe. It's not going to be healthy for you here."

She didn't speak for a moment. "You know? It was nothing personal, Alex. I truly like you."

"I know. Nothing personal."

He hung up the receiver. His initial relief was quickly being replaced by guilt and self-disgust. He had only been amusing himself, toying with his damn puzzle, fighting boredom when he had taunted Ledford. Now the game had become serious. A woman could have died to make sure Alex would reject any bid to work for Ledford's "associate." He had underestimated Ledford, who wouldn't make him the one to suffer for it.

But Angela hadn't been hurt. Why not?

Alex closed his eyes, trying to put the pieces together.

Because Ledford knew her death would not have affected Alex in any meaningful way.

But why offer an empty threat? Why make sure that Alex would immediately make a call to Rome?

"I left my driver and two of my subordinates in the living room."

What had Ledford's men been doing while he had been talking to Alex in the study? Why did he want to make sure Alex would remain in the study and give him a chance to leave the chalet?

Alex felt a sudden cold sickness in the pit of his stomach.

Who was the only person in the entire world Alex gave a damn about?

Angela was the red herring. . . .

"Christ!" Alex's eyes flicked open. "Pavel!" He whirled and ran across the study toward the door. "Pavel? Where the hell are—"

The first thing Alex saw was the blue cashmere scarf looped around Pavel's throat.

Pavel was strapped in a white suede easy chair facing the study, a leather gag in his mouth. His black eyes bulged from their sockets and his heavy features were frozen in a rictus of agony.

He had been castrated—then carved from belly to breastbone with the butcher knife that still protruded from his chest.

2

"Someone wants to see you, Caitlin." Jacques knelt beside her on the ground, holding the rosebush Caitlin was planting while she gently pressed the earth around the roots. "He's waiting up on the hill."

Caitlin stiffened, the muscles of her shoulders going rigid before she forced herself to relax. She pressed more earth around the bush's roots. "A man from the bank?"

"I don't think so. He doesn't look—" Jacques stopped and shrugged. "I don't know how to describe him. He's hard to fit in a mold."

Caitlin glanced up the hill at the man who was only a dark silhouette against the setting sun. "He's probably selling fertilizer." She lifted her arm and wiped her perspiring forehead with the sleeve of her blue cotton shirt. "Can't you get rid of him?"

Jacques shook his head. "I tried, but he won't go." He chuckled. "And I doubt if he'd be hauling fertilizer in that Lamborghini he parked in front of the house."

"Oh, damn, he *is* from the bank."

"If he is, you can bet the auditors keep an eagle eye on him," Jacques said dryly. "Go and see what he wants. I'll take over here. You need a break anyway."

"So do you." Caitlin stood and stretched to ease her back. *Merde*, she was tired. She had been working since before dawn and there were still two rows to be planted. "I'll be back in a few minutes."

"It will be dark soon. Go on to the house and we'll start again tomorrow."

Caitlin shook her head as she wiped her hands on her jeans. "There's too much to do tomorrow. You'll be finished with the rosemary in the north field and we'll have to start picking the lavender. I'll finish up here tonight." She moved down the row of newly planted rosebushes, her gaze fixed on the man standing watching them from the hilltop. "What's his name?"

"Alex Karazov."

She frowned. "I don't think I've ever heard of him. I know I've never met him."

"You would remember if you had."

She understood what Jacques meant the moment she saw Alex Karazov. He was an exceptionally good-looking man in his mid-thirties with an athlete's slim and supple strength. He had the deep tan of a man who spent hours on the ski slopes of St. Moritz or the beaches of Antibes and, as he watched her approach, he revealed an easy smile. She tensed as she suddenly realized she might well be looking at a younger version of her father. Her father's dark hair was now touched with gray, but it had the same luster as Alex Karazov's, his smile was just as charismatic, and he wore his clothes with the same careless elegance. It was only as she studied Karazov more closely that she became aware of the keen intelligence in his ice-blue eyes, the intensity and confidence he exuded. Why wouldn't he be confident? she thought ruefully. The sport jacket he wore probably cost more than her entire wardrobe.

But, intuitively, she knew he wasn't really like her

father. Denis Reardon had no hidden depths, everything was right on the surface for everyone to see and admire. She had an idea a great deal went on behind Karazov's urbane smile. He rather reminded her of a beautiful jasmine in the first stage of blooming, closed tight, secret, full of promise. The thought made her smile. How insulted a man as blatantly masculine as Karazov would feel to be compared to a flower.

The smile still lingered as she stopped before him. "I'm Caitlin Vasaro, Monsieur Karazov." She started to hold out her hand and then stopped and made a face as she looked down at the grime on it. "You'll forgive me if I don't shake hands. I've been working and I'm filthy. I understand you wish to speak with me?"

He didn't answer her question, his gaze fixed intently on her face. "Do you always work in the fields like a common laborer?"

"There's nothing common about the laborers of Vasaro, Monsieur Karazov. They're good people, doing a good job." She met his gaze. "And I do work in the fields quite frequently."

"No offense. I merely wondered. I'm afraid I have an insatiable curiosity." He looked down at the field. "What were you doing down there?"

His French was perfect, but the accent was odd; flat like an American's yet with an Englishman's precision. She switched to English. "Planting rosebushes. The storm last month destroyed half the bushes and we have to plant new ones."

"Shouldn't roses be planted in the spring?"

He wasn't either English or American, though he appeared more at ease with the language than French. "Usually January or November. But the weather here is almost ideal for the major part of the year, so we can plant—" She broke off before adding impatiently, "I'm sure you're not interested in Vasaro's planting seasons. How can I help you?"

"It's how we can help each other. And you're wrong, I'm very interested in everything about Vasaro. I intend to invest a great deal of money in one of its products."

She stiffened. "I beg your pardon?"

"It's very simple. I have money to invest. You have a project that requires capital."

She frowned suspiciously. "What project?"

"Your perfume. I believe you applied at several banks in Cannes for a loan to market your new fragrance."

"And I was refused."

"You have to admit that launching a perfume is risky business."

"And you're familiar with the perfume industry?"

"I know a little about it. I've just finished spending a week touring several packaging houses in Paris. Before that I put in two days at the advertising agency that created the campaign for Obsession, and I spent another week with your neighbors to the south who grow roses and jasmine for Chanel No. 5. Of course, I realize it's not enough to make me an expert," he said briskly. "But I learn fast and I'm accustomed to weighing variables. I once did it as a career."

"A stockbroker?"

"I've played the stockmarket on occasion." He lifted a brow. "I thought you'd be more enthusiastic."

She shook her head dazedly. "I feel as if I've been run over by a truck. I can't think—there's something wrong. Things don't happen like this. Men in Lamborghinis don't just drop out of the blue and offer—what *are* you offering?"

"You have a new perfume to market. You've tried to borrow four hundred thousand dollars for the project."

He shook his head. "By the way, that won't be nearly enough."

"Do you think I don't know? I thought I'd try to start small, and later, when the perfume caught on, I could show figures to persuade them to lend me more. I knew four hundred thousand was the most I could borrow with the collateral I have to offer. If you're so friendly with my banker, you must know Vasaro is mortgaged."

"Ah, but your banker and other bankers in Cannes are most discreet. No, my information came from other sources, sources that also tell me you're behind in your mortgage payments." He grinned. "It does sound like an old-time melodrama, doesn't it?"

"I'm afraid I don't see the entertainment value." Caitlin wished desperately that she weren't so exhausted. She had to think calmly and clearly. "Are you comparing yourself to the villain in the piece?"

"I don't believe anyone views himself as a true villain." His gaze shifted to Jacques working in the field below, then back to Caitlin. "And I have no intention of trying to persuade you into blindly agreeing with my proposition. That would be incredibly stupid of me when you're obviously an astute businesswoman."

"Incredibly stupid."

"So why don't I go right down the line and tell you what I'm offering and what I expect in return? I'll bankroll the marketing of your new perfume to the full extent of my resources. In return, you'll give me full control of all facets of the launch of the perfume for the first year. In addition, I'll receive twenty-five percent of the profits from the sale of the perfume for the first five years it's in production. Agreed?"

"No." She felt as if someone had kicked her in the chest and knocked the breath out of her. "I have to think about it. I can't just... It's too good to be true. Something has to be wrong."

"What could be wrong? I'm not asking you to give me anything but what my money earns for both of us. Aren't you looking a gift horse in the mouth?"

She leapt wildly toward the only conclusion she could imagine possible. "You're a total stranger who knows my business intimately. It is frightening, monsieur. I can guess only you're in some illegal activity. Drug money? You're trying to launder drug money."

He burst out laughing. "There are better ways to launder drug money than through the chancy proposition of launching a perfume. Better and safer."

"You seem to know a great deal about it."

"It's not drug money. I write mystery novels." He pulled a card from the inside pocket of his jacket. "The money for the launch will be drawn from my account at the Bank of Geneva." He took out a gold Mont Blanc pen and scrawled a number on the card. "Call this number and ask for Monsieur Ganold. He's vice president of the bank and will verify both the account and the fact that the money's transferred there directly from my publisher's bank in New York."

Her hand trembled as she took the card. It was no wonder she felt almost sick with excitement. He might be a genuine investor. She mustn't let her hopes soar. This man was a stranger; his motives were obscure. This might be some sort of awful trick. *Merde*, and she was probably being too eager even to speak with him. Still, she couldn't stop herself. "Twenty-five percent is too much."

"Take it or leave it. Seventy-five percent of a successful venture is better than a hundred percent of nothing. If you don't accept my offer, you may lose Vasaro as well as any chance to launch your perfume." He paused. "Suppose I sweeten the deal by giving you an additional two hundred thousand dollars in the loan. That won't entirely pay off your mortgage, but it will keep them from worrying you until you have money coming in from the perfume."

Vasaro safe and her own again. She felt another wild leap of excitement at the thought. "You mean it?" she whispered.

He nodded, his gaze fixed on her face. "Call the bank and check me out. Then we'll talk some more."

"I will." Her heart was pounding so hard, she could scarcely speak. "Will you come up to the house and meet my mother? She actually owns Vasaro and would have to sign the papers."

"So I learned. But you run the estate?"

Caitlin nodded. "My mother isn't interested in business. Come," she said, setting off quickly toward the two-story stone manor a few hundred yards away. "But," she added, "she won't object to any agreement we reach. Mother wants only what's best for Vasaro." Had she been too hostile to him? Dear heaven, what if he were legitimate . . . and he changed his mind? To come close to saving Vasaro and then fail would kill her. "Things were different when my mother was growing up here. She doesn't understand that—but she's really very supportive." She climbed the three stone steps and opened the mahogany double doors. "I promise there will be no difficul—" Her doubts came flying back to her, and she whirled to face him. "Why are you really doing this?" She rushed on, the words tumbling out. "I know it was rude even to suggest you might be involved in some criminal—"

"Very rude." A smile tugged at his lips. "It must have been the Lamborghini."

He was laughing at her, but she didn't care as long as he wasn't angry. She mustn't risk angering him if there was the slightest chance he could save Vasaro. "Why an investment in perfume? And why did you go to the trouble to learn about Vasaro?"

He hesitated, wariness flickering for an instant in his expression, and then he was smiling again. "I didn't ask specifically about Vasaro. At first I wasn't even interested in investing. I was only doing research for a book set in a place like Vasaro. But the more I found out about the perfume industry, the more I realized the possibilities. The profits resulting from a successful perfume are astronomical."

"*Successful* is the key word."

He nodded. "Why do you think I came to you? Word has leaked that some people in the business are very impressed with your perfume, if not your bankability. You have the most fertile ground in the province and you're on the verge of bankruptcy. Actually, a takeover of the property was recommended, but I haven't the time or inclination for that type of deal. I'm a writer, not a farmer." He paused. "Trust me, I'm not interested in harvesting anything but the profits from your perfume. I don't believe there's anything illogical about wanting to make money and do research for my book at the same time, do you?"

"No." She felt a little reassured. His reasoning and motivation appeared valid on the surface. "But there's no place *like* Vasaro. There is *only* Vasaro." What he said fit together perfectly, and yet there had been that instant of hesitation. "Your accent is peculiar. Are you American?"

He nodded. "I'm an American citizen but I grew up in Romania. My father was Russian and my mother Romanian. I now live in Switzerland."

"What kind of books did you say you wrote?"

"Mysteries. My pen name is Alex Kalan."

She shook her head. "I've never heard of you."

"Pity. I'm exceptionally good."

"I don't have much time to read."

He smiled faintly. "Too busy planting rosebushes. I understand." He stepped into the flagstoned foyer. "Fortunately, there are a modest number of readers in the world who are not so occupied." He looked admiringly around the cool, airy hall, from the copper chandelier to the small landscape on the white stucco wall. "This is charming." He moved across the foyer to touch the gleaming oak banister of the staircase leading to the second floor. "And very old. Early sixteenth century?"

"Vasaro was built in 1509." Caitlin's smile lit her face. "Some of the outbuildings were built later but nothing past 1815. Many of the pieces of furniture in the house are more than three hundred years old." She raised her voice and called, "Mother."

"Here, Caitlin." Katrine's light, cheerful voice issued from the salon to the right of the foyer. "I'm glad you decided to stop early. There's no sense in your..." Katrine trailed off as she came into the foyer and caught sight of Alex Karazov. Her face brightened. "We have a guest?"

She could put Karazov safely into her mother's hands to entertain while she made the telephone call, Caitlin realized with relief. No one could be more charming and warm than Katrine when she was playing the hostess. "This is Monsieur Karazov, Mother. My mother, Katrine Vasaro. Monsieur Karazov is a novelist and may decide to invest in Vasaro."

"Really?" Katrine's smile was radiant. "How delightful, Monsieur Karazov. I'm sure Caitlin is pleased. She seems to worry so much about money these days. I always tell her that everything—"

"Will you give Monsieur Karazov a glass of wine

while I make a telephone call, Mother?" Caitlin asked quickly, her fingers toying nervously with the business card. "I'll be back in a few moments."

"Take your time." A dazzling smile in place, Alex turned to her mother. "I'm very happy to meet you, Madame Vasaro."

He was displaying the same easy charm he had shown Caitlin, and her mother was positively glowing under his smile. But then, Katrine was susceptible to attractive men of all ages.

He took her mother's hand and said over his shoulder, "I'm sure your mother and I will get along very well without you. Ask any questions that occur to you. I told Ganold to be perfectly open with you."

"I will." Surely he must be legitimate, she thought, to be so frank. "It's not that I don't trust you, but I—"

"Don't trust me." His eyes glittered in the dim light of the hall as they met her own, and the words came crisply and with none of the charm with which he'd spoken to Katrine. "You'd be a fool to trust a man who walks in and offers to solve all your problems. Self-interest rules the world. If you can prove that it's in my best interest to bail out Vasaro, then trust me. If not, send me on my way."

"I'm sure Monsieur Karazov isn't serious," Katrine said, smiling uncertainly.

And Caitlin was quite sure he was entirely serious for the first time since she had met him. She shivered uneasily as they gazed at each other. She could sense a quiet power that had been hidden before and had a feeling this was the real Alex Karazov, not the charismatic man who had reminded her of her father. This man was bold, coldly incisive, ruthless... and honest. The last quality marginally reassured her even while the other characteristics gave her pause. If Karazov was honest, what did she care if he wasn't warm and wonderful? What did she care about anything as long as he could save Vasaro?

"I'll ask my questions and, if I'm not satisfied, you'll certainly be sent away." She gave him a cool smile. "But I think we can afford to give you one glass of wine while I decide." She ignored the sudden flicker of interest in his expression and waved him and her mother toward the salon. "I'll join you shortly, Monsieur."

She closed the study door behind her and wilted back against the polished panels. Her knees were unsteady and she felt light-headed. *Mon Dieu*, she was frightened. Not of Alex Karazov, she assured herself. She was afraid for Vasaro, afraid he wasn't what he claimed to be, afraid this chance to save Vasaro would vanish as quickly as it had appeared.

There was only one way to put her fear to rest.

She straightened away from the door and moved slowly toward the telephone on the Louis XIV desk.

Caitlin Vasaro's face was radiant with excitement when she walked into the salon twenty minutes later.

Alex stiffened with shock as he looked at her and felt a purely sexual stirring. Christ, he hadn't expected this reaction. He had thought Caitlin plain when he had first caught sight of her kneeling in the dirt in her grubby jeans and sweat-stained shirt, her shoulders bent with weariness. Later, he had revised his opinion to moderately attractive when he had seen her delicate features, the glowing skin of the same tawny shade as her hair. Now, with her expression charged with vitality and her green-gray eyes blazing with emotion, she came close to beauty.

He set his glass down on the table next to his chair and rose to his feet. "I take it you're satisfied I'm not a drug dealer."

She nodded eagerly. "Monsieur Ganold has even read your books."

"Of course. He has excellent taste. Why do you think I give him my business?"

"He says you've written two books and that they're extraordinary."

"I'm strong on plot, weak on character."

She laughed. "You said before that you were wonderful."

"But now that I have someone else to praise me, I can go back to being becomingly modest."

Caitlin gestured impatiently. "We have to talk about the perfume."

He lifted a brow. "You're going to agree to my proposition?"

"Of course I am. Do you think I'm a lunatic?"

"No." He gazed at her thoughtfully. "But I think you may be that rare creature, a woman without subterfuge."

"Is that bad?"

"Not bad. Just disconcerting."

Katrine lifted her glass of wine. "Caitlin has always been very blunt. One always knows where one stands with her."

"When do I get the money to pay the bank?" Caitlin asked.

Mother of God, the woman was as open and vulnerable as a child. All her previous wariness had vanished, and Alex felt an inexplicable irritation at the knowledge she was now completely malleable. "We can go into Cannes tomorrow and transfer the money into your account. However, I'd like to get this made final tonight." He reached into the inner pocket of his jacket and brought out a document. "I had a contract drawn up with the terms I outlined. I'd appreciate it if you'd sign on all pages, Madame Vasaro. The first four are mine, the last four are your copies." He laid the contract down on the table and gestured for Caitlin to seat herself in the chair he had just vacated. "The terminology is very clear-cut, but you'll want to read them before you advise your mother to sign."

Caitlin gazed at him in surprise. "You were so sure?"

"I like to be prepared. Is there any reason you wouldn't want to conclude this business tonight?"

"No, I suppose not." She slowly sat down, picked up the contract, and began to read it carefully.

At least, Alex thought, she wasn't telling her mother to sign the contract without reading it. It had all been too easy. *She* was too easy.

"Everything appears to be in order." Caitlin looked up from the papers. "As you said, it's fairly cut and dried." She set the papers in front of Katrine. "Sign them, Mother."

Alex offered Katrine his gold pen. "On the left bottom line of each page."

Katrine nodded and signed her name neatly on every page.

"Now you." Alex turned the contracts and slid them toward Caitlin. "Right below your mother's signature on the witness line."

Caitlin hesitated an instant before quickly scrawling her name on all the pages. "There." She pushed the papers away from her with a sigh of relief. "I suppose this means we're partners."

"Yes, we're partners." He gathered up the contracts. "Now let me tell you what my partners do not do." He separated the contracts and gave four of the pages to Caitlin. "My partners do *not* sign even a grocery list without having it gone over with a magnifying glass by a lawyer. My partners do not let themselves be rushed into making decisions. My partners, most particularly, don't base a business judgment on a telephone call any fledgling con man could have set up."

Caitlin's smile faded. "And did you set it up?"

"No, but that doesn't mean—why the hell weren't you more careful?"

"I was desperate," she said simply. "What if you'd changed your mind?"

The reply only fueled his exasperation. "You shouldn't tell me you're desperate. For God's sake, *protect* yourself."

"Why? I've already signed the contract. I have to trust you now." She met his gaze. "And besides, you told me you weren't a con man."

"And you believed me?"

"I believe you. I'm a fair judge of character. God knows, I've had to be, since I've had to manage Vasaro for the last four years." She studied him for a time. "And I think you're a hard man but not a cheat."

"Of course he's not a cheat, Caitlin." Katrine was shocked. "I'm surprised at you. Monsieur Karazov is obviously a gentleman."

Alex bowed mockingly to both of them. "Thank you for your vote of confidence."

"I'm not confident," Caitlin said gravely. "I'm scared and excited and not at all sure what you want from us."

"What I want from you is in the contracts. It couldn't be more clear."

She made a face. "I may be desperate but I'm not stupid. I doubt if you've done anything since you were an infant that could be considered simple or clear."

"You disappoint me. And after that touching declaration of faith."

"I said I didn't believe you were a cheat. I guess you never let anyone know what you're thinking or what your motives are. I realize you think signing that contract wasn't a good move on my part." She shrugged. "I know how to grow the flowers and I love creating perfumes, but ledgers and accounts drive me crazy."

"Then you should have pulled in your accountant."

A faint flush rose to her cheeks and she straightened her shoulders with a touch of bravado. "All right, do you want to know the truth? I may not like that side of Vasaro, but I'm a damn good businesswoman when it's necessary. I know very well the contract could be contested in court, and I think you know it too." Her words came with cool precision. "As you probably know, French juries get very emotional about helpless women on their own being taken advantage of by foreign investors. So I figured we'd be safe enough. Tomorrow morning I'll have those contracts gone over by my lawyer *and* my accountant. If there are any difficulties, we'll add riders. If you don't agree, we'll go to court."

His expression became suddenly intent. "Why did you sign it if you didn't think it was valid?"

"For the same reason you drew up the contract in the first place. A court case is a hassle most people prefer to avoid. My signing the contract made it very difficult for either of us to back out of the deal. I also made another call besides the one to Monsieur Ganold while I was in the study. I called Henri LeFabre, the loan officer at my own bank in Cannes, and asked him to verify that the telephone number was really that of the Bank of Geneva and that Monsieur Ganold was an officer of the bank." She met his gaze directly and she added fiercely, "And I don't *care* what you hope to get out of this deal as long as you give me the money to save Vasaro. I've protected Vasaro from everything else and I can protect it from you too. I'm glad you rushed me into signing, because now you're committed to Vasaro as much as we're committed to you."

She was alive again, all coolness gone, burning with such an intensity of emotion he felt as if he could feel its heat. One moment she had seemed naive and uncertain and the next she was a powerhouse.

He stared at her for a moment longer and then threw back his head and started to laugh. "My God, and I thought you were guileless as a lamb. You were trying to snare me."

"No, I was merely letting you snare me. You were right, I do hate subterfuge. But I do what I have to do for Vasaro." She turned to Katrine, who was staring at her with trepidation. "I imagine Monsieur Karazov will be staying for supper. Is Sophia preparing the meal tonight?"

Katrine immediately shook her head. "Of course not. I wouldn't think of allowing her to do it. I'll take care of it myself. This is a very special occasion."

"My mother is a Cordon Bleu cook, Monsieur Karazov. You're in for a treat. Don't you think you'd better start the preparations, Mother?"

"Oh, yes, I'll do that."

"She's very obedient," Alex said as soon as Katrine disappeared from view. "It must make things easy for you."

"Sometimes," Caitlin said absently, and then, when she realized what he meant, added defensively, "I don't manipulate her. You don't understand. My mother likes everything to be easy. She doesn't want to have to worry about—" She dismissed the subject as unimportant. "Perhaps I assumed too much. Are you going to stay for supper?"

"I'd be delighted."

"Where are you staying? Cannes?"

He nodded.

"A hotel?"

"The Majestic."

"We can offer you a room here if you'd really like to use Vasaro for your research."

"You're most obliging."

"I've signed a contract. It's only honorable to try to keep to the spirit as well as the letter of an agreement."

"Not many people conduct business in that way any longer. I'm afraid the 'spirit' has fallen by the wayside."

"Not at Vasaro. Do you wish to come here?"

He nodded. "For a little while. It will probably be more convenient for me to be on the spot since we need to make plans."

"Plans?"

"The marketing of the perfume. By the way, does this fragrance have a name?"

"*Vasaro.*"

"After the property? Don't they usually name a perfume something more exotic?"

"It's my perfume and it belongs to Vasaro." Her face was suddenly alight. "Don't you see? Vasaro has marketed perfumes before but never under its own name. I worked for four years creating this perfume and I want it to mean something." Her eyes widened with sudden apprehension. "You wouldn't want me to change the name?"

"I don't care what you call it. If a perfume called Poison could become a success, I don't see any problem with Vasaro."

"You're a strange man. You purposely set out to get exactly what you wanted from us with the least possible effort to yourself. Then you get angry when I let you."

"I'm not angry. I just don't see—" He wasn't telling the truth. He had been angry and uneasy since the first moment she had introduced herself. Something about the simplicity and forthrightness of the woman had aroused in him an odd urge to protect. Very odd, he thought cynically. He hadn't felt any urge but the most basic and sexual toward a woman since he had been a boy in Bucharest, and he certainly had no use for any softer emotion now. "I don't know any better than you why I'm reacting this way. You certainly appear to be able to take care of yourself."

"The perfume is mine and I had a right to take a chance with it as long as it didn't affect Vasaro." She met his gaze directly. "But it's best you realize I know the element of chance exists."

No, she didn't deliberately blind herself to chicanery or crookedness. She accepted the possibility, even the probability, that he meant her harm and then tried to live with it for the sake of her precious Vasaro. God, how long had it been since he had felt that deeply about anything?

Her grasp tightened on the copy of the contract he had handed her. "If you'll excuse me, I'd like to shower and change before supper. Help yourself to another glass of wine. It's our own vintage."

"It's very good."

"We like it." She moved toward the door. "It's not as smooth as the wines from some of the better-known vineyards in Champagne, but then, at Vasaro we grow the grapes only as a sideline. Flowers are our business."

"And what if you'd put your entire effort toward the vineyards?"

"It would be the best wine in the world," she said matter-of-factly. "Just as Vasaro grows the finest flowers."

He chuckled. "You think well of your Vasaro."

"It's my home. Vasaro is—" She stopped, and her eager smile faded. "But you're not interested in how I feel about Vasaro."

"I wouldn't say I was totally disinterested. I told you I had an insatiable curiosity."

"Oh, yes... curiosity." She gave him a polite smile over her shoulder. "I'll try to hurry. Make yourself comfortable."

The next moment she was gone and he slowly sank back down in the chair. The room felt cold without Caitlin Vasaro's vibrant presence. She radiated a fiery nervous energy that was at odds with the cool control she tried to maintain. He impatiently dismissed the thought and reached for his wineglass. He didn't give a damn about Caitlin or her Vasaro, and he would make sure he stayed in that frame of mind. She was only a piece in his puzzle. If he felt anything for the woman, it was a biological stirring and nothing else. It was no wonder the response had surprised him, for she wasn't really to his taste. Her breasts were magnificently Junoesque, but her tall, graceful body was far too thin and well muscled to be termed voluptuous. The answer must be that he had been a long time without a woman and the emotion he was feeling was tomcat common. Well, why not indulge himself? She was no child but a woman in her middle twenties, and it would be interesting to see if she could feel as much passion for a man as for her Vasaro.

He lifted the wineglass thoughtfully to his lips, his mind dwelling on the possibilities.

Karazov's manner was different toward Caitlin after she came downstairs for supper.

All through the meal Caitlin had been conscious of the subtle nuances of the change, but she couldn't quite put her finger on its composition. He was charming to

Katrine, courteous to Caitlin, and the talk at the table was politely impersonal. Yet something was definitely *there*.

Then he suddenly shifted his gaze to her and she realized he was acutely, physically aware of her. She felt a ripple of shock, and her eyes widened in surprise before she could hide the reaction.

Alex smiled and returned his attention to Katrine, complimenting her on the arrangement of the flowers on the table.

He left directly after supper to go back to Cannes and, after saying good-bye to Katrine, asked Caitlin to walk with him to his car in order to make plans for meeting at the bank tomorrow.

The white sports car parked in the driveway gleamed in the moonlight, arrogant and showy... and wrong.

"Why a Lamborghini?" Caitlin looked up at Karazov as they walked down the stone steps.

"Why not?"

"It doesn't seem like a car you would buy. It's too ostentatious."

"Perhaps it satisfies a quirk in my character."

"Really?" She thought about it. "But you don't impress me as a man who would need toys to express himself."

"You're right." He opened the door of the car. "I bought it because I was angry."

She looked up at him, puzzled.

"I'd just come into some unexpected money and I wanted to flaunt it."

"I see."

He smiled grimly. "No, you don't. You haven't the slightest idea what I'm talking about. You don't understand why I'd want to rub anyone's nose into the filthy lucre just to get my own back."

"No, I guess I don't. Revenge has always seemed a little futile to me."

He shook his head. "You're wrong. You can't ever let a slight go unpunished. It always encourages a repeat performance."

"An eye for an eye?"

He met her gaze. "Exactly."

She instinctively took a step back at the iciness of that glance. *Dieu*, what kind of man was Karazov? "You believe in revenge?"

"Everyone believes in revenge."

"I don't. I think people should try to forget and get on with their lives."

"Admirable." His lips twisted. "And completely unrealistic. You just haven't had the knife go deep enough to make you want to pull it out and turn it on the enemy."

"But you have?"

He was silent a moment. "Yes."

The silence stretched between them, and Caitlin searched for something to say. Then, abruptly, the awareness was back, stronger than before. She was suddenly conscious of the solid warmth of his body only a step away. She reached out blindly and touched the cool, smooth metal of the Lamborghini and said the first thing that came to mind. "My father would love this car."

"Would he? I've heard he's a connoisseur of fine things. He's in London now, isn't he?"

She stiffened. "Evidently you learned more about my mother and me than just our financial condition."

"Variables. Emotional response can make a perfectly reasonable human being do completely unreasonable things. Since your mother had to sign the papers, it was necessary for me to learn something about her." He shrugged. "Nothing in depth really—only that she married an Irishman named Denis Reardon whom she divorced thirteen years later."

"He divorced her."

"You didn't answer me. Your father's in London?"

"I think so." Her tone was reserved. "I received a card from him two Christmases ago. We don't correspond regularly. He divorced my mother when I was only twelve."

"I know." He gazed searchingly at her as if deciding whether or not to leave it at that before adding bluntly, "After running through her money and almost ruining Vasaro. You can't tell me you've never wanted to turn the knife on the charming Mr. Reardon?"

"No."

"Never?"

"What good would it do? He can't help what he is."

"A gigolo and a user."

"It's none of your business what he is," she snapped.

"I'm wondering how deep your turn-the-cheek philosophy goes."

She gazed at him in wonder. "You're trying to hurt me."

"No, I'm trying to wake you up."

"Why should you care? I'm nothing to you."

"You're my business partner." He smiled recklessly, his eyes glittering in the darkness. "I'm very solicitous of my business partners. I want them clearheaded and free to function in all the areas in which I need them."

The words were spoken with a silken sensuality that was in sharp contrast to the cool crispness of their import. The paradox again, catching her off guard. "You'll find I can function without any psychological spurring." Caitlin's hand fell away from the fender of the Lamborghini. "Now, if you'll excuse me, I have to get back to the house and change into my work clothes."

His smile faded. "You're going back to work? It's almost ten o'clock."

"I have to finish planting the roses."

"For God's sake, you don't have to work all hours of the day and night—especially since I've just agreed to pay you—"

"The lavender has to be picked tomorrow. That means the roses go in tonight." Caitlin could see he couldn't understand. "I don't have the money yet. It's not *real* to me. And even after I do have it, it won't be safe to ease off working until the mortgage is paid and I have a cushion in case we have another year like this one. I have to protect Vasaro."

"Christ," he muttered. "You're obsessed."

"I don't expect you to understand."

"I understand." His lips twisted. "I can be fairly obsessive myself at times." He slipped behind the wheel of the car. "I'll be at your bank at noon tomorrow. I hope you can spare the time to come to Cannes to pick up your money."

She frowned. "Two o'clock would be better for me. Even then I'll have to quit work early. We usually stop picking at one but I'll need to clean up and drive—"

"Two." He turned the ignition key and the car growled sensually to life. "I wouldn't think of interfering with your schedule."

Caitlin watched the sleek car glide down the driveway.

"Is everything all right, dear?" Her mother called from the doorway. Her full-skirted turquoise silk dress glowed jewel-bright against the lighted hallway behind her. Her gaze wandered to the sports car as it reached the blacktop and streaked down the road toward the turnoff for Cannes. "What a lovely car. Do you suppose he might let me drive it sometime?"

"Why don't you ask him?" Caitlin climbed the steps. "He seems quite taken with you."

"I was taken with him too. It's not often I meet such an attractive man. He rather reminds of that Australian actor with the eyes…"

"I imagine most of the actors from the land down under have eyes."

"You know what I mean." She snapped her fingers. "Mad Max."

"Mel Gibson."

Katrine beamed. "That's right. Anyway, he's a perfectly beautiful man and I'm sure everything's going to be fine, Caitlin."

Caitlin's lips brushed her mother's cheek as she passed her and went into the foyer. "I hope so. Good night, Mother." She moved toward the stairway. "I'll need the car tomorrow to drive to Cannes."

Her mother frowned. "I was going to have lunch with Mignon Salanot in Nice." She added quickly, "But I could cancel it."

"Don't bother. I'll take the pickup instead."

Katrine wrinkled her nose in distate. "Don't park near the bank. That old hulk is a disgrace."

Caitlin smiled. "I like it. It has character." She started up the stairs. "And it suits me. We're both plain and less than elegant."

"You're not plain. And you make no attempt to be elegant, dear. Take that dress you're wearing. It's at least five years old and the hem is an inch too long." Katrine added sternly, "It's a woman's duty to take the trouble to make herself attractive."

Caitlin shook her head in amusement as she said gently, "I'm afraid we live in different worlds."

Katrine sighed and then gave a resigned shrug. "Sleep well, Caitlin."

Caitlin didn't bother to tell her mother she was going

upstairs only to change. She had learned over the years it was always less wearing to avoid imparting any information Katrine might find distressing. "Are you going to bed?"

"Soon. I thought I'd browse through my new copy of *Elle*. Do you suppose now that Monsieur Karazov is being so generous I could buy a few dresses?"

"We'll see after we pay the bills."

"You are happy about all this, Caitlin? At first I thought you were but you—"

"I'm happy," Caitlin said quickly.

An expression of relief banished Katrine's anxious frown. "I don't always know what you're thinking. I do want you to be happy, Caitlin."

Katrine had always wanted everyone to be happy, Caitlin thought sadly. She couldn't understand happiness sometimes had to be paid for with work and sacrifices. She had spoken truly when she had told her mother they lived in different worlds. Katrine would have loved to have a daughter like herself to pore over fashion magazines, gossip over lunch, and get excited over the prospect of new dresses. In many ways Katrine's life was harder and lonelier than her own. At least Caitlin had Jacques and her friends among the workers who understood her problems and goals. She paused on the landing to smile down at Katrine. "I think we'll be able to afford at least one new dress. Why don't you look around when you're in Nice tomorrow and see if you can find something you like?"

Katrine's face lit up. "I'll be very careful not to be too extravagant. There's that lovely shop up the street from the Negresco Hotel that has the most exquisite things at the most ridiculous prices." She hurried toward the salon. "Something with a lowered waistline, I think. I saw something in *Vogue* last month that..." Her voice trailed off as she disappeared into the salon to find her precious store of fashion magazines.

Caitlin's smile faded as she continued up the stairs. They couldn't afford the dress, but perhaps by the time the bill came, their financial situation would be eased. Besides, Katrine's dress was a drop in the proverbial bucket. The advance Karazov would give her tomorrow would go toward the mortgage, but that would still leave the expenses of actually running Vasaro.

Karazov. Uneasiness surged through her as she thought about those moments by the car. She couldn't deny the man disturbed her physically. The chemistry between them had been as stark and blatant as the man himself.

But just because the sexual chemistry existed didn't mean it had to be acted upon. She wasn't an inexperienced child and she had felt the pull of physical attraction before. Not lately, of course. She had been too busy to think about men since she had left the university and taken over the running of Vasaro. There had been no one since Claude Janlier, and that awkward affair of her university days could never have been termed a grand passion. Still, it had definitely been an affair.

She was kidding herself, she thought with sudden impatience. She wasn't experienced enough to hold her own with any man as practiced as Alex Karazov even if she were willing to indulge in an affair. No, it would be best to avoid anything warmer than friendship. A sexual relationship between them might cloud their business dealings, and that must not happen. Nothing must get in the way of safeguarding Vasaro.

3

The statue on the pedestal gleamed in the pitch darkness of the room, its emerald eyes glittering with inhuman wisdom.

Caitlin studied it, adjusted her chair, then sat down at the desk and opened her notebook.

"Christ, it's the Wind Dancer!" The voice came from the doorway of the perfumery.

Caitlin went still, her fingers clenching the notebook. Dammit, this was *her* place. She didn't want him here. "Monsieur Karazov?" She stood up and moved toward the light switch. "I didn't expect you."

"What the hell are you doing with that statue here in—" He broke off as she flicked on the lights and pressed a button on the remote in her hand.

The statue on the black marble pedestal disappeared into thin air!

Caitlin smiled as she saw his expression. "Abracadabra."

His gaze quickly zeroed in on the three projectors set about the pedestal. "Holographic film?"

She nodded. "Guaranteed three-dimensional."

"So I noticed." He moved into the room, and Caitlin

saw he had discarded the elegant dark blue business suit he had worn when she had met him that afternoon at the bank in Cannes and was dressed in faded jeans and a white sweatshirt. "Your mother told me you'd be out here, but I never thought you'd be playing with projectors when you didn't show up for supper." He smiled faintly. "Not very polite. Does this mean you're willing to take my money but not my company?"

"I had some studying to do and I was sure Katrine would entertain you."

His gaze wandered to the pedestal. "You were studying the Wind Dancer?"

"You know it?"

"Doesn't everyone?"

"I think so, but then, I'm prejudiced. I did a paper on it when I was at the Sorbonne."

"I saw a picture of the statue in a book recently. You studied antiquities at the university?"

"I majored in agriculture with a minor in antiquities."

"A curious combination."

"Not necessarily. Vasaro is my blood, my life."

"And the Wind Dancer?"

"I suppose you could call it my passion."

His gaze narrowed. "Why?"

"The Vasaros have been connected with the Wind Dancer for over four hundred years. Naturally, I've been fascinated by the—" She shook her head. "You wouldn't understand."

"I could try."

"I bought a copy of this holographic film from the Metropolitan Museum in New York when I was doing my paper. The Andreas family funded the original project, but it cost me the earth to have the film duplicated. Holographic film is still in the experimental stages, and

I felt terribly guilty about taking the money from the operation here."

"But you did it anyway."

"A passion," she repeated. "And that was before I knew how much trouble we were in here. Whenever I have time I sneak off here and study it."

"At least you're not slaving in the fields." He closed the door behind him. "I suppose I should apologize for disturbing you."

She smiled. "I suppose you should."

"I apologize." He grimaced. "Now that we've gotten that over with, may I stay for a while? I'm restless as hell."

She could tell, almost sensing the disturbing waves of tension he radiated. She moved back across the room, sat down at the desk, and set the remote beside her notebook. "I'm afraid there's not much to amuse you here, Monsieur Karazov."

"Alex." He looked around the singularly comfortless room. "What is this place? It looks like a small airplane hangar."

"It's my workroom, the perfumery. This is where I create new perfumes."

"When you're not sitting in the dark, studying the Wind Dancer." He looked at the circular desk at which she was sitting. "Interesting." A multitude of shelves containing hundreds of glittering vials towered high above her head, and a small scale and notebook rested directly in front of her. "You look like you're about to play an organ."

"Close." She smiled. "That's what this desk is called. All these vials on the shelves contain *essence absolue*, oils of different flowers and plants. They're all carefully labeled so that I can blend and measure until I get just the right mixture." She indicated the scale and notebook. "I have to keep very precise records in case I stumble on something that's worth keeping. Scents are so subtle that the most minute change of ingredient can alter the entire chemistry of a perfume."

"I thought you'd already created your perfume."

"Ah, but that's the magic of fragrance. You can always create something new, something different. Millions of scents in the world and yet there's always the chance of—sorry, I get a little carried away. You can't be interested in all this."

"Why not? Why is this workroom in a special building instead of the main house?"

She nodded to the wide barnlike doors on either side of the room. "So that I can open the doors and windows and let the breeze clear it of lingering fragrances. It's very difficult keeping your nose from becoming desensitized. The olfactory nerve goes jaded, then dead rather quickly, reviving only in fresh air. This is a primitive setup compared to some of the streamlined workrooms of other perfumers, but I prefer it."

He prowled to the bookcases lining the far wall. "Your mother said you were very good at this."

"I love it," she said simply.

"More than growing your flowers?"

"It's all a part of the whole."

"And the whole is Vasaro?"

She nodded. "Michel said it was like a circle."

"Michel?"

"Michel Andreas. He lived here at the time of the French Revolution. He married the eldest daughter of Catherine Vasaro and François Etchelet."

He lifted a quizzical brow. "They weren't married? Wasn't that a bit shocking back then?"

"The names? No, Catherine and François were married. According to the terms of the inheritance of Vasaro, the property can be passed on only from the eldest daughter to the eldest daughter, and then only if the woman retains the name Vasaro even after her marriage."

He pulled down a copy of *Fragrance* from the shelf and leafed idly through it. "The eighteenth-century women's libbers must have been ecstatic."

"Michel created Vasaro's first successful perfume. It was said that every lady in Napoleon's court had a bottle of La Dame." Caitlin's face was aglow with eagerness. "You should read Catherine's journal. It's a journey back in time. She raised Michel as her own son and..." She saw his indulgent smile and stopped. "I know I get too involved when I talk about the history of Vasaro. It can't be of interest to anyone outside the family."

"On the contrary, I find it fascinating. It must feel very comfortable to have roots."

"Everyone has roots of some sort. Vasaro's roots just run deeper than most."

He was silent.

"I mean, parents and children form a bond that—"

"I know what you mean." He crossed to her. "For some people it's better to live without roots." He picked up a vial from the third shelf of the desk and held it up to the light. "What's this?"

The vial was labeled; it was clear he wished to change the subject.

"That's lilac."

"Do you use it in your perfume?"

She shook her head. "I use a top note of jasmine and a middle note of—"

"Note? Are we back to the organ again?"

She laughed. "Creating a perfume is a little like creating a symphony. There's a top note that you perceive at once, then the middle note, and then the basic note. But there are really all kinds of notes in between that blend and enhance. A good perfume unfolds for you from moment to moment until it fades away."

"Like the strains of the symphony."

"And it can't fade away too soon. There are all kinds of things to consider. Is it intense but not too intense? Will it be sharp or soft? Does it have body? Does it linger behind when the wearer walks away?"

"And how does your perfume answer those questions?"

"Judge for yourself. This is Vasaro." She took a vial from the lowest shelf of the desk and poured a drop on the absorbent surface of one of the white blotters stacked on the desk. She handed the blotter to Alex. "I wanted something as spicy and memorable as Opium but with other notes as well. I wanted the freshness of the fields after a rain and the faint scent of the lemon trees and..." She made a helpless gesture. "I just wanted it to be Vasaro."

He lifted the blotter and breathed in the scent. "It's different from any perfume I've ever smelled on a woman."

She had a sudden vivid picture of Alex standing close to a woman, his face buried in her hair. She pushed the image firmly aside. "A perfume should be distinctive. Do you like it?"

He set the blotter on the desk. "I can't tell. A perfume smells different on a woman's skin." He picked up the vial of Vasaro. "May I?"

He didn't wait for her to answer but took a tiny drop on his thumb and rubbed it into the sensitive flesh of her left wrist. He lifted her wrist and sniffed experimentally. "Good."

His tone was impersonal, but his grip on her wrist

was hard, warm, excruciatingly intimate. "One more place. It's the best possible test." He took another drop of perfume on his other thumb, then set the vial back on the desk. He gently pushed aside the collar of her shirt and encircled her slender neck with his hands. With both thumbs he slowly massaged the perfume into the hollow of her throat. "Your heartbeat is strongest here, and it spreads the scent. . . ."

His hands felt heavy, her throat fragile and vulnerable. She swallowed. "How do you know? I thought you said you didn't know very much about perfume."

"I don't. But I read a research report a few years ago about the olfactory system."

Her heart was accelerating beneath the pads of his thumbs as he rubbed leisurely back and forth. "And do you always remember what you read?"

"Most of the time. If it might prove useful. Otherwise I try to deep-six it. Memories can become jaded too." His hands left her throat and he pulled her to her feet. She found herself staring up at him like a stupid ninny, unable to look away from those glacier-light eyes. Dammit, she could feel her heart beating harder, her skin warming as the blood ran faster in her veins.

"That's right," he muttered, encouraging, praising the purely involuntary response that caused the fragrance to rise. "Great." No part of his body was now touching her, but she could feel his body heat. He stood perfectly still, his head bent, breathing in the scent.

She could see the pulse drumming in his temple, and the feathery curve of his dark lashes half closed to hide the blue of his eyes. She caught the faint fragrance of his own scent, lime cologne and something deeper, muskier. There was something starkly primitive about the two of them standing there, breathing each other's scents like two animals getting ready to mate. She tried wildly to think of something to say that would bring an end to the tension.

He inhaled deeply and she felt the soft warmth of his breath on her throat as he exhaled. *Dieu*, he wasn't even touching her and she was beginning to tremble.

"Extraordinary." He stepped back, his lowered lids still veiling his eyes. "I think we may have a winner."

Her knees felt suddenly weak, and she dropped back down onto her chair. She knew her face was flushed and she wished desperately for the aura of cool remoteness Alex seemed to be able to produce at will. She laughed shakily. "A good businessman would have found that out before he agreed to launch it."

"It wouldn't have helped. I know nothing about what a woman would like in a perfume." She thought the faintest glimmer of humor appeared in his expression. "But I know what I like."

And he liked her, he liked the way she smelled and the way she felt and the fact that she was female to his male. Sex, pure and simple. She quickly looked down at the vial of perfume. "What are you going to do about it?"

He didn't answer, and when she lifted her gaze, she saw that his eyes were twinkling.

"The perfume. You said we needed to talk about the marketing."

"We do."

"Well?"

"Not now. I have a few ideas, but I'm waiting for some additional information before I'll be ready to discuss them. I should be receiving a phone call within the next few days that will give me what I need and then I'll be ready to move."

"A phone call from whom?"

"A research specialist. You'd better tell your mother

I'll probably be receiving packets in the mail every day. I hire several agencies to gather information for me."

"For your novels?"

"Sometimes. I, too, have a passion." He smiled. "For trivia. I'll also be making a number of long-distance calls while I'm here. Send the bills to Monsieur Ganold when you get them." He glanced up at the volumes on the shelves. "Are all these books on perfume?"

How did he do it? She knew damn well he had been aroused only a few moments before and now he was behaving as coolly as if he had never touched her. However he managed the trick, she was grateful for the time it gave her to regain her composure. Her heartbeat was almost normal again, and soon she would be just as cool and remote as he. "Yes, the main library is at the house. Except for Catherine's journal, most of these are reference books."

He took down a leather-bound Bible from the shelf and looked at her inquiringly.

"Several passages are marked in the Song of Solomon. The Old Testament is full of references to perfume."

His glance fell on a worn, faded book in the second row. "This one isn't about perfume," he murmured. "*Facts and Legends of the Wind Dancer*." He ran his fingers exploringly over the faded blue binding. "It's very worn, practically falling apart."

"I've had it for a long time."

"How long?"

"Years." He had already invaded too many corners of her life in the short time she had known him, and it was time she set up barriers around this most private corner. "It's very fragile. Please, put it back on the shelf."

He lifted a brow but carefully set the book back where he had gotten it. "Interesting."

She wasn't sure he was speaking of the book itself or her

reaction, for he immediately went on. "May I take some of these perfume books back to the house? I think it's time I learned a little more about our common interest."

"Of course."

He turned and began pulling down volume after volume until he had eight books cradled in his arms.

"You can always come back tomorrow," she said dryly. "I'm not going to change my mind and lock you out."

"Thanks." He moved toward the door. "I don't sleep very well and I read fast."

"You must."

"I taught myself to speed-read several years ago. It was useful in my former profession." He slanted her a sly glance. "That should be a comfort to you. I shouldn't imagine the skill would be of any benefit at all to a drug dealer." He shifted the books and managed to open the door. "Shall I leave the door open? The room smells to high heaven."

"It's too late. That's why we use blotters. They can be put in sealed containers and disposed of after we've used them." She made a face. "Now I'll have to take a bath to rid myself of the fragrance."

"Yes, it's too late." He smiled curiously. "I lied, you know."

She gazed at him, startled. "What?"

"The hollow of a woman's throat isn't the best place to test a perfume."

"No?"

He shook his head. "There's another spot that's much more interesting. We'll have to try it sometime." He closed the door behind him before she could answer.

She gazed blankly at the door for a moment and then started to chuckle.

• • •

Alex went directly to his room when he returned to the house and immediately placed a call to Simon Goldbaum in New York.

Goldbaum was less than pleased to hear from him. "Jesus, Alex, what do you expect? Jonathan Andreas is a very private person and he's got the bread to protect his privacy. It's gonna take time."

"I need a hook." Alex sat down on the bed, flipped open the notebook, and picked up the pen he had placed by the phone when he had unpacked. "Give me what you have."

"Not much more than you can read in *Time*. He's forty-two years old, an industrialist who turned shipping on its ear and reversed the downward profit trend for the cruise ships. Gets along with the unions but he's sure not crazy about them. They interfere with his incentive plans for the workers. Active in politics. Republican. He has a compound just north of Charleston, South Carolina. Well liked by practically everybody. No family problems. Kind of patriarch of the clan."

"Married?"

"No, he's had a number of discreet affairs. The key word is *discreet*. The guy likes his privacy, I tell you."

"Is that all?"

"No." Goldbaum hesitated. "I've been nosing around Republican headquarters. They like him a lot. He's smart, diplomatic, but has the balls to ram in the shaft when it's needed. He's sort of Lee Iacocca meets Jack Kennedy."

"What does that mean?"

There was a silence on the other end of the line. "It means he could be the next president of the United States."

Alex examined the information for value, then discarded it. No help there. "What else?"

"Goddammit, Alex, you're not going to find a hook. A man who has a chance of becoming president is going to be damn careful not to make a wrong move."

"Dig."

"I think maybe he's a good guy, Alex."

"That doesn't mean he doesn't make mistakes. I need a hook."

"All right, all right. I'll call you next week. Are you at the chalet?"

"No, I'm in France." Alex gave him the number. "Don't leave any messages."

"For chrissake, I'm not an amateur. Pavel never made the mistake of thinking—" Goldbaum stopped and then said gruffly, "Sorry."

"So am I." Alex's voice was bleak. "And I want the bastard who killed him. Ledford's gone underground. To get him I need—"

"The hook," Goldbaum wearily finished for him. "I'll get it for you."

"What about Ledford's whereabouts? Anything new?"

"I'm working on it. He's smart. You're right, about a year ago he dug a hole and then pulled the hole in after him."

"Then go back further than a year. He had to have made some preparations before he went underground."

"If he did, he buried them pretty damn good." He went on quickly. "I know, dig!"

"Right."

Alex replaced the receiver and looked down at the few notes he had made. Damn few. He had expected more from Goldbaum. The man was a former newspaperman and good at his job. If he hadn't been able to find out all Alex needed to know about Andreas, it was probably because there wasn't anything to find out.

But there *had* to be something.

Alex could feel the familiar frustration and fury

welling up in him. He stood up and moved restlessly toward the casement window across the room. His hand clenched the aqua silk drapes as he gazed blindly out at the moonlit fields of Vasaro. He had thought it would be easier. He had thought he could remain remote and untouched, manipulate the events at Vasaro to suit himself and further his own aims without being affected. Yet he had been in contact with Caitlin Vasaro and her mother for only two days and he found himself—what? Touched, concerned—guilty?

He had no reason to feel guilty, he quickly assured himself. He may not have been completely open with Caitlin, but the influx of his money would save Vasaro, and that was the only thing Caitlin Vasaro really wanted. She had told him herself she didn't care what his purpose was in investing in Vasaro. As for his other emotions, he'd be very careful not to let Caitlin beneath his defenses.

His grip tightened on the curtains as he remembered the smooth, silky feel of Caitlin's flesh beneath his fingers, her gray-green eyes wary and wondering as she looked up at him. Why hadn't he gone further than that teasing foreplay? She had been ready for it. He had seen the faint tremor that shook her as he touched and felt the heat of her. Caitlin might be wary of him, but her response had been purely elemental.

He whirled and pulled his sweatshirt over his head as he strode back to the bed across the room. He would go to bed and forget about Caitlin and Vasaro and think only of Ledford and what he would do to him when he got his hands on the son of a bitch.

"Martinique, Alex," Pavel coaxed. "A little sun. That's all I ask. A little sun, a little sex, a gourmet meal now and then."

"Now and then? You haven't stepped on a scale lately."

Pavel strapped to the chair, his eyes looking at Alex, the dead lips moving. "Martinique. A little sun..."

"Pavel!"

Alex jerked upright in bed, his heart pounding, his body coated with a cold sweat.

Another dream. But it hadn't felt like a dream... none of them ever did. He had felt the same explosion of rage and sorrow as the moment when he had seen Pavel strapped in the chair.

He closed his eyes as he tried to control the shudders racking his body. The dreams came every night, but when he got Ledford, they would stop. He couldn't think of Ledford without thinking of Pavel, and to think of Pavel was unbearable. God, he missed that big bear.

The shaking was easing now. He lay back down on the bed and closed his eyes, feeling the tears sting behind the closed lids. He wouldn't think about Pavel. He couldn't think of him and keep the guilt and pain at bay. He searched desperately for something, anything to block the thought.

Caitlin Vasaro.

While he was with her he hadn't once thought of Pavel. He had been intrigued, touched, impatient, but at every moment totally involved. He could use her presence and the lust that accompanied it to distract him. He could use Caitlin to keep the pain away, to keep the dreams away.

Use? Jesus, he hated users. He had been used too often himself over the years.

But he needed something, someone. He needed the woman.

He could be honest with Caitlin, make his position clear. She had wanted him as much as he had wanted her. Why wouldn't she be willing to give him what he needed?

Forgetfulness.

• • •

"May I help?"

Caitlin looked up to see Alex standing beside her in the field. He was dressed in faded jeans similar to the pair he had worn the previous night and a white T-shirt.

"What?"

"I'd like to help, if I may."

He watched Adrienne, the woman next to her, pick the lavender. "This doesn't look too difficult."

"It's not. It requires practice and a certain rhythm." She frowned. "But it's hard work."

He smiled. "I don't think I'll collapse from exhaustion. I ski every day when I'm at my chalet, and I'm in pretty good shape."

She could see he wasn't boasting. His bare arms were corded with muscle, and he didn't appear to have an ounce of fat on his body. "If you're bored, why don't you write something?"

He grimaced. "The muse isn't whispering in my ear. I feel like doing something physical. If I work hard enough, I'll sleep better." His shoulders moved restlessly beneath the thin cotton of his T-shirt. "Well, are you going to let me help, or not?"

He was telling the truth. She could sense that same restlessness she had noticed the previous night. "Go to the truck and get a basket from Jacques."

"Caitlin told me to come to you and get a basket, D'Abler."

"Did she?" Jacques reached down and took a full basket of blossoms a picker was holding up to him before turning to face Alex. "Now, what would you be wanting with a basket?"

In spite of the overseer's casual tone, Alex could sense his antagonism, and a fierce surge of joy pounded through him as he looked at the man standing on the bed of the truck. He had heard that goading tone before in other men's voices, and it always preceded violence. After all these weeks of frustration, here at last was something to strike out against.

And Jacques D'Abler was a very formidable something. Though not a young man, the powerfully muscled overseer looked hard as a rock and held himself with the easy confidence of a man who had known few physical defeats. Alex's gaze ran over him, assessing, picking his spots for the battle to come. "What do the rest of the pickers want with them?"

"To earn a decent living." Jacques met his gaze. "But Caitlin tells me you don't need to earn a living, that you're rich as Midas and going to save Vasaro."

"And you don't believe her?"

"I believe you told her that." He shrugged. "She's not stupid. We'll have to see."

"Could I have a basket?"

"To show her you're one of us? You're not one of us, Monsieur Karazov. I've seen your kind before. You're too smooth and easy for Vasaro."

"I asked only for a basket, not your opinion."

"I'm a generous man. I'll give it to you anyway." Another picker had appeared beside the truck and Jacques reached down and took the woman's brimming basket. "As I said, Caitlin's not stupid but she wants to believe. I think she's beginning to trust you." He emptied the basket into the larger casque on the truck. "That makes me uneasy."

"Regrettable."

"Yes, it is. She doesn't trust many strangers. I'd be very upset if you disillusioned her."

It was coming. Alex took an eager step forward, his gaze narrowing on Jacques's face. "How upset?"

Jacques didn't answer him directly. "When Caitlin was a little girl, her father gave her a necklace, a golden Pegasus with emerald eyes. Everyone knew how fascinated she was by the stories of the real Wind Dancer, and Reardon was always clever about pleasing the ladies. She loved that necklace and wore it everywhere." He returned the empty basket to the picker and watched the woman stroll back into the field, waiting until she was out of earshot before continuing. "The night he left Vasaro, the necklace disappeared with him." He smiled sardonically. "God knows, by that time there wasn't much else left for him to take."

"I assure you I'm not a jewel thief. Is there a point to this story?"

"Oh, yes." Jacques's toothy smile widened, gleamed, in his brown face. "I followed the son of a bitch to his hotel in Cannes and tried to get the necklace back. I tried so hard, I broke his nose and three of his ribs."

"Interesting. And did you retrieve the necklace?"

"No, he'd already sold it to one of his jet-set friends. I tried to track it down, but the woman had left the country. So I went back to the hotel, broke both Reardon's arms, and came back home to Vasaro. He was the last man who disillusioned Caitlin."

Alex tried to hold on to his antagonism but found it impossible. Something about the man's frank, earthy ferocity reminded him of Pavel during those first days he'd known him in the Spetznez. "I can see why it might have discouraged all comers. Did Caitlin ever find out what you did?"

"No, she wouldn't have understood."

"But I do. Now that I've been properly intimidated, may I have my basket?"

"You're not intimidated."

"No, actually I'm disappointed." He met Jacques's gaze and told him the truth. "I needed something to fight, but I don't believe it's going to be you. We think too much alike."

Jacques stood looking at him for another moment and then reached down, took a basket from the stack, and tossed it to Alex. "Third row. I'll be there in a minute to show you what to do."

Caitlin had expected Alex to come back and pick with her after Jacques showed him the rudiments of gathering the blossoms. Instead, he chose a place beside Pierre Ledux and stayed there until afternoon, when Jacques called a halt to the picking. He tossed his empty basket on the bed of the truck and strode off toward the house without a word.

Alex was up and ready to go with her at dawn the next morning when she went down to the fields, but again he chose to pick in another row. When it was time to break for croissants and coffee at ten, she saw him sitting on the bed of the pickup truck, talking to Jacques.

On the third day Jacques made a point of stopping by the row where Caitlin was working. "He's pretty good, eh?"

Caitlin looked over to the row where Alex was picking beside Renée Boisson. "He's fast."

"And strong. He has great energy."

That was without question. She had noticed that volatile energy seething just below the surface for the past two days. He couldn't seem to work fast enough.

"At first I wasn't sure about him, but I ... I think he's a man to trust."

Caitlin looked at Jacques in surprise. Jacques didn't make snap judgments, and she had thought a man as enigmatic as Alex Karazov would pose a problem for him. "He's not an easy man to understand."

"He's hurting."

"How do you know?"

He shrugged. "I know. He works too hard." Jacques turned and strode off down the row toward the truck.

Caitlin gazed at Alex thoughtfully as she went back to work. He was laughing at something Renée had said, his face alive and expressive. He didn't look like a man who was troubled or in pain. He looked earthy, thoroughly male, and as distant from the polished man she had first seen waiting for her on the hill as Earth was to Neptune. A lock of dark hair hung over his perspiring forehead, and his blue shirt was darkened with sweat. He stood with his legs slightly astride, and the material of his faded jeans clung to his muscular thighs and hips.

Caitlin felt a tingle of heat move through her and hurriedly lifted her gaze back to his face. What had passed between them in her workroom had been only an episode to be forgotten by both of them. Alex Karazov had evidently succeeded, and so must she.

Yet Jacques was right about Alex's labor having an almost feverish quality. Not only did he work hard in the fields, but her mother had mentioned there was frequently a light under his door until after three in the morning. Well, his nocturnal habits were none of her business any more than those mysterious packets he received every day were her concern. A man as guarded as Alex Karazov would neither invite nor appreciate probing or sympathy. She firmly dismissed him from her thoughts and concentrated on the work at hand.

• • •

"Will you go for a walk with me?"

Caitlin turned from stacking her basket on the truck to Alex. She was again conscious of suppressed volatility and stiffened uneasily. "I don't have time to go for a walk."

"Just a short one. I've been exploring Vasaro by myself for the last few days, but there are questions I need to ask." He smiled. "Research."

"Perhaps tomorrow."

"Be fair," he said coaxingly. "Haven't I saved you any number of man-hours sweating in these fields? You owe me."

"You wanted to help."

He nodded. "And now I want you to walk with me."

"Where?"

He pointed to the south.

Caitlin hesitated, then started at a brisk pace in the direction he had indicated.

"Caitlin!"

Adrienne's small son, Gaston, was standing in the road, gazing pleadingly at her. His face was dirty, his brown hair tousled, gleaming, in the sunlight. "Tonight?"

She shook her head. "I have no time tonight."

His blue eyes filled with tears of disappointment and, as usual, she melted. "Tomorrow night. But you must ask your mother first and you must get all your chores done before you come."

His face brightened. "I will. Can I press the buttons?"

She smiled. "But of course. What would I do without you? You're a great help to me."

He gave her a toothy rainbow smile, and the next minute he was gone, racing down the road after his mother.

"What was that all about?" Alex asked.

"He likes to come to the perfumery when I'm studying the Wind Dancer and work the remote." She gave him a sly glance. "He thinks it's magic."

"Abracadabra." Alex echoed her own word to him. "I'm surprised you put up with him. I received the distinct impression intruders aren't welcome in your Wind Dancer domain."

"Gaston's no bother." She shrugged. "Well, maybe a little bother, but children usually give more than they receive. They teach us wonder."

"Do they? I've never been around them much."

"And he loves the Wind Dancer. Children always do."

"Whom does he belong to?"

"Adrienne and Étienne. He's one of my godchildren."

"How many do you have?"

"Twelve."

"Quite a family." He fell into step with her. She was almost as tall as Alex and their strides matched comfortably.

"What do you want to ask?"

"Wait."

The sun was shining, the scent of earth and blossoms heady in her nostrils and Alex's presence oddly companionable. It had been a long time since she had walked with anyone merely for the sake of walking. She always had something to do, somewhere to go, someone to see.

"You don't chatter," Alex observed after ten minutes of silence.

"Neither do you." She looked at him quizzically. "Was that a sexist judgment? Chattering isn't only a female characteristic. Pierre Ledux shoots words out like bullets from a machine gun."

He made a face. "I noticed."

"Jacques says you're a good worker. If you ever lost your money, he'd hire you on in a minute."

"I'll keep that in mind. Has Jacques been the overseer here long?"

"Since before I was born. Jacques grew up on Vasaro. I can remember him lifting me onto the bed of the truck with the blossoms when I could only toddle."

He nodded to the white flowers growing in the field to their left. "That's jasmine, isn't it?"

Caitlin nodded. "It will be ready for picking by the end of next week."

"What else do you grow here?"

"Orange blossom, geranium, bergamot, tuberose, hyacinth, cassia, mimosa, lemongrass, palmaros—"

"Wait." Alex held up his hand. "Perhaps I should ask what you don't grow?"

She smiled. "Not much. The ground is very fertile. We limit our output to meet demand, but Vasaro has experimented with almost everything over the centuries. We've even had a small success with some of the tropical plants like the vanilla orchid." She took a deep breath and closed her eyes. "Dear God, I love the smell of jasmine."

"Is that why you made it the top note of your perfume?"

"I don't know." She stared bemusedly at the white climbing jasmine. "Perhaps. I remember coming down here to the fields with Jacques at twilight when I was a little girl, and it was as if we entered a magic world. A golden haze seemed to hang over everything. The light turned the blossoms to rich cream and the sky was lavender and pink and scarlet. Sometimes I'd play hide-and-seek with Renée and Pierre and I'd run through the fields and shriek and—" She stopped and thought about it. "Memory. I guess that's why I used the jasmine. I wanted to hold on to a memory." She turned and smiled at Alex. "I suppose that's what perfumes are all about. We want to relive an old memory or create a new one."

"Jacques brought you down here? Not your father?"

Her smile faded. "Jacques brought me here only on the nights there was a party at the house. My father always said a grown-up party was no place for children." She glanced away and her pace quickened. "There were lots of parties at Vasaro in those days."

She could feel Alex's gaze on her face, but he didn't pursue the subject. They both fell silent again.

Alex didn't speak again until they had crested the next hill and a breathtaking panorama of sea, sky, and mountains lay before them in the distance. "What city is that?" He pointed far below them at the city curving along the coastline of the Mediterranean. "The cities along the Riviera all seem to jumble together."

"That's Cannes." She pointed to the gravel road leading around the cliff and down the hill. "About five miles away that road joins with the main highway that leads to Cannes. You brought me here to ask about those little towns?"

"No, I wondered about that house." He waved his hand to indicate a small stone cottage with a thatched roof a few hundred yards distant at the foot of the hill. "Who lives there?"

"No one." Caitlin smiled. "That's the Cottage of Flowers."

"It looks very old."

She nodded as she started down the hill toward it. "Philippe Andreas built it on the property before the French Revolution. He managed Vasaro for Catherine Vasaro."

"Was it used for a storage shed?"

"No."

"Then why did he build it?"

She chuckled. "He was the local Don Juan. He used to bring the peasant women here for romps."

"Droit du seigneur?"

"Oh, no, the women were willing enough." She opened

the door and entered the cottage, wrinkling her nose at the musty smell of dust and decayed wood. Cobwebs were everywhere. The only article of furniture was the single bed beneath the window across the room. The cotton spread covering it was mildewed and yellow with age. The wooden floor seemed to be in good shape but as filthy as the rest of the cottage. The hearth of the brick fireplace at the far end of the room was as cobwebbed as the rest and looked as if half the thatching from the roof had fallen through the chimney. "It's pretty dilapidated, isn't it? No one ever comes here anymore. We've always tried to keep it in good shape, but I haven't had the time or money to have it repaired lately."

He strolled over to the small brick fireplace. "Why bother if you don't use it?"

Her eyes widened in surprise. "It's part of Vasaro's history."

He turned to look at her and bowed mockingly. "Forgive me, I should have realized that anything connected with Vasaro was sacrosanct. Even the love nest of a libertine." He glanced around the cottage. "Where do you think he had his way with his paramours? On the bed over there?"

Caitlin was suddenly acutely conscious of the dimness of the cottage, how alone they were, Alex's blazing energy. She glanced toward the bed in the corner. "No, the bed wasn't here then."

Alex looked intently at her. "Where?"

"According to Catherine's journal, there was a sort of pallet. Philippe would spread a satin coverlet over the pallet, strew it with petals, and then make love on top of the petals." Alex's intensity was making her nervous and she laughed shakily. "That's why they call it the Cottage of Flowers."

"But it wasn't love, was it, Caitlin?" His voice was

very soft. "They came with him because they were hot and lusty and wanted him to give them what they needed. And he brought them here to do just that."

She smiled with an effort. "No, I guess he didn't make love to them. A poor choice of words."

"Choosing the right words is important. Honesty is important." Alex paused. "I want you every bit as much as Philippe did his peasant women. More."

She went still. "What?"

"You heard me." He met her gaze. "And I think you want me too. I'm saying I want to have you, but that it would be sex. Not love. Damn good sex and nothing else. I won't lie to you. I don't think there is such a thing as romantic love. I've certainly never run across it. Have you?"

"No." She stared at him, stunned. "You're certainly not trying to sweep me off my feet with sweet words."

"But they're honest words." His next words were halting, almost awkward. "Sometimes I may seem a cold man, but I'm not. I know many ways to please a woman." He paused. "And I would be kind to you. Kindness is important too."

"Yes, kindness is very important," she said abstractedly, still grappling with the main issue. "I didn't expect this. I'm a little . . . confused."

"I thought I'd made myself clear." That almost Slavic awkwardness of phrasing again. "Shall I be more explicit?"

"You've been explicit enough." She backed away from him. "I don't think we should have come here. The atmosphere must have taken you a little off balance."

"Philippe's lair didn't bring this about. For the past three days. I've been intending to ask you to sleep with me."

"You've scarcely looked at me."

"Because I hurt when I do," he said simply.

Her eyes widened in surprise, not so much at the

information as the fact that a man as guarded as Alex admitted such a thing.

"I've wanted you from that first night, but I didn't want it to come to this. I thought if I worked hard enough I'd be so tired I wouldn't—" He shook his head. "It didn't help. It's worse than before, and I knew I had to put an end to it. I considered seducing you, but that wouldn't have been fair. You deserve honesty."

"Thank you," she said dazedly. "Are you finished now?"

"Almost. I've told you only that I want you."

"What else is there?"

"I *need* you."

The word was spoken with such intensity, it sent an electrifying shock through her. He was telling the truth. For some reason, he did need her, and so urgently, the raw power of it was acting as a magnet drawing her toward him.

She took an impulsive step forward and then stopped. *Sacrebleu*, what was she doing? She didn't want this. "No."

He drew a deep breath and then exhaled it slowly. "Think about it. No ties, just mutual respect and nonstop erotica until we both grow tired of it."

"I don't want to think about it." She turned to leave. "The whole idea confuses me."

"I'll wait until you get used to the idea." He opened the door and stepped aside to let her precede him. "But I'll try again, Caitlin."

She knew he would. She had watched the single-minded drive he had exhibited in the fields for the past few days. "I won't change my mind." She met his gaze directly. "You're too intense. You drive too hard. You'd interfere with what I want for Vasaro."

"Try me. What can it hurt?"

She had a notion it could hurt a great deal. She had already acknowledged to herself she didn't have the right psychological makeup for a casual relationship. Alex seemed to be certain he could keep emotionally uninvolved, but she wasn't as sure about herself. In the short time he had been at Vasaro he had exerted a strong fascination and stirred her imagination more than any man she had ever met.

"Try me," he said again.

She didn't answer him as she started quickly up the hill.

Neither of them spoke again on the way back to the manor.

He was watching her again.

Caitlin's glance sidled away from where Alex was working to the stem of lavender she had just snapped off the branch.

He wasn't trying to make her aware of him. She knew instinctively he was as helpless to keep himself from looking at her as she was to keep from looking at him. She tossed the blossom in her basket and reached out blindly for another flower.

Dieu, it had gotten to the point that she didn't need to look at him to still see him in her mind's eye. It was hot today, and he and the other men had stripped off their shirts. A gleam of perspiration gilded the tanned flesh of his chest and shoulders, and she had glimpsed small, hard nipples through the dark triangle of hair thatching his chest. He had tied his black hair back from his forehead with a blue and white handkerchief he had borrowed from Pierre, and the band gave him an air of primitive savagery. As he bent and twisted with the rhythm of picking the flowers, the muscles of his flat stomach rippled and pulled with every movement.

"Not bad." Renée slanted Caitlin a mischievous glance.

"Now, if I weren't married to my gorgeous Pierre, I'd envy you."

Caitlin's nostrils should have been filled only with the scent of the lavender she was picking. Yet she could swear even across the field she could smell the faint fragrance of lime and musk that was distinctively Alex's. "There's no reason to envy me."

"No? Having that hunk just down the hall?" Renée tossed a blossom into her basket. "Or is he still down the hall?"

"He's down the hall."

"You always were a little crazy in the head. Why not enjoy him?"

Caitlin didn't answer.

"He looks at you like he wants to eat you. Maybe he does. Did any man ever—"

"I don't want to talk about him."

"You probably didn't. That Claude you told me about was pretty much a kid, wasn't he? Missionary position?"

"I hope you're enjoying yourself."

"Oh, I am." Renée looked over her shoulder. "He's looking at you again."

She *wouldn't* look across the field. It would only disturb her more and there was no sense to it. She would ignore Alex and keep on working.

Slowly, helplessly, she looked across the field at him.

He was staring at her.

She forgot to move.

A breeze stirred, touching her face and throat with its hot breath, pressing the cotton of her shirt against her breasts.

She heard a low whistle from Renée. "If it's that bad, you'd better move down the hall, my friend. A bed's softer than the ground."

Caitlin pulled her gaze away from Alex and started to pick again.

She wasn't waiting for him to come back, she told herself. It was only that she couldn't sleep and needed some fresh air.

Caitlin shifted on the cushions of the window seat, her gaze on the fields below. She was lying to herself. If she couldn't sleep, it was because Alex was out there somewhere.

For the past two nights she had stood at her window and watched him stride down the hill and into the fields, his steps charged, restless. Both nights he had been gone for hours and, sleepless and tense, she'd waited for him to return.

He was coming now, moving swiftly, lithely, up the hill. The night was so still, she could hear his passage through the grass and the even tempo of his breathing. The moon highlighted the luster of his black hair and outlined the definitive line of his body. Then, just before he reached the stone steps, he stopped and his head lifted to gaze at her window on the second floor.

She drew back into the shadows of the alcove in sudden panic.

"Caitlin?"

She didn't answer.

"I know you're there. I saw you."

She didn't speak.

He bit the next words out, each one weighted with pain. "Don't make me wait any longer. I need you."

He had said that once before.

Dear God, she was beginning to think she needed him too.

He stood there for a moment longer, perfectly still,

every muscle of his body rigid with tension. Then he moved slowly, heavily, up the stone steps and out of view.

She found herself holding her breath as she heard his step on the stairs leading to the second floor.

He passed her door and continued down the corridor to his own room.

"Perhaps you'd better skip picking in the fields this morning. Aren't you feeling well, Caitlin?" Katrine asked with a frown as she handed her the cup of coffee she had just poured. "You've been very quiet lately."

"I feel fine." Other than being in heat, she thought desperately. She wondered what Katrine would say if she actually burst out with those words. She imagined sex for Katrine would have to be as candy-box pretty as the other elements in her life. She wouldn't understand this almost animalistic craving. "Perhaps I'm a little tired."

"Alex was saying just last night at supper that you work too hard. After all, you could stop for supper when we have a guest."

"Alex isn't a guest. He's our business partner." She wished Katrine would quit talking about Alex. She took a hasty sip and put the coffee cup down. "I have to go now."

"Aren't you going to wait for Alex? You haven't waited for him for the last two days. I'd think since he's being nice enough to help you in the fields that you'd have the courtesy to—"

The kitchen door slammed behind Caitlin, cutting off Katrine's words.

Two minutes later Alex caught up with Caitlin and fell into step with her as they walked toward the field. She didn't look at him.

"It can't go on." Alex's voice was low. "There's no sense to it. Why are you fighting me? I won't hurt you."

She swallowed to ease the tightness of her throat and kept her gaze straight ahead.

"I'm healthy and not particularly kinky. You'll like me."

The sun was rising, spiking the lavender fields with purple splendor, but she was scarcely aware of the beauty spread before her.

"I can't eat. I can't sleep. I lie in bed and think of all the things I want to do with you." The words were only a level above a whisper, but each one scorched her. "I won't interfere with your Vasaro. All I want—" He stopped, and when he spoke again his voice was rough with frustration. "You know what I want." His stride lengthened and in another moment he had left her far behind.

4

It was almost midnight when she saw Alex walk away from the house and down the hill toward the fields.

She closed her eyes as she leaned her hot cheek on the cool glass of the windowpane. *Merde,* she wanted to go after him. Why did she have to feel this way? Lust wasn't supposed to be this all-consuming. She couldn't think or work or concentrate on the things that mattered to her. Alex's presence had come to dominate every action, every moment. Soon she would be no good at all to Vasaro. He interfered with every—

But it wasn't Alex Karazov who was interfering with her work, it was the way she felt about him.

She stiffened at the realization. Her lids flicked open as she straightened on the window seat. The enemy wasn't the man himself, but the lust she felt for him. If the lust was satisfied, she would be herself again. Why had she been so stupid as not to understand so simple a fact?

Her heart was pounding so hard with excitement, she could scarcely breathe. She could *have* him. It would even be good for Vasaro if she had him. Rationalizaton? So what? To *hell* with it.

She jumped to her feet and moved quickly toward the door.

She didn't allow herself time to think as she ran down the stairs and out the front door. The warm breeze brought the scent of the last of the lavender they would harvest the next day and pressed her white cotton nightgown against her body.

Alex was almost out of sight down the road and she hurried after him. He passed the newly planted rose field, his stride lengthening.

She didn't know why she didn't call out. She knew he would have stopped and waited for her.

She didn't have to call out. Just before he reached the jasmine field, he halted and looked back over his shoulder as if he had sensed her presence.

His expression frightened her.

Her pace faltered before she reached him, and she paused uncertainly.

"No." Alex's voice was guttural. His gaze traveled from her tousled hair to the flowing cotton of her sleeveless nightgown to her slippered feet. He held out his hand. "It's all right. Come."

She moved slowly toward him.

He stared down at her, the line of his cheeks hollow with tension. "Yes?" he asked thickly.

She could barely get the answer past her dry lips. "Yes."

His hand clamped on her wrist and he jerked her across the road and into the jasmine field.

Caitlin was vaguely conscious of the feel of the soft earth beneath the thin soles of her slippers, the heavy scent of jasmine, the moonlight edging Alex's dark hair with silver as he dragged her farther into the field.

"Alex, where—"

"Here." He stopped and turned to face her. "I can't

wait any longer." His hands fumbled as he undid his belt and unzipped his jeans. "Get rid of that nightgown."

She stared at him uncertainly. The flesh of his cheeks was pulled taut over the bones, and she suddenly felt the same fear she had known when he had turned to face her a few moments before.

"Hurry." He stripped off his clothes frantically, his gaze on her face. "For God's sake, no second thoughts now." He was naked, starkly, boldly, aroused. He took a step toward her. "I couldn't take it."

He pulled the nightgown over her head and threw it aside. "Come here."

She took a step toward him and was suddenly pressed against him, her naked breasts hard against the coarse hair of his chest. He rubbed against her, making low, choked sounds deep in his throat.

Her nipples were on fire. *She* was on fire. She moved against him, trying to get nearer. She felt as if she were being devoured. There was something wildly exciting about the intensity of his lust for her. "Alex, this is..." She drifted off helplessly. She didn't know how to describe what they were doing.

He pulled her down to the ground. "It's no good," he said thickly. "I can't hold—" He pushed her back on the earth and spread her thighs, his palms running feverishly up and down her flesh, feeling the textures of her. His fingers touched her, probed, sank deep.

She cried out, the muscles of her stomach clenching, convulsing.

"Tight," he muttered, "God, you're tight." He moved closer. He said through clenched teeth, "I—want—in."

She wanted him in. Her heart was pounding so hard, she couldn't get her breath.

He stabbed deep into her with frantic force.

Caitlin's entire body tensed as his presence in her body sent shock waves through every muscle.

He stopped, his face flushed, his eyes glazing with an expression of primitive pleasure. "Lord, that's good."

"Move." She could barely force the words from her dry throat as her hands plucked futilely at his shoulders. "I can't stand it." She undulated her hips against him, trying to take more of him. "Don't stop."

"I'm afraid to move." His eyes closed. "I've never felt like this before. I want to rip you apart, I want to—"

"I don't *care*." Caitlin lunged upward. "*Move*, dammit."

A shudder went through him and his lids slowly opened to reveal light eyes shimmering blindly in the moonlight. "I ...told you." His voice sounded like a low growl.

Caitlin's spine arched up from the ground, and she gave a low cry of wild satisfaction as he plunged deep.

"You like me? You like this?" His voice was hoarse, rasping as he thrust again and again. "Tell me."

"I ... like it." She moved against him, trying to meet his thrusts with her own.

He went wild, beyond control. He covered her like a stallion would a mare and rode her. It was incredible, basic, elemental.

She felt his fingertips smoothing, massaging her abdomen, feeling the muscles jar and tense with each movement. It was almost as if he were measuring the textures and depth of their joining. It was an unusual caress, all the more erotic for its oddness.

"Now." His hands delved beneath her body to cup her buttocks in his palms and lift her to each thrust. "Caitlin, give me—" He spoke through grated teeth, his nostrils flaring with each harsh breath. "No! I haven't had enough. I—want—to go—on." He moved desperately, his hips twisting. "Help me to go on."

She couldn't help him. She could barely help herself. Her head thrashed back and forth in the dirt of the field, and she could hear herself give frantic little cries as the tension coiled tighter and tighter with each movement of his body. She could no longer think coherently, but her senses were sending shards of messages.

Moonlight. Earth. Jasmine. Lime. Musk. Alex.

Alex froze, his chest rising and falling with the force of his breathing. "Damn, damn, damn...," he muttered desperately, and then something else in a language she didn't understand as he began to thrust again.

Caitlin climaxed, the tension exploding with a force that sent a fiery release through every muscle and vein in her body. An instant later she could feel Alex spasm again and again within her, shuddering helplessly.

He collapsed on top of her, his hips still moving yearningly, as if he couldn't stop even though he had already reached satisfaction. A moment later he lay still, breathing heavily, his flesh hot against her own.

Sweet Mary, what had happened between them? Caitlin wondered dazedly. She had never experienced anything like this intense encounter with Alex.

Alex's breathing gradually steadied and slowed. "I'm sorry." His voice was still uneven. "I was too rough. I lost control."

"We both lost control." She looked up at him. "You were very... primitive."

"I come of peasant stock." His lips twisted. "I have a tendency to be earthy."

"It was... like something out of the jungle. Savage..."

"But good?" His hands were playing with her breasts, stroking, lifting, before cupping them in his callused palms. His speech again had that faint Slavic intonation. "You have wonderful breasts. I've been wanting to do this since the first night I met you. You liked me?"

"Yes." She laughed shakily. "I seem to be pretty earthy myself." She was suddenly conscious of the cool ground beneath her naked back and the rows of sentinellike jasmine stakes with their coiled bounty of climbing white jasmine standing tall on either side of them. "Renée said a bed would be softer, but this isn't so bad. At least it's good Vasaro dirt."

"You talked to Renée about me?"

She shook her head. "She talked to me about you. She thought I was a bit retarded not to do this before."

He moved off her and raised her to a sitting position. "And I thought you were a sadist. You nearly drove me crazy. Another day like today and I might have dragged you down on the ground in front of the workers. God, I'm glad you've come to your senses." He helped her into her nightgown and began to button it. His expression suddenly sobered. "I didn't hurt you?"

"No. Did I hurt you?"

He chuckled. "No, but Renée is right, a mattress will be a lot easier on the knees. Let's go back to the house and wash off this dirt and—" He stopped as he saw her expression. "No?"

She nervously moistened her lips with her tongue. "I'd rather not."

He stiffened. "Rather not go back to the house or rather not go to bed with me? I'm not always like this, Caitlin. I'll try to be gentle with you next ti—"

"It's not that. I just want to keep this . . . separate."

His muscles relaxed slightly. "In what way?"

"I don't want my mother to know. I'd prefer that no one knows. I don't want it to change anything."

"You're still afraid I'll interfere with your running of Vasaro." His gaze narrowed on her face. "I told you I wouldn't let what we do hurt you. If you want to keep me in the background, that's fine."

It was going to be all right, she realized with relief. "You don't mind?"

"I'll mind when I wake up in the middle of the night and can't move on top of you. And you're going to mind the next time I'm inside you when I'm so frustrated I nearly tear you apart like I did tonight."

"I won't mind." She felt a deep tingle between her thinghs as she remembered the mindlessness of their joining only minutes before. "You'll see that it will be better this way." She frowned. "Though I don't know how we'll manage to—"

"Don't worry about it. I'll work it out."

Caitlin could already see difficulties looming on the horizon. "We could forget about this," she said tentatively. "It would be the sensible thing to—"

"No!" He tempered the violence in his voice as he continued. "I told you I'd work it out. We both need this." He buried his face in her hair and his voice was muffled. "I'll make it all right for you." He paused. "I didn't protect you. Is it okay?"

Mother of God! She had completely forgotten about the possibility of getting pregnant. Stupid. How could she have been so stupid? She knew the answer, dammit. She had been in such a fever of heat that she hadn't been able to think of anything but the act itself, and she hadn't needed contraceptives since she had left college.

"Caitlin?"

"It's fine. No problem." From now on she would make sure there was no problem. It was perfectly natural for Alex to assume she would have protected herself. She was twenty-five years old and a responsible woman even if she hadn't acted like one.

"You're sure?"

"No problem."

"Good." He gently pushed her back down on the

ground. "Then you won't mind if we go back to the jungle and I indulge my peasant instincts."

Alex didn't join them in the fields at dawn the next day. At eight o'clock Caitlin saw the Lamborghini slide down the driveway and turn onto the road leading to Cannes.

"Where's he going?" Renée's gaze followed her own.

Caitlin tried to shrug unconcernedly. "How should I know?"

"Maybe you played too hard to get?" Renée shrewdly studied Caitlin's averted face. "If a man doesn't get what he wants from one woman, there are always others to play his game. I'd make sure he gets a big welcome when he comes back from the city."

"I don't care—" Caitlin broke off as she realized she did care that Alex had left without telling her, and Renée's remarks were abrasive. Hard to get? She had given Alex exactly what he had wanted last night. Perhaps she had even been too accommodating. They had not returned to the house until close to three in the morning after innumerable feverish couplings. Now that the first edge was off his libido, Alex was no doubt less eager for her company and was going about his own business. She supposed she should have expected it. Men often grew bored when they got what they wanted from a woman. Her father had been the same with her mother.

Well, she had gotten what she wanted too, and she had no right to complain.

Still, he could have told her he wouldn't be picking with them today.

• • •

Alex had changed from his suit to his work clothes and was sitting on the bed of the truck, talking to Jacques, when Caitlin brought her final basket of the day to the truck.

He smiled at her. "Hello."

"Hello." She kept her face expressionless as she emptied the blossoms into the tub.

"Come with me." Alex levered himself down from the bed of the truck, grabbed Caitlin's hand, and pulled her away from the truck. "Hurry."

"I'm busy," she said curtly, trying to pull her wrist away from his grasp. "I have to go to the maceration shed."

"You're not busy, you're angry." He waved at Jacques on the truck as he pulled Caitlin down the road. He lowered his voice to a teasing, melodramatic whisper. "You think I used you and threw you aside."

"Don't be ridiculous. I don't have any right to be upset with you. We both know what drew us together."

"You have the right." He stopped in the middle of the road and grasped her shoulders in his hands. "I promised to be kind to you. And to behave as you think I've done wouldn't be kind." He smiled and shook her gently. "Now, stop being angry and come with me."

She could smell the familiar scent of him and felt her body react as mindlessly as it had last night to his touch. What did it matter about kindness or courtesy if he could give her this? "Where?"

"The Cottage of Flowers."

The first thing Caitlin noticed as she opened the door was the crisp cotton sheet covering the mattress on the floor in the center of the room.

She paused in the doorway, her eyes widening in surprise.

"Come on." He pulled her into the cottage. His blue eyes sparkled with boyish eagerness as he waved his hand with a flourish. "I scrubbed everything down and bought the linens in Cannes." He nodded at the cooler by the far wall. "Wine on ice." He grinned. "I even swept the birds' nests out of the chimney so we could have a fire if the nights turn cool."

She looked around dazedly. The cottage had been cleared of all debris and was pristine. "I see that you did. Why?"

"I told you I'd take care of it," he said simply. "You said no one ever comes here, so no one will know if we do. You can have your Vasaro." His hand gently stroked the tawny curls back from her face. "And I can have you. It's a wonderful solution, isn't it?"

It must have taken Alex hours to clean out the dirt and rubbish from the cottage. He had worked alone and in secret to protect her from anyone becoming aware of their association because that was what she had told him she wanted. He had said he believed kindness was important and she could see the truth of his belief in those words as she looked around her.

"The sheets are wash and wear and I chose not to spread them with petals." He met her gaze gravely. "I'm not a man who does that sort of thing. I hope you don't mind."

No, he would not give her romantic gestures because they would be a lie in their relationship. She felt a tiny twinge of sadness that she immediately dismissed as foolish. She had no need of romantic gestures when he gave her honesty, consideration, and the same lust that had brought them together. Her father had never given her mother anything but falsehoods and romantic trappings. She was much better off without satin sheets and rose petals.

She went into Alex's arms as naturally as if she had done it a hundred times before and laid her head on his chest. "No," she said. "I don't mind. I always thought Philippe went a little overboard anyway. I'm sure his ladies were more interested in who was on top of them than what was underneath."

"I'll go first." Caitlin quickly finished buttoning her shirt before tucking it into her jeans. "Give me ten minutes before you leave."

"Why is it so important to you that no one know about us?" Alex asked idly as he raised himself on one elbow on the mattress to look at her. It was really a shame to cover up those luscious breasts and sinuous hips. Yet the coarseness of her work clothes was sensually evocative when he knew the smooth, glowing flesh that lay beneath it. And after these last five days of intimate exploration he felt he knew that flesh very well indeed. "I feel like the other man in an illicit triangle."

"It's not really important." Caitlin avoided his gaze. "It's just more . . . comfortable."

"You think your mother would object?"

"No, not exactly."

"Jacques and the other workers are earthy as hell. You wouldn't get any flak from them."

"I know."

"Then, what is it?"

"I prefer to keep our relationship private."

He shook his head, studying her. "It isn't logical."

"Does everything have to be logical to you?"

"No, but I have to understand it. All kinds of actions and emotions cause us to act the way we do, but there has to be a cause and effect." He pushed the sheet aside and rose naked to his feet. "We have the effect. What's the cause?"

"Lord, you're tenacious," she said in exasperation as she moved toward the door. "You went to all the trouble of cleaning up this cottage to assure me of privacy and now you—"

"Want to know why," he finished, his brow furrowing as he began to dress. "It just occurred to me that it was odd. It doesn't matter to me one way or the other that you want me to be your backstreet man. I'm curious."

"About everything on the planet."

"Almost." His narrowed gaze searched her face. "It's your father, isn't it?"

She stiffened. "I don't know what you mean."

"The cause." He nodded. "That's it. He came to Vasaro, became involved with your mother, and, when he left, Vasaro was almost in ruins. You're seeing some correlation."

She tried to laugh. "That's not true. What we do together couldn't hurt Vasaro."

"Your mind knows that, but—"

"Mother of God, are you trying to dissect me for one of your books?"

"I write mysteries, not psychological thrillers." He suddenly smiled. "Sorry. You posed a puzzle and I have a passion for puzzles. No more questions."

"Because you think you have the answer."

"Yes," he said quietly. "There was never a possibility of my not giving you what you want, Caitlin. I merely have to understand why you wanted it." He opened the door for her and brushed a kiss on her cheek. "Ten minutes. Will I see you at supper?"

She shook her head. "I have to go to the perfumery."

"Why?"

"The Wind Dancer. I haven't had a chance to go there more than twice since the first night you came."

"I'm glad I'm such potent competition. Why are you studying it? What are you doing with—"

"It's none of your business." Her tone was suddenly fierce. "Stay out of my head, Alex."

There it was again. Every time he mentioned the Wind Dancer, she shut him out, guarding her attachment as if she were a priestess tending a sacred temple fire. "As long as you don't tell me to stay out of your body." He affectionately patted her bottom. "Did I ever tell you what a magnificent derriere you have?"

She laughed and he could see some of the tension ebb from her taut muscles. "Good-bye, Alex."

His smile gradually faded as he watched her walk briskly away from the cottage and up the hill. He had almost blown it. Caitlin obviously had some king-size hang-ups regarding her father and didn't take kindly to probing, and her passion for the Wind Dancer was also clearly out of bounds. Why the hell hadn't he been able to leave either subject alone? The last week that they had been meeting at the cottage had probably been the most erotic and fulfilling he had ever known. He had expected their lust for each other to dim within a few days, but they still came together with the urgency they had the first night in the jasmine field. Caitlin was a natural voluptuary, a stimulating companion.

He wanted more.

The realization surprised him. He wanted to *know* her. At first he had thought Caitlin was exactly what she appeared to be—an earthy, direct woman whose strength lay in her love for Vasaro and the people it sheltered. Yet soon he had become aware that she was also a creature of intense passions and impulses she tried to hold tight beneath a cool exterior. She displayed lightning flashes of humor that surprised him, and she was clearly more mother than daughter to Katrine. With Jacques there existed a deep bond, but there was nothing fatherly about it; they were equals and partners. She was one of the workers and yet was often forced to stand apart from them. Every time he studied her he saw a new facet that intrigued and drew him to uncover more.

She was coming too close.

The knowledge sent a chill down his spine. He had deliberately brought her to this point to give him something to challenge himself. But something had gone wrong.

He left the cottage and closed the door behind him. As he started up the hill he tried to think of a solution.

Vasaro.

He was too near Caitlin at Vasaro. They worked together in the fields, sometimes saw each other at meals, and now they were involved in physical intimacy. He had nothing else to think about but Caitlin, so naturally she was assuming too much importance in his life. Anywhere else but Vasaro he would be able to control his emotional response.

When he got back to the house he would call Goldbaum. It had been almost two weeks since he had talked to the investigator, and the man had to have discovered some new information that would give Alex reason to leave.

He hoped to God Goldbaum had found out something.

"I'm not sure," Goldbaum cautioned Alex. "Andreas is canny. There's no evidence. Just . . . an impression."

"I don't have anything else. I'll use it and see what happens."

"Probably zilch."

"Maybe. Anything on Ledford?"

"I've been retracing his steps for the last two years. Nothing's sending out any red flags."

"Keep working on it in case I don't hit pay dirt with Andreas."

Goldbaum sighed. "I do have other clients."

"Not ones who let you gouge them the way I do."

"That does help me to put up with you," Goldbaum agreed more cheerfully. "I'll be in touch."

"No, I'll call you. I'll probably be on the move."

Alex hung up the phone, adrenaline zinging through his veins.

A hook. Maybe not a good hook but a hook nonetheless.

He stood up and strode across the bedroom toward the door. After these weeks of sitting at Vasaro with his hands tied, he could *move*.

He hurried down the hall, taking the steps two at a time as he went to the perfumery in search of Caitlin.

Caitlin was kneeling on the floor directly in front of the pedestal on which the hologram appeared. He could see her shadowy form in the darkness and the gleam of light from the projector burnishing her tan curls as she tilted her head back to look up at it.

He experienced a twinge of uneasiness as he remembered the comparison he had made only hours before between Caitlin and a priestess at a shrine. "What the devil are you doing?"

Caitlin jumped and lowered the binoculars she had been holding to her eyes. "*Merde*, you startled me. Go away. I told you I couldn't see you tonight."

"So you can worship before the altar?"

"Don't be ridiculous." Her tone was impatient. "If you won't go away, come here and kneel down beside me."

He moved slowly across the room and dropped down beside her before the pedestal. "So?"

She handed him the binoculars. "Look at the base of the statue. Is the base seamless and of the same kind of gold as the statue?"

He lifted the binoculars to his eyes and focused them on the base of the hologram. "If it's not, it's pretty close."

"But is it the same?"

"You're the expert on antiquities."

"I don't *know*." Caitlin's voice was sharp with frustration. "I need more. All I have is Catherine's journal and that book Lily Andreas wrote in the twenties. The Andreas family have two journals that go much further back, and a good deal of that information has never been published." She flung out her hand at the hologram. "Just look at me. I'm staring at a damn hologram with a pair of high-powered binoculars. I need equipment. I need to see the statue itself."

Alex smiled. "Perhaps I can make a suggestion?"

Caitlin looked at him. A reflection of the Wind Dancer shimmered in her eyes in the diffused light from the projector. It was strange to see that inhuman power and beauty shining boldly out at him from such an earthy human being as Caitlin. She could probably see the same reflection in his own eyes. It was as if, for a brief instant, they had both been caught, possessed, by the statue.

"I'm not in a mood for jokes, Alex." Her tone was edged with impatience. "This is important to me."

"Obviously." He reached out and took the remote from her. "If you need to see it, let's go see it."

She stiffened. "What?"

He clicked off the projectors and the Wind Dancer disappeared from Caitlin's eyes. He felt a totally unreasonable flicker of relief as he rose to his feet, crossed the room, and switched on the light. "Pack a suitcase. Enough for a five-day stay. I don't know how long it will take, but we can always buy more if—"

"Pack? Where am I supposed to be going?"

"The United States. Is your passport in order?"

"I think so. I'll have to check."

"We can take care of it in Nice if there's a problem. Will you call Air France and book our reservations? I'll have to make a few calls and have some additional information delivered to me at the airport so I'll be ready for the presentation."

"What presentation?" Caitlin asked. "And I just can't run off to America. I have responsibilities here at Vasaro."

"And one of those responsibilities is marketing your perfume."

"Is that what this is all about?"

He nodded. "We have to have a hook to launch the perfume in a big way."

She slowly rose to her feet. "And this hook is in the United States?"

"South Carolina, to be exact." He smiled. "The Wind Dancer."

Her eyes widened in surprise as she realized what he was planning. "You're trying to get the Andreas family to let you use the Wind Dancer in a publicity campaign?"

"Can you think of a more evocative or romantic symbol?"

"No." She added flatly, "But it will never happen."

"Why not? You're distantly related to the Andreas family, which will give us an entree. I'll do the rest."

"What can we offer them? They don't need money." Caitlin nibbled worriedly at her lower lip. "And they've never permitted the statue to leave the U.S. since they lost it to Hitler at the beginning of World War Two." She met his gaze. "You'd want a world tour?"

"At least a European tour, starting in Paris."

She made a face. "If you expect familial feelings to soften any Andreas heart, you're going to be disappointed. Why do you think I've never approached them before about studying the Wind Dancer at close quarters? It was my grandmother who talked Jonathan's father into lending the Wind Dancer to the Louvre. When the Wind Dancer was stolen by the Nazis, the Andreas family was furious and blamed Vasaro for not protecting it."

"That was fifty years ago."

"I've heard the Andreas clan have long memories."

"We'll have to see." He took her hand and pulled her toward the door. "It's worth the gamble."

"You're really going to do it?"

He stopped and looked down at her. "Do you know how much it will cost to launch a major campaign to sell your perfume?"

"I was afraid to check into it. A small fortune, I suppose?"

"Try a bigger fortune. Between ten and fifteen million dollars."

She inhaled sharply. "Do you have that much money?"

"I have it. But with any luck we won't have to spend that much. The Wind Dancer would generate its own publicity. We wouldn't have to create a mystique for it."

"A mystique?" She smiled. "You seem to know the buzzwords."

"Courtesy of your library and those bundles of information I've been receiving in the mail every day." He stepped aside to let her precede him through the door. "And I guarantee I'll know a hell of a lot more before we reach Charleston."

Her smile faded. "If the campaign will cost this much money, will we be able to make a profit?"

"How much does it cost to make an ounce of Vasaro?"

"About twenty dollars. We use the best oils and ingredients."

He grinned. "Then we'll make a profit. We'll charge two hundred dollars an ounce."

"That's too much," she said, shocked. "That's more than Passion or Opium or—"

"Not for bottled mystique. Is your perfume good?"

"Yes."

"Wonderful?"

"It's Vasaro," she said simply.

He chuckled. "Which means it could become a classic. A classic perfume can easily earn fifty million dollars a year."

"I've never seen you like this," she said, bemused.

"That's because you've only seen me spinning my wheels. I'm basically a problem solver, and now I have a problem to solve." He muttered, "At long last."

"And you love it, don't you? It makes you come alive."

He shrugged. "At least it makes me feel I'm alive." He grasped her elbow. "If there's nothing direct to Charleston, ask Air France if there's a night flight to New York. And you'll want to give instructions to Jacques and say good-bye to your mother."

"I think I can handle that by myself," she said dryly.

"Sorry. I get carried away when—why are you laughing?"

"Because I remember saying that to you when I was talking about Vasaro. Perhaps we have more in common than I thought."

Her face was alight with laughter and he found himself caught and held. He wanted to reach out and touch her lips, gently trace the smile with his finger.

Tenderness.

He turned away without touching her. "Besides bringing along a copy of your paper on the Wind Dancer, you might look up any family history in case Andreas is a history buff. We'll need every advantage we can get if we're going to pry the Wind Dancer loose from him."

"What are those?" Caitlin glanced curiously at the clippings Alex had spread on the tray in front of him. "Is that what was in the envelope that man gave you at the departure gate?"

He nodded. "They're clippings from the U.S. papers for the last six months. I wanted to see how much space they'd given to the art thefts in Europe. Andreas isn't going to be overjoyed about lending the Wind Dancer if the newspapers have been on a feeding frenzy." Alex shoved the clippings back in the manila envelope as the attendant paused beside him, offering a smile and a cup of coffee. He returned the smile and accepted the cup. "Unfortunately, from what I can see they gave them plenty of coverage."

"Naturally, a theft like the 'Mona Lisa' would get world coverage." She shook her head. "It's incredible that they haven't been able to recover it after all this time. Those people at Interpol must be bumbling idiots."

He sipped his coffee. "Is that your opinion of Interpol?"

"What do you mean?"

"Have these thefts made you lose faith in the police?"

She thought about it. "I suppose . . . I don't know."

"And these terrorist attacks by the Black Medina frighten you?"

"They don't make me feel very secure."

"Interesting. You're probably more insulated at Vasaro than nine tenths of the population of Europe, and you're beginning to be angry and afraid. I wonder how those people who don't live in a sheltered garden are reacting?"

"I have no idea. Why are you so interested in all this?"

"I'm just—"

"Curious," Caitlin finished with a chuckle. "I've never seen anyone so curious. Remind me to tell you about the sad demise of a pussycat with that very failing."

His expression became shuttered. "I've heard it before."

Her smile faded as she looked at him. She had hurt him in some way. Behind that expressionless mask she could sense his pain and felt an answering ache deep within her. She glanced out the window into the darkness, trying to think of something to distract him. "I'm glad they didn't think 'Boy in the Field' was worth taking when they stole the 'Mona Lisa.' It's in the same section in the Louvre."

"'Boy in the Field'? I've never heard of it. Who painted it?"

"It's unsigned." She paused. "But it was painted by Juliette Andreas, Jonathan Andreas's, great-great-grandmother." She frowned. "Maybe I should have thrown another *great* in there. I always get confused when it comes to the greats."

"If it's unsigned, how do you know that Juliette Andreas painted it?"

"It's in Catherine's journal. Juliette left a painting of

Michel at Vasaro when she immigrated to the United States. Juliette was a fine artist, but there was a terrible prejudice against women painters at that time and there was no way she would have been accepted by the Louvre." She leaned back in her chair. "So Catherine decided to take matters in her own hands. Most of the great paintings from Versailles had been brought to the Louvre by 1793, but with so much confusion during the Terror, Catherine decided it wouldn't be illogical that a hidden cache of art treasures would have been overlooked."

A slow smile lit Alex's face. "I can't believe this."

"It's true. Somehow she and François managed to smuggle Juliette's paintings together with a Fragonard and a Del Sarto into one of the queen's apartments at Versailles. Then François arranged for the hidden masterpieces to be 'discovered' by the National Guard and they were immediately whisked to the Louvre with the others. Since the unsigned painting was in such prestigious company, it was immediately assumed to be painted by someone of immense stature."

"And so Juliette Andreas's painting hangs in the Louvre with the masters." Alex looked thoughtfully down into his coffee. "Does the Andreas family know this story?"

"I'm sure they do. Catherine said she wrote to Juliette to tell her."

"They must have been great friends for Catherine to go to so much trouble."

"Read the journal."

"Perhaps I will." His gaze lifted. "In the meantime, it wouldn't hurt for you to mention the incident to Andreas if the occasion presents itself."

"It's water under the bridge. That happened in 1797."

"You said the Andreases had long memories." He finished his coffee. "We can try."

She was no longer sensing that terrible pain in him, she realized with relief. Perhaps Catherine's story had helped as she had hoped it would. "You're certainly determined. You'll try anything, won't you?"

"And everything," he said flatly.

She glanced at his face. "Do you really think we have a chance of getting the Wind Dancer?"

"We'll get it."

"How can you be so sure?"

"Because I've got to get it."

She shook her head. "So there is no question of your doing it?"

He didn't answer.

"I don't suppose you'd like to tell me why it's so important for you to get the Wind Dancer?"

He smiled. "Why, to save me a barrel of money."

"But that isn't the only reason, is it?"

"Isn't it reason enough? We can't all have a passion for antiquities."

She wasn't going to get another answer from him. She didn't know why the realization hurt her. She didn't want to confide her own feelings about the Wind Dancer and she had told Alex in the beginning she didn't care what his reasons were for saving Vasaro. Yet now something had changed. She found she did care when he shut her out.

His fingers laced through hers, his strong grip companionable, a soothing caress after the hurtful evasion of the moment before. "Try to get some sleep. We have another four hours before we get to New York, and then another two to Charleston. You'll be exhausted by the time we get to Port Andreas."

"I can't sleep. I'm too nervous. Will he see us?"

"We have an appointment for three tomorrow afternoon. I called from Vasaro before we left and set it up with Andreas's personal assistant, Peter Maskovel." He shook his head. "It was almost too easy. I mentioned your name and Maskovel practically jumped through the phone."

"It's all moving so fast."

"We'll have to move even faster once we get Andreas's okay."

"I know we're doing the right thing, but it scares me." She smiled tremulously. "Wheeling and dealing isn't my area of expertise. I just want to run home and grow my flowers."

"You'll be fine once we start the wheels rolling. It's the waiting that's hard." He smiled. "And why be scared of Jonathan Andreas? You're practically cousins."

"It means too much. The Wind Dancer, the perfume, Vasaro . . ."

"Well, if you can't sleep, tell me a story."

"A story?"

"Catherine's journal. Start at the beginning and tell me all the scandalous details of your family history."

She looked at him doubtfully. "You really want me to?"

Alex's hand tightened. "I really do."

She leaned back on the headrest of the seat. "The journal opens on September 2, 1792, when Catherine is in the convent of the Abbaye de la Reine . . ."

5

"I'm Peter Maskovel. Is Miss Vasaro with you?" The deep voice rang boyishly eager over the intercom at the front gate.

Alex shot an amused glance at Caitlin in the passenger seat beside him. "Right here."

"I'll trigger the gate and meet you at the front entrance. Don't get out of the car until you reach the house."

The intercom shut off and the iron gates swung slowly open.

Alex drove the dark blue rental car through the gates. "I'm sure he would have turned me away if I'd told him I'd left you at home at Vasaro. Are you certain you've never met the man?"

"No, I've never even heard of him."

The tall iron gate clanged shut behind their car and the huge bolts slid electronically into place.

Caitlin looked back over her shoulder at the iron gates. "I feel like I've just breached a maximum security prison. Where are the bloodhounds?"

"Dobermans."

"What?"

"Andreas has six Dobermans patrolling the grounds.

That's why Maskovel told us not to get out of the car before we reached the main house."

"How did you know about the dogs?" She answered the question herself. "It was in those research packets."

He nodded. "The layout of the compound wasn't important to our purpose, but I didn't think it would hurt to know something about it."

"Why is it called a compound?"

"Several members of the Andreas family have their own residences on the grounds. Jonathan's two sisters and their husbands have beach houses on the shore and his father has a cottage farther inland. The mansion itself is surrounded by guest cottages and servant quarters."

They rounded a curve in the road, and an immense brick mansion with huge round white columns came into view.

"Very impressive," Caitlin murmured. "Southern aristocracy and mint juleps." She nodded to the flag flying from the pole in the middle of the grounds. "But shouldn't that be a Confederate flag?"

"Andreas's family fought on the Union side and he's very patriotic." As Alex started up the curving driveway he saw the wide double doors open and a slender man come out on the veranda. "That must be Peter Maskovel. He could be important to us."

"How?"

"He's worked for Andreas for eighteen years and Andreas trusts him completely." He studied the man coming down the steps. "They went to Yale together. Maskovel's family are coal miners in West Virginia and he earned a scholarship. There was something else. . . ." His brow cleared as he brought that final paragraph in the report into focus. "That's right, Maskovel has a bad heart. He had a triple bypass operation about five years ago."

"He doesn't look ill."

Peter Maskovel was a little over average height and, though not muscular, looked fit and tan in a white summer sweater and gray slacks. His carefully barbered light brown hair shone soft and baby fine in the sunlight, and his features were nondescript except for wide-set brown eyes that sparkled with intelligence.

"He's not ill. He just has to be careful." Alex parked the car and turned off the ignition. He turned to face her and smiled reassuringly. "Don't be nervous. We'll get what we came for."

"As I said, I'm out of my element." She smoothed her skirt. "Do I look all right?"

Alex glanced casually at the navy blue suit she was wearing. "Fine."

She grimaced. "I'm not sure my mother would agree. This suit is five years old."

"Andreas won't be looking at your clothes." He opened the door and stepped out onto the driveway. "Let's go get him."

"Mr. Karazov?" Peter gave Alex a polite nod as he opened the passenger door for Caitlin. "I'm Peter Maskovel." He helped Caitlin from the car, his gaze eagerly searching her face. "And you must be Caitlin Vasaro. I've been waiting a long time for this."

Caitlin looked at him in bewilderment. "How do you do, Mr. Maskovel?"

"Peter." He smiled. "I hope we'll be very good friends. I read your research paper that you contributed to Beaujolis's doctorate. It was the sharpest and most insightful part of the entire thesis." He paused. "I'd like to use you."

"Use me?"

He slammed the door. "You have Catherine's journal. I have Caterina and Sanchia Andreas's journals, but I've never read Catherine's. You see, I didn't even know—"

"Wait." Caitlin held up her hand to stop the flow. "*You* have the Andreas journals?"

He looked sheepish. "Well, Jonathan actually owns them, but I feel as if they're mine. I've been intending to phone you for the last year and ask if you'd make a Xerox copy of the journal at my expense and send it to me."

"I couldn't do that. The contents of the journal are confidential."

He made a face. "I was afraid you'd say that. There are quite a few family secrets in the Andreas journals too."

"Why would you be interested in Catherine's journal?"

"The Vasaro and Andreas families were bound together for centuries. I guess my interest began because I've lived for years with the Wind Dancer and I wanted to find out more about him." A gentle smile illuminated Maskovel's features, and suddenly they were no longer nondescript. "One thing led to another. I don't have any close members of my own family alive any longer, and the Andreas family and their ancestors have become my family now." His brow knotted in a thought. "And then, too, I wondered if there might be something in the journal about the inscription on the statue."

She stiffened. "The inscription?"

"You must know it's never been deciphered?"

"Of course, but I—"

"Excuse me, I wonder if we could discuss this later," Alex cut in. "I don't want to keep Mr. Andreas waiting."

Peter nodded. "Jonathan's in the study." He took Caitlin's elbow and began to climb the steps. "As I said, I started to read the journals to find out more about the Wind Dancer." They passed through a gracious foyer with gleaming oak floors. "Then last year I ran across some correspondence in the family records that mentioned Catherine's journal."

Caitlin caught a glimpse of Alex's amused gaze on Peter and she knew how he felt. Peter's eagerness was almost childlike and yet she had the impression that here was a man who was entirely mature and worldly-wise. The contradiction made Maskovel's enthusiasm all the more appealing. Yet, much as she liked the man himself, she was beginning to feel a fierce sense of envy and resentment. He had the two early journals, he had the Wind Dancer itself to study every single day, and he still wanted more.

Peter paused before a paneled mahogany door. "Could we talk about it later?" he asked quietly. "I really do need to see that journal."

"We'll talk. But I can't promise anything will come of it."

"Good enough." He smiled at her as he threw open the door. "Mr. Karazov and Miss Vasaro are here, Jonathan."

He stepped aside for them to enter before following them into the study and closing the door behind them.

Jonathan Andreas was big.

Caitlin's first impression was of the sheer magnitude of the man who turned from the window at their entrance. He was at least six feet five, with massive shoulders, a deep chest, and the build of a construction worker. His nose and mouth were hammered on the same large scale, broad cheekbones, eyebrows that slashed above eyes nearer to black than brown. Gray threaded Andreas's dark brown hair at the temples, but he looked no older than in his early forties. He was dressed with the same casualness as Peter in a navy blue cotton sweater, black twill trousers, and loafers.

A smile lit Andreas's face and caused the laugh lines to fan out around his eyes as he came toward them. Caitlin stared at him, mesmerized. He wasn't at all a handsome man, but there was something—

"Miss Vasaro." His hand enfolded Caitlin's in a firm, secure grasp and she experienced an overwhelming ense of well-being. "I hope you'll let me call you Caitlin. I don't know why you're here, but I'm glad you decided to come. I've heard about the Vasaros all my life and it's time we got together."

She suddenly understood Jonathan Andreas's attraction. He projected an aura of *goodness* that gave one a feeling nothing bad could happen in his presence. How extraordinary.

She smiled. "I wasn't sure we'd be welcome. I remember hearing stories about how furious your father was about the loss of the Wind Dancer."

"He still is." Andreas's black eyes twinkled. "That's why I've only *heard* about Vasaros all my life." He released her hand and gestured to one of the two brown leather chairs before the huge rosewood desk in the center of the room. "Sit down. I suppose Peter attacked you as soon as you stepped from the car?"

"Guilty," Peter admitted as he dropped down onto the cushioned leather couch across the study. "But Mr. Karazov rescued her before I could drag her off."

"Mr. Karazov." Andreas turned to Alex. "Forgive me for being rude. It's not often that I have a chance to knit a rift of fifty years."

"Perfectly understandable," Alex said. "From what I've heard, you're admirably suited to rift mending."

Andreas's cordial expression underwent only the slightest change, but Caitlin was conscious of a new element of wariness as he appraised Alex more carefully. "I've done my share. You can't run a business successfully unless everyone works together. Won't you sit down?"

Alex seated himself and smiled easily. "You'll notice I'm not waiting for you to be seated. I'm perfectly willing for you to occupy the position of power."

Andreas nodded. "You told Peter this was pertaining to a business matter." He turned to Caitlin. "Vasaro?"

She nodded. "We need your help."

"Money?"

"Not exactly." She nodded at Alex. "I'd prefer that my business partner explain."

"What do you want from me?" Andreas asked Alex.

"The Wind Dancer."

Caitlin heard Peter Maskovel murmur something, but she didn't take her gaze from Alex and Andreas.

Andreas chuckled. "You're joking."

"We'd like you to lend the Wind Dancer to us for a short time. Perhaps six months. Caitlin has a new perfume that needs to be suitably launched and—"

"You want to use the statue for a publicity gimmick?" Andreas interrupted. "So do half the entrepreneurs in the world. Do you think you're the first to come to me? We don't use the Wind Dancer for that purpose, Mr. Karazov."

"Not generally," Alex said quietly. "But the circumstances are different in this case. Miss Vasaro could lose everything she owns unless the perfume is a success, and she is your kinswoman."

"*Distant* kinswoman."

"I think it still might make a difference to you. You're reputed to be very protective of your family," Alex continued. "We wouldn't expect to use the Wind Dancer indefinitely. A short tour in Europe to launch and then a slightly longer tour here in the United States. After the tour the statue would be returned to you here at Port Andreas."

"How kind of you."

Alex ignored the irony in Andreas's tone. "Naturally, since we're limiting the use of the Wind Dancer, we'll have to use a secondary draw in the launch campaign."

"And why would you believe I'd actually do this?"

"I told you, family feeling." Alex smiled. "And the

added inducement that I'll give you six percent of my twenty-five percent of the profits for the next five years. I estimate those profits should be in the neighborhood of three hundred million dollars."

"Quite a respectable neighborhood." Andreas leaned back against the desk. "But even if I decided to help you, sending the Wind Dancer to Europe is out of the question."

Alex nodded understandingly. "The thefts. I give you my word that you won't lose the Wind Dancer if you choose to give us your cooperation. It goes without question that security would have to be incredibly tight."

Andreas looked at him skeptically.

"You're right, it's still a danger. Perhaps we should use your security people and do the tour under your personal supervision."

Andreas laughed in disbelief. "You expect me to go on tour with the statue? I'm a busy man, Karazov."

"It's the logical way to assure the safety of the Wind Dancer. Anyone could see that."

There was an odd emphasis on the last sentence, and Andreas's gaze narrowed thoughtfully on Alex's face. "What are you trying to say?"

"I've said it."

"Not enough." Andreas turned to Caitlin and said regretfully, "I'm sorry, but the risk is too great."

Caitlin felt her hopes plummet. *Merde*, she should have known it couldn't happen.

"At least listen to our plans for the campaign." Alex unsnapped his briefcase. "As soon as we return I'll find a packager to create a bottle. I thought perhaps the stopper could be a small figure of a Pegasus, reminiscent of the Wind Dancer, made of frosted Baccarat crystal." He pulled a sheaf of drawings, notes, and photographs from his briefcase. "As I said before, we'll need another draw, and that's usually provided by a celebrity. Elizabeth Taylor had Passion; Cher, Uninhibited; Baryshnikov, Misha." He stood up and crossed the study to stand before Andreas. "Here are some pictures and biographies of several actresses we might consider as spokeswoman."

Andreas hesitated before accepting the sheaf of papers.

Caitlin watched him seat himself at the huge rosewood desk and put the papers on the blotter in front of him. It was clear Andreas had no intention of letting them use the Wind Dancer and was merely being polite. Yet she knew Alex wouldn't give up. He had the same expression of single-minded intensity as he had when he had worked in the fields.

Andreas began to flip impatiently through the photographs.

"What we need is someone with glamour, intelligence, and strength, someone the public will perceive as a survivor as well as a sex symbol." Alex's tone was without expression. "My personal choice is Chelsea Benedict. I've always liked her pictures. Probably any of the others would do as well. Glenn Close is gaining a certain following and rep—"

"Chelsea Benedict?" Andreas didn't look up from the photographs.

"I agree she's controversial, but I think her good points outweigh her bad."

Andreas looked up, and Caitlin was surprised at the coolness of his expression as his gaze met Alex's. "You seem to have thought out your campaign very thoroughly."

"It's only a preliminary plan, but I didn't want to waste your time by coming totally unprepared." Alex smiled. "You'll think about it? If you'd like any other information, we'll be at the Hyatt in Charleston for the next two days."

"I'll think about it. You're a very clever man, Mr. Karazov. I wonder if Caitlin knows exactly how clever."

Wariness flickered in Alex's expression. "I beg your pardon?"

"When you made this appointment to see me, I asked Peter to contact an old friend of mine who is on the appropriation board of the National Security Agency to see what we could find out about you."

"Why? That appears to be a trifle unusual for a simple business appointment."

Jonathan smiled faintly. "My reputation regarding my protectiveness toward my family is entirely valid. I didn't like the idea of even a distant kinswoman being used to further the ambitions of a confidence man."

"Alex isn't a confidence man," Caitlin said.

"No, he's not." Jonathan opened the middle drawer of his desk, drew out a manila folder, and flipped it open. "Our Mr. Karazov is something of an enigma. Peter had a good deal of trouble compiling this dossier. It seems the CIA doesn't want any inquiries made about him. The NSA and the CIA aren't the warmest of associates under any circumstances, but the senator said they battened down all the hatches when Karazov was mentioned. Still, we did find out a few things."

"I'm sure you did," Alex said without expression.

"You're thirty-seven, born Romanian but became a naturalized citizen of the United States six years ago. You defected from the USSR five years before that with a man named Pavel Rubanski." Jonathan paused. "With the enthusiastic help of the CIA. They appeared to want you very badly indeed."

"You're saying he was an agent?" Caitlin asked, startled.

"No, I don't think so," Jonathan said. "The CIA stuck him into a think tank at Langley, Virginia, and he worked for them for six years. Whatever he was, they found him valuable enough to give him everything he wanted, ranging from renting him a private jet for weekend pleasure jaunts"—he glanced away from Caitlin to the dossier on the desk before him—"to the services of thousand-dollar-a-night call girls."

"You seem to have found out a good deal about me," Alex said dryly. "If they treated me so well, why did I leave?"

"A blow-up," Jonathan said. "Another question mark. For some reason you walked and left a hell of a lot of angry people behind at Langley. Now, angry people generally rant and rave, but the CIA has put a blanket of silence over everything concerning you."

"I assure you that I wasn't some sort of mad scientist concocting chemical warfare experiments."

"I didn't think you were. The scientist theory doesn't gibe with your military background in the Spetznez."

"The Spetznez?" Caitlin asked.

"I was in the military," Alex said. "The Spetznez is the Russian equivalent of the Green Berets."

"And also one of the best-trained killing machines in the world," Jonathan added.

"No more so than the U.S. Special Services," Alex said. "I understand you served with them in Vietnam, Andreas."

"Yes," Andreas said. "But I didn't serve with the KGB." He paused. "You were with the Spetznez only two years when you were tapped by the KGB for special duty."

"What kind of special duty?" Caitlin asked. She felt as if she were caught in the middle of some kind of cat-and-mouse game between Alex and Jonathan, and it was beginning to frighten and frustrate her.

"Why not ask him?" Andreas leaned back in his chair,

his gaze narrowed on Alex's face. "It's classified. The KGB is never forthcoming, but they're practically paranoid about Karazov. There's no question he's brilliant. He has a photographic memory and his library at Langley ranged from nuclear physics to ancient history. Yes, he's a very popular man. The Spetznez, the KGB, the CIA...they all wanted to keep him as a pet."

"You'll find no one keeps me as a pet these days," Alex said.

"No, you live in Switzerland in a deluxe chalet, apparently have money to burn, and several Swiss bank accounts."

"He writes novels," Caitlin said. "He's Alex Kalan."

"I'm aware of his pseudonym. As a matter of fact, I've read his books and have a great admiration for them. He's a mental wizard when it comes to plotting. But I doubt if the CIA or the KGB kept him on hand to provide them with reading matter." Jonathan smiled. "And he must have had a sizable fortune before the royalties started pouring in or he wouldn't have been able to buy the chalet."

"What he's trying to say is that I'm obviously a disreputable fellow and dangerous to deal with, Caitlin," Alex said lightly.

"Not exactly safe." Jonathan turned to Caitlin. "I believe everyone should make his own decisions, but you should have something on which to base a decision."

"So he's using you to ask the questions; he doesn't think I'll answer if he puts them to me."

Merde, she'd had enough of them talking around and over her head. "To me there appears to be only one pertinent question to ask. What did you do for the CIA, Alex?"

He didn't reply at once, and for a moment she didn't think he was going to answer. Then he said curtly, "I solved puzzles."

"You're joking."

"Oh, no." Alex's lips curved in a bitter smile. "It was no joke. I was the best in the business. In fact, I *was* the business. No one could do it like Alex Karazov."

Jonathan's expression was suddenly arrested. "Do what?"

"It's very simple. I have a talent. Give me a piece of information here and another there and I see relationships. I weigh the probabilities and the variables and project what's going to happen two or three steps down the road. Sometimes more than that."

"It sounds like hocus-pocus," Caitlin said.

Alex shook his head. "It's like a master's chess game on a bigger scale. Only I was never involved in the game itself. I just told them what moves to make to win the game." His smile faded. "They won a lot of games with me. Ninety-two point four percent to be exact."

"Intelligence field operations?" Jonathan asked.

"Most of the time. Sometimes they lent me to other departments."

"What departments?"

Alex shrugged. "I think we'll skip any more delving into my iniquitous past. I've told you what was important." His expression wasn't merely cynical, but wary. "Well, have you decided that I should be cast out into the darkness?"

"What?" She scarcely heard the question. Something he had said had sparked a mental chain reaction and her excitement was growing by the second.

"I said, have you decided—"

"Can you really work puzzles? All kinds of puzzles?" she interrupted.

He blinked, disconcerted. "Yes."

"It's a unique talent? No one is better at it than you?"

"I assure you that I'm truly one of a kind."

She scarcely noticed the irony in his tone. "Good." Eagerness and excitement soared through her as she told Jonathan, "Then we have something else to throw into the deal. The inscription on the base of the Wind Dancer has never been deciphered. Mr. Maskovel's obviously interested in doing so. Do you feel the same way?"

Jonathan went still. "Of course. It's a mystery that's plagued the family for centuries."

"Then Alex and I will solve it for you."

Alex's brows rose. "We will?"

"Of course." Caitlin frowned impatiently at him before turning back to Jonathan. "I have a background in antiquities and Alex is a problem-solver. Who has a better chance?"

Jonathan didn't answer for a moment. "It's an interesting offer. But may I remind you the inscription hasn't been deciphered in some thousands of years of attempts?"

"But Alex said he was unique."

Alex chuckled. "I'll watch my words next time. It can obviously be dangerous around you."

"Jonathan, if Karazov could help..." Peter spoke for the first time from the couch across the room. "If we could get a start..."

Jonathan stared speculatively at Alex. "Is it possible?"

"I'd have to study the inscription."

"Through the years the Andreas family has had some of the greatest experts in the world working on it. I think we need something more. A fresh approach." Jonathan smiled faintly. "I think we may need a puzzle breaker."

"I do analysis and projections for the future; you're talking about something else entirely."

"It's still a puzzle," Caitlin said. "We'll do it."

"I'm glad you have such confidence in me," Alex drawled. His gaze shifted back to Jonathan. "However,

I'd certainly try to do it if it meant your acceding to our request."

"I'll have to think about it." Jonathan rose to his feet. "I'll ask Peter to call you one way or the other tomorrow morning. Good day."

"It was kind of you to see us." Caitlin stood up. "We wouldn't have bothered you if it hadn't meant so much to Vasaro. Please. Believe me. I can—we *can* translate the inscription." Her expression held desperate earnestness. "And if you let us have the Wind Dancer, I promise we'll keep it safe, Monsieur Andreas."

"Jonathan." Andreas's expression softened as he turned to her. "Regardless of my decision, I hope this isn't good-bye. Perhaps you could come for a few weeks in the fall when the family gathers for my father's birthday." He grimaced. "The kids get pretty rowdy, but I think you'll like my sisters."

"Thank you, but I'm not sure your father would appreciate my barging into his party, and I have Vasaro to think about."

"And your new perfume."

She nodded and turned to Peter. "I suppose we'll be speaking tomorrow?"

Peter smiled as he rose to his feet. "You can bet on it."

She hesitated. "I wonder . . . while we're here, could I possibly see the Wind Dancer?"

"Certainly." Jonathan nodded at Peter, who immediately started toward the door of the study. "Peter will show you to the salon."

Alex grasped Caitlin's elbow and they started to follow Peter.

"Karazov." Jonathan stopped them as they reached the door. "One more question. What happened to your friend Pavel Rubanski?"

Caitlin felt Alex's grip tighten on her arm.

"What did your dossier tell you?"

"That the Swiss police filed a report he suffered a heart attack and died at your chalet last June."

"Then why should you question it?"

Jonathan was silent an instant. "I suppose I shouldn't. Just curious." He closed the dossier on his desk. "Send me the other information about your promotional plans."

Alex nodded. "As soon as I get back to the hotel."

Peter proceeded down the hall, but as soon as the door closed behind them, Caitlin whispered to Alex, "What plans?"

Alex propelled her down the corridor after Peter. "I'll type a few suggestions and send them back by messenger."

"A few? Shouldn't we have a detailed plan before—"

"We should, but I don't." He added, "Yet."

"He's reputed to be a very sharp businessman, Alex."

"Brilliant. But I think—"

"Here we are." Peter had opened a door to the left of the foyer. "The Wind Dancer is on that pedestal over there."

"I would have thought you'd keep it in a vault," Alex said as he entered the large, high-ceilinged room.

"Would you keep a member of the family in a vault?" Peter made a face. "Come to think of it, I have a great-aunt whom I wouldn't mind walling up. Don't worry, security at the compound is impregnable."

Caitlin's gaze went at once to the pedestal that held the place of honor in the middle of the salon. She felt the breath leave her lungs as she froze in the doorway. "Dear God." She had thought she had been prepared, but she knew now she hadn't been.

"Hits you like a fist in the belly, doesn't it?" Peter asked inelegantly. "I know how you feel. He still makes me feel a little uneasy sometimes."

He didn't make Caitlin feel uneasy. After the first stunning impact she felt a rush of overwhelming *rightness*. As if everything in her life had led her to this moment. She moved slowly across the salon until she stood before the statue, drinking in the sheer beauty of the Pegasus. "Hello, boy." She didn't realize she had spoken the words aloud as her hand reached out and hovered over one delicate filigree wing, almost afraid to touch it. The gold was light, cool, beneath her palm, and yet she felt as if—

"Caitlin?" It was Alex's voice.

"Yes." How strange. In her holograph those glittering emerald eyes had appeared cold, but there was nothing cold about the reality. They seemed to hold wisdom, understanding, even compassion.

"It's time to go."

"No, it's been only—" She turned to protest and saw both Alex and Peter were gazing not at the statue but at her own face. Her hand fell away from the wing of the Pegasus, and she forced herself to take a step back and smile at Peter. "Thank you for allowing us to see it. I've been waiting for this moment since I was a small child."

"You're welcome." Peter was still looking at her strangely. "It was very . . . interesting."

An odd air of protectiveness charged Alex's movements as he strode forward, took her arm, and pushed her gently toward the door. "It's magnificent. A private viewing is always more impressive. We'll expect to hear from you, Maskovel."

"Right." Peter stepped past them and started back down the hall toward Jonathan's study. "Have a safe trip back to Charleston."

"I think you almost blew it," Alex murmured to Caitlin as they walked down the hall toward the front door. "Maskovel was wondering if you were going to snatch the statue and run for it."

"It's so beautiful, Alex."

"We got the impression you thought so. You stared at it without saying a word for five minutes."

"Five—no, it couldn't have—" It had seemed only seconds she had stood before the pedestal. "Really?"

"Really. We both thought you were mesmerized." Alex opened the front door. "But on the whole I believe the meeting went very well." He suddenly chuckled. "Though I think you threw Andreas a curve when you didn't respond with proper horror when he revealed my wicked past." His smile faded as he glanced at her. "I admit you surprised me too."

"Why? It was all very interesting, but I always knew you had secrets." She started down the stone steps to the car waiting in the driveway. "Actually, it was far more innocuous than I'd been imagining."

"So you zeroed in on what was important to you and attacked." Alex followed her down the steps. "Pretty good for a lady who was shaking in her shoes before we walked into that library."

"It was important. I forgot about being nervous." She glanced at him gravely over her shoulder. "And we'll give good value to him, Alex. I'll decipher that inscription."

"Correct me if I'm wrong, but didn't you volunteer my services as well?"

"That was only because your credentials sounded impressive and I thought he might not go along with mine." Caitlin added quickly, "Don't worry about it. I'll deal with the Wind Dancer inscription by myself."

"Oh, I don't know. I'm beginning to become intrigued with the problem."

She whirled on him fiercely. "He's *mine*, Alex."

He broke out laughing. "Just teasing. I was curious to see how you'd react."

"'That damn curiosity." She relaxed. "I'm sorry. It's just that I never thought I'd have the opportunity to study him at close range." She suddenly frowned as another thought occurred to her. "And I still think Jonathan's going to balk if we don't give him a detailed promotional plan."

Alex shook his head. "I think this time all Andreas wants is paperwork."

"I don't understand what you're talking about."

"He has to have an excuse to give us what we want."

"Do you think he might really change his mind?"

"No." Alex opened the passenger door and helped her into the car. "I believe he's already changed it."

"What's your opinion, Peter?" Jonathan leaned back in the leather executive chair, his fingers toying absent-mindedly with the photograph of Glenn Close on the desk in front of him.

"About what?"

"Karazov."

"Smart. Hard. Subterranean."

"And Caitlin Vasaro?"

Peter smiled. "I thought she was a gentle pussycat until she clamped onto the idea of deciphering the inscription and wouldn't let go. There's definitely more there than meets the eye." His smile faded and his expression turned thoughtful. "And she's in love."

"With Karazov?"

"Maybe." Peter shrugged. "But definitely with the Wind Dancer. You should have seen her face when she was looking at it. I've never seen anything like the way she lit up."

"Then she'd be all the more careful not to endanger it."

"True." Peter studied his expression. "You're thinking about letting them use the Wind Dancer."

"You think I'm stupid to consider it?"

Peter grinned. "If you expect me to try to talk you out of it, forget it. If we take the Wind Dancer to France, I'd have a chance of getting my hands on Catherine's journal and we get a brilliant problem-solver to work on the inscription."

Jonathan chuckled. "And run the risk of losing the statue entirely."

"I'd see that the security is foolproof if you did decide to go through with it."

"You must want to decipher that inscription pretty badly."

"I thought I did until I saw Caitlin Vasaro looking at the statue. With me it's a hobby; with her it's something else entirely."

"It's not likely either of you will be able to do anything with it. Scholars have been trying to interpret that inscription on the Wind Dancer's base for centuries." Jonathan's tone was gentle. "Most of them decided it was a language dead long before the time of the pharaohs."

Peter shook his head. "The first reference we have on the Wind Dancer is in Troy. If the statue had appeared on the scene before that time, we'd have heard about it."

"Inscribed on the cave walls of the Neanderthals?"

"We'd have heard about it," Peter repeated stubbornly.

"Peter, you can't know—" Jonathan laughed and shook his head. "God, you're obstinate. Call Maddox and see if you can find anything more about Karazov. That report was damn skimpy. If we're going to deal with the man, we'd better know as much as we can about him."

"And are we going to deal with him?"

Jonathan's gaze wandered to the stack of photographs

and drawings on the blotter of the desk. He was silent a moment before saying slowly, "I think perhaps we might."

When Peter left the study he went directly to the large salon where he had recently brought Caitlin Vasaro and Alex Karazov to view the Wind Dancer. The room was normally used only for formal entertaining, but six years earlier Peter had persuaded Jonathan to let him move his office from down the hall to the salon.

He crossed the salon to his desk, picked up the receiver of the phone, and flipped the Rolodex to *M* and then to Maddox Investigating. He placed the call, gave Maddox the information he had on Karazov, and hung up.

He leaned back in the chair, his gaze going to the emerald eyes of the Wind Dancer across the room. He felt his heartbeat quicken and the familiar tension grip him. He had told Caitlin the statue had made him uneasy at first, but he had not told her it still had that effect. She would not have understood. It was clear from that first moment she had felt an unusual affinity for the Pegasus.

What did he feel? Why had he had his office moved so that he could be close to the Wind Dancer? He had told Jonathan it was because of the beauty of the statue, and it was partly true. The Wind Dancer dazzled and fascinated him, but it also held him in thrall.

Thrall? Nonsense. The Wind Dancer fascinated him because it was interwoven with the history of the Andreas family, and if Caitlin felt an affinity for the statue, he felt the same bond with the Andreas clan. His bum heart kept him from living an entirely normal life, but he had only to open Caterina's journal and he was able to soar instead of crawl along at the "reasonable" pace recommended by his doctors.

He sat up straight in his chair and reached into his

desk drawer for the leather-bound journal. He opened the fragile pages of the book with the utmost care to his favorite legend and soon was lost in the world of Paradignes, Andros, and Jacinth on that last day when Troy fell to the Greeks.

After dinner at the hotel Alex escorted Caitlin back to her room, unlocked the door, and handed her the key. "I'll order breakfast for both of us in your suite for nine tomorrow morning. What would you like?"

"Anything. I don't care."

He was going to leave her. In spite of the fact that he had booked two single suites, until that moment Caitlin had assumed he would spend the night in her bed. She averted her face so that he wouldn't see her disappointment. "What time do you think they'll call?"

"As early as Andreas considers civilized. He knows you're anxious and won't want to stretch out the suspense." He opened the door. "He likes you."

"I like him." She turned to look at Alex. "Don't you?"

Alex hesitated. "Yes, it's hard not to like him. Under other circumstances I think we could become friends."

She gazed at him, puzzled. "Is there a better opportunity for friendship than in a business partnership?"

Alex brushed a light kiss on Caitlin's forehead. "You be friends with him. You're the same kind of people."

"What kind is that?"

"Open. Gentle." He smiled down at her. "I lost the knack for being either a long time ago." He started to turn away. "Sleep well."

"Not likely." She wrinkled her nose at him. "My nervousness is back with a vengeance. You may be certain everything's going to turn out well, but I'm not so sure. This hasn't been my lucky year."

"I told you not to worry."

She curtsied. "Yes, sir."

"Take a hot shower, go right to bed, and you'll be asleep in five minutes." He turned away. "You haven't slept in almost thirty-six hours. If you need me, I'll be right down the hall."

But not in the same bed.

"I won't need you." She smiled with an effort. "You're right, I'm not being sensible. Good night."

He stopped and turned to face her. "Dammit, I'm not rejecting you. You don't understand. It's just that I... like you."

"And that's a reason for you to back off?"

"It's becoming too complicated." He met her gaze. "Because I'm not open and kind and decent like you and Andreas. I've lived for myself and by myself for too long."

"Are you warning me?"

"Yes. I'm giving you space tonight but I can't count on my good sense not being swamped by my sex drive. I'm leaving it up to you to protect yourself."

She watched him walk away from her before quickly entering the suite and closing the door behind her. She shouldn't be hurt that he had chosen not to stay with her. Now that they were involved in launching the perfume, any closer relationship was bound to fall by the wayside.

She glanced restlessly around the small sitting room. She supposed the suite was quite nice as suites went. The white satin drapes framed a huge picture window that overlooked the sea, and the room was all that was comfortable, elegant, and... impersonal. She suddenly felt a million miles from everything she knew and loved, a million miles from Vasaro.

She was being perfectly idiotic. In another minute

she would be howling like a homesick child. Caitlin straightened and moved briskly across the sitting room toward the adjoining bedroom. She would have that shower Alex had suggested, go right to bed, and be asleep in minutes.

And if she couldn't sleep, she would lie awake and think about those magical moments when she had gazed into the eyes of the Wind Dancer.

6

Peter Maskovel called Caitlin's suite promptly at ten o'clock the next morning. Caitlin listened on the bedroom extension while Alex spoke from the phone on the desk in the sitting room.

"Jonathan has decided to let you use the Wind Dancer." Peter's tone was crisply businesslike and betrayed none of the boyish enthusiasm it had contained yesterday. "For ten percent of the profits for the first five years and a guarantee of approval on every aspect of the itinerary of the tour. We'll provide full security. Jonathan or I or both of us will accompany the statue when it's outside the continental U.S."

"Agreed." Alex kept his tone as level and cool as Peter's. "There's no objection to the European launch and tour?"

"He doesn't like it, but he can see the necessity. He's okayed your ideas for packaging of the perfume, but he wants to see a prototype of the bottle before you commit to it. How soon do you plan on launching Vasaro?"

Alex covered the phone and asked Caitlin. "How soon could you have enough perfume for a limited launch?"

"I don't know." She covered her receiver and tried to think. "I have an agreement with Monsieur Serdeaux's factory in Grasse for the production of the perfume. I'll have to call him and see if he can start production immediately."

"If he agrees, give me an approximate."

"Three months."

"Three months," Alex told Peter, ignoring Caitlin's shocked expression. "But we need to start the hype before that time. We'll introduce our spokeswoman for the perfume in five weeks in Paris. I'd like to have the Wind Dancer on hand at that time to draw more press coverage."

"I'll have to check Jonathan's schedule." Peter paused. "Jonathan went over the list of spokesperson possibilities you furnished him and he decided you were right and Chelsea Benedict would be the best of the lot."

"I'm glad we agree."

"She won an Academy Award last year and is probably in high demand. The profile on her states she's never endorsed a product before. Can you promise us you can retain her services?"

"I believe I can make that assurance. None of the actresses I submitted for Mr. Andreas's approval were committed for a film in the immediate future."

"On a project like this, everything has to come together to make it work," Peter said. "No contracts will be drawn up regarding the Wind Dancer until we see the packaging prototype and a contract signed by Chelsea Benedict."

"That's reasonable. You'll have both within the next month. In return, I'll expect you to make sure Mr. Andreas's schedule remains open so he can accompany the Wind Dancer to Paris in five weeks' time."

There was a hesitation on the other end of the line.

"The Wind Dancer will be in Paris on October third *if* everything is in order."

"It will be."

The call was obviously drawing to a close with no mention of her offer to decipher the inscription, Caitlin noticed with panic.

"The inscription," she quickly reminded Peter.

"Oh, yes, we definitely want your assistance in the matter of the inscription. I'm something of a photography buff, and I have a slew of photographs I can send you of the Wind Dancer. I'll also see if I can arrange to send you a hologram we had commissioned for the Metropolitan."

"I understand Caterina's journal has all the legends. I'd like to have it, please. I already have a copy of the hologram."

"You do?" Peter was silent an instant. "Of course you'd have it. I should have guessed—"

"Will you send me the journal?"

"Do you read Italian?"

"No, but I speak it enough to get by."

"That won't help you. Caterina's journal dates back to 1497. I read Italian fluently and I have problems with translating sections of it. The Italian is archaic and you wouldn't be able to do any definitive work with it in its present form. It would be more efficient for me to have is translated for you. I'll get right on it."

"How soon can I expect it?"

"I have no idea. As soon as I can get it done. After you receive it, we'll expect bimonthly reports regarding your progress in deciphering the inscription."

"Which may be zilch at first," Alex said.

"We'll still expect a report." For the first time Peter allowed a hint of warmth to enter his voice. "Good luck to both of you. I hope you pull it off."

He hung up before Alex could reply.

"I can't believe it." Caitlin's eyes shimmered as Alex walked into the bedroom. "I never thought it would happen."

"I told you not to worry. The odds are on our side."

"Perhaps you could see that but I certainly couldn't." She jumped to her feet, her arms clasped across her chest as she hugged herself with excitement. "The Wind Dancer. I never thought—"

"You're repeating yourself." His smile widened indulgently. "You look as if you're ready to fly up to the ceiling."

"I am." Caitlin shook her head. "It was only a dream before. I was afraid to hope." Her smile suddenly faded. "But we still have to get the packaging prototype. How could you promise it within the month? It takes ages to create a package and a campaign built around it."

"Money is a great spur."

"It would take a great deal of money."

"I have a great deal of money."

"But Jonathan said—" Caitlin's tone was hesitant. "You obviously don't want to talk anymore about your past, but I'd like the assurance that this grand plan of yours isn't going to crumble when the police attach your assets . . . or something."

He chuckled. "The police aren't going to touch my accounts. I'm not a criminal, Caitlin."

Relief flowed through her, making her feel light as air. He had told her before he wasn't a drug dealer, but *criminal* was a more general word. "That's good." She switched back to the main topic. "Even if you manage to get the package in that time, what about Chelsea Benedict?"

"She may be more difficult. We'd better get to work on bringing her into the fold as soon as possible."

He was speaking as if Chelsea Benedict were a wandering

lamb just waiting for them to extend a welcoming hand, Caitlin thought apprehensively. According to the tabloids, the actress was much more like a raging tiger. Bawdy, irreverent, and completely individualistic, she had been a top star of stage and screen for the past thirteen years and had won two Oscars and a Tony. Her private life was very private indeed, but she still managed to stir up storms of publicity whenever she decided to take a stand on an issue. Caitlin vaguely remembered reading some scandal regarding the actress, but she couldn't recall the details. But Alex would probably be as well versed on her as he had proven to be on everything else. "I suppose you have a report on her too?"

He nodded. "I know a little about Chelsea Benedict."

"Only a little?"

"Enough." He stood up and brushed her cheek with his lips. "But right now the most important thing I know is where we can find her. She and her daughter are on a Save the Whales expedition in cooperation with Greenpeace. You'd better go shopping and pick up a warm coat while I make the reservations and get us checked out."

"Where is she?"

"Reykjavik."

"Iceland?"

Chelsea Benedict wished to hell the reporter would take the picture before she threw up.

She glanced over her shoulder and watched the crustacean-encrusted back of the gray whale disappear as he slid like a massive bullet beneath the ocean's gray-green surface. At least he was safe, and maybe Marisa would think this nightmare worthwhile. Running interference between his prey and a whaler that was four times as large as their small ship wasn't Chelsea's idea of a grand way to spend a day.

She stood at the helm of the ship, her hands clenched on the rail, glaring at the captain on the deck of the whaler three hundred yards away. Oh, God, she hoped she was glaring. She felt so miserable, she could just as well have been grinning at the bearded captain and the sour-faced idiot leveling the spear gun at her.

"Take the picture," she said between her teeth.

Paul Tyndale smiled maliciously. "I'm waiting to see if he'll shoot you."

She gave the reporter a poisonous stare. He looked plump, unrumpled, and disgustingly well. His trench coat was as crisp and dry as when the *Rescuer* had left Reykjavik that morning, while she was soaked to the skin from standing at the helm. "You volunteered to come along. Now make yourself useful."

"We're not close enough for an interesting picture. But I'm recording all this for posterity." He patted the pocket that contained the notebook he hadn't brought out during the entire encounter with the whaler. The Nikon camera hung around his thick neck like an albatross.

"My deal with *Time* was an article and a chance at the cover. That's why they sent a photojournalist along. A picture's worth a thousand words."

"He doesn't have to take a picture." Marisa took a step closer to Chelsea, her voice soft, urgent. "We've succeeded in what we wanted to do. The whale's safe for now and the Greenpeace boat will be here tomorrow."

Chelsea's gaze shifted to Marisa's worried face and her expression softened. Marisa's thin face was pinched with cold, her long, straight hair darkened to almost black by the wet spray. These hours hadn't been easy for Marisa either. Her daughter had probably not even noticed the discomfort in her worry over that damn whale. Chelsea said gently, "It's all right, baby. I'll take care of this."

"You have your publicity quota, Chelsea," Tyndale said. "Next week the magazine will have a small write-up about brave, environment-conscious Chelsea Benedict and her confrontation with the Icelandic whaler. You mustn't be greedy."

For a moment Chelsea was so furious, she forgot about the nausea making her stomach heave like the ocean waves over the bow. "Look, Tyndale, you've been taking potshots at me ever since we left Reykjavik. Say it."

Tyndale's smile faded. "I don't like movie stars who use serious issues to fuel their careers. The environment's a major problem and it should be taken seriously."

Christ, of all the reporters in the world, she had to land a pompous ass who had a grudge against movie stars. "You came along, dammit."

"Because you're news and I'm not averse to seeing my name on a *Time* photo. But I have no intention of giving you more than I have to."

"The deal was for pictures so that I could have a shot at the cover."

He shrugged. "So sue me."

Chelsea felt as if even the roots of her hair were flaming with the fury streaking through her. "I don't give a damn what you think of me, you son of a bitch," Chelsea said softly, each word enunciated with great precision. "But Marisa thinks this publicity will keep those whalers from killing more whales, and we're going to give her the whole nine yards." She called to Captain Desquares in the wheelhouse, "Move us closer to that whaler."

"Mother, no!" Marisa grasped her arm. "We don't need to do this."

Captain Desquares nodded. "It's not smart, Chelsea.

That captain was mad as hell when we cut in front of the whale."

Chelsea stared at the stocky, short man leaning over the side of the whaler and glaring at them. Desquares was right, the whaler's captain looked as mad as she felt. "We didn't come out here to make them happy." Chelsea turned back to Tyndale. "You think we're too far away to make a picture interesting? Let's see how near we can get. Go up in the wheelhouse with the captain, Marisa."

"No," Marisa said quietly.

"Then get on the starboard side of the ship. I don't want you anywhere near me."

Marisa hesitated and then obeyed with a sigh. "I wish you wouldn't do this, Mother."

"So do I," Captain Desquares muttered.

"More power," Chelsea ordered. "And you, Tyndale, stay right where you are and get that camera ready."

Tyndale straightened. "What do you think you're doing?"

"If you miss *this* picture, I guarantee your editor will cut off your balls."

Chelsea heard the liquid silken hiss of the water parted by the *Rescuer* as it edged even closer to the whaler. Now she could clearly see the bearded captain's stunned expression. He shrieked with rage and shook his fist at her.

"Mother, please." Marisa's voice was tense.

"Quick. Give me some Icelandic curses," Chelsea said over her shoulder to Captain Desquares. "Something obscene enough to make him testy."

"He's already testy," Tyndale said.

Desquares murmured something in a foreign tongue.

"Slower. I didn't catch it." Chelsea kept her eyes on the captain of the whaler, who was talking to the sailor manning the speargun. "Too many syllables."

The captain repeated the words more carefully.

"I've got it." Chelsea had always had an excellent ear for dialogue, but she had never thought she would put the talent to use in quite this way. Without looking at Tyndale she ordered, "Get ready. And if you don't take this one, I'll stick that camera where the sun doesn't shine."

"You're practically in the bastard's lap. He can't miss you."

"If he wants to hit me. I doubt if he's that stupid." She earnestly hoped he wasn't that stupid. She took a deep breath, raised her voice, and shouted the obscenities Desquares had furnished her at the whaler captain.

The next moments were a blur of noise and action.

The outraged scream of the whaler captain.

The soft explosion as the spear shot from the whaler's gun.

The whistle as the spear cleaved the air and catapulted toward Chelsea.

Marisa's low cry as she started across the deck toward Chelsea.

The spear burying itself in the wooden mast two feet from Chelsea's head with a solid thunk.

Every muscle in Chelsea's body vibrated with fear and rage as she whirled to glare at Tyndale. "Did you get the goddamn picture, you son of a bitch?"

Tyndale's face was pasty pale, his hands trembling on the camera. "I got it."

"Then let's get the hell out of here."

Captain Desquares obeyed with desperate speed, twisting the wheel ninety degrees. "Cut that line or we won't be going anywhere."

A sailor rushed forward and cut the line attached to the spear embedded in the mast.

Chelsea took a last look at the deck of the whaler. Though the captain was still glaring at her, he seemed a little calmer and they weren't reloading the speargun.

Two minutes later the *Rescuer* chugged southward toward Reykjavik.

Three minutes after the whaler was lost to view, Chelsea ran to the rail and was very, very sick.

She stayed there a long time. Through a dark haze she could see chunks of white ice the size of her fist floating on the frigid green water. Christ, all she needed to make her day complete was to hit an iceberg.

As soon as she lifted her head, Marisa was beside her, handing her a wet handkerchief. "Thanks, baby, I may live now." She shot a suspicious glance at Tyndale. "Did he shoot any pictures while I was upchucking?"

Marisa shook her head. "I think you've squelched him." She pulled Chelsea closer and gently stroked her hair. "I didn't mean to cause you all this trouble, Mother."

"You weren't to blame. The whaler and Tyndale caused this brouhaha." Chelsea made a face. "And my temper. I spoiled your peaceful confrontation, didn't I?"

"Maybe it's time we got more warlike," Marisa said. "No one seems to be listening to us." Her wide brow creased in a troubled frown. "The whales and dolphins are still being killed in huge numbers. Why won't anyone pay attention to us?"

"Maybe they will this time." Chelsea doubted if the confrontation would do any good, but she couldn't say that to Marisa. Her daughter didn't understand greed and was young enough to believe the world could still be changed if she worked hard enough at it. "Anyway, we'll get enough publicity to shake some of them up."

Marisa chuckled. "You should have seen Tyndale's face when that speargun went off."

"I hope he was scared witless." Chelsea grabbed the rail of the ship as her stomach started doing flip-flops again. "Oh, Christ, I thought I was over it." She closed her eyes and started to take deep breaths. "Marisa, you've got to promise me something."

Marisa took the handkerchief and dabbed at her mother's temples. "What?"

"That we'll save the elephants next time." Chelsea lurched forward and hung her head over the churning waves. "Lord, I hate being seasick."

The *Rescuer* was docking when Alex and Caitlin's taxi drew up beside a large warehouse. Down the dock a uniformed chauffeur leaned on the bumper of a long black limousine, his gaze on the incoming ship.

"Just in time," Alex said as he handed the taxi driver a bill and motioned for him to wait. "Now to see what kind of humor the lady's in and whether we should choose another time."

"You said she and her daughter were trying to stop the whalers?"

Alex nodded. "Iceland and Japan still hunt whales commercially. Iceland is supposedly tapering off, but there are still whalers plying their trade, and they're very hostile to outside interference."

"There she is. I recognize the hair." Caitlin jumped out of the car before the taxi driver could open the passenger door and hurried across the dock and down the pier.

The hair of the woman coming down the gangplank was a distinctive shade between rich honey and red and hung past her shoulders in a wild riot of curls that could only have been achieved by a master hairdresser. Chelsea Benedict looked small at first glance, but she moved with such swift, economical grace and vitality that an onlooker was conscious only of presence, not size. She was dressed in a white Irish fisherman's

sweater, a rust-colored suede jacket, and her green corduroy slacks were tucked into beige suede ankle boots.

Alex and Caitlin stopped and waited at the bottom of
the gangplank. Alex stepped forward as the actress
reached the pier. "Ms. Benedict? I'm Alex Karazov and
this is Caitlin Vasaro. I wonder if we could speak to you."

Chelsea lifted her head and Caitlin inhaled in surprise. She had not expected the actress to be this stunning in person. Chelsea Benedict wore no makeup, but
her smooth olive complexion clearly didn't need it. She
possessed high cheekbones and deep-set sapphire-blue
eyes. Her bold features lay no claim to classical beauty.
It was a face that set its own standards and dared all
comers to match it. "Hell, no." She scowled. Her voice
was throaty, almost hoarse. "I'm cold and I'm wet and
seasick and that bastard behind me on deck has an exclusive. Sorry."

For the first time, Caitlin noticed the lines of strain
beside Chelsea Benedict's famous mouth. Alex drew
Caitlin forward. "We're not reporters, Ms. Benedict. We
have a business proposition for you."

"I don't know you from Adam. See my business
manager." Chelsea looked over her shoulder. "Marisa,
let's get out of here."

A young girl a full head taller than Chelsea and
dressed in a yellow windbreaker and jeans hurried
down the gangplank. "Sorry, Mother. Mr. Tyndale was
asking me some questions."

Chelsea stiffened. "About the project?"

Marisa avoided her mother's gaze. "Partly."

"Go get in the limousine." Chelsea muttered a curse.
"I'll talk to Tyndale."

"It's all right, Mother. I didn't mind."

"I mind." Chelsea glanced past Marisa to the man

coming down the gangplank. "Your story is about Project Rescue, not my daughter, Tyndale."

Paul Tyndale smiled slyly. "You wanted the additional coverage. The cover story has to be much more in-depth and your daughter is a part of it." He looked at Marisa. "Maybe we'll take a few pictures of her too. If not, I'm sure we have some film from the court case that we can dredge up."

"They'll dredge you out of the Atlantic Ocean if you—"

"It's not important, Mother," Marisa interrupted. "I don't care what he writes about me. It's the whales that matter."

"You see?" Tyndale asked. "Your daughter has her priorities in order." He smiled mockingly at Chelsea. "Saving an endangered species is worth a little mud . . . if I choose to sling it."

He strolled past them down the pier toward the dock.

Chelsea gazed after him and defined his character and heritage in explicit Anglo-Saxon phrasing.

"I don't believe he's as bad as you think. He's just angry because you made him look foolish." Marisa put an arm around her mother. "Come on. A hot bath and a nap and you'll be fine."

"But you won't." Chelsea reached out and touched Marisa's cheek with her index finger. "I should have left it alone. What difference does one blasted cover make?"

"You always have been an overachiever." Marisa grinned. "And how can I complain when you did it for me?"

Alex stepped forward again. "This doesn't seem a good time to discuss our business. Could we meet you at your hotel this evening?"

"We'll be taking a flight back to New York tomorrow."

Chelsea started up the pier toward the black limousine. Contact my business manager."

"We need a quick decision." Alex and Caitlin fell into step with Chelsea and her daughter. "It will take only ten minutes for us to outline our offer."

"I don't think I'd be—"

"Please reconsider." Alex paused. "My partner, Jonathan Andreas, will be very disappointed if you won't even listen to our plans for you and the Wind Dancer."

Chelsea didn't speak for a moment, her face averted and half hidden by her bright fall of hair. "The Wind Dancer?"

They had reached the car and the chauffeur was opening the door.

"Could we call on you at seven this evening?"

Chelsea hesitated as Marisa got into the limousine. Oh, what the hell? Why not? Come to my suite at the Kravitz for tea at four."

She climbed into the car, and the chauffeur slammed the door and quickly walked around the car to the driver's seat.

Alex and Caitlin watched the limousine glide away from them down the dock.

"She's certainly larger than life, isn't she?" Caitlin jammed her hands down into her pockets of her fleece-lined coat. "How do you deal with someone like that?"

"Like you do everyone else." Alex took her arm and urged her toward the taxi several yards away. "You find out what they want and then give it to them." He grinned. "In exchange for what you want."

Chelsea listened intently to Alex's outline for their promotional campaign, her face without expression. She sat curled up on the cream-colored couch in her suite, dressed in loose silk lounging pajamas of a pale beige shade that made her wild, tousled hair shimmer in bright contrast. After Alex had finished, she was silent a moment, her long lashes lowered as she looked down into the amber depths of the tea in her cup. "I've never endorsed a product before. I'm an actress, not a huckster."

"An actress can always use the exposure." Alex leaned forward in his chair. "And I can assure you, everything will be handled tastefully. It's to our advantage to make sure the commercials and public appearances only enhance your popularity."

Chelsea didn't look up from her cup. "Yes, I can see that." She was silent a moment, and suddenly her head lifted and she shot a lightning glance at Caitlin sitting in the chair beside Alex. "Why the hell aren't you talking? It's your perfume, isn't it?"

Caitlin felt the color rise to her cheeks at the sudden attack. "Yes, it's my perfume."

"Then why aren't you trying to persuade me to pitch it?"

"I don't...I suppose I..." She stopped stammering and told the truth. "I guess you intimidate me a little."

Chelsea lifted a brow and shifted her glance to Alex. "And *he* doesn't?"

Chelsea was evidently a very shrewd judge of character. "I've never met a movie star before." Caitlin's lips were suddenly twitching as she added, "And the devil you know..."

Alex chuckled. "Caitlin realizes we have common interests."

"And do we also have common interests?" Chelsea asked Alex.

Alex met her gaze. "Close enough."

Chelsea turned back to Caitlin. "Do you have a sample of this perfume?"

"Of course." Caitlin opened her handbag and drew out a small vial. "I call it Vasaro."

Chelsea opened the vial and sniffed experimentally before rubbing a few drops on her wrists and then sniffing again. "God, that's wonderful stuff."

"You like it?" Caitlin's hopes soared as she eagerly leaned forward. "I created it. It's my first perfume."

"With a perfume this good, you won't have to create a second." Chelsea sniffed at her left wrist again. "Why Vasaro?"

"Vasaro is my home. We grow flowers for the perfume trade."

"Hmm." Chelsea returned the vial to Caitlin. "Where is it?"

"The South of France, near Grasse."

"We intend to shoot the television commercials at Vasaro," Alex told Chelsea. "The countryside is unbelievably beautiful."

"Touristy?"

"No, very secluded."

Chelsea sniffed her wrist again. "You say you'd want me in Paris in a month?"

Caitlin stifled a sigh of relief. The actress had to be interested or she wouldn't be asking questions.

Alex nodded. "We'll introduce you as the spokesperson, make a big fanfare about the Wind Dancer returning to its homeland, and announce the date of the launch of the perfume."

"And take a zillion pictures of me with the Wind Dancer." Chelsea made a face. "I've never been upstaged by a statue before."

"But what a statue," Alex said softly. "And what a woman. Together you'll rock the world."

Chelsea threw back her head and laughed. "Lord, you're persistent."

"Will you do it?"

Chelsea's lashes lowered to veil the glitter of her sapphire eyes again. "If we can come to an agreement."

Caitlin's hand nervously tightened on the vial of perfume.

"You haven't talked money," Chelsea said. "I hate to be crass, but—"

"Two million dollars," Alex said.

Caitlin inhaled sharply. She hadn't dreamed they would have to pay so much for a mere endorsement.

"Not enough," Chelsea said.

"It's more than you get for a picture."

"I'm asking three million next time."

"We're talking about commercials and a few personal appearances. It isn't as if you'll have to work hard."

"But I'm endorsing the product. It's a responsibility."

Alex was silent a moment. "Three million."

Chelsea's gaze narrowed. "I would have taken two million seven. You were too easy."

"Yes." He smiled. "But you would have made conditions. I don't have time for conditions."

Chelsea nodded slowly. "But I still have conditions." She nodded at the vial of perfume in Caitlin's hand. "I want my name on the bottle. We'll call the perfume Chelsea."

"No!" Caitlin, shocked, blurted out.

Chelsea's jaw set stubbornly. "I want it. It's built-in publicity for me to have my name on that bottle. Some perfumes stay popular for a half century. Look at Chanel No. 5."

Alex was silent.

"Tell her she can't have it." Caitlin whirled to face Alex. "Dammit, she *can't* change the name."

"I'll go down to two million seven," Chelsea said, "if you put my name on the bottle. Otherwise it's no deal."

"Alex." Caitlin's hand desperately clutched his arm. "*Tell* her."

"We need her."

"Not that much."

"Dammit, yes, that much." Alex's voice rang with intensity.

Despair made Caitlin's throat tighten with tears. Why hadn't she put a clause into that contract guaranteeing she would retain control of the name? It hadn't seemed necessary after Alex had told her he had no problem with calling the perfume Vasaro. "You said I could have my name. You said it didn't matter."

She could feel the muscles of Alex's forearm tighten through the tweed of his jacket. "You don't understand. Every part has to work together. One piece missing and I'd have to start over."

"But it's not right." She turned to Chelsea and said fiercely, "You can't have your name on my perfume. The perfume belongs to Vasaro. It *is* Vasaro."

Chelsea smiled and looked at Alex, waiting.

Alex's gaze moved to Caitlin's tense face. He didn't speak for a moment. "Okay." He turned back to Chelsea. "No deal. You can't have the name."

Caitlin went limp with relief.

Chelsea's eyes widened in surprise. "You're sure?"

"We'll find someone else for the job."

Chelsea smiled curiously. "You're not as hard as I thought you were, Mr. Karazov. I was almost sure you'd sell her down the river."

Alex stood up. "I'm sorry we've wasted your time. Let's go, Caitlin."

Chelsea gracefully unwound herself and rose from the couch in a slither of gleaming silk. "It hasn't been wasted. I find you both very interesting." She turned to Caitlin. "Your Vasaro must mean a great deal to you."

Caitlin nodded as she stood up. "There's no place on earth like it."

Chelsea laughed. "No place like home." She wrinkled her nose. "I wouldn't know. I've really never had one." Her smile faded. "And neither has Marisa." She suddenly turned again to Alex. "Three million," she said briskly. "And you keep the name."

Alex went still. "Agreed."

Stunned, Caitlin stared at Chelsea.

"But I still have a condition," Chelsea said to Caitlin. "I don't think you'll find this one particularly difficult to meet. I'd like you to accept my daughter, Marisa, as a houseguest at Vasaro until after the official launch of the perfume." She smiled. "She's only sixteen, but she won't cause you any trouble. She usually gets along with everyone. She's very quiet... not like me at all."

"She'll be very welcome." Caitlin meant the words. She had liked what she had seen of Chelsea's daughter at the pier. She appeared to have a grave maturity unusual in one so young. "I'm generally quite busy in the fields, but my mother can care for her."

"She doesn't need taking care of. At least, that's what she's always telling me." Chelsea strode toward the door. "Naturally, I don't listen to her. The only thing I ask is that you keep the reporters away from her for the next month or so. Tyndale's article is going to set off ripples, and I don't want any of them touching her."

"Ripples?"

"Ask your friend." Chelsea's shrewd gaze shifted to Alex. "I'll bet he knows all about Marisa. He seems to be privy to a good deal of information."

"As it happens, I do know about what happened to Marisa." Alex's expression was grave. "And I admired your response to it."

"I couldn't do anything else." Chelsea glanced at Caitlin. "You've got guts and you're not greedy. I like that."

"You've got guts too." Caitlin found herself smiling at Chelsea. The woman was loaded with charisma and it was difficult not to respect the actress's frankness. "But I can't say you're not greedy."

Chelsea's full-bodied laugh rang out. "It comes from growing up in the slums. No matter how rich you get, there's never enough."

Alex reached into the inside pocket of his jacket. "I've had a contract drawn up for you to sign. We can make the necessary changes and you can initial them and—"

"No way," Chelsea said flatly. "Send it to my business manager."

Alex smiled faintly and turned to Caitlin. "Smart lady. Now, that's what you should have done, Caitlin."

"But I didn't have a business manager. I can't trust anyone but myself," Caitlin said. "Unless it's you."

Alex grimaced. "Then heaven help you."

"Amen," Chelsea said dryly, opening the door and waving them out.

"What did she mean about you knowing about her daughter?" Caitlin asked Alex as they walked down the corridor toward the elevator.

"Nothing that most of the world doesn't know too," Alex said. "It's not something anyone could sweep under the carpet. Chelsea Benedict was in jail for fourteen months."

"Jail?" Caitlin turned and looked at him.

"Chelsea grew up in the slums of New York. Her mother was a hooker and her father—" He shrugged. "Who knows? He wasn't around long enough to matter. She went to a performing arts high school and was well on her way to a promising career, when she met Harry

Pernell. Pernell was an older man, a rich Wall Street mogul. He got Chelsea pregnant when she was sixteen, married her, and she had Marisa six months later." He pushed the button for the elevator. "She filed for divorce four years after Marisa was born and sued for custody. She didn't get it."

"The mother usually gets custody," Caitlin said. "Why didn't Chelsea?"

"Harry Pernell evidently was a prime son of a bitch. He was rich enough to hire witnesses and manufacture evidence against her. He received sole custody, but Chelsea didn't give up. She went back to work and hired lawyers. Marisa was attending a private school in Manhattan and Chelsea bribed servants and school officials to let her spend time with Marisa."

The doors of the elevators slid open. They entered the cubicle and Alex pushed the lobby button. "When Marisa was six, Chelsea found out that Pernell was sexually abusing her."

"His own daughter?" Caitlin felt sick.

Alex nodded. "Incest. Back then the subject was taboo. No one would believe Chelsea when she went to the police."

"Dear God," she whispered.

"So Chelsea kidnapped Marisa and hid her away with friends out of state." Alex's lips twisted. "And Pernell had Chelsea arrested and thrown in jail for kidnapping. She stayed there for fourteen months. She said she'd rot there before she let Pernell have Marisa."

"That took great courage."

Alex nodded. "The lady has style. Her lawyers eventually found evidence against Pernell on another child molestation charge, that one involving vicious and obvious assault, and Chelsea was pardoned."

"What happened to him?"

"He was sent to prison. He didn't last seven months in jail before he had a fatal 'accident.' Convicts don't like child molesters."

The feelings of fierce satisfaction that surged through Caitlin shocked her. She had always thought revenge was futile, but the idea of a helpless child being victimized in any way, but especially by her own father, made her sick with fury. If she felt such a strong reaction just hearing about it, what must have Chelsea gone through? Caitlin suddenly felt a strong sense of kinship with the woman.

"And this is the story Chelsea thinks the reporter will resurrect?"

"When she first made it big in Hollywood, everything about her past was dug up and spread in the tabloids. But she faced up to it and told the media and the public to back off. She said that if what she gave them on the screen wasn't enough for them, they could all go to hell."

"Sounds like her."

"She's a survivor." The elevator opened and Alex propelled Caitlin into the bright, noisy lobby. "She catches the imagination and yet she's earthy enough for most women to identify with her."

"Like Vasaro." A sudden memory of Chelsea as she had first seen her rushed back to Caitlin—beautiful, weary, and yet still ready to do battle. Yes, Chelsea *was* like Vasaro. She could take whatever the elements threw at her and still endure and flourish. "I'm glad she's going to be our spokeswoman." She grimaced. "Not that anyone asked my opinion."

"The promotion was to be left in my hands," Alex reminded her.

"I know. I'm not complaining." She gave him a radiant smile. "And you did fight for the name."

"Stop looking at me like that," Alex said roughly. "I fought her because I knew she'd back down."

"You couldn't have been certain." She slipped her arm in his. "Chelsea's right, you're not nearly as tough as you pretend."

Alex shook his head, warning her. "Don't make the mistake of thinking I'm something I'm not, Caitlin."

"I don't know what you are." Her smile widened. "But I think I'm beginning to find out."

He looked at her with a mixture of exasperation, frustration, and tenderness before he managed to tear his gaze away. "We'll fly directly to Paris from here. We have an appointment day after tomorrow with Pierre Desharmes."

She was immediately distracted. Pierre Desharmes was one of the premier packagers in the perfume industry, but he wouldn't have been her choice. "No."

Alex looked startled. "No?"

"I want Henri LeClerc."

"He's very much in demand." He lifted a skeptical brow. "We may not be able to persuade him to put Dior and Coty on the back burner to create a package for us."

"I want to try." She hesitated. "I read something about him in a magazine two years ago that may help."

"You can't rely on anything in the media."

"Well, it may be nothing . . . but I still want to try."

"Then we'll try. I'll call his office from the airport and set up an appointment." Alex smiled as he opened the glass doors of the front entrance and a chill blast of wind touched their faces. "We can only look the situation over and see how we can twist it to suit ourselves."

"Find out what LeClerc wants and then give it to him," Caitlin quoted, experiencing a thrill of excitement surging through her. In spite of the feeling that she was an alien in this fast-moving world in which

Alex seemed so comfortable, she couldn't deny the exhilaration of jetting from country to country and dealing with high-powered people like Chelsea Benedict and Jonathan Andreas.

"Exactly." An odd expression crossed Alex's face as he looked down at Caitlin's flushed cheeks and shining eyes. He stopped in the street to gently draw the collar of her coat closer around her neck and shut out more of the bitter chill.

Chelsea knocked and then opened the door of Marisa's bedroom. "Hi, they're gone."

Marisa looked up with a smile. "Good. Now you can order room service and then get to bed." She was curled up on the bed, her algebra book open, making notations in an open spiral notebook. She wore her old faded blue pajamas that made her tall, slender body look almost boyish. "Did you eat any of those scones they brought with the tea?"

Chelsea shook her head as she strolled toward the bed. "I couldn't face them. My stomach still feels on the quavery side. Scoot over."

Marisa moved across the bed and Chelsea lay down beside her. Chelsea gave a contented sigh and closed her eyes, letting all the tension of the day seep out of her. "This is good. God, I'm tired."

Marisa tossed her notebook aside and lay in companionable silence, waiting for Chelsea to stir.

It was pleasant lying there with no need to struggle, no need to be strong or clever or sparkling. Chelsea knew she would be herself in another moment, but just then she wanted only to lie next to Marisa. She could hear the light, even sound of Marisa's breathing and smell the fresh fragrance of the bouquet of iris and white lilac on the nightstand. The management of the hotel had sent up the bouquet when they had checked in, and Chelsea remembered how Marisa had smiled her slow, luminous smile when it had arrived and touched one of the velvet-textured petals of the iris with a gentle finger.

Chelsea was beginning to relax as the serenity Marisa always projected flowed into her. How did she do it? Chelsea thought in wonder. All the pain Marisa had suffered had wounded but never scarred her. "You know, sometimes I believe in all that reincarnation crap."

"You do? Why?"

"I think maybe some people may be born with their souls already in high gear and ready to roll." Chelsea opened her eyes and gazed thoughtfully at a picture of the aurora borealis on the opposite wall. "So that nothing that happens to them can change or destroy what they are. Do you know what I mean?"

"I think you're talking about old souls."

"Am I?" Well, Marisa would know. She devoured books like a chocoholic let loose in a Godiva shop. Chelsea turned on the bed to look at her. "I think you must be an old soul, baby."

Marisa chuckled. "You must be tired. I've never heard you wax philosophic before."

"Philosophic? Me?" Chelsea looked at her, startled. "Oh, my God, you're right. I sound like Shirley MacLaine." She sat up on the bed. "I must be light-headed. I'd better have something to eat. I'll order us both a salad and soup. Okay?"

"Okay." Marisa leaned back against the headboard as Chelsea placed the order with room service.

"There." Chelsea replaced the receiver and stood up. "Now I'll go and let you get on with your homework until they bring the food."

"You don't have to leave."

"Yes, I do." Chelsea moved toward the door leading to the sitting room. "I'm disturbing you, but you're too polite to tell me."

"Mother, that's not true."

"Yes, it is." Chelsea paused at the door and looked back over her shoulder. Marisa's expression was half concerned, half rueful, and Chelsea suddenly felt such profound love, it took her off guard. God, how had she gotten so lucky? With all the mistakes she had made, she must have done something right. "I'm not hurt. I know you love me." She made a face. "It's probably not easy having an actress for a mother."

"No." Marisa smiled. "But it's very entertaining."

"What a ghastly pun." Chelsea looked away from her. "I've decided to endorse a perfume."

Marisa's eyes widened in surprise. "Why?"

Chelsea shrugged. "It's a good deal." She paused. "The woman who created the perfume also grows flowers at a place called Vasaro in the South of France. I'm sending you there for the next few months until the perfume is launched."

Marisa went still. "The reporter."

"It's best, baby."

"I'm already behind and I'll miss the first few months of school."

"You can make it up. Your grades are good."

Marisa looked intently at her mother. "I don't need to run away from this."

"It's not running. Just a little selective ducking."

"It's the same thing. You always try to shelter everyone you care about. You don't have to protect me, Mother."

"Yes, I do. You don't know how those tiger sharks can shred you." Chelsea smiled. "Don't give me a hassle, baby.

You're pretty protective, too, or we wouldn't have been out in that boat, running interference for that blasted whale."

"That's different."

"Yeah, you don't weigh eight tons." Chelsea coaxed, "Go to Vasaro?"

For a moment she thought Marisa was going to refuse, then her daughter nodded. "All right, I'll go to Vasaro."

7

"I thought we'd never get through customs." Caitlin got into the taxi and settled back on the cushioned seat with a sigh of relief. "They were all so grim. Did you see those soldiers with the machine guns?"

Alex nodded as he got into the taxi and handed the driver a slip of paper. "They have a right to be nervous. The Black Medina killed two people at a Bach festival in Vienna yesterday."

Caitlin shivered. "I hadn't heard."

"I read about it in a newspaper on the plane," he said as the taxi pulled away from the curb.

"It's terrible. All this violence doesn't make any sense. What do they want?" Caitlin looked out the window. "The terrorists haven't even made any demands yet, have they?"

"No, but I'm sure they'll be forthcoming."

"It's a new Reign of Terror." Caitlin tried to dismiss the thought from her mind. "What hotel are we staying at?"

"No hotel."

"But you were on the phone for an hour at the airport in Reykjavik."

"Oh, we have a place to stay." Alex smiled at her.

"That's why I had to pick up that envelope at the ticket counter. A small surprise."

Forty minutes later the taxi pulled up before a house on the Place des Vosges in the Marais section of Paris. The two-story house facing the square had a steep slate roof, stone and brick facing, and the genteel air of another century.

"We're staying here?" She clutched at Alex's arm excitedly. "I can't believe it. It's the Andreas town house. I came to see it once when I was studying at the university, but it was occupied and I couldn't go through it."

"It doesn't belong to the Andreas family any longer." Alex paid off the taxi driver. "It was confiscated by the National Convention after Jean Marc Andreas and his Juliette fled the country." He picked up the bags and carried them up the stone steps. "Since then it's never been occupied by an Andreas." He took out a key from the envelope he had picked up at the airport and unlocked the front door. "Or a Vasaro, for that matter. It now belongs to a banker who's been living in Kenya for the past two years."

"Why did you do it?" Caitlin entered the foyer, her gaze traveling in wonder to the crystal chandelier glittering overhead. "You went to all this trouble for me?"

"I had my reasons. I told you, self-interest rules the world."

"Alex Karazov, why can't you just say it?" Caitlin put her hands on her hips and stared at him in exasperation. "Dammit, *tell* me you did it for me."

A grin lit his face. "All right, I did it for you." He started toward the staircase. "Partly."

Caitlin chuckled and hurried to his side. "Mother of God, you're stubborn." She passed him and took the stairs two at a time to the second floor. "I wonder which room was Catherine's?" She ran down the hall, throw-

ng open the doors to the bedchambers. "I wish I'd paid
more attention to her description of the house in the
journal."

"You mean you didn't memorize it? Incredible. On
the plane I thought you'd given me every detail page by
page."

"You don't have to be sarcastic. If you had any respect for history or roots..."

"I'm not being sarcastic," Alex said as he followed her
down the hall. "I'm joking."

"Oh, well, I don't care if you're sarcastic or not.
What a wonderful thing to do—this room." Caitlin
paused in the doorway of a large bedchamber and hurried over to the window. "I think it must have been this
room. It overlooks the garden. Catherine said her room
overlooked the garden." She threw open the casement
window. "Could we use this room, Alex? Look at the
view. We can see over the garden to all those lovely
slate roofs. So typical of Paris, don't you think?"

"I have no idea." Alex set down the suitcases and
came over to stand beside her at the window. "I've
never been to Paris before."

"You've never been—" She broke off as she turned to
look at him in astonishment. "You live in Europe and
you've never been to Paris?"

"I realize it's sacrilege," Alex said solemnly. "I haven't
gotten around to it."

"You don't 'get around' to Paris. You go on a pilgrim-
age." Caitlin smiled exuberantly. "Never mind, I'll show
you everything. We'll go for walks. Paris should always
be seen on foot. I'll show you the sidewalk café where I
used to go after class and we'll walk across the Pont de
Sully." Her eyes shone with eagerness. "You have to see
Notre-Dame. The stained glass of the rose window is
wonderful. And Saint-Antoine's. That's my favorite

cathedral in all of Paris. And we'll go to the Hôtel Carnavalet, where the Marquise de Sévigné—"

"Do you suppose we'll have time to see Monsieur LeClerc in between all this sight-seeing? A meeting or two?"

Caitlin's smile faded. "Of course, I realize that's what we're here for. I just thought we might... Perhaps you wouldn't even like my Paris. I never had much money when I was a student and I don't know any five-star restaurants or—"

"I'll like your Paris," Alex interrupted. "And we'll have plenty of time to kill once we've put the packaging problem into LeClerc's hands."

Caitlin's expression cleared and the eagerness returned. "Then could we go out right away? We can always unpack later. I want to show you the view from the Sully Bridge at sundown."

He smiled. "For the country mouse you call yourself, you're amazingly enthusiastic about a big city."

"But this isn't a big city, this is Paris. Well, I suppose it's a big city, but it's not the—" She stopped as she saw he was laughing at her and made a face at him. "You'll see what I mean after you have been here awhile."

"No doubt." He smiled and leaned forward to dust a kiss on the tip of her nose. "I'll call and confirm our appointment for tomorrow with LeClerc and then we can leave."

Caitlin nodded. "I'll change my shoes." She looked out over the city. "It seems different now. Isn't it strange how our viewpoints change as we get older?"

"You're not exactly Madame Methuselah."

"But I'm not in my teens any longer."

"When did you leave the university?"

"When I was twenty-two. I wanted to go on for an advanced degree, but the bank—Vasaro needed me."

"So you gave up your education."

"It was no real sacrifice. I've always known it was my duty to guard and preserve Vasaro, and the only thing I missed were my antiquity studies. Vasaro was what counted."

Alex gazed at her silently for a moment. "Why?"

"Because it's—" She stopped and then said slowly, "I suppose it's because Vasaro's always there and never changes. It's not a terrifically wonderful world, is it? There are crazy people like those terrorists and wars and drug pushers. The world keeps hurrying and changing and there's no place to get off. Except Vasaro. Everything in the world changes but Vasaro."

"There are no exceptions. Everything changes, Caitlin," Alex said gently.

"Not Vasaro. Not really. The years pass but every season there's the blossoming and the harvest. . . ." Caitlin felt suddenly awkward as she saw the intent manner in which he was looking at her. "I guess what I'm trying to say is that it's important to be able to hold on to something in this world."

"It's dangerous to let anything become too important to you. It's too easy for things to be taken away from you."

"Vasaro isn't a thing."

Alex nodded. "Not to you."

"What do you hold on to, Alex?"

"Myself. What I am."

"And that's enough?"

"I told you I didn't believe in roots." Alex moved toward the door. "I should be finished with the call in ten minutes. Why don't you meet me downstairs after you change your shoes?"

"All right."

He glanced back over his shoulder. "Do you know where I'd like to go first?"

"Where?"

"The Louvre. I want to see Juliette's painting, 'Boy in the Field.' "

Caitlin nodded eagerly. "We'll go to the museum before we go to the bridge. It's a wonderful painting, Alex."

"I'm sure it is."

Caitlin turned back to the window after Alex left the room. It was only a little after noon, the sun shone strong and bright, and the air was crisp and clear. Yet Caitlin felt suddenly as she had when she was a little girl running through the twilight fields of jasmine. The world seemed enveloped in a soft golden haze in which life was newly born and brimming with possibilities.

"I think that man's following us," Caitlin whispered as they moved past the large glass pyramid on the courtyard of the Louvre. "I'm sure I saw him in the square when we left the house."

"Which man?"

"The one wearing the mirrored sunglasses and red shirt."

Alex glanced casually over his shoulder. "The fat one with the guidebook?"

"Yes."

"Hmm. Do you suppose he wants to kidnap you and sell you into white slavery?"

"Alex, I'm serious."

"So am I. I understand they like them tall and blond in the Middle East. And those magnificent boobs would be a definite plus."

"I'm not blond."

"You are in the sunlight. Otherwise you're sort of streaked like a tabby cat or—"

"Shouldn't we do something?"

"Dye your hair?"

"Call the police."

"You haven't been kidnapped yet."

"Perhaps he's a pickpocket."

"I like the white-slavery idea better. It brings to mind all sorts of lascivious thoughts. Jewel-studded leather manacles, aphrodisiacs, naked houris dancing to arouse my libido."

"You don't need any arousing." Caitlin laughed. "You're outrageous. Dammit, I tell you I saw him at the square."

"The Place des Vosges is the oldest square in Paris and probably in every guidebook. And do you really think a pickpocket would wear a red shirt and mirrored sunglasses, for God's sake?"

"I guess not."

"If we see him again after we leave the museum, we'll alert the gendarmes. Good enough?"

She nodded.

"Now lead me to Juliette's painting. I need to inundate my overcharged libido with a cool stream of cultural pursuit. I keep seeing visions of you in nothing but a harem veil, bent over with that lovely ass wriggling..."

Caitlin giggled. "Kinky. Definitely kinky."

"You're the one who brought up the subject. I wonder if the Louvre has Delacroix's odalisque on display. We'll have to take a look at it and see if you'd really suit the life. Personally, I think you'd look very sexy leaning against a pile of silk cushions. Or, better still, on them, positioned just right for fun and games."

Still chuckling, Caitlin tried to sift through his nonsense. "Delacroix? There's an odalisque here, but it was painted by Ingres."

"There are several odalisques. Artists through the ages seem to have been caught up in the harem fantasy. Ingres's harem girl is very cool and self-contained, while Delacroix painted his nude as totally abandoned to sensuality. You're much more Delacroix than Ingres." He opened the door and allowed her to precede him into the museum. "It's a great painting. We'll have to find out if both are here so you can compare them."

Alex could hear the sound of Caitlin's shower running in the bathroom as he moved quickly past it, down the stairs, and into the salon.

He picked up the receiver of the telephone and stabbed in the number in Langley, Virginia, with a decisive finger.

After three rings the phone was picked up on the other end. "Charles Barney."

McMillan's ever efficient second in command. "Barney, put me through to McMillan."

"Alex?" Barney's soft, hesitant voice held a note of reproach. "What is it? You know I can't disturb him without good cause."

"Barney." Each of Alex's words were enunciated with icy precision. "Put me through."

Barney sighed. "Very well."

He was put on hold and a moment later Rod McMillan picked up the phone. "McMillan."

"McMillan, get rid of my tail or hire someone who has the sense to do it right."

"Alex?" Rod McMillan's voice was silky smooth. "You can't expect to get top-notch surveillance for such routine work. You've been hopscotching all over the place and we had to call in outside help. I hear you have a lady."

"Get rid of him or I'll take him out."

"I wouldn't advise that." McMillan's tone lost some of its evenness. "You could be a little more cooperative. After all, we did fix that nasty business of Pavel's death with the Swiss police for you." He paused. "You know the tail is only insurance, Alex."

"If she sees him again tomorrow, he's gone."

Alex's lips set grimly as he replaced the receiver, turned, and left the salon. Caitlin hadn't indicated she had seen the CIA tail after they had left the museum, but he had to make sure she had no suspicions. He had been lucky she had taken Jonathan's revelations so well, but facing his past was different from confronting his present.

Nothing must go wrong now that he was coming so close.

The little blue flowers on the Delft tile on the walls surrounding the tub were enchantingly pretty and exactly matched the flowers on the shower curtain, Caitlin thought dreamily. She lifted her face to the warm spray and sighed contentedly as she let the heat sink into her. Of course, the tiles weren't in keeping with the age of the house, but then, neither was the claw-footed bathtub, or a bathroom itself, for that matter. To judge by the decor, this room must have been converted from a dressing room to a bathroom sometime in the 1930s. Her great-grandmother had performed the same face-lift at Vasaro in 1935. Tradition was all very well, but it didn't replace the joys of modern plumbing and—

"Hello." Alex drew back the heavy shower curtain, stepped naked into the tub, and pulled the curtain closed behind him. "I could hardly fight my way to the tub through all this steam."

She gazed at him over her shoulder, startled. "I . . . like hot showers. They relax me."

"You don't look relaxed."

"You surprised me. I'm used to showering alone."

"We're not showering." He leaned forward, his gaze on her face. The tanned flesh of his cheekbones gleamed with a moist luster through the steamy mist, and his light blue eyes were narrowed and intent. Strange, how she had first thought those eyes were icy. "Give me your tongue."

Her heart began to beat harder. "What?"

"Stick out your tongue."

She slowly obeyed him. He leaned still closer and touched her tongue with his own for only a few seconds. The very brevity of the action somehow made it unbearably intimate.

"Nice." His palm cupped her cheek. "Now turn away again, lean forward, and put your hands on the tiles."

Caitlin laughed shakily. "Perhaps we'd better get out and go to bed."

"What a lack of imagination," Alex murmured as he took a bar of soap from the blue marble holder affixed to the wall. "Don't look at me and do exactly as I tell you."

Caitlin turned around and rested her palms on the tiles. "Is this a game?"

"Oh, yes, a very pleasurable game." With lazy circular movements he rubbed the soap into her breasts and belly. "Now part your legs, Caitlin."

He palmed the bar of soap and dipped between her thighs, rubbing slowly back and forth. The muscles of her stomach clenched as she felt the alien slickness of the soap, the warm hardness of his hand caressing that most intimate part of her. Then she heard the bar of soap hit the tub. "You've dropped the—"

She inhaled sharply as two fingers entered her and began to move in and out.

Her breasts were lifting and falling as she tried to force air into her constricted chest. The steam was hot, filling her lungs as he was filling her body. "What— brought this on?"

He leaned forward and his teeth nibbled at her left earlobe as his fingers left her. His palms began to massage her buttocks. "I suppose I got to thinking about white slaves and harems and how nice it would be to have my own."

"Harem?"

"I'm not greedy. One concubine would do." He began gently pinching the rounded flesh of her bottom between his thumbs and forefingers. Erotic sensation sent a long shiver through her body and caused her hands pressed on the tile to curl inward.

His warm, moist tongue entered her left ear. "Want to play?"

"I'm not sure I'd be good at it."

"You have a very passive role." He widened her stance, pressing against her. "I guarantee you'll be fantastic." He entered her in one deep plunge and she gave a low cry. "Let me do it all. Pretend you're a slave and I'm the sheikh who's just bought you. Let me play with you as if you were a pretty toy." His lips brushed the sensitive place just behind her ear. "We're in the middle of the Sahara Desert. You tried to run away from me, but I caught you before you reached the door and pushed you against the wall of my tent. No one can hear you or help you."

"It sounds barbaric."

"I suppose most men have a touch of barbarism." He moved still deeper inside her and then was still. "Now you're bound to me. Can you feel it?"

Her upper teeth sank into her lower lip. "Yes."

"Are you frightened?"

"No."

"Do you want the cavalry to come along and rescue you?"

She drew a deep, shaky breath. "No."

"That's good. Unfortunately, the Sahara is deplorably low on cavalry troops." His hand slid around and pressed hard on her belly as he slowly rotated his hips. "Do you like this?"

"Yes." Her eyes closed tightly and her palms splayed against the smooth, wet tile. She could barely force the words from her dry throat. Tight. So tight.

"Then stand very still. If you move or look at me, I'll stop."

He pulled slowly out and then sank back to the hilt with excruciating deliberation. Her teeth sank into her lower lip to keep from screaming.

He began to pull out again, and she made an involuntary movement to keep him.

"No." His hands pressed her shoulders to keep her facing forward and totally withdrew from her. "I told you that if you moved, I'd stop."

She felt an aching emptiness. She wanted him back. She clenched yearningly. "Alex, for heaven's sake . . ."

"You want it?"

"Yes!"

"Then be perfectly still." He entered her again with the same maddening deliberation. "Don't move a muscle."

She gritted her teeth hard together. It was like nothing she had ever experienced. She felt totally subjugated, not by him but by her own sexuality. The slow, torturous seduction continued for minutes that seemed like hours. She could hear Alex's heavy breathing behind her, felt the slickness of his wet hands on her shoulders, glimpsed the wisps of steam coating the blue flowers of the tiles on either side of her spread palms. She began to make low, whimpering sounds deep in her throat.

"Do you want to move?" Alex whispered in her ear.

"Yes." She swallowed. "Oh, yes."

"How much?"

"A . . . great deal."

"Then tell me how you feel." His hands moved around to cup her breasts. "Here."

"Full . . . swollen."

One hand wandered down and began to rub. "And here?"

"Hot . . . I—ache."

"And it would be better if you could move?"

"Yes."

"Then move." He swatted her lightly on the buttocks. "Now!"

She bucked backward as if released from tethers, taking him wildly, deeply, desperately.

He held her hips firmly, keeping them sealed, and stood motionless, letting her expel all the frustration and desperation that had built in those moments of enforced stillness.

She could feel the tears run down her cheeks as she moved in a frenzy until the wild climax forced her to collapse forward against the tiled wall.

"Shh." Alex's wet cheek was pressed to her own, his chest pressed against her back. "Easy."

"Easy?" She laughed tremulously. "There was nothing easy about that."

"But you liked it?"

She was discovering she liked anything and everything he did to her. "It was like riding a tornado."

Alex chuckled. "Thank you. I've never been compared

to a force of nature before." He turned off the shower, drew back the curtain, and steadied her as he stepped out of the tub. "I think we've had enough water for the time being." He grabbed a towel from the rack, lifted her out of the tub, and began to dry her. "I'll really have to get you a harem outfit."

"The hell you will."

He was gently rubbing her hair dry. "No?"

"No. Playing a harem slave is strictly a one-time occurrence. The role wouldn't suit me at all in real life. I'd find a way to castrate any bastard who did that to me."

He sighed. "Pity. You're spoiling my fantasy, you know. Maybe I'll have to hire our red-shirted friend to kidnap you and whisk you away to my tent in the Sahara. Of course, first I'll have to buy a tent to put in the Sahara, and then—"

"Red-shirted..." she repeated vaguely, scarcely remembering the fat tourist who had caused Alex so much amusement and triggered these moments of erotica.

"I'm sure the poor man would be devastated if he knew you'd dismissed him so quickly." Alex enveloped her head in the towel and began to rub her hair dry. "You seem to have forgotten his existence since we left the museum."

"Because I didn't see him again. And if you say I told you so, I'll—"

"Would I be so dastardly after you've let me play sheikh to your concubine?" He wrapped her in the towel and pushed her toward the door. "Into bed with you before you catch cold."

Henri LeClerc was bored.

Caitlin looked at his long, graceful fingers toying idly

with an ivory-handled letter opener. Since she and Alex
had been ushered into LeClerc's office ten minutes before, the packager's expression had reflected first politeness, then impatience, and now he was definitely bored.

Caitlin nervously fingered the fastening of her purse.
Alex finished outlining his offer. LeClerc was a slight
man whose narrow, triangular face laid no claim to
good looks with the exception of a pair of wide-set gray
eyes of exceptional brilliance.

Now a faintly sardonic smile lifted one corner of his
mouth as he shook his head. "You're very eloquent and
I can't deny your offer is very attractive, Monsieur
Karazov. That's why I'm sitting here listening to you
when I should be working." LeClerc shrugged his thin
shoulders. "After all, I'm only a poor artist who must
think of practicalities."

A poor artist who wore a Rolex watch and used a
Lalique dove figurine for a paperweight, Caitlin noticed. She glanced around the office at the wine-colored
carpet and beige drapes that formed a soothing background for the starkly modeled pine furniture. An Erte
painting in tones of black, gold, and rose occupied the
west wall. Situated against the wall facing her was a six-
foot lighted glass collector's case containing row upon
row of antique scent bottles. She had tried to get a
closer look at the case when she had come into the office, but LeClerc had seated them immediately.

Alex smiled and leaned forward in his chair. "We're
here to convince you how practical it would be to put
off your other commissions and take on ours." Alex
smiled. "If the money is insufficient, we—"

"The money is extraordinary," LeClerc interrupted.
"But I have no time for new projects. I'm working on a
package for Coty and after that I've promised to consider

a project for Guerlain. After all, I can't create a design out of thin air. It requires inspiration. I believe we're both wasting our time."

For once, Alex wasn't reaching his goal. LeClerc was going to refuse them. Even though the result of the interview had been evident for some minutes, Caitlin still felt a sharp pang of disappointment. LeClerc was truly the best.

Her desperate glance went again to the scent bottles in the display case across the room. If only she could examine the bottles at closer range.

Alex was saying, "I'm not asking you to give up Coty. Just let us have—"

"Monsieur LeClerc," Caitlin interrupted Alex. She gestured to the case across the room. "Please, may I take a closer look?"

Both men turned to her in surprise.

"I'm sorry." Caitlin rose to her feet, her gaze on the case across the room. "You go on with your discussion. I'll only..." She trailed off as she moved across the office to stand before the lighted case. There it was! Shimmering under the lights with blue fire.

"I apologize for the interruption, Monsieur LeClerc. I'm afraid my partner is mad about antiques." Caitlin could tell Alex wasn't pleased with her, and for an instant she felt a twinge of guilt before she dismissed it. LeClerc wasn't buying the deal, and she had to do something.

"I'm flattered she considers my collection so fascinating. I'm very proud of it." LeClerc rose and followed Caitlin to the case. "I've been acquiring those pieces since I was a boy. Not many people realize what artistry is required to create a scent bottle." He pointed to a ceramic castle complete with embattlements and chimneys. "That's an incense burner, the scent drifts up from the chimneys." He pointed to a small pottery vase. "And that ointment jar was found in the tomb of an Egyptian queen."

"And this one?" Caitlin pointed to the silver container resting on the third shelf of the case whose stopper was a large pear-shaped sapphire.

LeClerc smiled. "You have good taste. I finally managed to acquire that beauty two years ago at an auction." He made a face. "I would have been glad to have your money then. It cost me over a year's work. It belonged to—"

"Marie Antoinette," Caitlin finished for him, still staring at the bottle. "But there was another scent bottle with a ruby stopper in the set, wasn't there?"

LeClerc went still. "It was lost, undoubtedly stolen, when the National Guard took the queen from Versailles to Paris. How did you know of the other scent bottle? You're a collector, mademoiselle?"

Caitlin shook her head. "I read about your acquisition in a magazine and I have a personal interest in this particular bottle."

Alex was suddenly standing by them at the case. "Jean Marc Andreas, Caitlin?"

She should have known Alex would remember every detail of what she had related to him of the contents of Catherine's journal. "I think so. It exactly fits the description in the journal."

LeClerc said, "The scent bottles were supposed to have been given to Marie Antoinette by her brother Joseph."

Caitlin grinned as she shook her head. "And no doubt the double royalty gave the bottle an extra cachet that sent the price soaring."

"You seem very certain." LeClerc looked intrigued. "I'm sure you are aware that one of the joys of collecting is knowing every historical detail pertaining to one's treasures."

"I'm not absolutely sure it's the same bottle. How can I be?" Caitlin asked quietly. "But it fits the description of my scent bottle."

"And you knew there were two bottles." LeClerc

studied her thoughtfully. "You truly know the history of this bottle?"

"Oh, yes. It was filled with rose perfume from Vasaro." She smiled. "And though it wasn't given to the queen by Joseph, I believe you'd find the real story much more fascinating."

"The auctioneer said rosewater was the queen's favorite perfume," LeClerc murmured.

Caitlin nodded. "Though she did like violet almost as well."

LeClerc smiled. "I think we must talk. Will you and Monsieur Karazov join me for lunch?"

His thin face was alive with eagerness, and Caitlin felt hope springing again. Due to luck or coincidence or some wild quirk of destiny, they were going to get another chance with LeClerc.

Find out what they want and give it to them.

But not before you get what you want for yourself.

Caitlin glanced at Alex to find him gazing at her with a faint, speculative smile.

She turned back to LeClerc. "I really believe we'd better complete our discussion regarding the packaging of Vasaro first." Caitlin smiled sweetly. "I believe you will like the scent."

Three hours later LeClerc had agreed to do all possible to furnish them with a preliminary prototype for the packaging of Vasaro within thirty days.

Two weeks later Caitlin swept into the study where Alex was studying Peter's photographs of the Wind Dancer that had arrived the day before. He glanced up in mock alarm and made a big show of hastily covering the photographs with his arms. "Don't kill me. I was only looking."

"You won't find anything. I checked those pictures yesterday when they came in the mail. They're even worse than the holograph." She frowned. "I called Peter yesterday and told him that it was ridiculous he hasn't sent me the translation of the journal yet."

"Again?"

She looked sheepish. "It's only the third time I phoned." When he continued to look at her with raised brows, she muttered, "Well, maybe the fourth." She rushed on. "But half the time I only got to talk to the answering machine. If Peter isn't stalling, then the person who's doing the translation is taking his money and not giving him an honest day's work. We wouldn't tolerate that at Vasaro. A day's wages earns a day's work."

"And did you tell Peter your work ethic?"

"I told him to get that translator off his ass and into gear."

Alex chuckled. "And Peter replied?"

"He made soothing noises at me." She made a face at him. "I can't help it if I'm a little overeager. I've studied the Wind Dancer so long, he's become a part of my life." She shrugged. "That's not what I came to talk about. I've canceled your arrangements to have the party for Chelsea at the Ritz," she announced. "I've found a better place."

Alex frowned as he pushed the photographs aside. "Are you crazy? Dammit, there is no better place. The Ritz is *the* place to give a party in Paris."

"I found a better place." Caitlin dropped down in the chair across the desk and grinned at him. "Guess where?"

Her cheeks were flushed with excitement, and she was so disarmingly childlike he found his annoyance ebbing away. "The Eiffel Tower?"

"Definitely déclassé. Anyone can have a party at the Eiffel Tower."

"A *bateau-mouche* on the Seine."

She shook her head. "Even worse." She leaned forward and whispered, "Versailles."

He shook his head. "It's impossible. The palace is a historical monument."

"It's possible. I did it." Her gray-green eyes were shimmering with excitement. "I asked myself, what place would draw the most important people to a party?"

He carefully kept his smile from appearing indulgent. "And you answered?"

"The Hall of Mirrors at Versailles." Her slim, nervous hands linked together on her lap. "So I checked into it and I found that though it was rare, permission was occasionally given to use the hall for a diplomatic party or—"

"You really got it?"

She nodded. "I called Jonathan and asked him to twist a few arms with some high-level types in the government and then I went to see the historical preservation people and offered them a five-hundred-thousand-dollar bond to guarantee nothing would happen to any of the antiques. Naturally, we'll have to take out the candelabras and put down carpets over the wood floors, but I think— why are you laughing?"

"I was thinking how nice it was of you to consult me before offering five hundred thousand dollars of my money."

Her eyes widened in distress. "You're not *angry*. It's only a bond and it's *Versailles*, Alex."

He shook his head, a smile still lingering on his lips. "I'm not angry. I'm very proud of you."

The pink deepened in her cheeks. "I'm proud of myself. I wasn't sure I could pull it off. A month ago I don't think I would have even tried." She unfolded her hands and smoothed her skirt. "I've always been... I'm not good at this kind of thing."

"You keep saying that. Have you ever thought the

reason that you haven't been good is that you haven't tried? The way to gain confidence at anything is to do it and then do it again until you get it right. Another two months and you'll probably be—"

"With the grace of *le bon Dieu* in another two months I'll be back at Vasaro, where I belong." Then she nodded thoughtfully. "But you may be right. Lately, I've felt—" She hesitated, searching for words. "Like I'm exploding inside, as if every day I'm learning—" She broke off and shook her head. "I don't know." She jumped to her feet and moved toward the door. "I've got to start making lists and you must call a lawyer and make sure we get the proper signatures guaranteeing the rental."

"*Oui, mademoiselle.*"

She stopped at the door and smiled cheekily at him. "I have found out one thing. I learn *very* fast, Alex."

A moment later the door closed behind her, but Alex didn't immediately pick up the telephone to call the attorney. Caitlin did learn fast, and he knew what she meant about the changes she was experiencing. For the past two weeks he had watched her evolve, grow. She had gained confidence, lost inhibitions, become bolder. He didn't flatter himself it had anything to do with their personal relationship. Hope aided growth in wonderful and miraculous ways, and Caitlin was glowing, blossoming in its sunlight. He had found himself watching, anticipating, waiting for the next change to occur.

He suddenly pushed his chair away from the desk and stood up. To hell with the lawyer and Caitlin's lists. The sun was bright and this was Paris. He and Caitlin would go for a walk by the Seine and he would see if he could coax another mischievous smile from her like the one she had tossed at him before she walked out of the study.

• • •

Caitlin was gone again.

And Alex knew exactly where she could be found.

He shook his head resignedly as he gazed at the empty pillow before he threw back the covers and got out of bed. He shrugged into his robe in passing and padded barefoot from the room.

A moment later he was walking swiftly down the stairs toward the foyer. For God's sake, it was four o'clock in the morning. It wasn't enough that Caitlin had been driving herself from dawn to dusk completing plans for the party at Versailles the following week. She had to creep down to the study in the middle of the night to stare at those damn pictures like a besotted groupie ogling a Mick Jagger poster. He strode across the foyer and threw open the door of the study.

Caitlin looked up, startled. She wore her full white pique robe, and with her face scrubbed to glowing cleanliness, she looked like a guilty child.

"Bed," he ordered. "Now." He crossed the study in three strides, took the magnifying glass from her hand, and tossed it on the desk. "You told me yourself you had an appointment with the caterers at ten this morning."

"I couldn't sleep. I wasn't tired enough. I'm used to more physical labor than this."

And the nervous energy always electrifying Caitlin had needed an outlet. "I can see that working in the fields would exercise a few more muscles than scavenging in those decorator rental houses all over Paris." His lips twisted. "So you decided to creep down here and stare at those pictures of the Wind Dancer again. This is the third time this week."

She blinked. "I didn't think you knew I was gone."

"I knew." He looked down at the dozen eight-by-ten glossies of the statue on the blotter. "You said these were less than useless."

"They aren't the same ones. This batch arrived two days ago."

"Any value?"

"They're better than nothing. I thought they might spark something."

"Exhaustion?"

"I told you I wasn't tired."

"Perhaps not physically, but your nerves are drawn taut as violin strings."

"Maybe." She wearily rubbed her eyes with the back of her hand. "I don't know. I'm probably just tired of waiting. I need the journal."

He came around the desk and half sat, half leaned against it as he looked down at her. "You keep saying that. What's so important about the journal?"

He expected her to evade the question as she usually did any queries about the Wind Dancer, but after a moment's hesitation she said, "The Andreas family has always been fanatically careful about not revealing the contents of Caterina's journal to outsiders. The closest they came was the book by Lily Andreas, and even that was very general."

"Yet you did a paper titled 'The Wind Dancer in History.' "

"Rumors, legends, a few documented accounts from German officers who served in the regiment that protected the Wind Dancer for Hitler. But I wasn't able to unearth any details about the origin." She nibbled at her lower lip. "As far as public record is concerned, the first mention of the Wind Dancer is at Troy, when Andros fled the city by a secret tunnel with the statue and a woman believed to be Helen."

"Andros?"

"The first Andreas. He was supposed to have been a sea raider who had been captured by the Trojans and was being held prisoner when the war broke out between Troy and Greece."

"A Greek?"

"I don't know. If he was, I would have thought he would have been put to death during the siege. Paradignes, the king's brother, gave Andros the statue and showed him the way to escape the city."

"Why?"

"I don't *know*." She couldn't keep the frustration from her voice. "There are so many questions that are unanswered."

"They may not be answered in the journal either, Caitlin," Alex said gently.

"But I'll have a chance."

"You're acting as if it's a matter of life or death. And you say *I'm* curious."

She shook her head. "It's not curiosity. It's—" She broke off and lowered her gaze. Then she said in a rush, "He's trying to tell me something."

"I beg your pardon?"

She grimaced. "Now you think I'm mad."

"Completely *folle*."

"That's why I don't talk about it." She kept her gaze fastened on the photographs. "I first saw a picture of the Wind Dancer when I was eight years old. It was in that Lily Andreas book you saw on my shelf in the perfumery. For a while I carried that book around everywhere with me. I didn't want it out of my sight. It *meant* something to me, Alex."

"A Pegasus is a fairy-tale creature. It would have captured the imagination of any child." Particularly a child as neglected by her parents as Caitlin had obviously been. "A flying horse that could take you away to the stars."

"No, that wasn't it. It was . . . it was as if we had a secret no one else knew." She shook her head helplessly.

"Only I don't know it yet either." She lifted her gaze to meet his own. "But he wants me to know his secret. He wants me to be the one to find out—" She stopped, searching for words.

"What?"

"Don't you see? The Wind Dancer has been regarded as an object of power by some of the most brilliant leaders in history. There had to be a reason for them to feel like that."

"It's very valuable. Priceless objects are often looked upon with reverence and almost religious awe."

"No, it's more—" Her eyes were suddenly shining brilliantly in the lamplight. "Oh, I'm not saying it was put on earth by aliens from outer space or that it's some sort of religious symbol. But it exists, someone created it, and there has to be a reason for it to have such an effect on all of us. The inscription *means* something."

"A recipe for chopped—" He stopped the flippant response in midsentence as he saw her expression. After months of silence on the subject she was at last talking to him and deserved better. "Time for bed." He straightened away from the desk and pulled her to her feet. "You can sneak down here to study those pictures another time. The Wind Dancer has been around for thousands of years. I think we can assume it will be around tomorrow."

She sighed. "You do think I'm crazy."

"No." He feathered a kiss on her temple as he propelled her toward the door of the study. "I believe you have an idiosyncrasy I have trouble accepting. But since Alexander the Great reputedly had the same quirk about the Wind Dancer, I can hardly criticize you."

"You don't believe it's possible. I didn't think you would."

"I can't believe what you believe. I didn't grow up

bedazzled by a statue or running through fields of flowers. My world has always been founded on hard, cold logic." He stopped at the foot of the curving staircase and touched the side of her throat with two gentle fingers. "But I want to believe you. Prove it to me. Show me, Caitlin."

She gazed at him gravely and then her face lit with a luminous smile. "I will." As she turned and started up the stairs she glanced back at him. "Aren't you coming?"

"I'll be right up as soon as I put the photographs away and turn off the light." He grinned. "That's one thing I learned a long time ago. Always put away your puzzle pieces safely so they're not misplaced."

"I won't have any worthwhile pieces to put away until Peter sends me that translation," she grumbled. "I always get the answering machine when I call now."

"And he doesn't call you back?"

"No, he just expresses me another batch of photographs in the next day's mail. Do you realize how many hundreds of photographs I have in that desk drawer now?"

"You don't suppose he's gently pulling your leg?"

"Of course he is." She smiled reluctantly. "And it's very bad of him. I need that journal."

"So you'll call him tomorrow."

"He's got to run out of film sometime. I think he's keeping Kodak in business." She proceeded up the stairs, but at the landing she stopped again and turned around. "I'm scared, Alex."

He frowned. "Now, that's ridicu—"

"Don't be silly. Not about the Wind Dancer." She motioned impatiently with her left hand. "You're going to pick up LeClerc's final prototype this afternoon. What if it's not any good?"

"And what if the Wind Dancer were born in a bolt of

lightning?" Alex chuckled. "The chances are just as likely. LeClerc's a magnificent craftsman. Stop worrying and go to bed."

She gave him a sheepish smile as she turned and ran up the stairs.

He stood watching her from the bottom of the staircase. As wary and grounded in practicality as Caitlin was, it had taken a good deal of trust for her to confide in him her feelings for the Wind Dancer. He felt as if she had given him a great gift.

He turned on his heel and entered the study again. He carefully stacked the photographs into a pile and slipped them into the middle drawer of the desk. He reached over to turn out the light on the desk.

The phone on the desk rang.

He stopped in midmotion, looking at the phone. Only Goldbaum and Katrine had been informed they were at this number, and neither would call in the middle of the night unless it was an emergency.

He picked up the receiver.

"Alex, my boy, I've heard you've been looking for me."

A bolt of shock ran through him. "Ledford?"

"Who else? Like you, I'm unique in the scheme of things."

Alex's hand tightened on the receiver until his knuckles turned white. "You son of a bitch. I'm going to cut your heart out."

Ledford chuckled. "I knew you'd be displeased with my little statement with Pavel. But it was for your own good, Alex. You weren't taking me seriously enough and I had to warn you. Though I guess I always knew it wouldn't do any good. I understand you've been running all over Europe trying to find me. I've been trying to resist calling you for months, but I've never been good at ignoring temptation."

"How did you know where I could be reached?"

"I have my own sources, just as you have. It wouldn't help if you did succeed in finding me, you know. I'm invulnerable to you."

"Then you won't mind telling me where you are."

"Oh, no, that would spoil everything. I'm beginning to look forward to the challenge."

"There is no challenge."

"But of course there is. It's just like the chess games we used to play, only with much higher stakes." He paused. "I wonder if you know what a lonely man I am, Alex."

"I wonder if you believe I give a damn."

Ledford didn't seem to hear the bitter sarcasm in Alex's tone. "It's true. Ambitious men are forced to keep themselves at a distance. One of the happiest and most relaxing times of my life was when we were together at Langley."

Don't let the anger keep you from thinking. Keep the bastard talking. Make him give you more information. "What kind of game are we supposed to be playing?"

"Why, hide-and-seek. What else? And perhaps cat-and-mouse on my part. I'm afraid I won't be able to resist teasing you a bit after all of those humiliating defeats you heaped on my head. I've been thinking a good deal lately about all you took away from me when you left Langley. It rankles, Alex." He paused. "Let's see, what little morsel shall I give you tonight? You asked where I am. I'm speaking from Athens at the moment, but of course I'll be gone by the time you fly here from Paris."

"Won't our little match interfere with your great master plan?"

Ledford clucked reprovingly. "Sarcasm doesn't become you. It really is a master plan and I'm going to pick up all the marbles this time."

"All? How about your 'associate'?"

"I was never one to work in tandem for very long. He bores me. He's very bright but not gifted as you are." Ledford suddenly laughed. "And, speaking of gifts, I have one for you."

"Your head on a platter would be nice."

"How cruel. Now, personally, I'm a great believer in gifts. They say so much. I believe your gift should have been delivered to your doorstep by now, so I'll bid you a good night, Alex."

"Wait. Tell me—"

"Good-bye, Alex." Ledford hung up.

Alex slammed down the phone, ran out of the salon and into the foyer, and threw open the front door.

Lying in a graceful swathe on the doorstep, embellished by a red satin ribbon, was a man's blue cashmere scarf identical to the one he had last seen wound around Pavel's neck.

8

"Have you got it?" Caitlin asked eagerly as she met Alex at the front door later that day. Her gaze flew to the briefcase in his hand. "Did you see it? What's it like?"

"Yes, I've got it." Alex shut the front door behind him. "And if you'll stop asking questions and come with me into the salon, you'll see for yourself."

"Sorry. I'm excited." Caitlin trailed after him into the gold salon adjoining the foyer. "You didn't let me see any of the preliminary prototypes and I've been waiting for this for four weeks."

"I wasn't complaining." Alex set his briefcase on the table in the center of the room and unsnapped the lock. "I like to see you excited."

Caitlin's gaze lifted from the briefcase to his face. The words had been spoken absently with no hint of sexual innuendo, and she was suddenly aware his manner was charged with a curious tension. "What's wrong? Don't you like LeClerc's package?"

"It's remarkable. You'll be pleased." He unwrapped a small object wrapped in Styrofoam. "This is the bottle."

The crystal container was an exquisite flow of sweeping, graceful lines in the form of a pyramid, and the glass itself possessed an oddly layered look that made Caitlin feel as if she were looking into a crystal ball or a clear lake with great depths. She touched the crystal with her index finger. "It's lovely. Why a triangle?"

"LeClerc thought it would evoke power images of the pyramids, eternity, mysteries, etc.," Alex said. "The golden script with the name Vasaro will have an Egyptian hieroglyphic look." He drew a small black box from the briefcase. "This is the box. What do you think?"

"Stunning." The cardboard box looked amazingly like wood and possessed a thickly lacquered veneer that shone with a dull sable luster in the afternoon light pouring through the windows. "And Vasaro will be in the same gold script on the box?"

Alex nodded. "And here's the pièce de résistance." Alex carefully unwrapped the last small object. "The Pegasus. LeClerc thought it better not to reproduce the clouds and the base. There was no way to create another Wind Dancer, so he created his own Pegasus. The running stance is the same as the statue and will bring the Wind Dancer to mind without looking like a cheap copy."

"LeClerc's a genius," Caitlin whispered as she took the crystal Pegasus and gazed wonderingly at the stopper. As Alex had said, LeClerc's Pegasus was not the Wind Dancer but it was all grace and exultant, fluid lines. "It's a work of art." Caitlin set the stopper in the bottle with great care and stepped back to look at it. "He got the effect he was looking for. It's . . . magical."

"You don't mind the emphasis being on the Wind Dancer instead of Vasaro?"

"Why should I mind? The Wind Dancer has had a great deal to do with Vasaro's history." Caitlin smiled. "It's all one."

Alex's stare lingered on her luminous face for another moment before he pulled his gaze away. "I'm glad you feel that way." He began to rewrap the bottle and stopper. "I've air-expressed a replica of the package to Andreas with a request for him to send the contracts. He should have it tomorrow and I don't see how he could object to LeClerc's work."

"Neither do I." Caitlin picked up the cardboard box and ran her finger over the smooth lacquered finish. How had LeClerc managed to get that woodlike texture? "We were lucky to get him."

"Luck?" Alex raised a brow. "You told me this wasn't your lucky year."

"Maybe my luck has changed."

"This wasn't luck." Alex took the box from her and replaced it in the briefcase. "LeClerc liked your perfume and wanted in on a good thing."

"And you paid him double what you should have."

"He would have done it anyway. Just not as quickly." Alex snapped the briefcase shut. "LeClerc is an artist in a business where his art is seldom appreciated by the public. The fanfare we're going to get with the Wind Dancer will give him a chance to show off his artistry and earn a little well-deserved praise. The money wouldn't have worked without the showcase."

"So you found out what he wanted and gave it to him."

Alex nodded. "*We* gave it to him. He was ready to show me the door before you stepped in and earned us more time to pitch. He also liked the idea that your perfume was good enough to attract a repeat buyer and keep his creation out there in the marketplace indefinitely."

"And he gave us what we wanted." Caitlin smiled. "I'm beginning to think your formula works."

"Yes, it works." Alex looked away from her as he set the briefcase on the floor by the table. "Sometimes."

Caitlin's gaze flew to his face. "Something *is* wrong."

"Baccarat is dragging their heels. Even with a hefty

bonus they still want another six months to produce the bottles."

"Six months? Can we give it to them?"

"No." Alex smiled grimly. "So I'm flying to Ireland tomorrow to talk to Waterford."

"I thought you were set on Baccarat."

"Oh, we'll get Baccarat. They know Waterford is capable of giving us what we want in our time span. We hold a carrot out to Waterford, and Baccarat will be there, snapping it away from them."

"It sounds a little ruthless."

"It's business." He looked away from her. "I've told Andreas to express the signed contract to you at Vasaro and I made a reservation for you on a flight to Nice tomorrow. You'd better call Jacques to pick you up at the airport."

Caitlin looked at him, bewildered. "What are you talking about?"

"You're leaving Paris." Alex still didn't look at her. "I have to stay here to fight with Baccarat and start arranging for media coverage for the arrival of the Wind Dancer and Chelsea Benedict. But you don't have to be here for any of that."

She hadn't had to be there while LeClerc was creating the package either, Caitlin thought dully, but Alex had wanted her with him. Now it appeared he did not. "No." She quickly lowered her lashes. "It will be good to get home to Vasaro. I've missed it. When will you need me back?"

"A week. October third. I'll complete the arrangements for the party and coordinate the news conference for the fourth."

The party. She had been so dazed by the pain of rejection, she had forgotten about the party. *Her* party, the party at Versailles she had worked so long and hard to make a success. She felt a flare of anger pierce the desolation. Why the devil was she being so meek? "The hell you will."

He stiffened. "What?"

"I'm not being sent back to Vasaro just because you've decided you want out of a relationship." She turned to face him. "It's my perfume and that's my party. I'm staying in Paris until after the party at Versailles."

"You can't, dammit."

"I can do anything I please." She glared at him defiantly. "I won't let the fact that you've become bored with me hurt my perfume or Vasaro."

"I'm not bored with you." Alex's voice was rough. "It's better if we're not together right now."

"That's right. You'll be busy." Caitlin forced herself to give him a bright smile. "I'll be busy too. We needn't even see each other while I'm here in Paris." She turned and moved toward the door. "I'll leave for Vasaro right now, but I'll stay there only overnight to make sure Mother signs the contracts. Then I'll bring them back to Paris and check into the InterContinental, where you made reservations for Chelsea and Jonathan."

"That's not good enough. I want you out of Paris until the day of the party."

"We can't always have what we want."

"Caitlin, I can't explain, but there are reasons that you can't stay here." Desperation tinged his voice. "Good reasons."

"There's a better reason for me to stay. Vasaro." Caitlin hurried out of the salon and up the stairs. A moment later the door of Catherine's room shut behind her and she moved quickly toward the armoire where her suitcase was stored. She would keep busy and the pain would go away. It was idiotic to feel hurt anyway. She had known from the beginning there was nothing between them but the lust that had drawn them together.

But there had been more between them.

They had taken walks together, eaten at sidewalk cafés, argued the benefits and drawbacks of the total lowering of the economic barriers between European countries, traded views on art and religion and bureaucracy. In these past weeks, besides passion they had shared laughter and a joint purpose that had forged the tentative links of friendship.

Yes, that was it. *Friends.* She seized on the word gratefully, desperately. It hurt when friends no longer wanted your company. Pain was to be expected in such a circumstance.

She slung the suitcase on the bed and began to pack. She would keep herself busy with the party and afterward she would be free to go back to Vasaro, where she belonged.

Alex was right, they would be much better apart for a while.

A knock sounded before Alex walked into the bedroom. His lips were set in a grim line as he closed the door behind him. "I have something to tell you, Caitlin."

"You used me?" she whispered.

He flinched at the word. "Yes, I won't deny it. I did it deliberately and with . . . considerable forethought."

"Why?"

"I told you that my friend Pavel was murdered last June. It was done because I had stumbled on a connection between— Anyway, it was my fault. I was working on one of my damned puzzles and I saw a connection between the Black Medina and the art thefts. The modus operandi was the same as one used by a man who had worked with me in the CIA, Brian Ledford. Pavel was killed to prevent me from going any further with the puzzle."

"And the Wind Dancer?"

"Ledford had always been fascinated by the Wind Dancer. I knew if I could get it here, he'd try for it."

"And you used me and Jonathan to get it here."

"Yes."

She shut her eyes. "Christ, I feel like a puppet."

"I didn't want to hurt you, Caitlin," he said hoarsely.

"Well, you did hurt me." Her eyes opened to reveal eyes glittering with tears. "You bastard, you *did* hurt me. Who gave you the right to manipulate us all like this?"

"I didn't only take," he said. "May I remind you that I gave you all what you wanted?"

She laughed huskily. "That's right, you did. A fair trade, because you gave us what we want—" Her voice broke on the last word and he took an impulsive step forward.

"No!" She took a hasty step back. "No, thank you. I don't want that any longer, so you don't have to pretend."

"I didn't lie about what we are together, Caitlin."

"I don't believe you." She shook her head dazedly. "So what do we do now?"

"You leave Paris. It's not safe for you here."

"Why not? You're the one this Ledford evidently hates."

"He's . . . twisted. I don't think he killed Pavel only as a warning. He did it because Pavel was my friend."

"Twisted? Well, tell him I'm nothing to you. Tell him you were only using me. That should satisfy him, don't you think?"

"Caitlin, I didn't—" He broke off and shrugged helplessly. "Why the hell did you think I risked everything to tell you? I told you about the scarf on the doorstep. I can't be sure of anything as far as Ledford's concerned. He knows I'm here and he may know about you. If you go back to Vasaro now and stay there, you may be safe."

"And if I don't?"

"The publicity about the Wind Dancer begins to hit in the media tomorrow. I can't guarantee anything after that."

"I'm not asking for guarantees from you." She sat down on the side of the bed and pressed her fingers to her throbbing temples. "I'm trying to think what's best."

"It's best for you to go back to Vasaro."

"No, that's not an option."

"Why not, for God's sake?"

"Because the Wind Dancer will be arriving in Paris next week."

He became still. "You're not going to call Andreas and tell him about Ledford?"

"No, I need the statue for Vasaro. I believe you knew I wouldn't tell Jonathan."

"I hoped you wouldn't."

"And you knew which buttons to push." She smiled bitterly. "You see, you've made me as guilty as you are."

"If I'm to blame, then let me take care of it."

"The hell I will. If I let the Wind Dancer come, it's my guilt and my responsibility." She stood up and took a step closer to him, her hands clenching into fists. "But we're not going to cheat Jonathan, Alex."

"That was never my intention."

"How do I know what your intentions were?" Her eyes blazed at him from her pale face. "That statue is *not* going to be stolen. I'm going to stay here and make sure of that, Alex. You can play whatever games you want with that maniac, but it's not going to hurt anyone but the two of you. Do you understand?"

"Perfectly."

"Good." She turned away with a jerky movement and resumed packing. "Then please wait outside while I finish packing and then you can take me to the airport. I don't want to look at you right now."

• • •

He had hurt her.

Alex watched Caitlin disappear into the lobby of the Charles de Gaulle Airport and his hands tightened on the steering wheel of the car. She didn't look back but maintained the same cool remoteness she had exhibited since they had left the Place des Vosges. He would make it up to her after it was all over. He could make it right and she would understand.

Christ, he wished she would stay at Vasaro. The only thing he could do was try to minimize the threat to her by keeping away from her until after the party. Perhaps Ledford would pigeonhole Caitlin's status in Alex's life in the same unimportant category he had given Angela, and she would be safe.

Perhaps.

It was too nebulous and dangerous a word and concept to tolerate. He had to make certain Caitlin wasn't harmed.

There was no way he was going to give Ledford a reason to make an "example" of Caitlin as he had Pavel.

"It's a brilliant prototype." Jonathan gazed musingly down at the crystal stopper on the desk. "LeClerc has the reputation of being difficult. I wasn't sure that Karazov could get him to do the job."

"But you're still uneasy," Peter said.

"We don't know anything more about Karazov than we did before. Why does he want this so much? Why is he involved with Caitlin Vasaro?"

"It could be personal. He doesn't appear to have any obvious ulterior motives."

"Obvious?" Jonathan laughed shortly. "I'd bet there's

nothing obvious about Mr. Karazov. What was the word you used to describe him? Subterranean?"

"You're worried about Caitlin?"

"I like her." Jonathan frowned. "And Karazov isn't a safe man."

"What about the Wind Dancer? Do you think he has anything to do with the art thefts?"

"Why should he? You said yourself he has money to burn."

"Then you're going to sign the contracts?"

"I'm not sure."

Peter hesitated before saying slowly, "It's dangerous. Jennings would tell you to pass. You know you're going to be under scrutiny when you accept the nomination. A business liaison with anyone questionable could cause an uproar."

"I haven't even decided whether to run."

"You know you want to."

"It would be a challenge." Jonathan paused. "But there are other challenges."

"Not one like running the greatest country in the world."

"True."

"Jennings will be—"

"Al Jennings may be a power in the Republican Party, but he doesn't run my life." An edge of steel had entered Jonathan's tone. "I won't be a puppet for any group. If I decide not to sign the contracts, it won't be because I'm afraid to displease the party."

Peter chuckled as he stood. "I think you're spoiling for a fight. You haven't had any fun since you squashed that lawsuit against Cunard shipping."

Jonathan found his annoyance ebbing away. "Maybe." He looked down at the sheaf of papers in front of him.

"If I decide not to go through with the deal, you won't get to see your precious journal and Karazov will stop working on the inscription."

Peter was silent.

"It means a lot to you."

"Not enough to cost you the nomination. I'll find some other way to see the journal."

"I told Karazov I'd sign the contracts if he came through with his side of the bargain. We received the contracts signed by Chelsea Benedict two days ago."

"Yes."

"And LeClerc *has* designed the package." Jonathan leaned back in his chair, his gaze fixed on the portrait of Louis Charles Andreas on the far wall of the study. "Karazov wants this deal to go through. If I refuse to honor my promise, what do you think he'll do?"

"Find another way to get what he wants."

"And we've already established the man's a genius at plotting. Wouldn't it be safer to deal with him in the open and retain control?"

"Jennings wouldn't think it safer."

"I told you that I don't let the Jenningses of the world run my life," Jonathan said impatiently. "My contract is going to be with Caitlin Vasaro, and any connection with Karazov will be extremely tenuous."

Peter rose to his feet. "I'm not going to be involved in this particular decision. You're on your own, Jonathan."

Jonathan grinned. "Coward."

Peter nodded soberly. "Personally, I believe you'd be one of the greatest presidents the country has ever had, and I don't want to see you jeopardize your opportunity to run."

Jonathan's smile faded. "I haven't said I'm going to sign the contracts."

Peter moved toward the door. "I can see it coming. You're teetering on the edge."

"Perhaps. I'll have to think about it."

"In the meantime, I'll redouble the security arrangements just on the off chance Karazov has a yen for the Wind Dancer that has nothing to do with its monetary value."

That same afternoon Jonathan signed the contracts and Peter sent them by courier service back to Caitlin at Vasaro.

"Marisa's such a lovely person. Very quiet and unassuming." Katrine followed Caitlin into her room and watched her place her overnight case down on the bed. "Not at all what you'd expect from the daughter of a movie star. I offered to take her to Cannes and Nice, but the only trip I could get her to take in the two weeks she's been here was to the Jacques Cousteau Oceanographic Museum in Monte Carlo. The rest of the time she spent in the fields with Jacques or wandering around the property."

Caitlin unsnapped her overnight case and opened the lid. "She's a nice child. I'm glad she hasn't caused you any trouble. I didn't think she would."

Katrine frowned thoughtfully. "A child? Oh, I don't think Marisa's a child at all."

Caitlin looked at her in surprise. "She's only sixteen."

"I still don't think..." She trailed off vaguely and then asked, "Alex didn't return with you?"

"He had business in Paris and he knew I was going to be here only overnight." Caitlin didn't look at Katrine. "Everything's going very well."

"I'll miss him." Katrine smiled. "But I'll enjoy still having the Lamborghini at my disposal. I felt quite grand tooling about Nice in it."

Caitlin turned to look at her. "Alex told you that you could drive it?"

"Of course. He gave me the keys before you left for the

United States." Katrine raised a beautifully plucked eyebrow and pouted. "I'd hardly take it without his permission."

"No. I didn't know . . ." Caitlin started unpacking. "He didn't tell me."

"He's very thoughtful."

"Yes." Caitlin had a sudden memory of the trouble Alex had gone to to lease the house on the square and felt a queer aching sense of loss. She looked down and saw that her hands had involuntarily clenched her navy blue skirt and impatiently released the material. The fields. She needed to get back to work in the fields and everything would be fine. "Mother, would you ask Sophia to finish unpacking for me? I want to change and go down to the fields to see Jacques."

Katrine nodded. "I'll do it. I'm not busy right now." She moved toward the bed and her brow knitted in a frown as she saw the navy blue suit on top of the clothes in the suitcase. "You surely didn't wear that old thing? And I don't see anything new in there. What on earth did you do in Paris if you didn't go shopping?"

Caitlin smiled. "I found a few things to occupy my time. It was a business trip, you know. I have to get back tomorrow to complete the arrangements for the party after you sign the contracts." Caitlin unbuttoned her blouse and stripped it off as she strode over to the bureau to get a work shirt. "But Paris is always enjoyable, and there were the museums."

And Alex, wreathed in steam, moving in and out of her body.

And the sound of Alex's laughter in the courtyard of the Louvre.

And Alex lifting his brows in surprise when the head-waiter escorted the old lady and her pet Afghan to the table next to their own.

"You always did like the museums." Katrine handed her a clean pair of denim jeans. "I heard on television that they've doubled the guards at the Louvre. I can't imagine why you'd want to go to a place with armed policemen all about."

"They were very unobtrusive."

"Anyway, I'm glad you're home." Katrine watched her tug on the jeans. "There was another of those attacks by the Black Medina in Athens yesterday and Lars Krakow announced he's formed an antiterrorist task force to capture them."

"Good. No one else seems to be able to stop them." Perhaps this horror with Ledford would be over soon.

Katrine smiled. "I remember hearing stories about Krakow when I was growing up. He was the hero of my childhood. All the children used to paste pictures of him and de Gaulle in their scrapbooks. Krakow beat the Nazis and he'll find a way of catching those *canailles*." She shivered. "Thank heaven you don't see anything like that happening in civilized cities like Cannes or Nice. The larger the city, the more chance for trouble."

"Paris was very peaceful while we were there." Caitlin fastened her jeans and sat down on the bed to tug on her boots. "The only difference I noticed were the soldiers at the airport."

Caitlin could think of nothing else to say and became conscious of the same awkward silence that usually fell between them after their few common interests were exhausted.

Katrine didn't seem to notice. She was still frowning at the navy blue suit. "You really must let me throw this dowdy thing away, dear. It's an abomination."

•   •   •

Marisa Benedict looked up and smiled as Caitlin walked toward her down the row of tuberoses. "You're Caitlin Vasaro. I saw you at the dock in Reykjavik." Her eyes twinkled. "And I'd recognize you anyway from all the pictures in the albums your mother showed me."

"My mother showed you those pictures?"

"Oh, yes, she's very proud of you." Marisa wiped her perspiring forehead on the sleeve of her shirt. "But I guess you know that."

"No." Caitlin glanced thoughtfully back at the manor house, remembering that moment of awkwardness before she had left Katrine. Her mother sometimes surprised her and she was always resolving to make more of an effort to understand her. Well, there was no time for that now. "No, I didn't." She turned back to Marisa. "You don't have to work in the fields. You're our guest at Vasaro."

"I like it." Marisa snapped off a blossom and tossed it into the basket. "And I'm used to working outside on my vacations. I spent the last two summers working with the dolphins at the San Diego Marine Institute. I'm going to be a marine biologist."

"I see." Caitlin began to pick. "Was that why you were in Iceland, rescuing the whale?"

"Someone has to do something." She paused in her picking to look out over the fields. "Vasaro is very beautiful. It was kind of you to let me come."

"My mother tells me you're no trouble and you've evidently been a great help to Jacques."

"You know, there's something very soothing about picking the flowers," Marisa said softly. "It reminds me of the way I feel when I'm snorkeling. It's another world. Everywhere you look you see fresh beauty, and it surrounds you and sinks in and takes away all the ugliness and pain."

Caitlin stared at the young girl's luminous face and

felt a strong sense of empathy. Marisa was scarcely more than a child, but she had known a good deal of the ugliness and pain she had spoken about. "Yes, it does help."

Marisa glanced at Caitlin and smiled gently. "My mother said I'd like you. I hope we can be friends."

Caitlin returned her smile. "I'm sure we can."

Turkey

The picture in the Sunday supplement of the London *Times* immediately caught Brian Ledford's eye. He stopped and whistled softly through his teeth. "Beautiful. My God, he's beautiful."

"Who?" Across the table from him, Hans Brucker lifted his golden head with the swift, dangerous grace of a lion scenting an intruder in his domain.

"You wouldn't be interested." Brian didn't take his eyes from the newspaper. "Eat your breakfast."

"I wouldn't ask if I weren't interested." Hans's well-shaped lips curled sulkily. "And I'm not hungry."

"I noticed last night when we went for that midnight swim you were getting a little on the thin side," Brian said. "I worry about you. You must take care of yourself, my boy."

"I'll do what I please." But a moment later Hans began to eat his toast.

He was becoming too tame, Brian thought with regret. It was always a challenge to break them, but once the task was done he usually felt this sense of sadness. He had recruited Hans Brucker when he had first formed the Black Medina over a year before, attracted as much by the boy's sleek blond manliness as his lethal talent with explosives. Brucker's combination of angelic good looks and cold violence had ignited in Brian an excitement greater than any he had known in years.

Hans had grown up on the streets of Munich, joined the Sons of Justice terrorist group when he was twelve, and killed his first man a year later. By the time he caught Ledford's attention he had killed nine more individuals in various skillful and unpleasant ways and become a genius at the art of building and planting bombs and plastic explosives. The boy was only eighteen, not overly bright, tough, swaggering, and immured with the male machismo Brian detested. He was quite perfect. How could he have possibly resisted him? Brian thought with amusement.

Physical seduction was out of the question with the boy, but mental and emotional subjugation were entirely possible. After he had decided Hans was a worthy challenge, Brian had set about "learning" him and found exactly how to manipulate him to the maximum. In his experience, orphans usually responded to a strong father figure more than a lover, even lethal orphans like Hans, and Brian was expert at playing the father. Within six months Hans had become completely dependent on him. It was a pity the challenge was over now.

"Who is he?"

The boy was jealous. He would have been both surprised and revolted to realize how close this passionate emotional attachment he had for Brian was to sexual bondage. Brian was tempted to let him stew for a while, but that wouldn't have been sensible. Hans was a bit psychotic and it would be wise to keep him stable.

"Don't worry, Hans. It's only a statue." He held up the newspaper. "The Wind Dancer. Isn't it pretty?"

"Yeah." Hans didn't look at the picture as he relaxed and smiled. "Are we going to take it?"

"Very likely."

"He said no more thefts."

"Then we'll have to change his mind, won't we?"
Brian looked down at the picture again. "Because I really must have it. Call the newspaper and see who released these articles about the Wind Dancer coming to Paris."

"Call them yourself. I'm not your slave."

"But you like to please me." Brian's voice was velvet soft, his gaze never leaving the newspaper. "And I really want you to do this for me."

Though he didn't bother to lift his eyes, Brian knew the hot color was flooding Hans's fair cheeks. The boy had become boringly predictable. Hans muttered a curse, pushed his chair back from the table, and strode over to the telephone.

Brian leaned back in his chair and gazed thoughtfully at the picture of the Wind Dancer. His partner would have to be persuaded that one more theft would do no major harm to the integrity of the plan. Perhaps he would be more amenable if Brian offered to underwrite the expenses of the operation. No, that probably wouldn't be enough. He would no doubt demand Brian's group execute the job he had repeatedly refused to perform for the last few weeks. Christ, he hated to do it. The man had no respect for the beauties of the past; he was as culturally sensitive as Attila the Hun.

Hans replaced the receiver. "Alex Karazov."

Brian threw back his head and roared with laughter. "Wonderful. He's really wonderful." He slapped his knee. "God, I knew it. I wonder how he managed to do it?"

"You know Karazov?"

"Don't pout. You surely recall my old friend Alex? I had to make an example of a good friend of his."

Hans frowned. "I remember now. June. You wouldn't let me go with you."

Why hadn't he let Hans go with him on that trip? Brian wondered. He had still been in the midst of subjugating Hans at the time, and he knew the boy would have enjoyed working on Rubanski. Brian could have arranged matters so that he and Alex needn't have met.

Yet, for some reason, he had wanted to keep the encounter with Alex entirely separate. Entirely his own. He had told Alex his feelings for him were ambivalent, but he wasn't sure exactly what they were these days.

He wondered if he could still feel love. Brian had closed that emotion away from him for so long a time, he wasn't sure what it was any longer. He hated Karazov, but he also wanted him and respected him. At times he had even protected him. Hatred was supposed to border on love. Did he love as well as hate Alex Karazov?

"Are you going to kill him?"

"Quite possibly."

"Let me do it. I'll do it for you." Hans's voice was fierce, his blue eyes shimmering with eagerness. "You're right. I do like to do things for you."

"That's because we care for each other. Like father and son." The boy was really exquisite, Brian thought impersonally as he reached out and gently stroked the golden hair back from Hans's face. Hans used to wear his hair clipped brutally short in an attempt to minimize those angelic good looks and appear more macho. It was a badge of Brian's success that after only five months he had been able to convince him to let it grow to its present length. Now he could feel the quiver of emotion that went through the boy's body as he touched that shining fall of hair. He would never have been able to break Alex to his will like this, he thought with dissatisfaction. "No, if it's to be done, I'll do it."

Rage flared in the boy's eyes. "You like him."

"Don't be silly. I don't like him." Brian smiled as he

glanced back at the picture of the Wind Dancer. Neither Karazov nor the Wind Dancer inspired any feelings as puny as liking. Yet, in a way, he felt a very similar passion for both of them. "But I think we should find out what else my old friend Alex is up to at the moment. Let's see now, who did I have make that little surprise delivery for me?" He snapped his fingers. "Ferrazo. Call Ferrazo in Paris and tell him that from now on I want Karazov kept under constant surveillance."

"I'll go. Let me do it."

Brian chuckled. "And in a few days we'd find Karazov split open like an overripe watermelon in some alley. Call Ferrazo."

"I don't like it."

"You don't have to like it, just do it. Now be quiet while I call Brussels and see if I can negotiate a deal with our charming friend." He went to the telephone. In minutes he was connected and had explained what he wanted to do.

"Impossible," his partner said.

"I've been most cooperative with your demands," Ledford replied. "I *want* this."

There was a silence on the other end of the line. "How much do you want it?"

Ledford sighed. "All right, it goes against my aesthetic principles, but you can have your big boom."

"It's a fair exchange, one antiquity for another. I don't know why you're so fond of those dinosaurs anyway. It's time we swept out the trash of the centuries to clear the way for a new world of clear thinking and clean, modern lines."

"I said I'd do it."

"I'll need four."

Ledford thought about it. "Four would deplete me too radically. I'll give you three."

Another silence. "If you'll do another job for me as well. Smythe's being obstructive. I may need the help of your companion to remove him."

Ledford glanced across the veranda at Hans lounging with one jean-clad leg gracefully flung over the arm of a white rattan chair. A faint smile touched his lips. "How?"

"Nothing violent. I believe a heart attack would suffice."

"Hans will be disappointed. He's feeling quite irritated at the moment and would relish a chance of releasing his ire. When?"

"Come to Liverpool tomorrow. I have to attend a meeting at the Hilton, and Smythe will be there. He's going to take a room for the night and won't return to London until the following day. I've arranged to meet him day after tomorrow for lunch and a final discussion."

Ledford chuckled. "*Final* being the operative word."

"If I shake hands with him on leaving, you'll know the job is canceled. Otherwise, I want him removed before he can talk to anyone. You understand?"

"Perfectly." Ledford's voice was gentle. "You persist in believing me to be thick-witted. I wonder how you would have survived trying to accomplish my end of our enterprise. It takes more than fine speeches and using the media to steal a 'Mona Lisa.'"

"It takes a one-point-five-million-dollar bribe."

"And months of weakening the moral fiber of a man who had never before taken a bribe. I'd say my psychological acumen equals yours, wouldn't you?"

Silence again, and Ledford could practically hear the mental cogs turning as the bastard tried to decide whether it was best to try to pacify or dominate him. "I've never questioned your intelligence, Ledford. Why else would I have offered you the opportunity to join us?"

Because you thought you could control me, you son

of a bitch, Brian thought without emotion. Well, he would accept the control as long as it suited his purpose, but it was time he demonstrated he could twist all those fine plans into knots if he chose to do it. "We'll be in Liverpool tomorrow."

"If I shake hands with Smythe, it's canceled. This is most inconvenient. We may need Smythe to get to Cartwright."

"We can manage without him." Ledford hung up the phone, feeling real pleasure as he pictured the outraged response that rude action would elicit. He hoped the arrogant twit had a stroke.

"I have a wonderful jaunt in mind for you, dear boy," he told Hans. "Our friend has a lagniappe he wants me to give him beside the big boom."

"Lagniappe?"

"It's a word used in Louisiana. It means giving something a little extra, as a baker might give a customer a thirteenth cookie. Lagniappe should be no trouble for you in this case. You're used to giving me something extra whenever I ask for it."

Hans frowned, puzzled. "What does he want?"

"A heart attack."

"Who does he want wasted?"

"The Honorable John Roland Smythe, an aide to Amanda Cartwright, the special envoy to the European Economic Community. He handles all her travel arrangements, among other things. It appears the gentleman is incorruptible, unbribable, and deplorably discreet. Evidently, he can't be seduced or blackmailed to the cause, and he's been told too much to leave alive unless he agrees to work with us."

"I've never killed a Britisher before."

"Then you have a treat in store for you, don't you?"

"Why a heart attack? I don't like using injections. There are other ways."

"That would doubtless be far more satisfying to you." Ledford traced Hans's beautifully shaped lips with the tip of his index finger. "But it has to look like a natural death."

Hans frowned. "I don't understand. One time he wants us to do jobs that will cause an uproar and the next we have to keep everything secret. Why?"

"You don't have to understand."

Hans's lips set stubbornly. "Why?"

Brian sighed. Hans could be regrettably obstinate on occasion. "Hans, dear boy, you don't even read the newspaper. How am I supposed to explain—" He stopped and then spoke slowly and clearly, as if to a small child. "The twelve European countries who belong to the common market are trying to lower all barriers. They're even trying to get a common currency, ridding the world of pounds, lire, francs, and so forth. For years there have been groups that also wanted to form all those countries under one government. Can you imagine the power and rewards anyone could reap if they controlled a united Europe?"

Hans frowned impatiently. "What does that have to do with us?"

"There was too much opposition to total unification. Now our people control fifty-five percent of the newspapers and two cable stations in Europe, and that helps to shape public opinion, but it might still have taken years to persuade the key figures in all those governments to come into the camp." He smiled. "So the Black Medina was born. You like cowboy movies. Have you noticed how the wagons gather in a circle for protection when the Indians are attacking?"

Hans nodded.

"Well, all those fine countries are the wagons we're

herding together. All we have to do is send a few more waves of Indians at them and they'll be screaming for any protection they can get. If they can't get it from their own governments, they'll turn to whoever can offer it. We've planned one final disruption to make that happen."

"The one you told me about here in Turkey."

Brian nodded. "Once they're ready for plucking, we'll scoop them up so fast, they won't know what hit them. Great Britain is quarrelsome on too many issues, and that disturbs our friend very much."

"Oh." Hans was silent a moment. "But why do I have to use the hypodermic on Smythe?"

Hans was back to square one, and Brian wondered in exasperation how much of what he had said had gotten through that beautiful golden head. "Because there must be no hint of threat surrounding Cartwright in the next few months. It will make it more difficult to replace him with a man of our own who will prove more cooperative."

"You're going to kill the old lady."

Brian flinched. "She's not an old lady, she's a woman in the prime of life. All of us can't be eighteen."

"I've never killed an old lady either."

"I doubt if you'll be chosen to do it."

"Why not?"

"It's a job that requires careful planning and coordination of all concerned."

"I can do it. Please." Hans took Brian's hand in both his own and brought it to his lips. "I . . . need to do it."

"Indeed? Why?"

"I used to be—" He paused, searching for words. "People used to respect me. I could walk into a room and feel as if I owned it. Before you made me so . . ." He trailed off and then whispered. "I used to *do* things."

Brian clucked gently. "Is your self-worth suffering

from our relationship? I thought I'd taught you that a proper son gives respect and obedience in all things. I have no desire to make you unhappy. Perhaps it would be better for you if I let you go."

"No!" Hans's grasp tightened on Brian's hand. "You know I didn't mean—just give me more to do."

"I'll think about it." Brian smiled. "Let's see how you do the day after tomorrow with Smythe." His smile faded and his expression became thoughtful. "And after you've attended to Smythe, while you're in jolly old England I may have you toddle around to Kilane Downs in Yorkshire on another job."

The son of a bitch didn't offer to shake his hand as they paused beside the bank of elevators, and Smythe felt relieved. He didn't think he could stomach touching the man after what he had just heard.

"Mull it over. It's the only way for us to go."

"I'll think about it." Smythe pushed the button for the elevator. "I'll let you know. I'm sure you believe you're doing the right thing, but it's not something to consider lightly." The doors of the elevator slid open and Smythe hurriedly stepped into the cubicle. "You understand that you caught me off guard. It came as a surprise. I have to—" He broke off as he saw the thin, contemptuous smile on the other man's face. Smythe panicked as he realized he was not deceiving him, that his revulsion had been too obvious.

The doors slid closed, blocking out that faultlessly elegant, threatening presence, and Smythe drew a deep breath as he pushed the button for the sixth floor. All he had to do was get to his room and call the office. They'd send men to accompany him to Downing Street and he could tell his story.

And what a story.

He felt the same anger he had known when he had been told what they wanted of him. Christ, Amanda Cartwright could be hell on wheels to work for, but goddammit, she kept the wheels turning and he liked the old girl. He had no intention of letting her be put down at that conference.

The doors slid open and he hurried from the elevator down the hall to his room. He thrust the key in the lock and opened the door.

"Herr Smythe, could I speak to you?"

His heart skipped a beat and his muscles tensed as fear swept through him. Then he relaxed as he glanced over his shoulder and saw a young boy strolling toward him from the direction of the elevators. He couldn't be more than eighteen or nineteen, the same age as his own son, Robert, who had entered Oxford the past year. The boy was dressed in tight jeans, a black turtleneck sweater, and white windbreaker, and his golden hair fell in a shining bell over his ears. Thank heaven, Rob always dressed with more conservatism than most of his age group and kept his hair carefully barbered. But this lad at least appeared cleaner and more attractive than most of Rob's friends. "I'm sorry, I'm in a bit of a hurry."

"But I've come such a long way, Herr Smythe." The boy's smile lit his handsome features with angelic radiance as he came even with Smythe. His left hand slid casually into the pocket of his windbreaker. "And I promise it will take only a moment."

Caitlin received a call at the InterContinental from Alex on the afternoon of September 30. His tone was terse and businesslike. "Chelsea Benedict is flying into Paris four days early. She wants you to make yourself available tomorrow and meet her in the lobby at one, when she arrives."

"Is that necessary?"

"She thinks it is. It would probably be good public relations to keep her happy. It's your decision."

"Very well, I'll meet her. Did you get Baccarat to escalate the production of the bottles?"

"No problem. They'll have enough for the launch."

"You've succeeded again. So, threatening to take away what someone wants works almost as well as giving him what he wants."

"I'm not apologizing for twisting a few arms, Caitlin."

Why was she arguing with him, when all she wanted to do was get off the phone and away from his voice? "I'm not condemning you," she said wearily. "It just seemed overly manipulative."

"It was." He paused. "And I am."

"Yes, you are." She dropped the subject. "And the publicity?"

"Haven't you seen the newspapers?"

"I haven't paid much attention lately. It seems as if I've spent half the time talking on the phone to Serdeaux at the perfume factory and the other half working on the arrangements for the party. Have we been in the newspapers?"

"The announcement of the Wind Dancer's journey to France is all over the newspapers and television."

"Then you've got what you wanted."

An odd thread of tension entered Alex's voice. "Yes, I've got what I wanted." He added deliberately, "What we both wanted. I'll call Chelsea back and tell her you've agreed to meet her."

When Caitlin went down to the lobby at one the next afternoon, she found Chelsea surrounded by piles upon piles of luggage, bedazzled bellboys, a man in a chauffeur's uniform, and the concierge. She looked completely different from the casually dressed woman Caitlin had met in Reykjavik. Today Chelsea wore a skintight brown dress, her bright hair blazing against the dark fabric. She looked superbly confident and utterly chic.

"Hi," Chelsea called to Caitlin. "Be with you in a minute." Miraculously, the actress proved true to her word. With lightning efficiency she arranged to have the concierge check her in, dispatched tips to the bellboys, and crooking her finger at the chauffeur to follow her, she strode briskly across the lobby toward Caitlin. "What a madhouse. Caitlin, this is George. He's going to be our chauffeur while I'm in Paris."

Caitlin barely had time to murmur an acknowledgment before Chelsea whisked her out of the front entrance and into a black stretch limousine parked on the Rue de Castiglione. "I hope you don't mind, but I told the concierge to have your stuff moved into my suite. I know I should have asked you first, but those damn VIP suites are always as big as a football field and you won't have trouble avoiding me if you like. I hate being alone in hotels."

"No, I don't mind." Startled as Chelsea practically pushed her into the backseat of the limousine, Caitlin asked, "Where are we going?"

"Shopping." Chelsea's gaze raked over Caitlin's tailored gray dress. "Though Christian Lacroix may never let you in the front door in that thing. Oh, well, we'll tell them you've been in the Congo for the past five years. They wouldn't dare throw out a missionary." She paused before she got into the limousine to take a deep breath. "Lord, I love the smell of Paris. It's not like anything else. Fresh-baked croissants, the flower carts, the carbon monoxide from the tourist buses..."

Caitlin laughed. "And the clicking of the cameras."

"That's sound, not scent. Let's get our senses straight." Chelsea stepped into the limousine and George slammed the door shut. "Come along and we'll breathe in the perfume-laden air of Lacroix."

Caitlin settled back on the plush seat. "I prefer the scents of Vasaro. I think you will too. When has Alex arranged to have the commercials shot?"

"Too soon, my dear, too soon. Shortly after the party. Alex has hired Pauley Hartland to direct the commercials." When Caitlin looked at her blankly, she continued. "Pauley won the Clio award two years running for the best television commercial."

Caitlin's eyes twinkled as she nodded solemnly. "You mean he's good."

"The best."

"Are any of the commercials being shot with the Wind Dancer?"

"Not the ones at Vasaro. Alex told Pauley he absolutely can't take the Wind Dancer to Vasaro for security reasons, so Pauley's shooting one interior commercial in order to use the statue in it." She made a face. "But the location scouts haven't come up with anything yet."

"What are you looking for?"

"A restaurant or club. Romantic rather than sophisticated."

"La Rotonde."

Chelsea looked at her inquiringly.

"It's a marvelous café at the Negresco Hotel in Nice. Carousel horses that go up and down on pedestals between the tables and booths. In the center of the room there's a life-size little-girl doll dressed in a white Victorian dress playing an organ grinder." She closed her eyes, trying to remember. "They play soft Viennese waltzes and the windows have those lovely pink Austrian blinds that drape so beautifully."

"It sounds wonderful."

"It is." Caitlin's eyes opened and she smiled reminiscently. "My father used to take me there every birthday when I was little." How strange she had forgotten those magic times and remembered only the bitterness after he had left.

"I'll call Pauley and have him send someone down to check it out." As the car began to glide down the street, Chelsea turned to Caitlin. "Marisa likes you. Every time I've talked to her on the phone she mentions you."

"And I like Marisa," Caitlin said. "She's a lovely child."

"She's not a child." Chelsea's gloved hands clenched her handbag. "She's never been a child since that bastard—" She broke off, and when she spoke again her voice was even. "She loved her father and he deliberately hurt her. Do you know what that can do to a child?"

"Yes."

Chelsea's gaze lifted to search Caitlin's face. "I think you do. Maybe that's why the two of you became friends so quickly. Two of a—why are you looking at me like that?"

"It just occurred to me to wonder why you let her come to Vasaro."

"I liked you."

"But you knew I'd probably be spending a good deal of time here in Paris." Caitlin studied her thoughtfully. "And you're obviously very protective of Marisa. I don't think you'd send her to a stranger's home just because you liked them."

Chelsea made a face. "You're not dumb." She looked a little sheepish. "I had you all checked out."

"What?"

"I had you investigated. Oh, I told them to be very discreet. I didn't want your neighbors suspecting you were an ax murderer or anything. They all like and respect your family, by the way."

Caitlin smothered a smile. "That's nice."

Chelsea glanced at her warily. "You're not mad at me?"

Caitlin chuckled. "No, I think it's funny."

Chelsea breathed a sigh of relief. "Great." She looked away from Caitlin and the next words were halting. "I'd like to say thank you for being kind to my daughter and making her feel at home. That wasn't in our deal."

"I'm glad we could help. Did that reporter cause the trouble you thought he would?"

Chelsea shook her head. "Tyndale never mentioned our backgrounds and we got the cover." She frowned. "How the hell do you figure someone like that?"

"Your daughter said she didn't believe he was as bad as you thought."

"It's better to prepare for the worst, and she's enjoyed her stay at Vasaro." The limousine stopped in front of a shop on the rue du Faubourg Saint-Honoré and Chelsea grinned as the chauffeur came around to open the door. "Come on, let's choose some working clothes."

"I'm not going to be much help to you. My mother thinks my taste is abysmal, boring."

"She's right. I knew the first time I saw you that you were just like Marisa. She thinks clothes are meant only to cover the body and provide warmth."

"And what do you think they are?"

"Tools to set a mood. Costumes to make a statement." She gestured to the brown dress she was wearing. "What do you think of me when you see this outfit?"

"Chic, bold, eye-catching."

"We'll have to get something more subdued for you. Elegance instead of pizzazz."

"Me?" Caitlin looked at her blankly. "I thought we were going shopping for you."

Chelsea shook her head. "I called and ordered my gown for the party from Lagerfeld at Chanel's when I went back to the States from Iceland and all I have to have is a fitting. This trip is for you."

"Then we're shopping in the wrong neighborhood."

"Nonsense." Chelsea moved toward the entrance. "You're selling a perfume for two hundred dollars an ounce. The public should perceive you as a woman who would wear her own perfume—ergo, you have to dress the part. Working clothes."

"I can't afford the—"

"I can," Chelsea interrupted gruffly. "You were kind to Marisa, and I pay my debts."

"Chelsea, I spent only two days with her. My mother has been caring for her. I can't let you do this."

"So we'll buy some things for your mother too."

"I don't even need—"

"My God, will you just shut up?" Chelsea sailed past the liveried footman holding open the door. "I charged you almost three million dollars for this gig. Relax and take me for a little of it."

Caitlin hesitated before hurrying after her into the store. She supposed she would need presentable clothes for the next few days, and she had never felt more dull or wraithlike than in Chelsea's vivid presence. "Only what I need. My usual lifestyle doesn't call for—"

Chelsea wasn't listening. "Jewel colors, I think." She studied Caitlin. "Burgundies, emeralds, and, of course, blacks. You'd look stunning in black with that hair. Draped bodices and a flowing Grecian look. Large breasts aren't fashionable and hell to dress." She frowned. "It's hard for me to tell what would suit you. I'm a peacock and you're a swan."

"A swan?" Caitlin laughed. "I'm no ugly duckling, but I'm definitely not a swan."

"Wait and see." An elegantly dressed saleswoman was fixing Caitlin with a supercilious stare as she glided across the deep silver-gray carpet toward them. Chelsea moved a protective step closer to Caitlin. "It's that god-awful dress. Don't let her scare you," she whispered. "These dragons get a bonus for every client they intimidate. It's part of the show. Simply look aloof and above it all and I'll do the rest."

Caitlin tried to look appropriately disdainful, but it was difficult with the saleswoman staring at her with such contempt.

Chelsea stepped aggressively forward, like a warrior going into battle, and when she spoke, her enunciation had lost any trace of Hollywoodese and became pure Royal Shakespearean theater. "*Bonjour, Madame.* This is Mademoiselle Caitlin Vasaro. You've heard of her, of course." Chelsea looked astonished as the woman shook her head. "No? How can that be? The president is to award her the Croix de Guerre next week for her self-less service in the Congo." She gazed at the woman pityingly. "Perhaps we should have gone to Dior after all, Caitlin. I realize you wished to try these new people, but there's something to be said for the old guard." She paused, locked glances with the dragon, and threw out the one irresistible challenge to a couture house. "Now, tell me, madame, what can Lacroix do for my friend that Dior cannot?"

9

"We bought too much." Caitlin leaned back in the limousine with a sigh of relief. After only three hours in that rarefied atmosphere of haute couture she felt more tired than if she'd worked a full twenty-four hours in the fields of Vasaro. "I'm glad we found those three dresses for my mother, but I didn't need—"

"Of course you did," Chelsea said. "Three evening gowns, two day dresses, one suit, two cocktail dresses. We didn't even buy you any shoes." She frowned. "I think you should wear the black velvet gown for the party. It's wonderful with your skin."

"And it shows so much of it," Caitlin said dryly. "You didn't buy anything for yourself."

"I needed only the two gowns I ordered for the party and the launch." She leaned forward in the limousine. "Take us to number fourteen Saint-Germain, George."

"We're not going back to the hotel?" Caitlin firmly shook her head. "No more shopping. I can't take it."

"Relax. We're not going shopping." Chelsea leaned back and grinned. "We're going to tea with a nice old man and his wife."

"I'd rather go back to the hotel and put my feet up."

"Later," Chelsea said. "You have to meet Monsieur Perdot first. Don't worry, you'll have a good time. They're two of the most charming people in Paris."

To her surprise, Caitlin found Chelsea was right and she did enjoy the next two hours enormously. Jean Perdot and his wife, Mignon, lived in a tiny town house that was probably almost as old as the Andreas house. The moment Caitlin walked into the parlor she became aware of a comfortable Victorian ambience that soothed her frayed nerves as much as the chamomile tea Madame Perdot served them from Sevres cups of almost transparent delicacy. The serpentine-backed couch was cushioned in crimson velvet, and a small fire burned in the grate of the white marble fireplace. The pattern of green vines and white roses in the Aubusson carpet covering the oak floor was echoed by several lush potted palms set about in strategic nooks and corners. By the tall arched window across the room a fine Venetian lace cloth covered a small table on which a cozy cluttering of framed photographs, silver and ivory snuffboxes, and an exquisite black ostrich fan rested.

The Perdots matched their surroundings in both warmth and elegance. Mignon was tiny, white-haired, and wore a superbly cut dress in a soft shade of blue that reminded Caitlin of robins' eggs and dawn skies. Her husband was tall, spare, with a leonine shock of gray-white hair and keen blue eyes. The couple was witty, well mannered, unabashedly affectionate with each other and with Chelsea, and displayed a warm interest in Caitlin.

When Chelsea finally rose to leave, Caitlin felt a definite twinge of disappointment.

Jean Perdot accompanied them to the door and kissed Chelsea's cheek. "That outfit is atrocious, you know," he murmured genially. "We all know you have a fine body without your flaunting it. That dress is not you at all."

Caitlin's eyes widened in surprise at the rudeness from a man who before had previously displayed only old-world courtliness.

"I hoped you'd feel like that." Chelsea gazed at him limpidly. "That's why I wore it, Jean."

Jean Perdot's eyes crinkled as he chuckled. *"Bon Dieu*, you're a wise child."

"I try." Chelsea gestured to Caitlin. "A swan?"

The old man shook his head. "A tall rose of deepest crimson, straight, strongly rooted." He studied Caitlin. "With thorns."

"Thorns?" Chelsea frowned. "I don't think so."

"Because you've never seen them?" Jean Perdot smiled faintly. "She may not even know she has them, but they're there." He lifted Caitlin's hand to his lips. "It was delightful meeting you, my child. Come back and see us."

"Thank you for having me, Monsieur Perdot."

He stood in the doorway and watched until they were ensconced in the limousine.

"He likes you," Chelsea said with satisfaction as the limousine pulled away from the curb. "I was hoping he might."

"For a moment back there I felt as if I were a bug beneath a microscope."

"It was a compliment. If you hadn't interested him, he would have told me he could see nothing in you."

"See? What is he? Some kind of psychic?"

"He's the greatest dress designer in the world."

Caitlin looked at her blankly. "But I've never heard of him."

"That's because he's also the best-kept secret in the world. Every one of his clients has to promise she won't divulge the designer of any dress he does for her."

"What?"

"He belongs to the Perdot banking family and has

never needed money. He's been in business for over forty years but he's never wanted to have the bother of an haute couture house because he says it would get in the way of his artistry. He designs to fit his client's personality and Madame does the sewing."

"Incredible."

"I thought so too. He refuses more clients than he takes." She grinned. "For example, the Duchess of Windsor's on his reject list. He tells me he may select only a few new clients in a decade."

"And you're one of them?"

"I got lucky. I was introduced by one of his oldest clients five years ago and he found me a challenge."

Caitlin could see how he would.

"He doesn't take orders; he creates a gown and then sends word that he's deigned to favor you. I wore one of his gowns to accept my Oscar."

"I didn't see the news of the awards. Sorry."

"I was a smash." Chelsea grinned. "When we get back to the hotel I'll show you what he had waiting for me when I arrived in Paris this time."

Caitlin thought she wouldn't want to see another gown as long as she lived after those hours at that high-fashion silken cocoon on the rue du Faubourg Saint-Honoré, but she was suddenly curious how the designer saw Chelsea Benedict. "I'd like that."

Chelsea cast a casual glance out the back window of the limousine. "He's really very good."

"Monsieur Perdot?"

Chelsea shook her head. "Your shadow."

Caitlin stiffened. "What?"

"The man driving the dark gray Renault."

When Caitlin continued to look at her blankly, Chelsea said, "The detective Alex hired to follow you around to protect you while you were transporting all those rented art objects back and forth to Versailles." Chelsea looked at her in puzzlement. "Didn't Alex tell you he told me about him? He didn't want me to think someone was about to kidnap me and knew I'd probably spot him myself." She grimaced. "God knows, the studios have hired enough people to tail me to protect their investment during filmings."

"No, he didn't tell me he had told you." He hadn't bothered to tell Caitlin about the detective either. Since she had returned to Paris she had purposely kept herself so busy, she fell into bed each night in a state of exhaustion that almost enabled her to forget Ledford, but the knowledge that Alex had not forgotten brought the threat rushing back to her.

"You okay?" Chelsea was studying her expression with concern.

She forced a smile. "Just tired."

When they arrived back at the hotel, Chelsea moved through the lobby acquiring bellboys like a general recruiting his troops, and in moments she had her small army depositing their multitude of boxes on the eighteenth-century brocade couch in the paneled sitting room of the suite. Chelsea distributed charming smiles and generous tips to the dazzled porters before waving them from the room. She walked quickly toward the bedroom, every movement graceful, coordinated, and full of vitality. "Come along. Jean's treasure is in the armoire in the bedroom."

"I'm coming." Caitlin kicked off her high heels. "As fast as I can limp along. How do you survive marathons like this?"

"All you need is a hot shower and you'll be fine."

Alex's intent eyes gazing at her through the haze of mist in the tub.

The memory came out of nowhere with painful suddenness. She would *not* think of Alex, Caitlin told herself desperately. He had used her and he had used Vasaro. The hurt would go away soon. It was the first time she had thought of him all day, and that must mean she was already healing.

Chelsea opened the armoire and reached into its dark depths. "I do like this. Isn't Jean a genuis?"

Caitlin saw what she meant as Chelsea pulled out the silver evening gown. No, it wasn't a gown, but a dress. A short dress with a high neckline and long sleeves. The lines were simple and would hang loose, barely skimming Chelsea's curves. It was the fabric that caught and held the eye. The silver sequins of which the dress was composed were patterned to resemble shimmering chain mail, and in it Chelsea would look like a young medieval knight—but fabulously sexy, feminine. It was clear Jean Perdot did not see Chelsea Benedict as the peacock she had called herself but as a warrior knight, an Amazon queen. As Caitlin recalled how Chelsea had turned ferociously on the reporter at the docks in defense of Marisa, and the protective step she had taken toward Caitlin when the saleswoman had given her that patronizing glance, she nodded slowly. "You're right. The man's a genius. Are you going to wear it for the party?"

Chelsea shook her head as she gently touched the glittering sequins. "Too ostentatious. A good spokesperson should show off the product, not herself. Besides, there's no way I can eclipse that bloody statue, so I might as well accept my fate with dignity." She hung the gown back in the armoire. "I'll save it for something special."

"Another Academy Award?"

"Maybe." Chelsea closed the door of the armoire. "You'd better get into the shower while I call room service. I thought we'd eat in the suite and relax tonight. We've got a news conference tomorrow morning and then tomorrow afternoon we need to buy shoes."

"News conference?" Caitlin forgot about the threat of another bout of shopping at this new threat. "Why do I have to be there?"

"Because you created the perfume, silly." Chelsea smiled. "Don't worry, I'll try to take the heat off you. Dealing with the press is part of my job."

"It will have to be almost entirely your job. I'll have to be at Versailles for most of the next two days."

Chelsea nodded. "Alex told me about your coup. He's very proud of you."

"Is he?" Caitlin's tone was reserved. "How nice. Actually, it wasn't too difficult to persuade them it was only fitting that the palace be used to welcome the Wind Dancer back to its former home."

Chelsea wrinkled her nose. "Forget about welcoming Chelsea Benedict."

"I'm sure more people will be looking at you than at the statue."

"You're very kind, but that's probably not true. At any rate, everyone wants to be on the A list for an invitation to a party at Versailles." She stared at Caitlin speculatively. "Do you know, I think you've changed since I first met you."

"Have I? In what way?"

"I'm not sure. Perhaps less easy to intimidate?"

"That woman at Lacroix managed to intimidate me."

Chelsea chuckled. "But then, the whole female population of the world trembles before Lacroix." Her smile faded. "Your partnership with Karazov has produced quite a powerhouse combo. As they say in your language, you and your Alex are *très formidable*."

"He's not my Alex and I'm hardly a powerhouse." Caitlin moved toward the door. "But, at least, you have the term right for him. *Très formidable.*"

"I'll see you later." Chelsea straightened the floating chiffon panels of her white gown as she paused in the doorway of the Hall of Mirrors and assumed an air of conscious majesty. She winked at Caitlin. "It's show time!"

Caitlin took a hasty step back as the reporters and television cameraman flowed across the hall toward Chelsea like nails to a magnet. She had been present at several of Chelsea's "show times" in the past few days, and she definitely preferred to be in the background, particularly at this party, which culminated all her efforts of the past weeks. The actress effortlessly dominated any situation by sheer personality alone. She combined glamour, humor, and an exuberant vitality that was the epitome of star quality.

Chelsea was immediately swept away into the throng of guests, and Caitlin eased herself into the room and gravitated to the far corner of the room. Other than assuring that the mechanics of the party went smoothly, her part was now over. On the far side of the hall a four-piece orchestra was playing Vivaldi, but only an occasional strain could be heard above the buzz of conversation and the delicate clink of glasses. White-coated waiters insinuated themselves among the crowd of guests, offering puff-pastry canapés, Roederer Cristal champagne, and orange juice for the nondrinkers.

Savonnerie carpets had been laid on the wooden floor of the hall, and the chandeliers glittered in crystal celebration high overhead. A splendid ice sculpture of LeClerc's Wind Dancer dominated the buffet of beluga caviar, lobster, and light pastry confections on the long damask-covered table next to the bank of long, arched windows.

Caitlin watched the guests' reflections in the seventeen mirrors lining the wall, ebbing and flowing, laughing and preening, and she suddenly wondered how similar this party was to the balls that had been given in Catherine's time. Catherine had never attended a ball here, but her friend, Juliette, must at some time have been in this very hall and gazed up at the arched ceiling at Le Brun's painted glorification of the Sun King just as Caitlin was doing now.

"There you are. I've been searching all over for you."

She looked down from the ceiling to focus on Jonathan looming larger and more impressive than ever. "Hello, Jonathan, I'm glad to see a friendly face in the crowd." She smiled. "I've seen three movie stars, a prime minister, and an oil sheikh, and I was beginning to feel overpowered."

"There's no reason you should feel anything but proud and happy tonight. You've done a splendid job." Jonathan took her hand and Caitlin felt again that sense of indescribable well-being she had experienced when she had first met him. "And besides, you look beautiful. Very regal. As if you belong in a palace."

She laughed and shook her head. "And I feel like I belong in an insane asylum. These past few days have been traumatic. I don't know how you manage to deal with all the spotlight."

"You get used to it." Jonathan took a glass of champagne from the tray of a passing white-coated waiter and handed it to her. "But sometimes one of these relaxes you." He sipped his own champagne and his gaze wandered casually over the crowd. "Ms. Benedict seems to be thriving on it."

Caitlin glanced at the number of people clustered around Chelsea in the center of the room. "She's amazing. She only has to be with anyone for five minutes and she has them in the palm of her hand. You should see the way she handled the press."

"I've heard she's not always so diplomatic." Jonathan turned back to Caitlin. "You like her?"

Caitlin nodded. "Very much. She's *real*. Would you like to meet her?"

"I've already met her. We both received an invitation for dinner at the White House last year." Jonathan finished his champagne and set his empty glass on the damask-covered table. "I know almost everyone here. Would you like an introduction to Mitterrand or Krakow?"

"Is Krakow here? I wasn't sure he'd come."

"Over by the potted palm."

Caitlin gazed with interest at the legend and was not disappointed. In Lars Krakow's newspaper photographs his close-cut hair had looked white, but she saw now it was a shade between pale gold and silver. His tall, thin form was dressed with the same elegant anonymity as the rest of the men in the room, but the scar twisting the flesh of his left cheek and those sad, deepest black eyes set him apart. He looked like a saint...or a martyr. Her mother had told her he had received that scar as a child when he had been tortured by the Gestapo for information regarding the whereabouts of the Danish resistance headquarters in Copenhagen. He had revealed nothing, and when they had released him his body had been so broken and torn, it had taken over two years to heal. He had become a national hero and after the war had risen to the heights of European politics. "I've heard a lot about him. My mother admires him very much. You know him?"

"I've met him at several trade conferences. He's very charismatic."

Caitlin caught a hint of reserve in his tone, and her gaze left Krakow to search Jonathan's face. "You don't like him?"

"As I said, he's very personable. I don't know him well enough to form an opinion." His gaze was on the man to whom Krakow was talking, and his expression became grim. "But I do know the good Monsieur Dalpré. He's head of Interpol and made both Peter's and my life miserable with his red tape about the Wind Dancer. I told him we were handling our own security, but he wanted to know every damn step of our itinerary."

Krakow's presence was so dominant, Caitlin had scarcely noticed the slight, dark-haired man standing beside him speaking with such intensity. "He appears to be trying to convince him of something."

"Raoul Dalpré's a passionate advocate for the consolidation of Europe. He's probably trying to persuade Krakow into his camp." Jonathan shrugged. "It would be quite a feather in his cap. Krakow's come out flatly against unity."

"What do you think about it?"

"A consolidation of all the countries of Europe under one governing body would produce a superpower that could be a threat in more than an economic sense. I think we'd all do well to keep an eye on Mr. Dalpré."

"According to the newspaper stories I've read lately, terrorist attacks and thefts would be virtually eliminated with better central control. Everyone's blaming bureaucracy and poor communication for the breakdown."

Jonathan shrugged. "Perhaps." He dismissed the subject. "You didn't answer me. Do you want to meet Krakow?"

She glanced at Krakow again. She really would have
liked to have told her mother she had met him, but the
poor man seemed to have his hands full with the volu
ble Monsieur Dalpré. She shook her head. "My mother
may never forgive me, but I don't think so. I believe I'l
just float around and make sure everything is going wel
and try to look inconspicuous."

"Impossible. Lovely women may be understated bu
never inconspicuous." Jonathan took her elbow and began
propelling her through the crowd toward the Peace Salor
at the far end of the gallery. "Forget about playing hostess
Come and say hello to Peter and put his mind at rest. He's
sure you're ready to skewer him like shish kebab."

She frowned. "I've been tempted. I need that translation and I still don't have it."

"Then let me take you over so that you can dress
down the poor man in person." His lips twitched. "I
will give you much greater satisfaction than talking to
an answering machine."

"How is Peter?"

"Fine. You'll see for yourself in a moment. It's not
enough for him that there are infrared cameras, trip
alarms, and security men all around the palace. He has
to stand guard too." He deftly maneuvered her around
an obese uniformed gentleman with an impressive array
of decorations on his massive chest. "Though he was
very impressed with Karazov's arrangements."

"Alex is usually very thorough. I'm glad you're
pleased."

"I could hardly be anything else. He met us at the airport this afternoon, double-checked on all our security
measures, and supervised the transportation of the
Wind Dancer to Versailles. He didn't trust our security
and hired additional guards of his own for the evening. I
saw him a few moments ago patrolling the hall as if it

were a battlefield." His brow knit thoughtfully. "Rather out of character. I would have judged him more likely to be behind the scenes, pulling strings."

"You make him sound Machiavellian."

"Do I?" Jonathan smiled. "In many ways Machiavelli was a much-maligned man. He was merely a product of his time and environment. Karazov may be the same."

They had come even with a square roped off with red velvet cords from the rest of the hall, and Caitlin saw Peter Maskovel standing vigilantly within the square. He was dressed in an immaculate tuxedo, but the formal wear didn't make him look bigger and more robust as it did Jonathan. Instead, he appeared paler and more finely drawn than when she had last seen him at Port Andreas.

Peter's thin face lit with a smile as he saw Caitlin. "Hi." He gestured to the Pegasus on the black marble pedestal by his side. "Have you come to see me or my buddy here?"

"Both." Caitlin smiled. "How are you, Mr. Maskovel? You look a little tired."

"Great." He grinned. "Well, almost great. A touch of jet lag."

Jonathan frowned. "For God's sake, go back to the hotel and rest. You've done your part here."

"Not until the evening's over and the Wind Dancer's safely locked up in the vault at the InterContinental."

"Are your accommodations comfortable?" Caitlin asked. "Chelsea and I are sharing a suite on the fourth floor."

Jonathan nodded. "Fine. Peter and I have suites on the same floor. Alex reserved the entire fourth floor to avoid any problems and to assure us privacy."

"Neighbors." Peter grinned coaxingly at Caitlin. "You can't flay a neighbor."

She tried to ignore the appeal and gazed at him sternly. "They did it quite frequently during the Middle Ages. I *need* that translation, Peter."

Peter sighed. "You're a worse slave driver than Jonathan. Father Domenico is almost finished, and I can do the rest from his notes. A week more and the journal will be completely translated."

Her eyes widened. "Father?"

"There aren't that many scholars who have the expertise to accurately transcribe fifteenth-century Italian. I had to go to a monastery in Virginia and beg Father Domenico to help us."

Caitlin guiltily remembered all those less than complimentary messages regarding the translator she had left on Peter's answering machine. "I thought you'd *hired* someone to translate them. Why didn't you tell me?"

"Naturally, Jonathan will contribute generously to the coffers of the monastery." Peter gazed at her limpidly. "And it was more amusing not to tell you. After a while I actually began to enjoy those barbed little messages you left on my answering machine. They added a certain zing to my day."

She started to laugh. "Lord, and I told you to tell him to get off his ass and get his butt in gear."

Peter's eyes twinkled. "I neglected to pass on your exact message to Father Domenico. He wouldn't have understood. You'll have your translation as soon as I have time to copy his notes on the last twenty pages. He did the translation all by hand and it's barely legible."

"Then I suppose I'd better provide you with peaceful surroundings to finish up. Can you spare the time to go to Vasaro for a few days?" Caitlin smiled as she saw the eagerness dawning on his face and added softly, "I couldn't consider having you read Catherine's journal anywhere else."

He went still. "You mean it?"

Caitlin nodded. "It's the least I can do after nagging you for the past month."

"When?"

"Whenever you like."

"Tomorrow?" He shook his head. "No, not tomorrow. I'll have to supervise the shipment of the Wind Dancer to Nice. The day after tomorrow?"

Caitlin laughed. "Fine. I'll call my mother and tell her you're coming."

"How long can I stay?"

"As long as you like. Chelsea and I have to leave for Nice tomorrow to shoot a commercial at the Negresco, but that shouldn't take more than a few days and then we'll be going home to Vasaro to shoot the rest."

"Now I do feel great." Peter took a step forward and grasped Caitlin's hand in both his own. "Thank you. You don't know what this means to me."

"I ask only one favor."

"The translation?"

She nodded. "And that you *please* don't send me any more photographs."

Peter laughed. "Deal."

"Catherine's journal isn't going to help, you know. There are no references to the inscription in the journal."

"The family history is really more important than the inscription. Deciphering the inscription would only be a plus for me." Peter smiled gently. "We can work together, Caitlin. I want to help you. I'm not trying to compete."

Caitlin reacted with warmth—and guilt. She really had been a demanding shrew about those translations. "I'll try to remember that." Caitlin's gaze followed Peter's to the Pegasus, and for a moment was caught in the same fascination that had transfixed her the first time she had seen it. She whispered, "It means so much to me. I have to do it, Peter."

"I know you do."

Jonathan touched Caitlin's arm. "Why don't you go tell Ms. Benedict I'm ready for the official announcement of her as spokesperson." His voice lowered to a barely audible undertone. "I'd like to get this over with so I can send Peter to bed to get some rest. He shouldn't become overtired like this."

Caitlin nodded. "I'll get her." She started down the hall toward the spot where Chelsea was holding court.

"You look different."

It was Alex's voice.

She stopped and consciously braced herself before she turned to face him. He also looked different: tough, sleek, panther-dark, elegant. "Hello, Alex."

"That's a lovely gown. I've never seen you in black." His gaze lingered on her breasts overflowing the black strapless bodice. "Your skin looks—" He stopped and shifted his gaze to her face. "How is it going?"

Dear heaven, she couldn't be feeling like this after all the lectures she had given herself about being over him, she thought desperately. Her mind condemned what he had done, but it clearly made no difference to her body's responses. She forced herself to smile. "Fine. Everything's moving like clockwork." She lowered her voice. "And you?"

"No sign of him."

Her lips twisted in a bittersweet smile. "I know that's a disappointment for you, but I can't say I'm sorry."

"He could still come."

Her tone hardened. "Then you'd better make damn sure you get him and he doesn't get the Wind Dancer."

His expression turned suddenly fierce. "Do you think

don't know that? You went over the security measures
with me last night. You know how careful I'm being."

"I don't know what—" She broke off and moistened
her lips. She had to get away from him. This bitter dialogue was nearly as painful as the knowledge of her
physical response to him. "I'd better go."

"Yes, that's a very good idea."

His voice was thick, the intonation faintly Slavic. Her
gaze flew to his face. She inhaled sharply as she saw his
expression, and her nails bit into her palms as her hands
clenched at her sides. Mother of God, she wanted to
touch him. She jerkily turned away. "I have to go get
Chelsea. Jonathan wants to have the announcement
over with."

"So do I." Alex's voice was tight with tension as he
whirled on his heel. "Christ, I want to get the whole
damn mess over with."

In another moment he had disappeared into the
crowd.

Where was he?

Alex stood in the corner of the hall, tuning out
Jonathan's speech introducing Chelsea, as he watched
the crowd.

Nothing suspicious.

The bait couldn't have been more prominently displayed.

The trap was set.

Where the *hell* was Brian Ledford?

Jonathan opened the door of his hotel suite to see
Peter standing in the hall. "Just thought I'd drop by and
let you know the Wind Dancer's locked up for the
night."

"In a safe?" Jonathan asked.

Peter nodded. "It's a walk-in safe and I've stationed two guards outside the vault room. He's as secure as if he were tucked in at Fort Knox." He frowned anxiously. "Can you spare me to go to Vasaro?"

"Why not? I'll probably be going to Vasaro myself when they start shooting the commercials."

Peter smiled with relief. "You will? I thought you'd be too busy."

"I have an investment to protect, and it's time I learned more about commercials. I've been thinking about authorizing a television campaign for the new cruise ship when it's launched."

"Pauley Hartland is supposed to be fantastic. He'd be great for the job." He smothered a yawn. "Chelsea Benedict looked good with the Wind Dancer, didn't she?"

Jonathan nodded. "They compliment each other. She was an excellent choice."

Peter started to swing the door shut. "Good night, Jonathan, I'll see you in the morning."

"Good night. And sleep late, dammit. You don't have to be up at the crack of dawn every day."

Peter covered another yawn with his hand. "Maybe."

As soon as the door closed behind Peter, Jonathan strode across the sitting room, tugging off his black tie. He threw it on the desk before taking off his tuxedo jacket and draping it on the back of the chair.

Christ, he felt like a kid on Christmas Eve trying to resist creeping downstairs to peek at the presents he knew would be under the tree.

He wasn't a kid any longer, and he didn't want to wait. He had waited too long already and life was too damn short.

He heard the sound of the key turning in the lock and whirled to face the door as it opened.

"Jesus, why aren't you undressed?" Chelsea slammed the door behind her and ran across the room, the filmy skirts of her white gown floating behind her like wings. "I would have been." She launched herself at him, her arms closing around his neck, pressing dozens of quick, fevered kisses on his face and throat. "Why can't men be—"

"Shut up, Chelsea." He stopped her words with a long, slow kiss. "I didn't have time." He picked her up and carried her to the bedroom. God, she was light in his arms. It always surprised him how slight she was physically when contrasted to the dimensions of her personality. So much spirit and vitality, so much strength and loving generosity. "I've waited eight months for this, and I'm not going to let your harping spoil it."

"Okay," she said meekly as she nestled closer. "But if you were as eager to ball me as I am to—"

"Make love," Jonathan corrected her as he laid her down on the bed and began to unbutton his shirt. During the last few times they had been together she had been using more and more street slang, and he knew damn well it was to point out the differences in their backgrounds. "You know what's between us. Stop hiding behind sex and say it."

"What's in a word?" Chelsea said airily as she kicked off her shoes and knelt on the bed with her back to him. "Unzip me."

"Say it." Jonathan slipped the zipper down and lifted the shining fall of her hair to one side to nuzzle her nape. "Please?"

She laughed tremulously as she turned around. "I can never resist a gentleman who says please. Make love. Is that prettier?"

"Yes, and a hell of a lot more truthful." Jonathan pushed the gown down to Chelsea's waist. Her naked breasts rose high and perfectly curved, the nipples as hard and pointed as he remembered. God, it had been too long. "Chelsea, love . . ."

His head lowered and he forgot all about semantics.

"I'm actually beginning to feel the stirring of gratitude toward Karazov," Jonathan said as he stroked a bright wing of hair back from Chelsea's face. "Very dangerous."

"How did he find out about us? We were so careful."

"Who knows? He has certain connections."

"I don't like it. If he can find out, so can any enterprising reporter."

"I don't think so. Karazov is . . . unusual."

"Can we trust him not to talk?"

"I think so."

"You don't sound very concerned."

"Frankly, Chelsea, I don't give a damn."

She giggled. "A quote from the man from Charleston."

"I am from Charleston."

"But you're much nicer than Rhett Butler." Her smile faded. "Well, I do give a damn."

"I know. That's what this stupidity is all about. Where did you get the key to my room?"

"Karazov. I found it in my purse after he left my suite this evening before the party."

"It appears he pays his debts."

"Well, he's no cupid."

"Chelsea, my love, I have no desire to talk about Karazov tonight." He studied her carefully. "You're thinner than you were in Kingston." His wide palm cupped Chelsea's breast and squeezed gently. "I thought you'd lost weight when I first saw you tonight at the party."

"Only a few pounds. You worry too much." Chelsea

nestled closer, tangling her legs between Jonathan's. "Stop frowning at me. I can take care of myself."

"Like hell you can," Jonathan said grimly. "I saw the picture on the cover of *Time* with that damn spear sticking in the mast beside your head. You damned well almost got yourself harpooned."

"I lost my temper," she admitted sheepishly.

Jonathan suddenly chuckled. "From now on, if there's any harpooning to be done, I want to do it."

"Well, you certainly have the weapon for the job." She reached down and her hand closed around him. "A whale of a weapon."

"Compliments will get you—" He gasped as her hold tightened around him and he swiftly amended, "Another harpooning."

She giggled and raised herself on one elbow to look down at him. "God, you're easy."

"I'm not easy. I'm passionate." He pulled her head down to kiss her lingeringly. "All men in love are passionate." He felt her stiffen against him and he kissed her again. "It's time you learned that, Chelsea."

She pulled away from him and sat up in bed. "I'm thirsty." She swung her feet to the floor and stood up. "I'm going to get some mineral water. Do you want something?"

"No." He watched her walk naked across the bedroom toward the sitting room door. He loved to watch the way she moved, the way she held her shoulders squared as if marching against a foe, the short, springy steps that breathed vitality. It was her walk that first attracted him when he had seen her moving ahead of him into the White House dining room. Then he had found himself sitting beside her at the long table, and before the evening was over he had known that something rare and beautiful had come into his life. "Wait." He picked up his pleated tuxedo shirt from the floor where he had dropped it. "The air-conditioning in here is too cool for you to run around butt naked." He tossed her the shirt. "Put this on."

She caught the shirt and slipped her arms into the sleeves, batting her lashes flirtatiously as she rolled up the cuffs. "Well, I do declare. I just love the caretaking ways of you southern gentlemen." She turned and left the bedroom, and her words trailed after her. "It makes my little heart flutter and my mind—"

"My love, you're a wonderful actress, but as a southern belle you're a total washout." Jonathan got out of bed, went to the armoire, and jerked his black velvet robe from the hanger. He slipped into it and followed Chelsea into the sitting room.

Chelsea was rummaging in the minibar across the room. "I'm glad you've finally realized that." She pulled out a small bottle of Evian and unscrewed it. "I'm strictly Hollywood and Beverly Hills."

"You're anything you want to be." Jonathan stood in the middle of the room and watched her pour the mineral water into a goblet. "You have limitless potential, my love."

Her hand tightened on the goblet. "Stop calling me that. I'm not your love."

He just stood looking at her, not speaking.

"I'm not," she repeated defiantly. "It's not love." She lifted the goblet to her lips. "And I wish you wouldn't keep saying you love me. It's just sex—a good, healthy roll in the hay."

He still didn't speak.

"I don't know why men have to get sentimental after they've been laid. For God's sake, orgasms aren't love. Sex isn't anything to me. I can have an orgasm with anyone, anytime." She snapped her fingers. "Just like that.

Hell, I can have an orgasm watching Baryshnikov do an élevé or Barry Bonds hit a home run."

Jonathan's lips twitched. "How very gratifying for you."

She appeared momentarily disconcerted and then began to laugh. "Damn you."

"Sorry, Chelsea, I know I'm supposed to be properly discouraged." He moved closer to her. "Now, when are you going to marry me?"

"Never." Chelsea took another sip of mineral water. "I told you that eight months ago and you accepted it."

"I didn't accept it. I just dropped the subject."

"Well, accept it now. As long as we can do it discreetly, I don't mind meeting you for a little ball—" She broke off as she met his gaze and then substituted, "Making love. But that's the end of it. I have my life to live and you have yours and they wouldn't mix."

"We mixed very well a little while ago." He smiled. "And I didn't even have to do a dance step or hit a home run."

"Listen to me." She put the goblet down on the cabinet with careful precision. "It's not negotiable."

"Everything is negotiable." Jonathan reached out and began to button the shirt. "It's not going to keep you warm if you don't—"

"I can take care of myself." She backed away from him. "I'm not one of your board members or a member of your family. You don't have to do anything for me."

"I don't have to," he said gently. "I regard it as my privilege."

"Oh, Lord." She shut her eyes tightly. "What am I going to do with you?"

"Come and live with me. Marry me. Let me give you another child as great as Marisa to love."

"I can't do that." Her eyes opened to reveal eyes glittering with tears. "And I wish you'd just shut up about it."

He shook his head. "Not this time. We're going to bring it out in the open. Talk to me, Chelsea."

"I don't want to talk." She took two steps and was in his arms, burrowing her face in his chest. "I've missed you. Lord, I've missed you, Jonathan."

"That's a good start." His hand gently stroked the back of her head. "Now the rest of it."

"Do you know the first thing I ever heard said about you?" Her voice was muffled. "I was talking to Gerald Tibbets, the ambassador to Venezuela, and he nodded at you and he said, 'Do you know who that is? That's Jonathan Andreas, and he's going to be the next president of the United States.'"

Jonathan chuckled. "Saying doesn't make it so."

"But you want it." Her voice was suddenly fierce. "And you *should* want it. You'd be a terrific president."

"And you'd be a terrific first lady."

She shook her head. "I'm a movie star."

"So was Ronald Reagan."

"It's different. And I spent fourteen months in jail. I was tarred and feathered by every tabloid from here to Timbuktu."

"And you rose above it and became a great actress. And you are a superb human being." He kissed her lightly. "Not to mention a fantastic lay."

"I'm serious." Her voice was shaking. "I'm not saying I'm ashamed of anything I've done." She shook her head. "No, that's a lie. I'm ashamed I was so stupid that I didn't see the bastard was a threat to Marisa."

"You were scarcely more than a child yourself."

"When I brought a child into the world I gave up my right to stay a child." She shook her head. "Anyway, I've made other mistakes, but I've never felt...I grew from them."

Jonathan quietly stroked her hair and waited for her to go on.

"But I don't have the right to make another mistake that would hurt someone else. There's no way the voters would accept you with me as your first lady."

"How do you know? The world is changing. People aren't nearly as narrow-minded as they used to be."

"Tell that to Gary Hart," she said. "Some of the tabloids claimed I was unfaithful to my husband and promiscuous later."

"Were you?"

"No." She shivered. "I couldn't stand anyone to touch me for years after my marriage to that son of a bitch. I thought I'd—" She broke off. "But that doesn't matter now."

"It does to me. Everything about you matters to me." He pushed her away from him and cupped her cheeks in his hands. "You want the truth? Yes, I'd like to be president. If everything went well, I was planning in a few months to announce I'd run."

She stiffened and forced a smile. "You see, my way is best."

He shook his head. "I've dealt in power all my life, and the presidency isn't the end-all of my existence. It's only a job I'd like to do. Four years in the White House isn't worth missing what we could have together for the rest of our lives."

"Eight," she said quickly. "They'd be insane not to re-elect you."

"Eight years isn't worth it either."

"Well, it will have to be." She turned away and moved toward the bedroom. "However, if you're extremely nice to me, I may let you slip me into the White House for fun and games as they say Kennedy did Marilyn Monroe."

"You're too flamboyant to be a president's mistress."

"So I'd work at it. I can do most things if I work at them." She paused in the doorway of the bedroom. "Now I feel in the mood for a little skillful harpooning." She grinned. "If you're up to it."

"With you I'm always up to it." He paused. "This isn't the end of the discussion."

"I know." She wrinkled her nose at him. "You don't know what's good for you."

"Yes, I do." It was no use trying to batter down her defenses. He would do better to stop arguing and use gentle persistence. Thank God Karazov had maneuvered them both into a position where he now had enough time and opportunity to try to persuade her to his way of thinking. He moved toward her across the room. "Milk, vegetables, and oat bran are all good for me." He slipped his arm around her waist and strolled back toward the bed with her. "And so is exercise. Long walks, swimming, tennis..." His hand dropped down to caress her buttocks through the material of his shirt. "And most particularly harpooning."

It was three o'clock in the morning, but the phone was ringing when Alex unlocked the door at the house on the Place des Vosges.

He slammed the door and hurried into the salon to pick up the receiver.

"Alex, my boy, you've outdone yourself." Ledford laughed. "But then, I knew you'd rise to the challenge. Anger and grief usually spur men to execute great deeds. Look at the way you managed to get the Wind Dancer here to bait me. Dazzling footwork, Alex."

"Try to take it, Ledford."

"Oh, I will." He paused. "You expected it tonight at

Versailles, didn't you? I can just see you wandering around that magnificent hall, looking behind potted plants and waiting for me to come. I admit I almost obliged you just so you wouldn't be disappointed."

"Why didn't you?"

"My associate objected to any trouble at the party tonight and I graciously acceded to his wishes. You see, he's not at all pleased with my insistence on stealing the Wind Dancer. I had to make a bargain with him that would please us both."

"Another theft?"

"No, the other side of the operation." His tone became mocking. "And one that involves a certain personal sacrifice for me. You know my love for antiquities. I hope you appreciate the lengths I'm going to please you."

"I want to see you."

"You will, in time. How can I stay away from you?" His tone lost its mockery. "Perhaps all my trouble is really for you and not the Wind Dancer. Perhaps all your efforts aren't for revenge but a way to bring us closer. Did you ever think of that?"

"No."

"No, of course not. You'd never admit it even to yourself." Ledford was silent a moment. "I was always a little jealous of Pavel. That's why I let them toy with him."

Alex felt the white-hot rage twist inside him. "You bastard."

"That's not kind and I'm always kind to you. In fact, I'm dedicating this business tonight to you. It's not every man who can inspire such a magnificent gesture of destruction."

"I don't want your gestures," Alex said with icy precision. "I want your life."

"Sorry." Ledford paused. "You should be able to hear the explosion quite well from the Place des Vosges. By the way, that's a lovely house you're leasing. I was tempted to come and visit you and see the decor. You have such exquisite taste."

"The door's always open."

Ledford chuckled. "I'll remember that." He paused. "I understand you had a female companion there with you for a time. I don't like that, Alex."

Alex felt a chill. He forgot to breathe.

"I hadn't been told about the lady when we last talked, or I would have reproved you then." Ledford went on softly. "Your attention should be entirely on me and our little competition. I'd think you would have learned with Angela."

"Angela?"

"You didn't know? They didn't move fast enough to get her out of reach, but I promise you it was very quick."

"My God."

"I considered forgetting about her. After all, there was no real reason it should be done. But after I saw you again I found I couldn't bear the thought of you two together, so I indulged myself. I was much happier once I knew she was dead." Ledford's tone switched to briskness. "Well, I really must go. It was stimulating chatting with you, but there's work to be done tonight. You can be sure I'll be in touch."

The receiver was replaced on the other end of the line.

Alex gazed without seeing at the mirror on the wall across the salon. Ledford was a maniac. No, it would be safer if he were a maniac. He was completely and coldly amoral. Alex's stomach twisted with sudden fear as he remembered how he had hoped Ledford would categorize Caitlin in the same innocuous position as he had Angela.

Caitlin!

He grabbed the receiver and dialed Caitlin's number

at the InterContinental. The phone was picked up on the fifth ring.

"Hello," Caitlin answered drowsily.

Relief poured through him in a dizzying stream. "Caitlin, are you all right?"

"I was until you woke me up. What's the—"

"Stay where you are with the door locked. I'm calling Jonathan to come to your room to stay with you until I get there. It shouldn't be more than a few minutes. Don't open the door to anyone but him."

"Alex, what's the—" she stopped. "Ledford?"

"He didn't mention you by name. He may not know who you are, but I can't be sure."

"Dear God," she whispered. "The Wind Dancer."

"I'm not worried about the damned statue. Keep your door locked." He hung up and dialed Jonathan's room number at the hotel. When Jonathan answered the phone, Alex said tersely, "Go to Caitlin's room and stay with her until I get there. Then phone Peter from her room and tell him to check on the Wind Dancer."

"What the hell's happening? Karazov?"

"Just do it." He pressed the hook again, dialed the operator, and asked to be connected to the police. When he was connected he said quickly, "The Black Medina will strike tonight. It involves an explosion. An antiquity." He replaced the receiver.

It had probably been a futile gesture to make that last call to the police. In a city as old as Paris, antiquities were the norm, not the exception.

He jumped to his feet and strode toward the front door.

An explosion rocked the house!

• • •

For over a thousand years prayers had soared to the heavens from this sacred place of worship. First it had been a Christian basilica, then a Romanesque church before it became a monastery during the fifteenth century. During World War II it had been a haven for fugitives from the Third Reich, and such was its splendor, Hitler had contemplated dismantling it and having it transported to Berlin for the glory of the fatherland. The cathedral had survived war and pestilence and the passage of time.

It had not survived Brian Ledford.

The Cathedral of Saint-Antoine was only two blocks from the InterContinental Hotel, and Alex had been forced to abandon his taxi when he had come within a block of the disaster. Now, as he tried to push through the crowd, Alex's throat tightened as he looked at the destruction. The famous tower was gone and the interior of the cathedral was a blackened, blazing inferno. Glittering shards of stained glass that had been created by the greatest artists of the Renaissance had been blown out to strew the street in front of him. He remembered the wonder on Caitlin's face as she had looked up at the sun shining through those windows only a few weeks before.

"Step back." A young gendarme, his face pale and eyes oddly bright, pushed the crowd surging forward against the ropes farther away from the burning building. "You can't do anything. Let the firemen through."

Three fire trucks were already at the disaster scene, and Alex heard a siren scream as another truck tore across the bridge toward the cathedral.

"It will do no good. It's gone." An old woman standing beside Alex looked at the burning church, her eyes as moistly bright as the young gendarme's. "I had my first communion here. I stood right here in this spot for

a requiem mass for General de Gaulle." She fell silent,
the tears running slowly down her face.

The rest of the people in the crowd were also silent
as they watched with tense faces and moist eyes as the
cathedral was inexorably engulfed in flame.

Ledford had chosen his target well if his purpose was
to shock and anger the world. Alex was not even a
Frenchman, and yet he felt with an aching keenness the
loss of this bastion of tradition and splendor.

"*Canaille*," the old woman muttered, wiping her eyes
on her sleeve. "Godless bastards."

Alex didn't answer as he pushed through the silent
crowd that stood watching while the walls of the
Cathedral of Saint-Antoine burned to the ground.

10

The reflection of the flames cast a malignant glow into the night sky.

Caitlin stood at the window of the sitting room, gazing at that fiery illumination and listening to the wail of sirens as the fire trucks raced toward the disaster.

"They really did it this time."

Caitlin turned. Standing in the doorway leading to the hall, Chelsea was still dressed in the white gown she had worn to the reception, her hair tousled, her face devoid of makeup.

Caitlin said, "I tried to call downstairs to the desk when I felt the explosion, but I couldn't get through. What's happening?"

"I don't know. Jonathan's calling someone at the embassy to try to find out. He sent me on ahead to tell you he'll be right here." Chelsea frowned in concern. "What's wrong? Are you sick?"

"No."

"Then why the hell did Alex—"

"I think it would be better to wait until Jonathan gets here to talk about it." Caitlin couldn't go on lying to them, and God knows she didn't want to confess twice to this deceit.

"You look like hell. It can't be that bad." Chelsea crossed the room to stand beside Caitlin at the window. She was silent a moment, her features lit by the red glow of the fire as she looked out into the darkness. "You didn't ask what I was doing with Jonathan."

"It's none of my business. I went to your room after Alex called and saw your bed hadn't been slept in." Caitlin didn't look at her. "You don't have to tell me anything."

"It's a little late to try to hide anything from you now. Since we're all going to be one big happy family until the launch, you probably would have found out anyway. Jonathan and I have been lovers for the last year." Chelsea continued haltingly. "I'd appreciate it if you didn't discuss this with anyone. Jonathan has political aspirations, and it wouldn't be good for his career."

"As I said, it's none of my business."

"Thank you." Chelsea was silent a moment. "He's wonderful, you know."

"I like Jonathan very much."

"Everyone does. He really cares about people, and they sense it. Whenever I'm with him I feel—" She stopped and said softly, "He's like a mountain that gives shelter and sustenance and beauty all at the same time."

"Is that why you agreed to the endorsement?"

Chelsea nodded slowly. "There was no question about my doing it the moment Alex mentioned Jonathan's name. It gave Jonathan and me the perfect opportunity to see each other that avoided suspicion. Alex was very clever."

"Alex knew about your affair with Jonathan?"

"He had to know. He played us both too well."

Yes, he had played them all well. "How did he find out?"

Chelsea shrugged. "I have no idea. Jonathan says he has connections."

And all those research agencies he used so prodigiously, Caitlin thought. "He found out what you wanted and gave it to you."

"I suppose that's one way of putting it."

"It's Alex's way of putting it," she said, her tone bittersweet.

"Alex has a habit of being—" Chelsea snapped her fingers. "I forgot something. I was so worried, I just tossed..." She hurried to grab a box from the table beside the door and bring it back to Caitlin. "It was outside in the hall in front of the door. Your name's on the card."

The box was open and the card was tucked beneath the red bow in the folds of a fine blue cashmere neck scarf.

Caitlin stared down at the scarf, and for the first time since Alex's call, the terror became real to her. Alex had told her about those other scarves Ledford had left, but this one was different. More delicate.

It was a woman's scarf.

"It's Saint-Antoine," Jonathan said as he entered the suite a few minutes later.

Caitlin's eyes widened in horror. "No," she whispered.

"Yes." Jonathan nodded grimly as he closed the door. "Enough explosives were planted in the cathedral to totally destroy it. They don't expect anything much to be left but rubble. It was the Black Medina. The police received an anonymous call several minutes before the explosion."

Caitlin's hand clenched on the velvet drape. "I hope they castrate the sons of bitches when they catch them."

Chelsea looked at her in surprise. "I've never seen you so venomous."

"It's Saint-Antoine." Caitlin looked back at the livid portion of the sky. "It *means* something. It's as bad as if they'd blown up Notre-Dame. You Americans don't understand. Here in Europe our history and culture are everything. We live with it. It's part of the foundation of our lives. What if someone blew up your Lincoln Memorial?"

Chelsea's hand gently touched Caitlin's shoulder. "Perhaps the embassy's wrong."

"I visited there only a few weeks ago. I wanted to show Alex the—" She broke off as she looked down at the scarf on the table beside her. Ledford had done this monstrous thing. "Madness."

Her whole life seemed tainted with ugliness. Why would anyone blow up anything so beautiful as Saint-Antoine? Why would a man want to kill a woman he had never met?

"Alex was very concerned for your safety when he called, Caitlin." Jonathan spoke very gently, but his expression was relentlessly determined. "Isn't there something you'd like to tell us?"

Fifteen minutes later Caitlin opened the door to Alex's knock. "I've told them everything, Alex."

Alex stiffened warily and then moved forward into the suite. "Good, that saves me from doing it." He closed the door, locked it, and turned to face them. "Have you checked on the Wind Dancer, Andreas?"

"It's safe. Peter just telephoned me. He'd gone down to the vault himself. The guards reported the alarms went off when the blast shook the building, but when they went into the safe the Wind Dancer was still there."

Alex went still. "Call him back. Those alarms shouldn't have been triggered by the explosion. I went over the vault mechanism myself when I heard you were going to place the statue in the safe there."

"Peter said he saw the Wind Dancer."

"Call him back. Tell him to check again," Alex said.

Jonathan gazed at him in silence for a moment before he crossed to the phone and dialed a number. "Peter? Do me a favor and check on the statue again. Yes, I know you've already done it. Do it again and call me back." He hung up the phone and turned to face Alex. "It's a waste of time. It seems the statue wasn't the target." He paused. "Tonight. There won't be an opportunity after tomorrow morning. I'm sending Peter back to the compound with the statue."

"I thought you would."

"And I'm calling the police to tell them about your friend Ledford."

"No!"

"He's a damned mass murderer," Jonathan said. "You don't have the right to keep his identity from them."

"Do you think they'd be able to catch him because they learned his name?" Alex asked. "I've been trying to find him for almost four months and haven't been able to get near him."

"They have means at their command that you don't."

"And I have means at my command that they don't," Alex said. "As long as Ledford thinks the game is between the two of us, I have a chance to get him."

"And he has a chance to get Caitlin," Chelsea said. "Jesus, can't you see she's scared to death?"

He didn't want to see it. He had been avoiding looking at Caitlin since the first moment he had walked into the room. "Calling the police wouldn't stop him. Don't you see? He was with the CIA, dammit. He has contacts and sources all over Europe. They wouldn't be able to keep her safe."

"And you can?" Chelsea asked sarcastically. "This entire floor was supposed to be secured, but he still managed to leave his little surprise package."

He went still. "What pack—" His gaze fell on the scarf on the table. "Christ," he whispered.

"My name was on the card," Caitlin said. "He knows who I am."

She *was* frightened, and who the hell could blame her? He wanted to touch her, to reach out in comfort, but he knew she would not accept it. "I never meant this to happen, Caitlin. It *shouldn't* have happened."

"You miscalculated," she said dully. "What a pity when you planned everything so—"

A loud knock on the door interrupted her. "Jonathan! For God's sake, open the door."

"That's Peter." Jonathan crossed the room, unlocked the door, and threw it open.

Peter strode into the room, his baby-fine hair mussed and his face pale. "They've got it, Jonathan. I could have sworn—God, I'm sorry. I should have known—should have stayed there myself."

"The Wind Dancer?" Jonathan went rigid, his gaze fastened on Peter in disbelief. "They've got the Wind Dancer?"

Peter slammed the door. "I swear I looked inside the safe myself, but it was dim and I—"

"What are you talking about?"

"A duplicate. When the alarm went off we thought

the explosion of the cathedral caused it. Every car and burglar alarm within three blocks of the cathedral went off too. It shook the entire hotel and—" Peter stopped and took a breath. "One of the guards ran out into the lobby to call me and see if the statue should be moved and the other stayed at the vault. That's when they must have taken the Wind Dancer and left the duplicate."

"How, with the other guard on duty?"

"He disappeared after I left the vault after checking on the Wind Dancer the first time. Ledford must have gotten to him somehow."

"What duplicate?" Jonathan demanded incredulously. "There's no duplicate close enough to the Wind Dancer to fool you."

"Yes, there is."

At Caitlin's words they all turned to look at her.

"There's one copy that's good enough if the statues aren't side by side." Caitlin's trembling hand rose to rub her lower lip. "A statue created by Mario Desedero, a Venetian artist. I saw it once when I was working on my paper on the Wind Dancer. In dim light very few people would be able to tell them apart."

"I didn't even know there was a copy," Chelsea said.

"Jean Marc Andreas commissioned its creation in the eighteenth century. It's now in the private collection of Alfred Connaught, an English industrialist who lives at Kilane Downs in Yorkshire."

"Christ, I *knew* that," Peter said miserably. "It was in your paper, Caitlin. Why didn't I remember—"

"But what's it doing here?" Chelsea interrupted.

"It would be much easier for Ledford to steal a copy than the real thing," Alex said. "Perhaps someone should check on the health and well-being of Mr. Connaught."

"Jesus," Chelsea murmured.

Jonathan shook his head dazedly. "It's gone. I can't believe it." He lifted his head and glared at Alex. "You bastard, that statue has been in my family since the beginning of—shouldn't—" He broke off and drew a deep breath, obviously trying to regain control. "I can't believe it's gone."

"I'll get it back," Alex said.

"How? You haven't done too well to date even finding Ledford."

"It's my fault the Wind Dancer was stolen. I'll find Ledford and I'll get it back."

Caitlin moved to stand before Jonathan. "I'm so sorry, Jonathan." Her eyes were bright with tears. "I can't tell you how terrible I feel about this. I promise you that we'll find it for you."

"We?" Alex shook his head. "Not you. You're a target."

"And where should I go to hide?" Caitlin whirled to face him, her eyes suddenly glittering with anger as well as tears. "Do you think I'd lead that monster to Vasaro? I let you do this. I could have stopped Jonathan from bringing the statue to Paris. All I would have had to do was pick up the phone." She drew a trembling breath. "But I didn't do it. I wanted the Wind Dancer here so badly that I took the chance."

"No one's blaming you, Caitlin," Chelsea said. "We know how desperate you were to make the perfume—"

"Then you should blame me. I'm just as guilty as Alex. Perhaps more guilty. It was all like a dream come true. The Wind Dancer...I love Vasaro so much, I wanted the perfume to succeed so badly, I couldn't bring myself to—" Caitlin had to stop as her voice broke. She swallowed and continued. "I told you that I wouldn't let Jonathan be hurt by this, Alex."

Alex turned to Jonathan. "The game's changed. Ledford has the Wind Dancer and he'll do anything to keep it. It's an obsession with him."

"Listen to him," Caitlin said with a bitter smile. "Alex is an expert on obsessions."

"She's right. Ledford is an obsession with me, but that's what you need. I'm your only chance. Tell the police anything about Ledford and we lose the only edge we have."

"You told me yourself that you don't have any clues," Jonathan said.

"I have a man working on Ledford's background. He may find something we can use." Jonathan looked unconvinced, and Alex could hardly blame him. "And if we can't find Ledford, maybe we could go after his partner. Ledford mentioned he didn't go after the statue at the reception tonight because his associate objected. The logical reason for him to object would be if he was attending the party."

"You're reaching for straws."

Alex couldn't deny it. "At least I have straws to reach for. Give me twenty-four hours to get a lead."

Jonathan hesitated and then shrugged. "Twenty-four hours. No more."

Alex turned to Caitlin. "You sent out the invitations. I'll need the guest list."

She went over to the desk across the room, opened the middle drawer, and drew out the papers. She brought them to Alex and handed them to him. "Can I help?"

"Not with this part of it." He met her gaze. "But I'll be better able to concentrate if I know you're safe."

She shook her head. "I'm not going home to Vasaro."

"We'll talk about that later. I'm not sure where the safest place would be for you." He turned and moved toward the door. "Stay with her until I come back, Jonathan. I'm going to arrange for two guards outside in the hall and move into the suite next door." He glanced over his shoulder at Caitlin as he opened the door. "For God's sake, stay here in the suite."

"Don't worry." Caitlin didn't look at him. "I want to live. I have no intention of letting that maniac kill me."

"I won't let him touch you." Alex closed the door of the suite behind him and strode down the hall toward the elevators.

It was after six in the morning and daylight was pouring through the window of the sitting room when Alex unlocked the door of his suite next door to Caitlin's.

Lord, he was tired.

Alex flexed his shoulders to rid himself of tension and then moved toward the desk across the sitting room and dropped into the chair. He couldn't rest yet. He took the guest list Caitlin had given him out of the pocket of his tuxedo and stared at it, trying to ignore the lethargy keeping him from thinking.

Twenty-four hours.

He began to go over the shorter list he had made. It was a column of distinguished names. At the end of an hour he had underlined only two possibilities; Raoul Dalpré, head of Interpol, and Benjamin Carter, English billionaire and art connoisseur. Dalpré had been surprisingly ineffectual in pursuing the art thieves, and Carter was known as a fanatic collector with underworld connections who was not above purchasing stolen art objects. He leaned back in his chair and rubbed his eyes. His choices were flimsy at best and wouldn't be enough to convince Andreas. He would have to think about them, try to place them in the picture, but he was too tired just then.

He reached for the telephone and dialed Simon Goldbaum in New York.

"Jesus, don't you ever sleep?"

"Time's running out. I have to have something on Ledford. Anything."

"A report came in yesterday afternoon, but I haven't had time to look at it. Call me back at the office at a decent hour tomorrow after I go over it."

"Go down to the office now."

"Do you know what time it is here?"

"Now."

"It will cost you triple."

"What else is new?"

"Okay." Goldbaum sighed. "But it's probably not going to be worth your money."

"I'm at the InterContinental in Paris."

"I'll get back to you." Goldbaum hung up the phone.

Alex replaced the receiver and leaned back in his chair. He had hoped Goldbaum would have something he could get his teeth into and block out the thought of Caitlin's wary, bitter expression as she had looked at him earlier that night. What was so different? All his life people had been looking at him with that same wariness and uncertainty. They seemed to sense his own cynicism and distrust and returned it tenfold. Except for Caitlin. At first she had been wary of him, but that had faded and become—

He pushed back the chair and stood up. He couldn't think of Caitlin now. Thinking about her made the hollowness and guilt rush back and engulf him, and he had to concentrate on Ledford and those names. He strode toward the bedroom. He'd take a shower, order coffee,

nd try to think of a new way to put the pieces to-
ether.

KRAKOW VOWS TO CAPTURE TERRORISTS WHO BOMBED
AINT-ANTOINE.

Alex studied the headline of the morning paper the
vaiter had brought with the coffee. Christ, that's all he
leeded, a do-gooder galloping around, tilting at wind-
nills, and getting in his way at every turn.

The phone rang just as he finished his third cup of
offee.

"I told you that you couldn't stop me," Ledford said.

Alex's grip tightened on the receiver. "Where are you?"

Ledford ignored the question. "And you left that
ovely house on the Place des Vosges. What a shame.
'm very much afraid the lady was to blame."

"Stay away from her, Ledford."

"Perhaps. The scarf I sent her was merely a teasing
ittle jest. However, it really annoyed me the way you
ushed to her defense. I'll have to explore my feelings
>n the subject of Ms. Vasaro. Tell me, is she—"

Alex threw out a name to distract his attention.
Why did Dalpré want Saint-Antoine blown up?"

"Dalpré?" Ledford was silent for a moment. "You've
>ut that many pieces together so quickly? Ah, I do love
hat mind of yours, Alex."

Alex froze with shock. Christ, he couldn't believe he
lad hit it lucky with such a wild shot. "Why?"

"I really didn't want to blow it up, but Dalpré has no
espect for antiquity and I had to have the Wind
)ancer."

"Then why did he order you to steal some of the
nost valuable antiquities in the world?"

"You don't understand. He didn't order me to steal

them. I had to persuade him the thefts should be an integral part of the operation." He laughed. "He wants to be Napoleon and I told him they'd form a solid monetary backup for the treasury of his new regime."

"Christ, and he fell for it?"

"Well, I think the darling man may have his own plans for my little treasure trove."

"You sound like you deserve each other."

"Certainly he deserves me, but I really think I rate something better than Dalpré." He paused. "I knew you'd be upset with me about Saint-Antoine."

"Upset? You're insane."

"No, I merely compartmentalize." Ledford paused. "But now I'm having trouble putting you back into a box. I suppose it's because I've never resolved how I felt about you. I do like things neat."

"Is Dalpré going—"

"I don't want to talk about Dalpré."

"What do you want to talk about?"

"Nothing." He paused. "I just wanted to hear the sound of your voice." His own voice lowered to a level above a whisper. "And to let you know there's nothing I can't take away from you."

He hung up.

Alex tried to rid himself of the rage tearing through him and assimilate what information he had received from the call.

Not much. Only two facts had emerged; he was still being watched and, if Ledford was to be believed, Dalpré was a confirmed conspirator. It was dangerous to believe Ledford and yet everything he had said fit. Dalpré had both the contacts and the muscle to initiate a coup, and his advocacy of a unification of Europe was no secret.

The phone rang again fifteen minutes later.

"It's pretty weak," Goldbaum said as soon as Alex picked up the receiver. "Istanbul."

"Go on."

"About fourteen months ago Ledford applied for a visa and went to Turkey. He did the entire tourist bit, toured the Dardanelles coast, and then spent two weeks in Istanbul." He hesitated. "He bought a house there."

"You're sure?"

"Yeah, and he didn't want anyone to know about the buy. It took my man weeks to sift through all the paperwork and dummy corporations, but Ledford was the purchaser."

"Does he still own it?"

"He did five days ago."

"Give me the address."

"Two fourteen Street of Swords. Now can I go home and go to bed?"

"Not yet. I want you to dig up all you can on a British industrialist named Benjamin Carter and on Raoul Dalpré."

"*The* Raoul Dalpré?"

"Interpol."

Goldbaum whistled. "That's kinda dicey. I hear he can get damned vicious, and he's got the power to pull out the stops."

"I need information and twenty-four-hour surveillance." Goldbaum started to object, and Alex cut him short. "I know. It's going to cost me. Whatever it takes."

"Desleppes is in Brussels. . . . Maybe I could put him on it. Anything else?"

Alex glanced at the headlines of the newspaper. "Surveillance on Lars Krakow. I want to know everything his investigation turns up on the terrorists."

"I'm surprised you don't expect me to find them before he does." Goldbaum's tone was caustic. "I'm not a miracle worker, you know."

"I wish you were. I could use a miracle right now."

There was a silence on the other end of the line, and then Goldbaum said gruffly, "Go to bed. Hell, you must be tireder than me if you're going the miracle route. I'll get what you need."

Before Alex could answer, he had hung up with his usual abruptness.

Istanbul. It made sense. Where better to hide priceless works of art than in a house in an Asian country with close ties to Europe? Ledford could be on his way to that house in Istanbul right now. The thought made the blood pound fiercely through Alex's veins. He could *have* the son of a bitch.

From the moment Goldbaum had mentioned Turkey, something had caught at Alex, tugged at his memory. Why the hell couldn't he put his finger on it? Oh, well, it would come to him and, in the meantime, he would be on his way.

He picked up the telephone receiver and called Air France for reservations to Geneva and then placed a call to Jonathan Andreas's suite.

By two that afternoon Alex was ready to leave and went next door to tell Caitlin what he had learned.

"I'm going with you," Caitlin said flatly.

"I'm not arguing with you," Alex said. "I've thought about it and I think you'll be safer with me."

"Good, I'll pack." Caitlin turned and moved toward the bedroom. "I can be ready in twenty minutes."

"Not yet. I want you to give me two days in Istanbul alone."

She stopped and turned around. "Why?"

"I have to find a house for you." As she continued to look at him suspiciously, he shook his head. "For God's sake, I'm being followed and I don't know how long it will take to lose him. I have to find a place that's safe for you."

"Is Paris safe for me?"

"No, but at least here I can surround you with guards and Jonathan will make sure nothing happens to you. Day after tomorrow he'll get tickets for the film crew, Chelsea, and you to fly to Nice. When you all arrive at the airport, I've arranged with Goldbaum to have a woman of your general description meet you in the ladies' rest room. You'll change clothes and she'll use your ticket to fly to Nice with the rest of the party, where she will conveniently disappear. Jonathan will put you on a flight to Istanbul before he leaves for Nice and I'll meet you at the airport in Istanbul. By the time any interested party discovers you haven't gone to Nice, I'll have you safely stowed away."

Caitlin was silent a moment. "You're not trying to deceive me?"

He flinched. "No, that's all over."

"All right, two days."

Relief washed over him. "Thank God you're being reasonable."

"Do you think I'm not frightened?" she demanded. "I keep seeing that blue scarf. . . . I don't want to die and I don't know anything about this. It's not my world."

"I could try to find a safe house for you somewhere else."

"No." She shook her head. "I promised Jonathan I'd get the Wind Dancer back. I keep my promises."

He hadn't expected anything else. Caitlin had a staunch and rigid sense of honor in a world that had almost forgotten its meaning. She was as bound by guilt and her promise as he was by his obsession to catch Ledford. Jesus, he had made a mess of everything.

"Jonathan checked on Alfred Connaught. Kilane Downs burned to the ground and he was killed in the fire. It was presumed his entire art collection was also destroyed." She smiled mirthlessly. "But we know better, don't we?"

"Yes."

"And Chelsea's agreed to go on with the launch. It's very kind of her. We don't deserve it."

"We paid her almost three million dollars to guarantee her kindness." He held up his hand as Caitlin started to protest. "Sorry. It *was* kind. She didn't have to go through with it. Since we don't have the Wind Dancer, she and Jonathan and the camera crew will skip the Nice shots and go directly to Vasaro to film the rest of the commercials." He added, "And I've had Jonathan send Peter ahead to Vasaro to keep an eye out for anything that doesn't look right."

"My mother." Caitlin's gaze flew to his face. "Will my mother be safe?"

"It's only a precaution," he said quickly. "Call and tell her you have to stay in Paris due to business and Peter will visit so he can study Catherine's journal. There's no real reason to suspect any trouble, and we don't want to alarm her."

Caitlin relaxed and nodded. "That's what I thought. There would be no reason for him to hurt anyone at Vasaro if I'm not there."

"I lost Karazov at the airport in Geneva," Ferrazo told Ledford as soon as he answered the phone. "I don't know how the hell he slipped away from me. One minute he was there and the next he was gone."

"I'll tell you how he slipped away from you," Ledford said caustically. "He's been tailed for five years by the KGB *and* the CIA. In that time a man becomes very skilled at eluding a tail when it suits his convenience. Why the hell weren't you more careful?"

"I tried to—" Ferrazo broke off and then said, "I went up to his chalet at St. Basil. The house was closed and there was no sign of him. Should I keep looking for him here in Switzerland?"

Ledford thought about it. "No, Geneva was a red herring."

"You want me to go back to Paris? He might try to contact the woman."

"I have plenty of people in Paris who can keep watch on the hotel, and Andreas has tightened security so we wouldn't know whether Karazov contacted her or not. Go to Vasaro and wait in case she goes back there."

Ledford hung up, frowning. Undoubtedly, Alex had laid a false trail and then made tracks for his real destination. Alex seldom acted impulsively or erratically, therefore he must have learned something to have galvanized him to leave Paris. Ledford carefully reviewed their conversations; no slips of any importance, so it followed Alex must have obtained information from one of his usual sources. Now, what possible loose thread had Alex managed to pull?

The hosue on the Street of Swords.

He must have shredded that mountain of paperwork and found out about the house. The knowledge should have upset Ledford, but instead he found himself experiencing an almost fatherly pride.

Pride and pleasure. Alex clearly had his priorities

back in order. He had deserted the Vasaro woman the moment he had seen a way to move forward in the joust between them.

"I told you I could do the job better than Ferrazo."

Ledford turned to look at Hans and felt a sharp jab of annoyance. He was not sure if his impatience was caused by boredom with the boy himself or the comparisons Brian had been making between Hans and Alex of late. "You did, didn't you? But then, you think you can do any job better than anyone else."

"Let me go after him. I'll find him."

"No need. I believe my friend Alex has gone to Istanbul. We'll just call someone to keep an eye on him. I need you here."

Hans scowled. "Why are we still in Paris? I thought all you wanted was the statue."

"We have to finish this job first."

"We've already finished it. You said I did a good job on the cathedral."

"Very good, but blowing Saint-Antoine's was only the first step." Ledford smiled. "There's another facet to the operation."

"And I can be part of it?"

"Oh, yes, dear heart." Ledford smiled benignly. "I have every intention of making you part of it." He reached for the telephone again. "Now be still while I make this call to Istanbul."

"I suppose you're going to get the Gypsy to watch Karazov?"

"Yes."

"Why haven't you ever let me meet him?"

"The Gypsy's a very secretive fellow. He prefers not to be the focus of attention."

"I don't like it."

"That doesn't surprise me, but I really don't know

why you should want to meet him. You have very little in common." Ledford was already dialing. "However, the man is quite efficient. Yes, I think the Gypsy will do very nicely."

The house on the Street of Swords was not a house at all; it was a palace.

The wooden building towered three stories high. Glittering leaded-glass windows punctuated the lower levels of the front facade of the palace, and on the upper level intricately carved filigree wood shutters veiled the area that once must have housed the harem quarters. Two golden domes, shimmering brilliantly under the strong sun, dominated the wings stretching on either side of the central building. Two fourteen-foot brass-bound doors led into the palace. The doors originally had been painted deep crimson but were faded now to a rich cinnamon color. A small courtyard with a graceful white and turquoise mosaic fountain fronted the entrance. A master craftsman had lavished time and artistry on the high ornamental black iron fence enclosing both the palace and courtyard. In the iron he had wrought flamingos pacing with majestic dignity, peacocks with plumage unfurled, falcons soaring in flight.

Alex had arrived in Istanbul late the night before, and this morning had managed to dig out the history and location of the house. He had spent all the rest of the morning standing across the street in this twisting, stinking alley intersecting the Street of Swords, sweating like a pig and waiting for someone to enter that impressive front gate.

Dead end.

There had been no sign of Ledford or anyone resembling the kind of criminal element with whom he

surrounded himself. Ledford's house was evidently
closed, and he hadn't even caught sight of a servant in
the courtyard. If Ledford was using the house as a cache
for the stolen artwork, he would have left a ring of
guards around the place.

Yet Ledford's purchase of the palace had to have
some purpose. Both the fact of the purchase and the re-
tention of the house indicated it must have some part
in Ledford's overall plan. But it was not only logic but
instinct that was nagging at Alex to stay in Istanbul.
Ever since Goldbaum had mentioned Ledford's trip to
Turkey, he'd had the frustrating feeling he always experienced when he saw a puzzle piece ready to be positioned but unable to find the right spot to slip it into.

Something was going to happen here, dammit.

But Alex couldn't wait around indefinitely for
Ledford to show up. He had to have facts or leads that
would put him on the initiative and, although he had
visited Istanbul several times in the past, he knew damn
well he wasn't equipped to ferret out what he needed
on this foreign terrain. He would have to find someone
who could supply him with the information he needed.

Alex left the alley and returned quickly by taxi to
the Hilton. The moment he reached his room he placed
a call to Rod McMillan at Langley. "I'm in Istanbul and I
need help."

"You arrogant son of a bitch. You expect me to give it
to you?"

"I need a native who knows the underbelly of the
city and all the snakes that crawl out from beneath it at
night. Either give me a name or I'll go looking for him
myself."

"Good luck."

"Catching snakes in Istanbul can be dangerous. Are you
sure you want me risking my neck in those alleyways?"

There was a silence on the other end of the line. "Someday I'm going to rid myself of you, Karazov. Very violently."

Alex mockingly echoed McMillan's words. "Good luck."

He heard McMillan mutter something to someone in the room with him. "Hold on," McMillan told Alex. "Barney's getting it."

Alex could almost see the amber light of the computer gleaming on Barney's balding head as he tapped with precision into the classified memory banks.

A few minutes later McMillan came back on the line. "Kemal Nemid. He's done work for us and for your friends in the KGB."

"How do I contact him?"

"He doesn't have a telephone. Barney will arrange a meeting with him. The dossier says Nemid prefers the first contact to be in a public place, usually an outdoor café called the Korfez on the Bosporus."

"When?"

"Tomorrow?"

"Today. I'm leaving the hotel now. I'll be at the café all day and all evening." Alex hung up the phone.

Alex sipped from the glass of coffee, his gaze never ceasing to travel from the umbrella-shaded tables of the sidewalk café to the stream of busy traffic on the street a few yards away and back. It was almost sundown, dammit. McMillan had had over six hours to contact his man and there had been no sign of this Kemal Nemid. It would be just like McMillan to let Alex stew here all evening before producing Nemid.

A cacophony of automobile horns broke the stillness and Alex's gaze flew to the street. A boy of thirteen or fourteen was riding a wobbling blue bicycle down the narrow thoroughfare. The automobiles behind him moved at a snail's pace.

The boy gave a calm glance over his shoulder at the traffic piling up behind him before smiling ingratiatingly and calling, "Please. Patience. Low tire."

Howls and curses answered him from the drivers. The boy's smile faded, and he turned and began to pedal industriously. The tire was losing more air by the second, the drivers of the cars in the parade grew more abusive, the boy more solemn and determined.

Alex smiled as he watched the bizarre procession.

When the boy came even with the café he jumped the bicycle onto the curb, slipped from the seat, and swept a low bow to the drivers. He motioned with an imperious gesture for the cars to proceed. The courtesy was ignored as the cars accelerated and whipped past him.

The kid had panache. Alex watched the boy kneel beside the bicycle to examine the tire. Not many people could have coped with those impatient drivers, much less in such style. Alex studied him, realizing the boy was older than he had first thought. A closer view revealed the tousled curly black hair and bright black eyes looked just as youthful, and the boy's ragged, faded blue jeans were certainly the preferred uniform of the students here in Istanbul, but his body was neither gangly nor adolescent. He was not more than five eight or nine inches in height, but his thighs bulged with sinewy muscle as he squatted by his bicycle, and his bright red sweatshirt covered well-developed shoulders.

The boy shook his dark head mournfully as he turned to Alex. "I think the frame is bent. I was in a hurry and rode it down a flight of a stairs in a street by the Grand Bazaar."

"Too bad."

The boy scowled. "It was a very fine bicycle. You will have to pay for it."

Alex's eyes widened. "Oh, I will?"

"But of course. You're the one who couldn't wait to see me. I had to rush from my last class at the university and I broke my—"

"*You're* Kemal Nemid?"

The boy nodded as he rose to his feet. "You must definitely buy me a new bicycle." He rolled the bicycle to the stand by the café entrance and walked back to Alex's table. "I must warn you, McMillan says he will not pay this time, and I'm very expensive." He grinned. "But you will find I am worth my pay. I am truly most excellent in every way."

Alex smothered a smile. The kid's panache was obviously equaled by his conceit. "I was expecting someone older."

"I'm almost twenty-three. Youth is good." Kemal indicated his bright black eyes. "The young see better and notice more. You're lucky to get me." He dropped down into the chair opposite Alex and crooked his finger for the waiter. "Now, what do you want me to do, Mr. Karazov?"

"How did you recognize me?"

"Good eyes, sharp intuition, keen wit." Kemal's eyes twinkled mischievously. "Besides, Barney faxed me a picture of you."

"A fax machine?"

"Oh, I'm up on all the latest technology. I gouged the machine out of McMillan on my last job for him."

"A fax machine with no telephone?"

He looked faintly shocked. "But I would have had to pay for regular telephone service. I went to the telephone company and made a deal with them that the equipment be used only for the fax. That way I can charge my clients for the service." He looked up at the hovering waiter. "*Raki*." He turned back to Alex. "You disapprove of me squeezing McMillan?"

"No, I'm all in favor of McMillan being gouged."

"Good. I don't like him." Kemal leaned back in his chair. "Barney says you're looking for someone."

"Brian Ledford."

Kemal made a face. "Nasty."

Alex stiffened. "You know him?"

"I've seen him a few times. He's not here in Istanbul now."

"How do you know?"

Kemal's smile was a flash of gleaming white teeth in his good-looking face. "I make it my business to know such things. That's why you're going to pay me a great deal of money. Ledford was here a few weeks ago, but he's gone now."

"How long was he in Istanbul?"

Kemal shrugged. "Off and on for over a year."

"And he stayed at the house on the Street of Swords?"

Kemal shook his head. "I know nothing about a house on the Street of Swords. From what I heard, Ledford stayed somewhere in the old city."

"Where?"

"I don't know."

Dead end again. Yet if Ledford had used Istanbul as the base for his operations, he had to have formed a network of some kind. "Who was his supplier?"

A delighted smile touched Kemal's lips. "Very good. A supplier would have to know where to deliver the merchandise."

"I'm glad you approve. Now, tell me who—"

"Oh, I have no idea, but I do believe keen thinking should be praised, don't you?"

Alex gazed at him blankly. "I want information, not praise."

Kemal nodded amiably. "Okay, what would he have had to supply?"

"Ledford would have needed weapons, explosives, false papers. Who's capable of handling that variety of load?"

"False papers too?"

Alex nodded.

"The other items are simple enough, but the false papers would require someone—" He stopped, frowning before he said slowly, "The Gypsy. Only the Gypsy could handle all of it."

"Who the hell is the Gypsy?"

"You want his name?" Kemal shook his head. "I don't know. When someone works with clients like Ledford, they don't want anyone to know more than they have to about them. I've heard the Gypsy works through several front men in town."

"Can you find him?"

"I'll try. I don't promise anything."

"Not even for this great deal of money you're going to charge me?"

"Ah, but I'll try *very* hard." Kemal smiled beguilingly. "In fact, I can take you to one of the Gypsy's front people tomorrow night, if you like."

"I like," Alex said. "I'd like it even better if you could take me there tonight."

"You're in too much of a hurry." The waiter set a glass and napkin before Kemal and moved away. "Life should be savored." He lifted the milky liquor to his lips. "Like *raki*. Have you ever tried it?"

"On my first trip to Istanbul. It can blow your mind."

"But so pleasantly." Kemal sipped the liquor and sighed contentedly. "Man should live only for pleasure, you know."

"Can you arrange for me to meet this man tonight?"

Kemal shook his head. "Impossible. Tomorrow, I promise." He took another sip of his *raki*. "But you won't be bored tonight. We have something to do."

"We do?"

Kemal nodded solemnly and looked around the café before lowering his voice. "We must go to a shop near the covered bazaar."

"To meet another one of the Gypsy's contacts?"

"No." Kemal beamed at Alex. "To buy me another bicycle."

11

"Catherine's journal is with the books on perfume in the perfumery." Katrine smiled at Peter. "Caitlin always liked to have it close by, and heaven knows, she always spent more time in the perfumery than she did in the house. I'll take you over there. You can bring it back and browse through it in comfort."

"I don't want to trouble you. Just give me directions and I'll find it myself." Katrine appeared to be a nice enough woman, but Peter didn't want to have to be polite and indulge in social chitchat once he got his hands on the journal. "Please. You've been kind enough to welcome me into your home. I don't want to burden you any more than necessary."

Katrine hesitated. "Well, if you'd rather... It's the second stone building to the rear of the manor house." Her expression brightened. "Marisa is wandering outside somewhere. If you run into her, I'm sure she'll be glad to show you where it is."

"Right. The second stone building. Is it locked?"

Katrine shook her head. "No one would steal anything here at Vasaro."

Peter grinned. "Shades of Shangri-la, I believe I'm going to like it here. Who is Marisa?"

"Marisa Benedict, Chelsea Benedict's daughter. She's staying with us for the next few weeks. I thought you knew."

Peter shook his head. "No one mentioned her to me. Not that it matters. I wouldn't want to bother her. I'll just find my own way." He started for the front door. "If the perfumery isn't being used, I wonder if you'd give me permission to study the journal there and copy some notes I have to send Caitlin."

"Of course." Katrine smiled indulgently. "But it's not as comfortable as the house. Don't become too involved and forget about meals, as Caitlin does. We have dinner early, about seven."

"I'll be back in time." Peter opened the door. "By the way, I'm something of a photography nut. I do the developing myself, but since I have no equipment here, I wonder if there's somewhere nearby I could have my film processed."

"The pharmacy in the village."

"Great. Thank you again, Madame Vasaro."

"Katrine. We're very informal at Vasaro."

"Katrine." Peter smiled over his shoulder. "Now I *know* I'm going to like it here." He closed the door behind him.

He stood on the top step and took a deep, heady breath of the fragrance-laden air. God, Vasaro was beautiful. The sun shone brilliantly in the hard blue sky, and everywhere he looked there were trees and plants and blossoms, signs of life and renewal. He had never felt stronger or more alive, and he could practically feel the blood sing in his veins.

Peter smiled. Blood didn't sing and he shouldn't be

this happy. Only moments before he had arrived at Vasaro he had still been weighed down by guilt about his part in the Wind Dancer's theft two days earlier. He had begged Jonathan to let him stay in Paris to handle the tedious job of dealing with insurance people and police, but instead of punishment he had been sent to Vasaro.

How the devil would he even know if something wasn't as it should be in this Garden of Eden? Everything seemed perfect to him. He supposed all he could do was wander around, talk to people, take pictures, and—

Pictures, Lord, this place was a photographer's paradise. He could hardly wait to unpack his Nikon and walk over the property. He found to his astonishment that Catherine's journal was suddenly fading in importance for him. From the first moment he had caught sight of the place he'd had a curious feeling that something for which he had long searched was waiting for him at Vasaro.

Foolishness. What was waiting for him was the job of getting the translation typed and ready to send Caitlin and the pleasure of inundating himself in another branch of the Andreas family through Catherine Vasaro's journal.

He walked briskly around the manor house and then hesitated. Katrine had said the second stone building, but he was facing a half-stone, half-wooden structure that obviously had once been a stable. Did she mean for him to count this as one of the buildings?

"Hello, can I help you?"

Peter turned to face a tall, slender girl dressed in a loose yellow shirt and soft, faded jeans. She met his gaze with an air of quaint gravity and, as he watched, an errant breeze lifted a few fine strands of her long, straight brown hair and blew it across her lips. She brushed it back with an unhurried gesture.

"I'm Peter Maskovel. I'm looking for the perfumery."

"I'm Marisa Benedict." She smiled serenely at him. "It's not far. I'll take you."

He caught his breath as he looked at her. He felt as he had when he had first seen the Wind Dancer over twenty years before—frightened, excited, filled with a sense of coming home.

And he had the curious feeling he had found what had been waiting for him at Vasaro.

"His name is Adnan Irmak." Kemal opened the wrought iron door and preceded Alex into the foyer of Irmak's *yali* on the shores of the Bosporus. "I must warn you, he won't be cooperative."

"Given a little pressure, most men prove cooperative. Fill me in on him."

Kemal shrugged as he crossed the foyer and started down a long, gleaming corridor. "He deals a little in drugs. Occasionally he can be persuaded to fence a few things. But he makes most of his money from the Harem."

"He owns the Harem?"

"You've heard of it?"

"How could I help it?" Brothels were legalized and controlled in Istanbul, but activities at Irmak's Harem were strictly beyond the realm of legality. Its infamous reputation was known worldwide. "It's not my cup of tea. I visited the Kafas once but I decided not to go on into the Harem."

"I've been there." Kemal looked away from him. "It's not a good place."

So Alex had heard. For the right price the Harem offered every kind of sexual debauchery and erotica from S and M to pedophilia. He glanced down at the expensive Persian carpet on the tiled floor and then to the exquisite Ming vase occupying the place of honor on a pedestal by the door they were approaching. "He seems to be doing well with his flesh-peddling."

"Oh, Adnan's very rich. He could probably retire." Kemal smiled crookedly. "But he won't do it. Why should he? He's greedy and he likes what he does."

"Irmak sounds like a fit cohort for Ledford."

Kemal nodded. "And Adnan has the contacts. For a while I wondered if he could be the Gypsy himself." He knocked on the door at the end of the corridor. "It's Kemal, Adnan."

"Come in, Kemal," a deep voice boomed. "You know my door is always open to you."

Alex followed Kemal into the office.

Adnan Irmak sat at his desk, smoking an ornate water pipe set on a low table beside him. The ruby-colored glass of the bowl glittered in the late afternoon sunlight, and the long scarlet cord attached to the pipe was inset with shimmering flecks of gold. Irmak was the first Turk wearing the traditional robes Alex had seen since he had arrived in Istanbul. But perhaps the flowing brown-and-white-striped garment was designed to hide the immense rolls of fat clinging to the man's small frame. Adnan Irmak must have weighed close to four hundred pounds.

"Come in. Come in." Irmak waved a chubby arm at the two chairs in front of the desk. "Sit down. It's been a long time since you came to see me, Kemal. But I forgive you now that you bring me a client." He stared at Kemal appraisingly before his plump cheeks dimpled as he beamed at the young man. "You're handsomer than ever, you young devil." His gaze turned to Alex. "Now, how may I serve you? Kemal tells me you have a special request and the means to purchase it."

"I need to find a man."

"That's no problem." Irmak giggled. He cast a mischievous glance at Kemal. "I supply all desires, don't I, Kemal?"

Kemal nodded.

Irmak sucked on his pipe. "I've always believed Allah put man on earth to have whatever he desires, and I've built my fortune on giving it to him. You might say I'm like the slave procurer of the royal seraglios of the past." He sighed. "How I envy those men. What power they wielded. A man could indulge himself in any way he pleased with no worry about the law. They were the law."

"I'm not looking for a whore."

"The Gypsy," Kemal said.

Irmak frowned, his lips pursing as he drew deeply on his pipe. "I've never heard of him."

"I can afford a sum generous enough to jog your memory."

"I said I didn't know him." Irmak's tone was peevish. "I'm not pleased with you, Kemal. You said he was a customer."

Kemal shrugged. "He's offering you money."

Alex said, "You don't have to take me to the Gypsy. I only want to know how to contact him."

"Go away." Irmak made a shooing gesture with the hand not holding the pipe. "I don't know anything."

"Kemal says you do. Name your price."

"I don't have a pri—" Irmak broke off, his expression becoming calculating. "You're reckless with your offers. Kemal said you had money." He suddenly smiled ingratiatingly. "I can't help you find this Gypsy, but perhaps we can still do business. You are a visitor to our city, and visitors are always lonely." He leaned forward. "Have you ever been to my fine establishment?"

"I've never had that honor," Alex said ironically.

"It's a place beyond imagination. Just like the harems of the past. Fine furnishings, sweet incense, satin cushions." Adnan's black eyes glinted like small glossy raisins, almost lost in the plumpness of his face. "But I have modern drugs to stimulate desire until my little darlings are wild to please their masters."

Alex felt a ripple of revulsion as he looked at the man. Kemal was right, the panderer enjoyed what he did. "I'm not interested in your—"

"Don't be hasty. I have something special for you." Adnan crooned. "A lovely little girl with long, golden hair and skin like velvet. Melis has tiny little breasts and just the hint of her woman's fleece." Irmak paused before announcing triumphantly, "Eleven years old and she's almost a virgin. Where can—"

"Christ!" Alex had a bellyful of him. He was abruptly on his feet and around the desk. "I don't want to screw one of your victims, you son of a bitch." He spun the chair around, grabbed the pipe out of Adnan's hand, and jerked the cord loose from the ruby-colored bowl. "But I do want to know how to find the Gypsy." He placed one knee on Irmak's genitals, letting them bear his weight. Ignoring Irmak's screech of pain, Alex wrapped the glittering gold-flecked cord around Irmak's neck and pulled it tight. Irmak made a gurgling noise in his throat, his pudgy fingers tearing futilely at the cord. "I want to know very much." Alex twisted the cord another turn, and it sank deeper into the rolls of fat. Irmak's mouth opened and his eyes bulged. "Tell me," Alex said softly.

"I—can't. I—" The cord tightened again, cutting off Irmak's helpless sputtering.

"You're really very good, Karazov." Kemal was gazing

with cool objectivity at the cord looped around Irmak's throat. He leaned leisurely back and flung one leg over the arm of his chair. "But may I point out he can't talk with that garrote around his neck?"

"He can nod." Alex smiled savagely down into Irmak's livid face. "Are we going to talk?"

Irmak nodded frantically.

"And are you going to tell me where to find the Gypsy?"

Irmak nodded again.

Kemal's foot swung lazily back and forth as he smiled admiringly at Alex. "Excellent. Truly excellent."

Alex loosened the cord.

Irmak drew a long-starved breath, his massive hands clutching at the cushioned arms of the chair. "You're a crazy man," he squeaked. "You almost killed me."

"The Gypsy."

"I don't know..." Hoarse words tumbled out as the cord began to tighten again. "As Allah is my witness, I don't know where to find him. But I know many people. I may be able to find out."

"When?"

"Soon. Tomorrow." He looked down at the cord around his neck. "Yes, tomorrow."

Alex studied his expression. The man was too frightened to lie. Irmak really didn't know where the Gypsy could be found. He unwound the cord and cast it aside before removing his knee from Irmak's genitals. "I'm at the Hilton. Call me."

Irmak nodded, his expression surly as he rubbed his neck with one hand while clutching at his genitals with the other. "You hurt me."

"I intended to hurt you," Alex said. "I enjoyed it. When you enjoy something, you look forward to doing it again. You might remember that." He moved toward the door. "Come on, Kemal."

Kemal slowly rose to his feet and followed him. "I couldn't have done better myself," he murmured. "I'm beginning to think we're true soul mates, Karazov."

"I'm not going to forget this, Kemal." Irmak glowered at him across the room as he massaged his throat.

"Forgiveness?" Kemal looked back over his shoulder and smiled. "When has there ever been any question of forgiveness between us, Adnan?" He followed Alex from the office and closed the door behind him.

"I've probably disrupted your business relationship with Irmak," Alex said as they started down the hall. "I'll make it up to you."

"Oh, I'm counting on it." Kemal smiled placidly. "As a matter of fact, I was just computing how much it was going to cost you. After all, Adnan and I go way back."

"How far?"

"I was only eight when Adnan took me to his bosom," Kemal said lightly. "I had run away from my home, but Adnan understood perfectly what every child needs. He gave me food and a bath and another, even more luxurious home—in the Harem."

Alex's eyes widened in surprise.

"Oh, yes, I was the sweetest little plum in Adnan's basket of child whores. I was as good at that as I am at everything else." Kemal shrugged. "However, I felt I wasn't really cut out for the occupation, so I ran away when I was fourteen and found another profession that would keep me safe from Adnan and give me independence. Independence is very important, you know."

"Yes, very important."

"I thought you'd understand. And money is the ultimate independence." Kemal opened the wrought iron front door and they stepped onto the street. "Someday I shall have a great home, big as a palace, and live like a caliph. I've decided I'm going to be the most independent man in this hemisphere."

"I'm surprised you don't say the world," Alex said dryly.

"I'm a realist," Kemal told him. "And a realist sets one goal at a time. Today the hemisphere, tomorrow the world."

"Was Irmak lying about being able to find out where to contact the Gypsy?"

"Possibly, but you scared him shitless. He's not a brave man." For an instant Kemal's smiled faded. "Except with helpless women and children. Then he roars like a lion." He shrugged. "But Adnan may come through for us. Meanwhile, I'll be diligently searching for another lead. Don't worry, together we will persevere until we get what you want."

Alex believed him. He had discovered a core of steely toughness and keen intelligence lay beneath Kemal's lighthearted facade. He also found he was beginning to like the scamp. "I have a friend arriving tomorrow. I'll need a house. A very safe house. Can you help me?"

"Of course. Have I not put myself at your disposal? Any particular location?"

"Just untraceable and unapproachable without warning."

"I know a few such places."

"I thought you would."

"Anything else?"

"Since I have to wait around for Adnan's call tomorrow, it seems I have an evening on my hands. Would you like to show me something of your Istanbul besides that damn bicycle shop?"

"It was a very fine bicycle shop," Kemal protested.

"A very expensive one, at least."

Kemal's brow knitted thoughtfully. "There's a club that has a band that plays great American rock. I like American rock. I play Bruce Springsteen all the time on my Walkman. The Boss is one great musician. I'm a great musician myself, and I know."

"Rock. Just what I wanted to hear in exotic Istanbul."

"You will like it. Trust me." Kemal's lids lowered and his long, dark lashes half veiled his eyes. "But my time is very valuable. I have exams this week and I'm sacrificing my study time for you. You will pay, of course."

Alex should have expected it. At this rate, he might be the one who made Kemal the richest man in this hemisphere. He sighed resignedly. "Of course."

Chelsea and Caitlin entered the elevator and the doors slid silently closed.

"Now you know what to do?" Chelsea asked. "After the mystery minx and I leave the john, you wait five minutes and then go to your own gate. Jonathan will meet you there with your papers and carry-on luggage."

"I should know. You've gone over it enough times."

"Sorry. I guess I tend to be a little overprotective."

If Caitlin had not been so nervous, she would have smiled at the understatement.

"Jonathan is meeting us in the lobby. He decided it would be safer for us to hire a mega limousine for the entire crew so that you could become lost in the mob." The doors slid open and Chelsea stepped out of the elevator. "Now, remember to move slowly and casually; body language is everything when you—"

"One moment, Mademoiselle Vasaro. I need a word with you. I am Raoul Dalpré."

Caitlin stopped short, her glance flying to Ledford's partner. When he had stood next to Krakow he had appeared rather commonplace, but now he exuded an aura of power and authority. His gray silk tie gleamed icy cool against the impeccable tailoring on his dark blue suit. *Icy.* The word suited him, she realized. Pale face, cold gray eyes, beautifully manicured, soft-looking hands...

Jonathan was suddenly there beside them. "I explained to Monsieur Dalpré that we had to leave for the airport, but he insisted on seeing you, Caitlin."

"It will take only a few moments," Dalpré said.

"We don't have a few moments," Chelsea said briskly as she gripped Caitlin's arm and started across the lobby. "You've chosen a bad time. Come on, Caitlin."

"We can talk while I walk you to your car." Dalpré fell into step with Caitlin. "I understand you're responsible for bringing the Wind Dancer to France, mademoiselle."

Jonathan said quickly, "I explained why the—"

"And that your associate, Monsieur Karazov, left Paris immediately after the theft. Where did he go?"

Caitlin shrugged. "He didn't tell me. Perhaps back to Switzerland. He has a home there."

"You didn't inquire? I fine that odd. What if you had needed to contact him?" Dalpré paused and then said softly, "He is not at his home in St. Basil. I took it upon myself to verify that fact."

"No? Well, I'm sure he'll be in touch." Caitlin's pace quickened as they neared the glass doors leading to the street. "Alex is rather unpredictable."

"Monsieur Andreas tells me you're returning to Vasaro today."

"That's right," Caitlin said. "Do you have any problem with that?"

"Not unless you decide to disappear like Monsieur Karazov." Dalpré smiled coldly. "I admit that would displease me exceedingly. I do not—"

"Oh, look, they're loading the luggage into the limousine." Chelsea pushed Caitlin out onto the street. "We'll have to check and make sure the porters haven't missed anything."

Dalpré followed them to the limousine. "I have a car down the street. Why don't I take you to the airport, Mademoiselle Vasaro?"

"That wouldn't be convenient. I've already made arrangements for us to be met by VIP personnel when we arrive at the airport," Jonathan said. "Good-bye, Dalpré."

"You seem eager to be rid of me, Monsieur Andreas." Dalpré smiled thinly. "And, as I recall, you weren't very cooperative when I tried to assure the safety of your property. Perhaps you should have listened to my advice."

"Perhaps." Jonathan's tone was noncommittal. "Don't you have anything else to do but question my cousin? Besides the Wind Dancer, I believe there are a number of other stolen art objects you've failed to recover."

Dalpré stiffened. "That's hardly my fault. My hands are tied without a closer unity between governments." He turned back to Caitlin. "You're taking the two o'clock flight to Nice?"

"Yes."

"Then may you have a safe flight. I'm sure I will see you again. Good day, mademoiselle."

He turned and walked down the rue de Castiglione.

Caitlin released her breath in a relieved rush.

"The iceman cometh," Chelsea muttered.

Caitlin nodded. "Do you think he suspects I'm not going to Nice?"

"Maybe." Jonathan shrugged. "But he can't know for sure."

"Pull the hood of your cape forward to shadow your face." Chelsea stepped back and looked at Caitlin critically before nodding. "I think that will do. That rose and cream plaid was a good choice."

"I don't exactly fade into the woodwork."

"We don't want you to fade away. We want everyone to remember you." She adjusted the rose-colored fringed tassels over Caitlin's shoulders. "Or at least the cloak. You have the dark blue jacket in your duffel?"

Caitlin nodded.

Chelsea nodded to the limousine. "Then let's go. It's show time."

When Caitlin arrived at the airport in Istanbul, Alex met her at customs and took her quickly to the house he had rented on the Bosporus. "Home," he announced as he held open the front door. "An Englishman and his wife have gone back to London for a visit, and Kemal managed to sublet it for me. Those French doors over there lead out to a postage-stamp-size garden. The gate has a foolproof security system. Two bedrooms, a living room and dining room combination, an office, and a bathroom. Tub, no shower. Not luxurious but adequate."

Caitlin didn't know what she had expected, but it was not this cool English gardenlike room. After all the exotic splendor of minarets and domed mosques on the way from the airport, the Western decor was both comforting and refreshing. Delicate violets imprinted the pale background of the chintz cushions of the couch and the large easy chair facing it. A long breakfast bar with four high stools cushioned in the same violet-patterned chintz divided the small living area from a tiny kitchenette. Two fair-haired children beamed at her from the framed photograph on the corner of the breakfast bar. "Nice. This Kemal you told me about must be a miracle worker."

"He's fairly incredible." He set her two suitcases down. "He said he buried the paperwork on the lease so deep it would take an earthquake to unearth it and the telephone is still in the owner's name. I've arranged with the desk at the Hilton to continue to accept messages and we'll retrieve them every morning. Any correspondence for us will go to the American Express office under Kemal's name and be picked up by him and brought here." Alex went to the casement windows. "There's a good view of the Bosporus from here." He opened the windows and cool air rushed into the room. "And five times a day you can hear the muezzin calling the faithful to prayer from that minaret in the distance."

"You sound like a real estate salesman." She turned to look at him. "It took us a long time to get here. Were we being followed?"

"I don't think so, but I wanted to be sure. Your bedroom is the one on the left."

"Who were you afraid was following us? Ledford?"

"Perhaps one of Ledford's men."

"Was that who was following us in Paris? The man in the red shirt?"

"God no," he said, stung. "Do you think I'd have let you stay with me if there had been that kind of danger to you?"

"I don't know. Would you?" Her tone was cool as she turned and moved toward the bedroom he had indicated. "Who was following us in Paris?"

"CIA. They were no threat to you."

"But you made sure that I didn't suspect anything, didn't you?"

"Yes."

"Why?"

"I didn't want to rock the boat. Everything was going well and I didn't want anything to upset you and make you back out of the deal."

"I doubt if I would have pulled out at that point." Caitlin smiled bitterly. "You had me blind and dizzy during those weeks in Paris."

"I was pretty dizzy myself."

"But not blind. You knew exactly what you were doing, didn't you, Alex?"

His lips tightened, but he said quietly, "Yes, exactly."

"Are you going to tell me why the CIA was following you?"

"Do you care?"

"No, I'm just curious. You can understand that. You're very curious yourself."

"Yes, I can understand curiosity." He turned, then picked up her suitcases and carried them to her bedroom. "Get unpacked. I'll make coffee."

"You're not going to tell me any more of your secrets?"

"It's a waste of time. It doesn't matter anymore."

"It matters to me."

Wariness flickered in his expression. "Why?"

"Because I want to know you."

"You do know me."

She shook her head. "No, I only thought I did. But you knew me, didn't you? I became more vulnerable to you than I've ever been to any other human being because you knew which buttons to push. That's why you were able to manipulate me, Alex." She shivered. "You know this world and I don't. I need to know how it works. I need to know how your mind works."

"Evidently not very well lately." He shrugged wearily and set her suitcases down inside the bedroom. "Hell, maybe you're right. I'll call you when the coffee is brewed and you can come in and interrogate me to your heart's content."

Alex leaned back on the cushions of the couch and smiled sardonically at her. "Well?"

Caitlin looked down into the depths of her coffee cup. "Why does the CIA follow you?"

"To protect me."

She glanced up at him skeptically.

He shrugged. "Oh, not because they're overly fond of me. They hate my guts."

"Why?"

"I'm a loaded pistol pointed at McMillan's head."

"Who is McMillan?"

"Rod McMillan is very high up in the CIA. Among other projects, he oversaw the activities of the department that arranged my exit from Mother Russia." Alex took a swallow of his coffee. "There are a good many honest and patriotic men who work for the CIA. McMillan's not one of them."

"He's crooked?"

"Dirty as they come." Alex shrugged. "Maybe at one time he was straight, but by the time I knew him he was using his position and the information the Company gathered to line his own pockets and make himself a very rich man."

Caitlin lifted her cup to her lips. "Go on."

"You want it all? Very well, when I first started working for the CIA I was under no illusions about McMillan, but I didn't care. The Company paid me well, they kept me from being sanctioned by the KGB, and they let me work my puzzles with no interference. McMillan promised me after ten years they'd relocate me and let me live my own life. It was a good deal."

"So why did you leave?"

"Something happened. . . ." He shook his head, his eyes bleak. "I don't think I'll tell you about that. It would make me a little too vulnerable to you at the moment. I find I do have some sense of self-preservation left." He sipped his coffee and set the cup back down in the saucer on the table. "Anyway, something happened and I knew I had to get away from the job I was doing. However, if I left the department, McMillan threatened to cancel my protection. I knew I wouldn't have lasted six months before the KGB chopped me. So I had my own puzzle to solve. How to keep McMillan from using me, without ending up dead meat."

"I'm sure a man as brilliant as you had no trouble coming up with the answer."

He ignored her mockery. "I began to monitor incoming information from the field to find an ace. Not only the projects that concerned me but the ones that were reported directly to McMillan. It took me six months and then I got lucky. I began to see threads of information that began to form a pattern. McMillan's big coup. The one that was going to set him up for life." He looked up and smiled at Caitlin. "You weren't far wrong. It is drug money in most of my bank accounts in Switzerland. But I didn't deal drugs, I stole the money."

"From a drug dealer?"

He shook his head. "From McMillan . . . and Ysborski."

"Ysborski?"

"A colonel in the KGB. That was one of the threads that kept reappearing. Both the CIA and KGB were zeroing in on a plot involving a Venezuelan drug kingpin, one Manuel Salazar. Salazar planned to overthrow the government of Venezuela and take control himself. Now, taking over a country is a very expensive proposition."

"How expensive?"

"Five hundred million dollars. To be paid to various Venezuelan officials and army officers who would stage a minor revolution and then discreetly hand over the reins to Salazar's puppets." He smiled. "Both McMillan and Ysborski thought it was their patriotic duty to deprive Salazar of the means to become a dictator, and they couldn't see why the confiscated money shouldn't go into their own pockets instead of being lost somewhere in the judicial process. So McMillan and Ysborski came to an agreement to work together toward a common end. As soon as they found out where the money was to be transferred, they'd step in and grab it for themselves. Fifty-fifty split."

"And you stepped in first?"

He shook his head. "That wouldn't have served my purpose. I had no desire to have Salazar after me, so I waited until McMillan and Ysborski stole the money from Salazar. I must admit they handled the theft very cleverly and got away clean. Then Pavel and I stole the money from them." He smiled. "And headed for Switzerland."

"Why didn't they go after you?"

"Because when I left Langley I took all the various bits of documented information I'd used to put together my puzzle, along with my analysis of those facts. I photocopied the lot thirty-two times and put the copies in safety deposit boxes scattered in several countries around the world with instructions that upon my death or disappearance they be immediately sent to various newspapers and politicians in both the U.S. and the Soviet Union." He smiled crookedly. "I also addressed one very detailed letter to Manuel Salazar."

"Very clever. They had to protect you or be ruined or murdered by Salazar."

"Or by their own people who didn't want the reputation of their respective organizations compromised."

"A plot worthy of you, Alex. Did you enjoy having all those men dancing on your string?"

"I did enjoy it, as a matter of fact. Did you expect me to deny it? They *used* me. The KGB used me. The CIA used me. I can't remember a time when someone hasn't used me to get what he wanted."

"Poor Alex."

He drew a deep breath and said quietly, "I'm not asking for sympathy. I just want you to understand. In my world everybody used everybody else. I opted out of that world, but then Pavel—he was my *friend*, dammit."

"So you used me to avenge him."

"You weren't supposed to be hurt."

"But you would have done it even if you knew I would have been hurt."

He didn't answer for a moment. "When it all started, I didn't care who got hurt as long as I got Ledford. Is that what you want to hear?"

She suddenly knew that wasn't what she had wanted him to say. She hadn't wanted him to be honest with her. She had wanted him to make weak excuses, to be less than the man she had known all these months. She had wanted fuel for maintaining scorn and anger. She felt a sudden sense of panic. Why was it necessary to fuel her anger? She quickly lowered her gaze. "That's what I want to hear."

"Then I admit it. You always knew that, Caitlin."

She had known that about Alex and been swept away by him anyway. The reminder caused her uneasiness to escalate. "As I said, you had me blind and dizzy. I don't remember what I knew or didn't know about you." She put her cup down. "What have you found out since you've been here? Is Ledford in Istanbul?"

"Kemal's man at the airport says there's been no sign of him."

"What about the supplier you told me about on the way from the airport?"

"The Gypsy?" Alex shook his head. "We've been in contact with one of his front men, Adnan Irmak, but Kemal said he dropped out of sight last night after I paid him a visit. Kemal hasn't been able to find out where he went."

"Then what can we do?"

"I'm waiting for a call from Kemal now."

"Maybe Ledford won't come back here if he knows you're looking for him."

"I've got a hunch he will."

"You operate on hunches? What about your much-lauded 'talent'?"

"I've never known how it works. Part of it is pure analysis and projection. The other part...who knows? Ever since I found out about Ledford's house I've had a feeling it should mean something to me."

"Do we take turns watching the house?"

"No, I'd certainly be recognized, and you might be too. Kemal has arranged for one of his cohorts to do it."

"When am I going to meet this Kemal? You said—"

Caitlin broke off as the phone on the end table shrilled.

Alex answered it. "Hello." He listened for a moment. "I've got it. Eleven o'clock." He returned the receiver to its cradle. "Kemal. He asked me to meet him tonight. He's going to try to find out where Irmak's hiding."

"Hiding?"

"Irmak was supposed to contact me today at the ho-tel about the whereabouts of the Gypsy, but he didn't

do it." Alex smiled faintly. "Irmak obviously has no desire to meet with me again. Kemal says there were two
bodyguards lurking outside his *yali* on the Bosporus.
I'm afraid I lost patience with him during our last encounter."

Caitlin felt a chill as she saw his expression. She had
told him she wanted to know him, but she wasn't certain she wanted to know this Alex Karazov. "Where are
you going to meet Kemal?"

"We're going to the club Irmak owns and see if he
shows or Kemal can dig out any information."

"Then I'm going with you."

"I thought you would. I don't suppose it would do
any good to tell you it's not a place in which you'll feel
in the least comfortable?"

"No good at all."

He smiled curiously. "Then I wouldn't think of keeping you from going along: Wear something dark, high-
necked, and conservative." He picked up both cups and
saucers and went into the tiny kitchenette, saying, "And
don't blame me if you don't like the floor show."

"*Kafas?*" Caitlin asked, reading the name scrawled in
gold on the brass-bound mahogany doors.

"It means 'golden cage' in Turkish." Alex knocked and
the door was opened by a tall, bearded man dressed in
flowing red robes and a white turban. Alex murmured
something to him in Turkish and the man allowed them
to enter into a mosaic-tiled anteroom. Another identi-
cally garbed man held a white robe for Alex to slip on.
Both men ignored Caitlin as they bowed to Alex and
gestured to a keyhole-shaped entrance to the left. Alex
grasped Caitlin's elbow and propelled her toward the
door. "Actually, the name's surprisingly fitting."

As they entered the club they were immediately assaulted by the odor of sweet smoke and strong coffee. "It doesn't look very golden to me." Caitlin's gaze wandered around the large room. The only golden touch was the soft, diffused glow lighting the panels of the high-arched ceiling. The room resembled a stadium more than a cage. The patrons' low tables and enormous satin cushions were located on six levels, looking down at a circular arena occupied by turbaned musicians playing exotic stringed instruments, bells, and drums. Waiters dressed in scarlet robes bearing trays with drinks and pastries hurried up and down the three flights of stairs bridging the six levels. No women, she noticed suddenly. The place was filled to capacity with men wearing robes like the one the doorman had given Alex, but she was the only woman in the room. "And that sweetish smell could mean big trouble here in Istanbul."

"You must have seen *Midnight Express*. Turkey's no tougher on drug users than a lot of other countries."

"I don't particularly want to do any comparison shopping."

"Don't worry, the Golden Cage is protected."

"By whom?"

"Someone very high in the government, I understand. It's never safe to inquire too closely into these things." Alex seated her on the cushions of a small low table close to the door. "However, I can assure you that you don't have to worry about a raid."

"I'm the only woman here."

"You won't be thrown out. This club caters to men but occasionally a woman is brought here."

"What did you say to the man who let us in?"

"The password Kemal gave me. You have to know the password or be a guest of a regular patron to be allowed in."

"You've been here before?"

"Once. Years ago." Alex motioned and one of the waiters hurried toward them up the stairs. "This place was designed to appeal to men who have a sultan complex. It's best that you keep a low profile."

"I wasn't about to get up and do a belly dance."

He must have noticed the edginess of her tone, because he turned to study her expression. "You're nervous. I told you that it wasn't a place for you."

"I'm not nervous. I'm merely—" She stopped. "So I'm nervous. I'll get over it."

Alex turned to the waiter now at his elbow and spoke rapidly in Turkish. The man nodded and a moment later disappeared into the crowd. "I told him to send Kemal here when he comes in and I ordered coffee."

She looked back at him. "You speak Turkish."

"How suspicious you sound. I visited Istanbul many times when I was with the KGB. I like it here. As I said, it's a city where rules can be bent. I've never liked rules."

She knew Alex hated rules. When he couldn't break them, he found a way of going around them. She had once found that lawlessness exciting. She quickly looked down at the copper brazier on the table. "Why is it fitting that this place is called the Golden Cage?"

"It's a historical term. It's named after an apartment in the Topkapi Palace that was once called the Golden Cage."

"Why?"

"Because the reigning sultan's brothers were held captive there for their entire lives and never permitted to leave."

Her gaze shifted to his face. "How terrible."

Alex nodded. "It was to protect the reigning sultan from assassination. Not pleasant but better than being slaughtered. They were occasionally allowed concubines, but only after the women had their uteruses cut out so that they could no longer bear children."

Caitlin shivered. "I don't see why anyone would want to name a place after a prison, golden or not."

Alex smiled faintly. "Because the princes were only *occasionally* allowed women. Now, what do you suppose healthy, sexually active males would do in circumstances like that?"

"This is a gay bar?"

"To be exact, it's AC/DC. I understand from Kemal that Irmak is homosexual, which is probably one of the reasons the Gypsy uses him as a front man to deal with Ledford. The Kafas is one of the most famous sex clubs in the world and would have attracted Ledford and—"

"Ah, you've brought a lady. I approve. There's nothing like combining business with pleasure."

Caitlin stared up at the startlingly handsome young man who had just spoken. He was dressed in the same white robe as the rest of the customers, but wore his with a verve and dash lacking in any of the others.

"Kemal Nemid. Caitlin Vasaro," Alex said.

Kemal Nemid dropped down onto the cushion next to Caitlin and addressed Alex. "I haven't been able to make contact yet. They keep the door to the Harem locked until after the show begins." Kemal gracefully crossed his legs tailor fashion and immediately took on the persona of a royal caliph perched on his satin cushion. He turned to Caitlin. "What a pretty lady you are." He took her hand and raised it to his lips like a courtier of old. "I'm honored to meet you. May I tell you what gorgeous breasts you have?"

Caitlin blinked. "Thank you."

"Like lovely, jutting mountains." He reproachfully eyed the high neck of her black dress. "You should not cover them up like that. Do you like me?"

She glanced in confusion at Alex. He only shrugged and she looked back at Kemal. "I . . . don't know you."

"But you like what you see?"

"Yes, I guess so."

"Then perhaps you could participate with me as well as Alex."

"Kemal," Alex said softly.

Kemal sighed. "She is here because of Ledford and not to participate?"

Alex nodded.

Kemal shook his head mournfully. "It would be very enjoyable if she were to participate. I do love big breasts. Psychological. I lost my mother when I was so young."

"Pardon me, Monsieur Nemid, but what—"

"Kemal. Call me Kemal. Even if we cannot perform together, we are going to be fast friends. I can tell. I have second sight, you know."

"No, I didn't know." Caitlin was having difficulty smothering a smile. The boy was both outrageous and irresistible.

"And if you decide to participate, I'm at your service."

It was the second time he had mentioned participating. "What is it I'm supposed to participate in?"

Kemal looked at Alex inquiringly.

"By all means, tell her," Alex said.

Kemal frowned as he turned back to Caitlin. "Alex should have been the one to tell you. It's too late for you to leave now. No one can leave or be admitted to the Golden Cage after eleven."

"She wanted to come," Alex said.

Kemal's gaze searched Alex's expression. "And for some reason, you wanted her to see it. You want her in the Harem?"

"We're here to find Irmak. The Harem is out of the question at the moment."

Kemal lifted a brow. "Yet you know what seeing it will do to her. It's not fair of you to—"

"I'm getting very tired of being ignored," Caitlin said forcefully.

"Forgive me." Kemal smiled at Caitlin. "It's rude of us. You must stay for the show now. The Cage's doors are locked. It's tradition, but no harm will come to you."

"Tradition?"

"Every night there's a reenactment of the debauchery at Topkapi." He squeezed her hand comfortingly. "That's why I thought Alex might have brought you. If a patron wishes to participate, he may do so."

"Naturally," Caitlin said faintly. "You're talking about a sex show. Right?"

Kemal nodded. "But not the usual show you would see in Paris. Except for a few women brought over from the Harem, these are volunteers who wish to exhibit themselves. You'll find it very stimulating."

A gong sounded and the lights were suddenly dimmed.

Caitlin's heart jumped to her throat as she looked down at the arena. All the musicians with the exception of the man playing the drum had left the center of the room, and three scarlet-cushioned couches had been positioned at intervals in the clearing. *Merde*, she was no child. There was no reason for her to be this nervous.

"You need not look." Kemal released her hand and rose. "If you can keep yourself from it. I never can, but then, I'm a sensualist. I'll see you both after the show. I'm going to see if I can get through to the Harem when they bring in the women." He started down the stairs toward the clearing in the center of the room.

The drum began to echo like a rhythmic heartbeat through the room. The darkness changed to rosy twilight as two men came on the stage. Both men were young, athletic-looking, beautiful, and completely nude.

The show went on for over an hour and featured not only homosexual but heterosexual couplings. The men and women were all young and attractive and there was no question of their enthusiasm. During the entire time Caitlin found herself fascinated, attracted, repelled, and yet helpless to turn away. It was sex and yet not sex, a sensual ballet, a feverish dream. No sound disturbed the fantasy, the men at the tables were silent in the darkness, the air charged with awareness.

She tried not to look at Alex, but she felt his gaze on her several times during the performance and she could not keep herself from glancing at him.

He smiled faintly as he caught and interpreted her expression. "Arousing?" His voice was low, almost guttural, with the Slavic intonation with which she had become so familiar when they had been involved in the same activities being performed before them.

"Yes." Caitlin swallowed and glanced away. He knew her responses too well for her to deny it. She could still feel Alex's gaze on her face but avoided looking at him again. "I wish Kemal would come back."

"Soon," Alex said. "The show will end in about ten minutes."

It couldn't be too soon. Her grasp tightened on her tulip-shaped glass of coffee on the table before her. Her heart was slamming frantically against her rib cage. "What is this Harem you and Kemal were talking about? Another part of the legend?"

Alex nodded. "The golden cage at Topkapi was across from the harem." Alex nodded at a door adjoining the stage. "That door leads to the apartments occupied by the men and women of the Harem. It's actually a bordello, but no one can enter it except through the Kafas. The patrons watch the show and then go on to the bordello. There are also several empty apartments that can be rented for the hour or the night."

"Incredible."

"Convenient," Alex corrected her. "After an exhibition like this, it's very difficult to wait." He paused. "Isn't it, Caitlin?"

The exhibition was ending onstage, thank heaven. She kept her face expressionless as she turned to look at him. "Why did you want me to see this? Is it supposed to be a turn-on?"

"Yes."

"And I'm supposed to fall into your bed as soon as we get back to the cottage?"

"I'm not a fool."

"Or perhaps you thought I'd try out the Harem?"

He smiled faintly. "If things were different, I'm quite sure you'd choose the Harem."

She glanced hurriedly away from him. "I'm not impressed."

"Yes, you are. I can see the pulse pounding in your temple. You're hot and aroused and angry as hell at me for knowing it."

"It has nothing to do with you."

Some indefinable emotion flickered in his face before he smiled self-mockingly. "It has everything to do with me. You're intelligent enough to know how self-serving I am. We can't continue living in the same house with you constantly on guard against me, and sex appears to be the only way I can reach you. I thought it wouldn't hurt to lay the groundwork."

She should look away from him. She knew how compelling Alex could be when he exerted himself. She finally managed to tear her glance away and shifted it back to the stage to find the performance had ended. "I think we'd better—there's Kemal." She experienced a rush of relief as she saw Kemal climbing the steps two at a time as he came toward them. She wanted to get out of there. The sensual atmosphere had knocked her off balance and she needed to regain her emotional equilibrium.

"Irmak?" Alex asked Kemal as he stopped beside their table.

Kemal shook his head. "Not here tonight. But he's still in the city. Melis says he was at the Harem this morning."

"Melis..." Alex frowned as if trying to identify the name.

"You remember Melis. 'Eleven years old with golden hair.'" He gestured to the men who were now streaming through the door leading to the Harem. "She's going to have a busy night."

"Eleven?" Caitlin felt sick. "They have children here? Can't we do something?"

"Perhaps," Kemal said. "But not tonight. Nothing's going to happen to her or the others that hasn't happened before."

"It's horrible that they can use children like that."

"It's worse than horrible, it's a death sentence."

"What?"

"The prostitutes are given physical checkups every other day to protect the clients and make them feel safe enough to come back." Kemal paused before adding softly, "But Adnan wouldn't think of inconveniencing his clients by giving them the same tests or asking them to use protection. In this day of AIDS, how long do you think Adnan's whores survive?"

Alex stood up, took off his robe, and threw some currency on the table. "Why don't we just go pay another visit to Irmak's *yali*?"

Kemal shook his head. "Melis says he's not there. Besides, you want the Gypsy before you kill Adnan. He may just be hiding until he can locate the Gypsy for you." He noticed Caitlin's startled face and gave her a dazzling smile. "But we're frightening the pretty lady. Enough of this sad talk." He reached out a hand and pulled her to her feet. "Come, I will go home with you."

"You will?"

Kemal took off his robe and tossed it on the cushions to reveal jeans and a white fleecy sweatshirt. "We will have coffee and I'll tell you of the many places you must see in my city." He snapped his fingers. "No, tomorrow I will take you myself."

"I'm not here to sight-see, Kemal."

"But what else can you do until I find Adnan? And because I find you so beautiful, I will charge you nothing." Kemal glanced at Alex and magnanimously added, "You may come if you like."

Alex said dryly, "How kind of you to include me."

"Yes, it is." Kemal beamed at him. "Particularly since it's clear you have no intention of letting me show the pretty lady what a magnificent lover I am."

"That's perceptive of you."

"Don't worry." Kemal airily waved a hand. "I need your money. I promise I will never show her what she's missing."

Alex's lips twitched. "Thank you, but I don't think a tour is wise." He turned to Caitlin. "However, you have no idea what a compliment he's giving you to make the offer gratis. No one likes money as much as Kemal."

"So very true." Kemal took Caitlin's arm and nudged

her toward the door. "Now we go back to your house. I live near here on the Street of the Turban Makers, but there are cockroaches. Ladies hate cockroaches."

"Yes, we do."

"Me, too, but the rent is cheap. We will stop by my place and get my guitar and I will play for you."

"I don't feel much like a party."

Kemal nodded understandingly. "You are still sad about the children. But you can do nothing to help them now, so you must not think of them. Enjoy the moment."

"Can you do that?"

Kemal gazed at her gravely. "Yes. I'm sorry you think me unfeeling, but I learned a long time ago how to put aside sadness until it was time to act." He smiled. "You are in for a great treat. I sing too." He struck a pose, knees bent, strumming an imaginary guitar. "I will sing 'Born in the U.S.A.' for you."

"Are you any good?"

"Oh, yes," Kemal said seriously. "I'm a superb musician. Almost as good as Bruce Springsteen. I'm better at sex, but the guitar takes more practice to reach perfection."

Caitlin chuckled. "Yet you have to manipulate certain chords in either." The words had tumbled out before she thought. She glanced sidewise at Alex to find him smiling faintly, knowingly. She looked hurriedly back at Kemal. "Alex tells me you work with the CIA."

"Part-time. I'm a student at the university." His black eyes twinkled. "I major in philosophy."

Caitlin shook her head. "I should have guessed."

The air was brisk with a hint of autumn chill as they left the Golden Cage and started up the twisting street.

"Socrates was a sensualist too," Kemal stated. "Most of the Greeks were. But they appreciated the beauty of men much more than that of women, which wasn't exactly fair. I'm far more democratic." He turned to Alex. "You go with us tomorrow?"

"No, and neither will Caitlin. I told you it wasn't wise."

Kemal's gaze narrowed on Alex's face. "You mean safe. There is danger for her?"

"Ledford."

"It is too bad." Then his expression brightened as he inclined his head in a slight bow to Caitlin. "But do not worry, pretty lady, I promise I will think on it and overcome this difficulty."

And, gazing in bemusement at his determined face, Caitlin knew Kemal would keep his promise.

In the next several hours Kemal proved to be the superb musician he claimed to be. His skill on the guitar was exceeded by a remarkable baritone singing voice. The moment he entered their cottage he sat on the floor and entertained them with rock songs, jokes, and wickedly witty stories of his life in the city. Caitlin found him to be a curious combination of boyishly appealing and tough worldly-wise. She was irresistibly drawn to him. Alex, on the contrary, was unusually silent.

It was close to three in the morning when Kemal put his guitar carefully in its case and rose to his feet. "I must go home and shower and dress for class. Today you will rest from your trip, but tomorrow morning at six o'clock I will call for you."

Caitlin blinked. "Call for me?"

"Of course." He moved toward the door. "I promised to show you my city."

Alex stiffened. "And I said it was too dangerous."

"But that is why we will go at dawn." Kemal turned

at the door and smiled. "That way we will be through before anyone else is stirring."

Caitlin shook her head. "Nothing will be open."

"I have friends. I will find a way to open closed doors." He turned back to Alex. "I will have her safely back by nine. Okay?"

"No," Alex said.

"Yes," Caitlin said at the same time.

Alex whirled to face her. "I don't like it, dammit."

"It seems safe enough. You said we weren't followed from the airport." She said to Kemal, "I'll be ready at six."

Kemal's brilliant smile flashed and the next moment the door had closed behind him.

"Why?" Alex bit out.

She avoided looking at him. "I find Kemal amusing. I've never seen anyone more enthusiastic or guileless in my entire life."

"Don't be fooled. He's one tough little bastard."

"Well then, that will make me safer, won't it? Besides, I don't think you would have taken me to the Kafas tonight if you thought there was any danger."

"You didn't give me much choice. This is no time for casual sight-seeing."

She didn't give a damn about sight-seeing. She had no intention of being cooped up in the same house with Alex for twenty-four hours at a time. Those moments at the Kafas had shown her how vulnerable she was to him. "Maybe I'm just subscribing to Kemal's philosophy of enjoying the moment."

"Then I'm going with you."

"No!" Alex's eyes flew to her face at the violence of her rejection, and Caitlin quickly turned on her heel and walked toward her bedroom. "I don't want you along."

"Too bad. You'll have to put up with me today. If I

see that Kemal's right and the risks seem slight, I'll rid you of my presence after that. Satisfied?"

"No, but I guess it will have to do. Good night."

She heard a muttered curse behind her and then Alex said wearily, "Wear shoes you can slip on and off easily."

She glanced back over her shoulder. "Why?"

"The city is filled with mosques and you'll have to remove your shoes before entering them."

"How do you know? Oh, yes, you told me you'd visited here before."

"Mosques weren't on my list of sight-seeing musts at the time. I was very young and as much a sensualist as our friend Kemal." He lifted his shoulders in a weary shrug. "I told you I had a passion for trivia. My head is crammed with the damned stuff."

He looked jaded and so terribly alone that for an instant she experienced a pang of sympathy. *Dieu*, how stupid. No one needed sympathy less than Alex Karazov. "What are we going to do after we get back to the cottage tomorrow?"

He shrugged. "Make a few phone calls. Study the photographs of the Wind Dancer. Maybe I'll try to make a projection about Ledford's next move."

"Can you do that?"

"Sometimes. Not often with this many variables in the picture."

She hesitated, oddly reluctant to leave him. She asked suddenly, "Why did you defect to the United States?"

"Oh, no, I'm not going to give you any more weapons against me tonight."

"Well, tomorrow is another day." She started to swing the door shut.

"It won't work, you know."

"What won't work?"

"You can't run away."

"I'm not running away."

"The hell you're not. You were scared to death in Paris, but now you're willing to risk your neck just to avoid me."

"I'm not—the risk is minimal."

"Maybe. But, dammit, you shouldn't take any risk." He paused. "Look, we have to work and live together if we're going to find Ledford. You can't stay bitter and angry at me twenty-four hours a day."

"Don't count on it." Caitlin shut the door and wearily leaned back against it.

Would it ever get easier?

12

Caitlin had a restless night and was up at seven the next morning. The first thing she did was call Vasaro.

Katrine answered the phone and Caitlin felt a rush of affection as she heard her mother's voice. "Mother? How are you?"

"Well enough." Katrine sounded distracted. "Really, Caitlin, it was most unfair of you to invite all these people to Vasaro and then not come home to help. They're supposed to descend on me at noon today, and where am I going to put them? Ms. Benedict and Mr. Andreas and this Pauley person...And what about the film crew? Can't you put off that tiresome business in Paris and come home until they leave?"

"You'll manage splendidly, Mother. You know you always do," Caitlin said. "And think of the stories you'll have to tell your friends about Chelsea Benedict. They'll be green with envy that you had her at Vasaro."

"That's true." Katrine was instantly mollified as she thought of that social coup on the horizon. "Do you suppose I could persuade her to go to Nice to lunch with me one day?"

"If she's not too busy."

"And Marisa has volunteered to give up her room here at the manor to stay in the village with Renée and her husband." Katrine was brightening more by the minute. "I have to hang up now, Caitlin. I don't have any more time to talk to you."

"Wait. Is Peter Maskovel around?"

"Oh, yes, we've just finished breakfast. Peter! He's coming. Good-bye, Caitlin."

"I'm sorry I couldn't be there to—"

"Hello, Caitlin." Peter Maskovel's voice.

"I just wondered if everything was going well with the translation."

"Fine. I should finish copying the notes today. Where should I send them?"

"The American Express office in Istanbul in care of Kemal Nemid. Tell Jonathan if he has any word for us to leave a message at the Hilton for Alex."

"Right. Anything else?"

"We may be here awhile. Could you send me my projectors and the hologram film you'll find in the perfumery?"

"I'll put the notes in the box and send them off together."

"Thank you."

Peter was silent, and she knew he was wondering why she didn't bring the call to a close. Dammit, she didn't want to break even this fragile link to home. "Have you been enjoying yourself at Vasaro?"

"Who wouldn't? It's heaven on earth. In the short time I've been here I've used up bushels of film." He went on quickly. "But I've been working in the evenings on the translation. Marisa has been helping me type it."

"She's rather special, isn't she?"

Peter didn't answer for a moment. "Very special."

She had no more excuse to continue the conversation. "Since I can't be there, I'd appreciate it if you'd help my mother cope. She doesn't like to have to worry about things."

"Marisa and I will watch out for her."

Another silence.

"One more thing." She tried to keep her tone light. "I know I told you not to send me more photographs, but I really wouldn't mind if you sent me a few prints of your shots of Vasaro."

"I'll send you a copy of every single one," Peter said gently.

"That's kind of you. Good-bye, Peter."

She hung up and drew a deep, shaky breath. She felt so cut off, so alone.

"Is anything wrong?" Alex stood in the doorway of his bedroom. She wondered how long he had been listening.

"No. Mother is a little harried because of the film crew coming, but she'll get along fine." She stood up, tightened the belt of her robe, and moved toward her bedroom. "I should get the translation in a few days. That's why I called Vasaro. I can't just spend my time twiddling my thumbs. I have to have *purpose*."

"Caitlin."

She didn't look at him. "I have to get dressed."

"Don't close me out. I want to help you."

She turned her head and stared directly into his eyes. "Tell me, can you help me not feel an exile from Vasaro?"

He shook his head wearily. "No, I can't do that."

"I didn't think so." She went into the bedroom and closed the door.

•   •   •

Peter turned away from the phone to see Marisa standing beside him. "She's homesick."

Marisa nodded gravely. "It's must be terrible having a home you love and know it's forbidden to you. My mother and I have moved around so much that we've never stayed long enough to become attached to any one place." She fell into step with him as he started for the front door. "I can help you for only a few hours this morning. I have to come back to pack and move to the village."

"Can you find a place for me with one of the workers? Katrine seems concerned about space."

"I'll ask Jacques. Louis lives alone and might like the company." Marisa smiled at him. "It will be nice being together away from the crowd, won't it? Neither of us is the celebrity type."

"Very nice."

She slipped her arm in his as they strolled down the steps. "I feel so comfortable with you, Peter."

He could feel his heart skip a beat and then accelerate as she touched him, but he carefully kept his face expressionless. Sixteen and forty, he reminded himself. A girl in the sunrise of a bright, active life and an aging crock whose condition might worsen and deteriorate at any time. She liked him. She confided in him. They had become friends who could talk and work together intimately. He should be grateful that he had been given these moments.

He covered her hand with his own and patted it affectionately as they walked toward the perfumery. "I feel comfortable with you too, Marisa."

•   •   •

"We will go for a ferry ride on the Golden Horn," Kemal said. "Did I tell you that they used to call the Golden Horn the sultan's pond? It used to be polluted, but now it is clear and beautif—"

"How far is it to this ferry?"

"Only a mile or two."

"And we'll walk?"

"Of course, it's the only way to see Istanbul."

Caitlin vaguely remembered telling Alex the same thing about Paris, but she had never been the indefatigable guide Kemal had proven to be. It was only a little after eight in the morning and she was exhausted. "Can't we take a taxi?"

Kemal decisively shook his head. "You have no need of taxis. You're a big, strong, beautiful woman." Then, as he saw her face cloud mutinously, he relented. "But maybe tomorrow we'll rent you a bicycle."

"No, thank you. Not in this traffic." She sighed. "Very well, I'll walk."

"A bicycle is good. Much better than an automobile. It goes places even the smallest car would not."

Caitlin shook her head. "Which way?"

Kemal started briskly down the street, and she fell into step with him.

They walked in silence for over a block before Kemal asked suddenly, "Why do you treat Alex with such coldness?"

Caitlin gave him an exasperated glance. "That's a very personal question, and it's none of your business, Kemal."

"Is it because you have been lovers and are no longer?"

Caitlin stiffened. "How do you know that—"

"Oh, Alex did not tell me," Kemal said quickly. "I

have great sensitivity of soul. Naturally, I would sense this feeling between you."

"Sensitivity *and* second sight?"

Kemal grinned. "The two go together." He studied her guarded expression. "Are you frightened of Alex?"

She was startled. "Why would I be frightened?"

"He's a man who can kill. Sometimes women fear that in a man."

She remembered the moment a few days before when she had felt a tiny ripple of fear as she had looked at Alex. "What happened between Alex and Irmak?"

"Alex became . . . irritated."

"And?"

Kemal shrugged but didn't answer.

"No, of course I'm not afraid of Alex," Caitlin said.

"Then why do you have a separate bed, when you wish to occupy his?"

"I don't wish to—Kemal, this conversation is closed."

"You're angry with me," Kemal said. "I spoke only because I like Alex Karazov. I like you too."

"That's not unusual. You seem to get along with everyone."

"Oh, yes, everyone likes me. How could they help it?"

"I have no idea." She smiled reluctantly. It was impossible to be annoyed with Kemal for long, and this occasion was no exception. The rogue blithely trampled on forbidden ground as if he owned the entire earth.

"But you should not stop yourself from taking what you want from each other," Kemal persisted. "Who knows what tomorrow will bring? You must savor every moment."

"Kemal, you're a complete pagan."

"But it's true," he protested. "Trust me. This is wisdom I speak."

She suddenly chuckled. "Philosophy according to Kemal?"

He nodded gravely. "When I was a small boy I was very poor and my family was much despised. So I ran away from them. I thought I was running to a better life."

"And it wasn't?"

"Alex did not tell you? No, it was not a better life. I should have clung to my family and enjoyed the good times and endured the—" Kemal broke off and smiled at her. "Enough. You do not want to hear my blabberings." Whether she did or not, she could see Kemal was done with confidences. He offered magnanimously, "If your feet are truly sore after we come back on the ferry, we will take a taxi back to the cottage."

She felt as if he had gifted her with a diamond tiara. "Really?"

He nodded. "You pay, of course."

"Of course." Caitlin had discovered almost immediately how right Alex had been about the compliment Kemal had paid her by not charging her for acting as her guide. "That goes without saying."

"I will *not* climb that tree, Pauley." Chelsea's tone was unequivocal. "You've had me riding bareback on the cliff, running through a field of roses, dancing on grapes." She made a face. "I'm going to get you for that. Do you know how squishy that stuff is between your toes?"

"But you have such divine toes, angel," Pauley drawled. His white teeth gleamed as he smiled coaxingly. "And you know we have to have one more shot before we pack up and go back to Nice." He gestured to an orange tree a few yards away. "Now, here's how I see it. You're a nymph sitting on the lower branches of that orange tree. We'll put the fans on you and your skirts will blow gently and the blossoms will fall on your hair and then drift down on the Wind Dancer on the pedestal below the tree."

"The tree isn't even in bloom."

"We can fix that. I brought props from Nice. Who says the blossoms have to be real? Silk is good. Silk is fine."

"We don't have the Wind Dancer."

"The magic of special effects, angel. I can transpose a picture of the Wind Dancer on the film and then shoot it surreal. Dream stuff."

Chelsea heard Jonathan's low chuckle but she didn't look in his direction. Pauley had been running her ragged with his demands for the past two days and she was not amused. "I do not do trees."

"It will be perfectly safe. We'll get a ladder and—"

"Pauley, I grew up in the slums of New York. The only trees I knew about were the coat trees at Ulysses S. Grant Elementary. I refuse to go swinging through this grove like Sheena of the Jungle."

"You're tired." Pauley's tone turned to a solicitous croon. "And I'm a bastard not to realize how hard you've worked today. Take a fifteen-minute break and we'll talk about it later."

"Fifteen minutes? I've been up since dawn and you give me—" Chelsea stopped as she realized she was talking to the air. Pauley had strolled away toward the cameraman on the crane, and the rest of the crew had dispersed and were wandering in the direction of the trestle table with refreshments Katrine had ordered set up at the edge of the orange grove.

"A nymph?" Jonathan lifted his brow. "Somehow I can't see you as a wood nymph. You're much too substantial."

"Tell that to Pauley." She moved across the grove to

where Jonathan was standing. "He suddenly seems to think I've become an earth mother." She lifted the hem of her gold tissue gown to show him her bare feet. "And I haven't seen a pair of shoes all day. I think he has a foot fetish."

"Interesting thought." Jonathan's eyes twinkled as he took her arm. "I don't suppose you want to go for a walk, then? Can I get you anything to drink?"

She shook her head. "I just want to get this over with. I'll never complain about going on location for a movie again. At least the studios give me a stunt girl."

"He got some wonderful shots though. I think I like the one where you're kneeling by the stream in that gold gown best." He turned and smiled gently at her. "You did a fantastic job. You looked like a Joan of Arc who had found the Holy Grail."

His expression was so loving that suddenly all her annoyance and weariness started to melt away. "Did I? It's all a blur. I'm not sure I remember it." She started to reach out and take his hand and then stopped. The atmosphere here at Vasaro practically breathed of Utopia, and she had continually to remind herself the outside world was only a few miles away and any one of Pauley's crew could be tempted by the tabloids to bring that world down on them again. Her hand fell to her side without touching him. "I missed you this morning."

"I was on the phone with Interpol and then Peter and I had to go over some contracts that my office sent by courier yesterday. I have to pay some attention to my business."

"Not too much." Chelsea tried to smile. "You can let it slide a little, can't you? We may not have a chance like this again."

Jonathan's smile faded. "The hell we won't. We'll have a chance all the time when you marry me."

"No. You know I can't." She turned away and looked blindly at the group of people gathered around the trestle table. "I like your Peter. He's as nice as you said he was. Does he know about us?"

"I haven't said anything to him, but he knows me well enough to read me. He probably realizes I love you." He paused before adding deliberately, "And that you love me."

"I never said that," Chelsea said, her pace quickening. "I told you I didn't—" She broke off and moved toward the table. "It's time we got on with the shoot. Maybe I'll let Pauley make me a Nereid after all. What the hell? I've done everything else."

"When are you going to stop running, Chelsea?"

"I'm not running. I'm just doing my job." Chelsea glared defiantly at him over her shoulder. "This is a job I can do. The one you have in mind for me wouldn't suit me at all."

"It would suit you very well," Jonathan said quietly. "Try it. It's not as if—"

"I'm sorry to disturb you, Jonathan, but you've just received a telephone call. I think you'd better return it."

They both turned to see Peter strolling toward them through the grove.

Jonathan frowned impatiently. "Can't you handle it?"

"It's Al Jennings. He's calling from Cannes."

Jonathan stiffened and his gaze narrowed on Peter's face. "What in the hell is he doing there?"

"Well, I don't think it's a pleasure trip." Peter's gaze shifted uneasily to Chelsea. "He says he wants to meet with you at his hotel tomorrow afternoon."

Chelsea quickly hid the panic shooting through her

She should have known their time together was too good to last. "Then you'll have to go, won't you?"

"Not unless I wish to go." Jonathan's lips tightened. "I don't run when Al Jennings crooks his finger."

"Don't be stupid," Chelsea said bluntly. "I know who Jennings is. He's the good senator from South Carolina and he's grooming you for the nomination. Of course you have to go." She met his gaze directly. "And we both know why he's here. He's trying to save your political skin. He must have seen those pictures of us together at the party at Versailles when you introduced me as spokesperson. I should never have let you do it. Christ, I should have known better."

"The decision wasn't entirely your own," Jonathan said dryly. "You may believe you have to carry the burden in every relationship, but I did have something to say about it."

Peter was trying desperately not to make eye contact with either one of them. "Shall I tell him you're unavailable?"

"No." Jonathan held Chelsea's gaze. "Tell him I'll be glad to meet with him." He paused. "And so will Ms. Benedict."

"No!" Chelsea shook her head. "Leave me out of it, Jonathan."

"Why? Are you afraid you may be wrong about the party seeing you as a scarlet woman?"

"I'm not wrong." Her hands opened and closed nervously at her sides. "I just don't see what good it would do for me to go."

"Then go because I want you to go," Jonathan said softly. "And because if you don't go, I'll tell the honorable senator to go to hell."

He would do it. Chelsea felt helpless and exasperated. "What if there are reporters there?"

"Chelsea, for God's sake, you can't hide—" He turned to Peter. "Tell Jennings the only way we'll meet with him is if he can arrange that there be no possibility of any media present." He turned back to Chelsea. "Okay?"

She nodded slowly. "Okay."

Peter breathed a sigh of relief. "Right. I'll call him back." He whirled and the speed with which he moved through the grove resembled flight.

Chelsea straightened her shoulders with a touch of militancy, her hands smoothing the delicate golden folds of her gown. "I suppose I'd better climb Pauley's tree if we're going to get the shoot wrapped up this afternoon. Otherwise he'll raise hell if I leave tomorrow morning." She glanced at Jonathan and asked haltingly, "Will you be around?"

"I wouldn't miss it. It's not every day that I get to see you up a tree." Jonathan's lips were twitching. "I'll definitely be around."

For now. For today.

Chelsea didn't look at Jonathan again as she strolled beside him toward Pauley and the crew. Well, nothing lasted forever. She should be happy nothing had happened to disturb these last two weeks they'd had together.

She wasn't happy, dammit. She wanted more.

"You look very fierce. What are you thinking about?"

"An old nursery rhyme that fits me perfectly." She quoted softly, " 'Greedy eyes, greedy gut. Eat the whole world up.' Caitlin once said I was greedy. She was right." He opened his lips to speak, but she went on quickly. "I'll have to go down to the village and see

Marisa before I leave. I've scarcely had a chance to talk to her since I got here. She's looking well, isn't she?"

"Blooming." Jonathan frowned uncertainly. "She was very quiet when you introduced us. Do you think she likes me?"

Chelsea looked at him in astonishment. She had never heard Jonathan sound so insecure. "She's always quiet. Of course she likes you. Everyone likes you."

"She's not everyone, she's your daughter," Jonathan said. "And I hope she's going to be my daughter."

Chelsea started to protest but restrained herself. If their meeting with Jennings went as she thought it would, their time together might well be coming to a close, and she would be damned if she'd spoil it by arguing with him. Instead, she smiled and said, "Don't worry. Marisa likes you. What's not to like?"

"Your mother and Jonathan are going to Cannes tomorrow for a business meeting," Peter said. "And the film crew is leaving tonight for Nice to start editing the commercials. Soon we'll have the place to ourselves again."

"Good." Marisa slanted him a smile. "If you can rule out Katrine, Jacques, and the workers."

"You know what I mean."

"Yes, I know. You want to get back to your journals." Marisa leaned back against the bole of an olive tree, her gaze on the orange and gold wings of a butterfly hovering over a bed of purple violets. "Why are these journals so important to you, Peter? You said Caitlin wants to know about the inscription on the Wind Dancer, but what about you?"

Peter shut Catherine's brown leather journal and

turned to face her. "I don't know. I guess I've always felt close to the people who wrote them and—no, that's not true. From the moment I started reading Caterina's journal I've felt as if I were somehow part of their story." He made a face. "Since I came to Vasaro I've even started dreaming about them."

Marisa picked a blade of grass and put it between her lips. "What kind of dreams?"

"Not good."

"About the Wind Dancer?"

"Not really."

She shook her head. "Am I going to have to pry it out of you?"

She would do it too, he thought ruefully. She had evidently caught the hint of disturbance in his voice and would persist. He had learned that Marisa's serenity cloaked an inflexible determination where the well-being of the people she cared about was concerned. "About Paradignes."

"Who?"

"Don't you remember? I told you that Paradignes was the brother of the king of Troy who gave Andros the Wind Dancer and helped him escape from Troy before it fell."

"Oh, yes. He decided to stay and died when the Greeks invaded the city."

Peter nodded. "I've been dreaming about him."

"What kind of dreams?"

"Just what you'd expect of me. Crazy dreams. Paradignes is sitting in a big chair that looks like a throne. His head is resting on the high carved back and his eyes are closed. He's waiting for something."

"How do you know?"

"I *know*." He moved his shoulder helplessly. "I'm

looking at him and yet I feel I *am* him. I can feel his sadness, and his patience and his waiting."

"That doesn't sound like such a bad dream. Why should it frighten you?"

"Because I know he's going to open his eyes and look at me." Peter shook his head. "I told you the dreams were crazy."

Marisa threw away the blade of grass she had been nibbling and knelt in front of him. "Listen, you're having these wild dreams because you've been staring at Caterina's journal for the past four days. Why shouldn't you be dreaming about the Wind Dancer legends? And when you have this stupid dream again, remember that you and Paradignes are nothing alike. You would never have been caught sitting waiting for those Greeks to break in and kill you. You're too much of a fighter. You'd have gone with Andros or saved Troy single-handedly."

He chuckled. "I'm glad you have such confidence in me."

"It's true. Tonight, if Paradignes comes knocking, send him packing. He has nothing to do with you."

"Right." Everything Marisa said made perfect sense. He couldn't explain to her how the dreams made him feel. Standing there before the old man, waiting in terror for him to open his eyes, knowing it was coming, because in some incredible fashion he knew he was a part of that proud, sad Trojan.

Marisa was wrong about Paradignes and him being totally different. She didn't realize it was she who was the fighter and was trying to instill that quality in him through sheer force of will. He was much more prone to accept fate and make the best of it, as Paradignes had done.

And the two of them had one more thing in common that he would not mention to Marisa. The old man had been unable to flee or do battle because, like Peter, he, too, had an infirmity.

Paradignes had been a cripple.

"You're right, I'll shoo him on his way." Peter stood up and reached down to pull Marisa to her feet. "Come on. Drive into Grasse with me. I've got Caitlin's box packed and I want to send it off this afternoon."

She nodded and fell into step with him.

"Wait a minute." He stopped and moved a few paces away from her. "The sun is coming through the trees and forming a halo around your hair." He lifted the Nikon dangling from the strap around his neck and aimed it at her. "What a fantastic dappling effect. Almost angelic."

"You've taken hundreds of pictures of me," she protested. "And pictures are supposed to be true to life. I'm definitely no angel."

"I know." Like her mother, Marisa could be surprisingly earthy at times. "I want the picture anyway."

Not angelic. Grave and sweet and all that spoke of life in its most radiant hour.

Sunrise.

Marisa and Peter stopped at the geranium field on their way to the village to chat for a moment with Jacques.

"You've hired some new people," Marisa remarked as she looked down at the field from the vantage point on the hill where she stood with Peter and Jacques. "Did you need them? The geranium harvest is almost over."

Jacques shrugged. "Anise is too big with child to work in the fields now and Pierre had to go to Lyon and help his mother in her shop for a while. So I hired a couple of transients day before yesterday to replace them." He grimaced. "They won't last long. Neither of them likes getting their fingers dirty and their backsides sweaty."

"Why didn't you tell me? I can come down and help pick in the mornings." She turned to Peter, who was sighting his camera down at the field. "I'll see you at the perfumery tomorrow afternoon instead of morning."

"What?" His tone was absent as he clicked a few more pictures. "Okay. Fine."

"Did you hear me?"

"You're going to slave in the Elysian fields." He grimaced as he focused the camera on Jacques's strong, weather-lined face and snapped. "I wish I could help."

"Forget it. You have your own work to do." Marisa's gaze went to the two men working at the far end of the row. Jacques was probably right, she thought. Neither of the men was moving with the smooth, coordinated rhythm of the other workers in the field and were doing more laughing and talking than picking. The tall, sandy-haired boy looked English and was probably on holiday. The other man was older, perhaps in his early thirties, short, stocky, and dark-complexioned. "Well, I think I could probably do a better job than they're doing, Jacques. They certainly don't look like they're working up a sweat."

"I'll stir them up." Jacques's lips tightened grimly as he started down the hill. "They'll get sweaty whether they like it or not." He called, "Hey, Kembro, you think it's a garden party? We pick the flowers, not smell them."

The tall, sandy-haired boy looked up guiltily and then began to pick swiftly.

"You, too, Ferrazo," Jacques called to the older man. "You wanted the job. Now do it."

Ferrazo lifted his head to look at Jacques and his teeth bared in an easy smile. His gaze wandered to where Marisa and Peter stood on the hill. He appraised them at leisure before looking down on the orange-red geraniums.

Late that day Ledford received a call from Ferrazo at his apartment in Paris.

"I think someone took my picture today. That Maskovel guy who is staying in the village," Ferrazo said as soon as Ledford answered the phone. "I don't like it."

"Did he seem suspicious?"

"No, he's been taking pictures all over the place."

"Then don't worry about it." Ledford leaned back in his chair. "Is that all?"

Ferrazo continued belligerently. "No, I don't like sweating my ass off working in these fields and taking guff. I've been hanging around here for almost a week now. I didn't sign on with you to work at a farm."

"Only for a little longer. What's the Vasaro woman been doing since she got there?"

"She didn't get here."

Ledford slowly sat upright in his chair again as shock spread through him. "What do you mean, she didn't get there? She left the hotel four days ago and took the plane for Nice."

"Well, she didn't come here. Only the film crew and Maskovel and—"

"Why didn't you tell me she didn't come back to Vasaro?"

"I thought you knew." Ferrazo's tone was defensive. "You sent me here *in case* she came back to Vasaro."

Alex had sent for her to come to Istanbul to be with him. He had taken the initiative and managed to deceive both Ledford's people and Ledford himself. How he must be laughing at them all now. Ledford was suddenly spiraling back in time to that ignominious period at Langley, and rage spiked through him.

Then shock was replaced by pain so great, Ledford could scarcely think. He felt betrayed. How could Alex do this to him? He had let that whore come between them and their grand and splendid game. No wonder he had gone underground, and the Gypsy had not been able to find him after those first two days. He was probably balling the slut even now. Ledford had held his hand when he could have ordered Ferrazo to kill him, and this was how he had been repaid. He spoke through clenched teeth. "*Damn* your stupidity. I wanted to know *everything* about the woman."

"I ain't stupid. I didn't know you—should I stay here at Vasaro?"

"What?" Ledford tried to think through the haze of pain enveloping him. "Where are you calling from?"

"The pharmacy in the village."

"Give me the telephone number and stay there. I'll call you back."

Ledford took down the number and then hung up the receiver.

Caitlin Vasaro. He had seen newspaper photos of her at the party at Versailles but could recall only a vague impression of a tall woman with delicate facial features. She had been a mere pawn, but now she was assuming importance. She had not stayed cowering and afraid in her proper place after his warning. She, too, must have been aggressively involved in this deception. It was *her* fault. She had taken advantage of Alex's shocked state after Pavel's death to seduce him, to try to distract him from his inevitable confrontation with Brian. She was the one who had caused Alex to betray him.

He started to reach for the telephone but then let his hand drop away. Lock it away. Compartmentalize. First, he must get this business at the Louvre out of the way. He mustn't do anything impulsive when so much was at stake. Since Alex had come back into his life, he had noticed it was becoming difficult to shut away his feelings and he recognized the danger. Once he shut away emotion, he could see it was irrational to blame Alex for betraying him because he had not known what Brian planned for him if he met the test. This irrationality had almost destroyed him as a boy, but he now had it firmly under control.

He sat down in the chair beside the table and tried to clear his mind of all emotion. He must think coldly and concisely of how to show Alex he had won nothing by this deception and correct the wrong done him.

Alex was standing by the French doors and whirled to face Caitlin as she walked into the cottage. "Where the *hell* have you been?"

"Easy, Alex," Kemal said quietly as he rose from the couch.

Caitlin took one look at Alex's grim expression and was immediately on guard. She put down her notebook and purse on the table beside the door and removed her sunglasses. "The Archaeological Museum." She strode around the bar, opened the refrigerator, and took out a bottle of ginger ale. Ignoring Alex entirely, she said, "Hello, Kemal."

"Good afternoon, Caitlin." He beamed at her. "Did you have a pleasant day?"

"No, I've had one hell of a day. I have a headache, my neck feels like one big knot, and I'm dead tired." She poured the ginger ale into a glass and put the bottle back in the refrigerator. "And I don't feel like facing an inquisition."

"Too damn bad." Alex glared at her. "You leave here before I get up and don't come home until almost three in the afternoon and you don't expect me to question you?"

"You sound like a cross between a headmaster and an irate husband. Neither role becomes you."

"He was worried," Kemal said quickly. "He thought you were with me until I dropped in for lunch."

"You should have been with him," Alex said. "But no, you go wandering around Istanbul by yourself without telling anyone where—"

"I left a note."

"Which said only that you'd be back in a few hours."

"I didn't expect to be this long. I went to the museum and I didn't want anyone hovering over me while I was working." She lifted the glass to her lips and sipped the ginger ale. "Besides, Kemal would have been bored."

"With you? Never."

"Shut up, Kemal," Alex said.

Kemal nodded. "It seems the wise course." He sat down on a stool and leaned his elbows on the breakfast bar. "Proceed."

Caitlin went around the bar and sat down in the Queen Anne chair across from the couch. "I'm not going to make excuses, Alex. I can't let Ledford make me a prisoner. There's no reason for Ledford to suspect I didn't take that plane to Nice, and he clearly doesn't know we're here or he would have made a move by now. I wanted to go to the museum, and I went."

"Without protection."

"I went out three days in a row with Kemal and nothing happened."

"But who would dare bother you with a tiger like me to defend—" Kemal intercepted Alex's stare and shook his head. "I think it would be better if I left. It's very difficult for me not to participate, and I am confused about which side to take." He slipped from the stool and moved toward the door. "And, of course, whichever side I chose would surely win, so it would really not be fair." He opened the front door. "Sort it out. I will see you tomorrow."

Caitlin stared at the door after he had closed it and suddenly started to laugh. "He's impossible."

"They created the word for him." His attempt at a smile faded. "Kemal was right. I was worried. It was bad enough when you went out with him, but this was a hell of a lot worse. You're getting overconfident."

"Maybe." She leaned her head against the back of the chair. "I couldn't just sit here. I need to feel that I was *doing* something."

"And what did you do?"

"Looked at every tablet and wall with any script on exhibit in the whole museum. Then I talked to the curator, Monsieur Moduhl, and persuaded him to take me downstairs and let me go through the stored artifacts."

"No wonder you're tired."

"There were a few tablets that had markings similar to those on the Wind Dancer, but the Wind Dancer's script looks more Greek."

"Did you expect to find it there waiting for you?"

"No." She sipped the ginger ale and turned her head in a circle to try to ease the muscles. "When the Wind Dancer was made, there were so many widely separated lands and cultures that there must have been hundreds of splinter languages. Three of the tablets at the museum had never been deciphered. Rosetta Stones don't fall from every tree. I don't even know where to start."

"You've already started."

"I guess I have, haven't I? The process of elimination is never satisfying. I showed the curator the pictures of the inscription and he said the glyphs looked vaguely familiar."

"Lean your head forward." His voice was closer. He was standing directly behind her chair.

"What?"

He didn't wait for her to obey him. His hands were on her nape, his strong fingers massaging while his thumbs moved up and down her neck.

She stiffened, every muscle rigid.

"Stop it," he said roughly. "I'm only trying to help you. Close your eyes and relax." The pads of his thumbs sank deep into the tendons of her neck, and a delicious shiver went through her as she felt a tiny burst of tension release. She melted back against the cushions of the chair. "Did he say where he thought he had seen it?"

She closed her eyes and the isolating darkness made the pleasure he was bringing her so exquisitely intense, she had to gather her thoughts before she could remember what they had been talking about. "No, he said he'd think about it. I told him I'd check back with him tomorrow."

"You don't think you're pushing him a bit?"

"It's not pushing to remind him to think about it."

"And if he doesn't remember by tomorrow?"

"I'll call him the next day."

"And the next day and the day after that." He chuckled. "Tell me, does the poor man have an answering machine?"

"I wouldn't go that route again. I'm in the same city with Monsieur Moduhl."

"Allah help the man."

"That's not fair. I was never rude to Peter."

"Just persistent." His thumbs pressed into the muscles in her lower nape. "Next time you go to the museum, make sure you have either me or Kemal in tow."

His hands had fallen to her lower neck and clavicle and she felt almost dazed with pleasure as he dug and massaged and soothed the twisted muscles. Spurts of released pressure mixed with pain sent the blood coursing through her body and turned her weak. "I can concentrate better when I'm by myself."

"Not if you're dead."

The soft words jarred her but not enough to bring her out of the haze. The skin of her throat and shoulders was beginning to heat and tingle beneath his hands. Strange, even though her eyes were shut she could almost see his strong, tan fingers moving rhythmically, deeply, on her flesh. "I know there may be a threat . . . but it's not real. It's never been real to me. How can it be? It seems impossible someone I don't even know would want to kill me. None of it makes sense."

"Caitlin, dammit, don't be reckless and stupid about this. A target's most vulnerable when he feels he's safest. I've seen it all before. First comes the fear, then, when nothing happens for a while, boredom raises its head. Boredom breeds recklessness." Alex's voice was deep, soft, persuasive. She could smell the faint scent of his lime aftershave in the darkness. "I won't interfere. Just let me be there."

Her muscles were now loose, fluid, tingling, but she still didn't move. She wanted him to go on touching her and then—she pulled away from him and stood up with a jerky movement. Christ, how stupid could she get? She whirled to face him. "God, you're good, Alex."

His gaze was wary. "I suppose you're not referring to my ability as a masseur?"

"Give them what they want, and they'll do anything you want. Isn't that the way it goes?"

"Yes."

"You can't control me with sex any longer, Alex."

"I wasn't trying." He met her stare directly. "Not at first. I wanted only to help you."

"But you would have done it."

He smiled bitterly. "Oh, yes, I'd use sex to control you if it meant keeping you alive. I'd use anything I've got."

13

The car glided slowly across the Pont Royal. "I don't like it," Hans said, staring out onto the dark waters of the Seine. "You haven't assigned enough men for a job at the Louvre, and it's too soon after the cathedral."

"Three will be plenty." Ledford glanced at Hans. "We're going to blow it up, not steal the paintings."

"I thought you didn't like blowing up paintings and stuff."

"The Winged Victory is not stuff," Ledford said with a grimace. "I really must make some attempt at educating you."

A vast wave of relief rolled through Hans. Lately Brian had seemed impatient with him, as if he were tiring of the relationship. But if Brian said he'd try to make him smarter, it meant he still cared. There was hope. "I don't know about any of that stuff, but I could learn."

Brian reached out and gently caressed Hans's hair. Hans held himself very still, hiding the revulsion he felt. Brian was always touching Hans's hair, fooling with it, winding it around his fingers. God, he hated that long, soft hair. He hated how he looked in the mirror now. He *wasn't* what was in the mirror.

"We'll have to give you the chance," Brian said. "As soon as this job is over." He turned right and stopped by the Quai des Tuileries. "You have your knife? You'd better take out the guard at the gate quietly."

Hans nodded.

"You'll be fine once you're in the courtyard. I've taken care of the other guards."

"Bribes?"

Brian nodded. "Cordoza and Brenter will meet you by the glass pyramid in the Cour Napoleon. They're carrying the explosives. Set the timers for ten minutes so you can make it here to the car."

Hans nodded. "I know my job." He started to get out of the car.

"Wait." Brian's eyes were gleaming brilliantly in the darkness as he leaned over and gently touched Hans's cheek. "I wonder if you know how much I care about you?"

Hans felt a shiver of joy run through him as it always did when Brian touched him lovingly. Before Brian had come along, no one had ever caressed him or taken care of him or disciplined him. He hated the discipline, but Brian said it was needed, that he did it only because he loved him like a father would a son and punishment was a part of loving.

"Go on," Brian whispered, his hand falling away from Hans's cheek. "It's time for you to go."

"I'll see you." Hans jumped out of the car and moved jauntily down the street toward the main entrance.

The guard at the gate was standing with his back to the street, peering into the courtyard as if he had heard something. It was ridiculously easy for Hans to slip up behind him. He grasped the guard around the throat, covering his mouth with his left hand while his right hand, holding the fourteen-inch combat knife, dug up under the man's rib cage to pierce his heart. Hans grimaced distastefully as the guard's death released the usual foul smell of urine and waste.

He dragged the guard into the courtyard and out of sight and then walked to the glass pyramid.

Brenter and Cordoza were standing by the pyramid, and when they caught sight of Hans they moved toward him. Hans tensed as he saw Cordoza's strong, good-looking features and thick black hair shining with a high luster in the moonlight. He had seen Brian looking speculatively at Cordoza once or twice in the past few months. Greasy spic. He'd never liked spics. He just hoped the bastard had the timers. On the last job he'd forgotten two of them, and if Hans hadn't been able to rig a—

Half of Cordoza's face blew away.

Something dark and soft splattered on the glass of the pyramid.

Cordoza's brains.

Brenter screamed and dove to the ground. It was too late. The front of his black jacket blossomed with blood from another spray of bullets.

Christ, what was happening?

Hans threw himself to the side and reached inside his jacket for his knife as bullets blasted the wall next to him.

What had gone wrong? It was supposed to be fixed. Brian said it was fixed. . . .

"Sorry, my boy."

Hans turned on his side. Brian was standing in the moonlight with an Ingram MAC-10 submachine gun in his hands and a gentle smile on his lips.

"You said it was fixed," Hans said dazedly.

Brian nodded. "It was fixed. No guards. Just me."

"Why?"

"It was part of the deal. A few sacrificial lambs were required, and I felt obligated to do the butchering myself. After all, you are my men." Brian raised the Ingram and aimed it at Hans's head. Fear burst through him. He had just seen Cordoza's brains splatter onto the pyramid and knew what that gun could do. Brian hesitated, lowered the barrel of the gun, and sprayed a short burst of bullets into Hans's body.

Pain.

Hans cried out, slumped over, and lay still.

"It was only part of the deal, Hans," Brian said regretfully.

Hans lay motionless, biting his lower lip to keep back the screams of agony that would bring another round of bullets.

He heard the click of Brian's footsteps on the cobblestones as he walked toward the gate.

He was dying. Brian had killed him.

Hatred boiled acid-black inside him.

He was going to die because Brian had wanted that goddamn statue and made a deal to get it.

He *wouldn't* die.

He wasn't as smart as Brian, but he was younger and stronger.

And Brian wasn't so smart. He hadn't done the job right. The one inflexible rule was that you made sure of the hit, and Brian had broken the rule. Hans could have done it better. . . .

His hysterical laugh was almost a sob as he began crawling toward the gate. Anything for Brian. Let me do it, Brian. Let me kill myself for you. I can do it better.

He crawled slowly, painfully, feeling the blood gushing from his wounds onto the cobblestones of the courtyard. As soon as he got out of the courtyard, he'd stop the blood.

He'd get himself help.

He'd live, goddammit.

Because he couldn't die while Brian Ledford was still alive.

As usual, after Alex and Caitlin finished breakfast the next morning, Alex called the desk at the Hilton to retrieve his messages. There was only one message that had been left at eight forty-five that same morning.

Alex crashed down the receiver and turned to Caitlin. "Jackpot. A message from Irmak."

Caitlin looked at him, startled. "What was it?"

He looked down at the message he had scrawled on the pad beside the telephone. "'I have something for you. Come to Selim the Great's mosque at ten o'clock this morning.'"

"I'll get my purse."

"Hurry. We'll have to find a taxi, and there are over five hundred mosques in Istanbul."

Caitlin picked up her kidskin bag and slipped the strap over her shoulder. "No one knows that better than I do. Kemal must have taken me to every one of them," she said dryly. "And an amazing number appeared to house the remains of a personage who was either termed 'great' or 'magnificent.' We'll be lucky to find a taxi driver who can find the place."

Selim's mosque was on the other side of Istanbul, and it took Alex and Caitlin over an hour to reach it from the cottage. Irmak was waiting outside, looking ridiculously out of place in his robes among the crowd of tourists milling about. Irmak spotted Alex, and as he drew closer, Alex noticed his fat brown face was coated with a greasy sweat.

"Here it is." Irmak's hand was shaking as he handed Alex a slim white oblong box. "A gift."

Alex looked down at the box impatiently. "You can't bribe me, Irmak."

"It's not from me. It's from Ledford."

Alex felt a chill as he remembered a drift of blue cashmere lying coiled on the doorstep of the house in Paris. "Ledford? He's here?"

"I don't know," Irmak muttered. "I don't know anything. Leave me alone." He turned and started to waddle away.

"Wait," Alex called after him. "Where is—" He stopped.

Irmak was fading into the crowd. Impossible to get to him now.

Caitlin stared at the box with horrified fascination, and Alex knew she was remembering the scarf left before her own front door. "Open it," she said hoarsely.

He slipped off the ribbon and slowly opened the box.

Lying like an exquisite wax blossom on its bed of tissue paper was a single black tulip.

Alex picked up the card that lay tucked beside the tulip.

"What does it say?" Caitlin asked.

"It's not a note from Ledford," Alex said. "It's just one of those typed cards with a brief history of the tulip that usually accompanies bouquets sold to the tourists." He read it aloud to her. " 'Contrary to popular belief, the tulip did not originate in Holland but was brought from Turkey to the court of Louis XIV in France by the French ambassador to the Ottoman court. The flower flourished and the bulbs—' "

"No!"

Alex's gaze flew from the note to her face.

She was marble pale, her eyes glittering. "Don't you

see? Black is the color of mourning. A black blossom brought to *France*."

"My God," he whispered.

The box fell from his hands. The black tulip tumbled out in the street and was crushed under his shoe as he ran out into the street to hail a taxi to take them back to the cottage.

A black blossom brought to France.

Vasaro!

"It could be only a warning," Alex said as he dialed the number for Vasaro. "Everything could still be all right."

"There's no reason for him to hurt anyone at Vasaro." Caitlin sat down in the chair, every muscle rigid, staring at the phone. "It doesn't make sense."

"No, it doesn't. But I'll just get in touch with Jonathan and warn him to—"

"I'm sorry, monsieur, there's trouble on the line." The operator's voice was bored as it broke in. "Please place your call again."

"Trouble on the line," he told Caitlin. He spoke quickly into the receiver again. "There's a pharmacy in the village. I don't know the number. Try there."

"It will do no good. My board indicates a cable malfunction in the area. Please place your call again."

Panic tightened Alex's chest as he hung up the phone. The phone lines to Vasaro had been cut. The certainty was overpowering. God, he could almost visualize the glint of sunlight on the stainless steel of the wire cutter as the line had been severed.

"What's wrong?" Caitlin whispered, gazing at his expression.

Alex didn't look at her as he checked in his jacket

pocket for his passport. "Maybe nothing. But I'm going to Vasaro anyway."

"You go out in the street and hail a taxi." Caitlin picked up the receiver of the telephone. "I'll call and make reservations for us on the first flight to Nice."

"It could be a trap for you."

"And it could be a ploy to draw you away from me so that they can kill me here."

Alex had thought of that possibility too. Catch-22. He could get Kemal to protect her while he was gone, but he knew he would be frantic with worry all the time he was at Vasaro.

"I'm going, Alex." Caitlin's voice was trembling. "No one can stop me. It's Vasaro."

Alex nodded and headed for the door. Vasaro was the focal point of her existence, and he had no right to attempt to dissuade her. He could only try to protect her.

Jesus, he felt helpless. His only hope was Jonathan Andreas. Jonathan was sharp, alert, and knew the situation. Thank God Jonathan was still at Vasaro.

It took Jonathan and Chelsea three hours to travel from Vasaro to the vineyard in the hills where Jennings had arranged to have their meeting at the home of an old friend.

In appearance Albert Jennings's slightly rotund frame and plump face bore a genial resemblance to the cozy stereotype of the old family physician. The only feature belying that impression was the sleek perfection of his white hair, cut with such skill that every wave lay fastidiously in place. The standard politician's haircut, thought Chelsea as she followed Jennings and Jonathan out onto the veranda overlooking the vineyards.

On the long drive Albert Jennings had been affable

to Jonathan, scrupulously courteous to Chelsea, and never once indicated this meeting was anything more than a get-together of compatriots in a foreign country.

"Why don't you sit here, Ms. Benedict?" Jennings indicated a comfortably cushioned white filigreed Empress chair positioned for views of the verdant hills and terraced vineyards. He turned and looked out over the vineyard in the late afternoon sunlight. The vines were overflowing with dusky purple grapes. "It's the time of the vintage. Wonderful view. I was stationed in France during World War Two and I remember when I first came back here after the war I took one look at these hills and swore I'd retire somewhere in this province." He smiled. "But things change, don't they? Now I want to be near my grandchildren. You should understand that because you have a daughter."

Chelsea smiled tightly. "Yes, I have a daughter. Her name is Marisa."

Jonathan seated himself in the chair beside her, facing Jennings, silently aligning himself with her against the enemy. "A lovely girl, Al. You'd enjoy meeting her."

Jennings smiled warmly as he leaned back against the stone balustrade. "I'm sure any offspring of Ms. Benedict's couldn't help but be charming. The entire world pays tribute to the beauty and talent of Chelsea Benedict."

Chelsea's hands tightened on the metal arms of the chair. "Let's get to it, shall we? I don't have much patience for this kind of bull. You're here because of me, aren't you?"

Jennings's smile lost none of its wattage as he nodded. "We deemed it wise to have a small discussion with Jonathan regarding his association with you."

Chelsea glared at him defiantly. "We've been careful. We've been seen together only in connection with the Wind Dancer and the launching of the perfume."

"Back off, Al." Jonathan's quiet voice had a steely undercurrent. "This is none of your business."

"It *is* his business." Chelsea turned fiercely on Jonathan. "Of course it's his business. You're public property."

"The hell I am."

"Actually, when I arranged this trip it was merely to issue a warning regarding any future involvement," Jennings said. "You're right, you've behaved with exemplary discretion, Ms. Benedict."

"We're going to be married, Al," Jonathan said.

"No!" Chelsea's voice was sharp, and she tried to temper it as she turned to Jennings. "Tell him. What the hell are you waiting for?"

For a moment a flicker of genuine sympathy transformed the smooth urbanity of Jennings's expression as he looked at her. "You realize this isn't a duty I'd choose to accept. Personally, I admire you tremendously."

"Tell him."

Jennings turned to Jonathan. "It won't do, Jonathan. Divorce, jail, the ugliness of the court case. She'd ruin your chances with the voters. There's no way we can promise you the nomination if you marry her."

"Yet you 'admire her tremendously,'" Jonathan said bitterly. "Are you aware that she got her GED in that jail cell and when she got out she worked until she received a bachelor of arts degree at Columbia? That she speaks four languages?" Jennings started to say something, but Jonathan gave him no opportunity. "And that she's chairperson for Safe Houses for Abused Children, gave five hundred thousand dollars last year to MADD, made four commercials and toured twenty-three cities in the campaign to solve the literacy problem in the United States?"

Chelsea looked at him, startled. She hadn't realized Jonathan knew that much about her life away from him.

Jonathan glanced at her face and smiled faintly. "Sorry to blow that rough-diamond image you're always trying to foist on me, but did you really think I wouldn't want to know all about the woman I love?" His smile faded as he turned back to Jennings. "And besides, it always pays to have ammunition when the shooting starts."

Jennings shook his head. "Every political campaign has to be aimed at the lowest common denominator of the population. There's a hell of a lot of prejudice running rampant out there, and it would show up at the polls." Jennings met Jonathan's gaze directly. "Even if we could overcome the stigma of that court case, there's still her public image to contend with. She may be as charitable as Mother Teresa, but she's still bawdy, impulsive, and says exactly what she thinks." He held up his hand as Jonathan opened his lips to protest. "I agree that last quality is one to be admired, but not in a first lady. Diplomacy is the name of the game."

"Are you finished?" Jonathan asked.

Jennings nodded.

Jonathan got to his feet. "Go to hell." He turned to Chelsea. "We're finished here."

"No, we're not." Chelsea jerked her thumb at the French doors. "Take a walk, Jennings. I'll handle this."

Jennings hesitated and then straightened away from the balustrade. "We want only the best for him. It's the right thing to do."

"I know it is," Chelsea said. "It's going to be fine. Just leave us alone."

Jennings nodded and moved toward the French doors across the veranda. "I'll tell Paul to delay tea."

Jonathan waited until the doors closed behind Jennings and then said with great precision, "No, Chelsea."

"Don't tell me no." Chelsea jumped to her feet and moved to look out over the vineyards. "You don't have anything to say about this. We're not going to see each other again until after you receive the nomination."

Jonathan was incredulous. "Jennings is wrong. The voters would accept you."

"Because you do? If the majority of the population consisted of an army of Jonathan Andreases, maybe we'd have a chance. But it doesn't. What did Jennings say? The lowest common denominator?"

"It appears I have more respect for the voters than either of you do," Jonathan said quietly. "I believe they respect intelligence and personal integrity more than a holier-than-thou pristine facade."

"You can't risk it."

"It's my career, Chelsea."

"And I won't ruin it." Chelsea's eyes were blazing as she turned to face him, her voice uneven. "So listen to me. This is what we're going to do. We separate and don't see each other again until the night of the launch of the perfume, then we go our own ways until after you win the nomination."

"Bullshit."

She ignored him. "When you're nominated we'll be seeing each other in public and legitimately because I'll be working on your campaign. After you become president it will be safe for you to—"

"Make you my mistress and sneak you up the back stairs of the White House," Jonathan finished for her. "Sorry, love, I find that totally unacceptable."

"It's all we're going to have," she said flatly. "I'm serious about this, Jonathan. I've never seen myself as a femme fatale, and I refuse to be the kind of vamp men deep-six their ambitions for. If you don't agree to my terms, I'll never see you again."

Jonathan gazed intently at her. "You're bluffing."

"I'm not a master negotiator like you, Jonathan. I don't know anything about bluffing. I have only one weapon, and I'm going to use it. If you want us to have anything together, you'll take your shot."

A flicker of anger crossed his face. "I don't like this, Chelsea."

"Do you feel emasculated because I won't let you play the big, noble hero?" Chelsea scoffed. "Too bad. That's not the way the world works any longer."

"You're trying to make me angry."

She turned away. "Maybe I am. That would be one solution."

"The wrong solution. I'm going to tell Jennings I'm not going to run."

"It will be only a waste of time to withdraw from this campaign. In five years, perhaps even less, you'll realize what we had is over and you'll run for office then. Because you *want* it, Jonathan." She met his gaze bleakly. "You know I keep my promises. Make me the bad guy and I won't see you again."

He looked at her a long time. "Christ, you're tough."

"You bet I am." She turned away from the balustrade. "Now, let's tell Jennings he doesn't have to worry about me any longer."

"No."

"Then I'll tell him myself." Chelsea moved toward the French doors. "And then I'll inform him in my impulsive, bawdy fashion that he can screw his tea party and take us back to the hotel in Cannes."

"He hurt you."

"Hell no. I know what I am."

"I don't think you do."

"Well, I know what we are." She opened the door and smiled bitterly over her shoulder. "We're history,

Jonathan." She added, "Until *you* become history, Mr. President."

He started after her across the veranda. "I'm not going to let you do this, you know. I'll find a way to block you."

That was the possibility that terrified her. Jonathan could be just as stubborn as she, and he had proved his brilliance and innovativeness time after time over the years. He had never turned that acumen in her direction, but she had no doubt he'd be a formidable adversary. She wanted desperately to keep the fragile contact she had suggested to Jonathan. Dear God, she hoped he wouldn't push her toward the final break.

"Don't do it," she said huskily as she walked quickly into the house. "For God's sake, don't do it, Jonathan."

Two hours after Caitlin and Alex left the cottage they were on an Air France plane bound for Nice. As the plane taxied down the runway, Alex saw the headlines in the newspaper the stewardess had handed him:

KRAKOW'S ANTITERRORIST TEAM BATTLE BLACK MEDINA AT LOUVRE

Caitlin's eyes were wide with fear as they met his own. "It happened only last night. The Black Medina has never struck twice in the same week. Maybe that flower *was* just a warning." Her hands nervously clasped and unclasped the arms of her seat. "Maybe it was some kind of macabre joke."

Alex's hand covered Caitlin's. For a moment he thought she would pull away. Then, slowly, her hand turned and held tight to his own. For the first time since he had told her how he had deceived her, she had voluntarily touched him.

He mustn't read anything into it. She would probably

have reached out to Satan himself at that moment. He gave her hand a squeeze, trying to impart warmth, comfort, anything to help her while he glanced down at the newspaper.

Above the story was a picture of a smiling Krakow fighting his way toward the gateway to the Louvre through a crowd numbering in the hundreds. Alex smiled cynically as he saw the glazed expressions on the faces of the people in that crowd, the way they reached out to touch Krakow as if he were some kind of saint. Well, why not? He had kept his promise. The great hero had brought down, if not the entire Black Medina, at least the dangerous segment that had destroyed their beloved Saint-Antoine's.

He was the savior. All he had to do was reach out and they'd give him anything he wanted.

A crown lies in the gutter, one need only stoop and pick it up.

Who had said those words? Oh, yes, they were attributed to Napoleon during the—

"*My God!*" He went rigid, his grasp tightened on the paper. Caitlin's gaze flew to his face. "What's wrong?"

"Ledford said his partner wanted to be Napoleon."

"So?"

"It's not Dalpré, it's Krakow who wants to be Napoleon."

"*Krakow* is Ledford's partner?"

"I guessed wrong and it amused Ledford to let me wander down a blind alley. He even supplied me with bits of motivation and pieces of half-truths to authenticate it."

Alex quickly scanned the story as the jet became airborne. Krakow's team hadn't captured the terrorists, they'd only blown them away. According to the article, the terrorists had killed a guard in an attempt to destroy the Louvre as they had Saint-Antoine's the previous week. Krakow's team had been patrolling the Louvre to prevent just such a tragedy from occurring and had stopped the three terrorists before they could plant the explosives. Unfortunately, they had resisted arrest and two of the three perpetrators had been killed in the resulting gun battle. The third had escaped but had been wounded and was expected to be apprehended in the next few days.

Caitlin was leaning forward to read over his shoulder. "But it doesn't make sense. Krakow is—it's not possible." She gestured at the paper. "His people just killed two of the terrorists."

"Which automatically puts him above suspicion, elevates him to enormous popularity, and places him squarely in position to make the next move."

"What move?"

"My guess is that he'll use this attack on the Louvre to motivate a 'reluctant' change of his position in the Consolidation for a United Europe and accept that some central form of government is needed to control the terrorists." He paused. "With himself at its head."

"It's all guesswork. You can't be sure of that."

"No, I can't be sure." But it felt right, as if a missing puzzle piece has slipped smoothly into place. "We'll have to wait and see."

"Krakow's a childhood hero of my mother's. She thought he would make everything..." Caitlin trailed off and looked blindly out the window. "God help us all."

Katrine sat at the kitchen table, her hands cradling the cup of freshly brewed espresso she had just finished preparing. She had made enough for Peter and Marisa, who often walked over from the village to chat with her in the evening, but they hadn't arrived yet.

She frowned critically down at her delicate fingers gripping the cup. This fingernail polish had a trifle too much beige for her fair complexion. After Peter and Marisa left for the evening she would go upstairs, remove it, and put on that lovely pink polish she had bought in Cannes the previous week. Nothing made a woman feel more feminine than pretty nails. She shuddered to think of Caitlin's close-clipped, unpolished nails. Caitlin really had nicer hands than her own, and Katrine had always tried to persuade her there must be some way for her to work in the fields and still maintain—

Lights in the sky.

Katrine set her coffee cup down on the table, her gaze on the window over the sink. How peculiar. She pushed back her chair and wandered over to the sink, her gaze on the two strong beams on the horizon, piercing downward like giant stilts. The beams looked a little like the searchlights one could see lighting the sky during the Cannes Film Festival. Denis had once taken her to Cannes during the festival and it had been very exciting. All those fast cars, glittering jewels, and famous faces. Denis had looked so handsome in his tuxedo, and she had felt very sophisticated and glamorous herself.

She frowned as she suddenly realized the lights couldn't be from Cannes when one had to go over the hills to the cliff to catch sight of Cannes from Vasaro.

"Madame Vasaro."

She jumped and looked over her shoulder to see a small, stocky man in denims and a frayed blue work shirt standing in the doorway. One of the new workers, she recognized. The Italian, Ferneo or Ferrazo or something. "You startled me. I didn't hear you knock."

He smiled at her and she saw a dull metallic glitter as
e moved his hand from its half-hidden position behind
im. A flashlight?

"I was just looking at those strange lights. Did
acques send—"

She never finished the sentence.

Peter and Marisa had reached the crest of the hill lead-
ng to Vasaro, when Peter saw the helicopter land on the
awn in front of the manor house. A stream of men wear-
ng dark clothing and ski masks poured from the craft's
epths like a Delta Force attacking an enemy outpost.

"What is it?" Marisa's hand clutched his arm. "What
o they want?"

"I don't know." But he was afraid he did know.

A flash of fire streaked across the rose field, and the
ushes burst into flames.

"Flamethrowers. My God, they're torching the fields!"

Peter could see the men from the helicopter spread-
ng out in all directions, the flamethrowers like fiery
cepters spreading destruction wherever they touched.

"Marisa, did you see—" Renée came running up the
oad from the village behind them. She stopped short,
er voice dying to a whisper. "Mother of God, the fields.
Ve have to save the fields."

"Stay where you are." Peter grabbed Marisa's hand.
Tell everyone to stay in the village and not go near—"

An explosion rocked the ground, and Peter instinc-
ively pushed both women to the dirt. His heart was
ounding, hurting. Don't die, you son of a bitch. Now
vould be a fine time to die, when Marisa needed him.
Another explosion and then another. The outbuildings
vere being blown up one by one, stone and wood and
ebris blown to the heavens.

"Katrine," Marisa whispered. "Where's Katrine?"

"I'll go after—" Peter raised his head from the dir
just as a glare lit the already-flaming landscape.

Vasaro's manor house that had stood for over fou
hundred years suddenly exploded in a flash of light.

Marisa was on her feet and running down the hill to
ward Vasaro. "Katrine!"

Nightmare. Peter saw Marisa's slim form outline
like a paper doll against the fire-engulfed landscape. Hi
heart pounded wildly, painfully, as he ran after her.

She was falling!

He hadn't heard the bullet, but he could see the dar
red splotch on her white shirt as her body twisted an
fell.

Oh, God, not Marisa.

Not Marisa.

Not Marisa.

She was alive, moving, trying to crawl to the side o
the road.

A squat, muscular man whose face was vaguely fa
miliar was running toward Marisa, a gun extended be
fore him.

"Don't!" Peter felt as if he were moving in slow mo
tion. He wouldn't get there in time. Marisa would die.

Peter hurled himself on top of Marisa's body.

He jerked as pain exploded inside him. Once. Twice
Three times.

"Lie still," he muttered to Marisa. Something warn
and salty filled his mouth. "Let him think we're—"

He stopped and lay limp and still.

No more shots. Maybe he had gone away. Mayb
Marisa was safe.

He was dying. Funny, to think how careful he had al
ways been. Proper rest, proper exercise, no stress, s
that his heart wouldn't give out on him. All for nothing

"Peter," Marisa whispered. She was scooting slowly, painfully, from beneath his body. "The man's gone."

She was covered with blood, but he didn't know how much was hers and how much was his own. He should try to help her, bandage her, but he couldn't seem to reach out to her. Renée had been on the hill. . . .

"Renée . . . get to . . . Renée."

She didn't move other than to draw closer to him. She wanted to help him.

"No . . . *live*," he muttered.

"We'll both live." Her hand reached out and tightly gripped his own, her eyes glittering brightly in the glare of the fire. "Fight."

It was too late. Marisa didn't understand. She was a warrior, like Andros, and warriors never fully understood. But they didn't have to understand. It was the warrior's duty only to protect and guard the Wind Dancer.

The Wind Dancer? Where had that thought come from?

Peter could feel the pain growing, exploding in his chest. He felt a moment of violent rejection. "Marisa!"

"I'm here."

He didn't want to leave Marisa.

And he was afraid.

Marisa was trying to sit up, fumbling at the buttons of his shirt.

The pain was worse and the fear was growing greater. He had to find a way to shut away the fear.

He gazed up into Marisa's eyes staring into his own with compassion and understanding. Beautiful, sad emerald eyes. No, that was the Wind Dancer again. But suddenly the two seemed to merge and become one, reaching out to him. His fear eased.

A dominion without end, limitless flight, clouds lined with golden light.

And more.

Paradignes. The old man sitting with eyes closed in his high-backed throne chair.

Paradignes's eyes were opening, and the old man was looking at him. Why hadn't Peter understood before?

And he was no longer afraid.

Vasaro was burning!

Caitlin stared in disbelief as the two-seater rental car rounded the curve in the road.

Fields, groves, vineyards—all were being devoured by flame. Great curling clouds of black smoke rose to the sky.

"No!" She didn't notice the raw scream that tore from her throat. "It's not happening!"

Alex jammed on the accelerator and tore down the road.

"Alex..." They rounded the curve to see the manor house engulfed in fire. The north side of the stone house had been blown away, and all that remained was a broken shell that reminded Caitlin of pictures she had seen of London during the blitz. Flame licked out of the upper windows like obscene tongues. "My mother."

"I know. I'm hurrying." The tops of the lemon and lime trees had caught fire, forming an arch of flame as Alex gunned the sports car up the curving driveway.

"Mother." Caitlin fumbled at the handle of the door as soon as the car stopped. "Mother's in that house."

"Stay here out of the smoke. I'll get her." Alex jumped out of the car, tore up the steps, and threw open the front door.

Death. Death was all around her. Vasaro was dying. The house was dying and death was still in that house, waiting for Alex. And he expected her to stay outside and *wait*?

Caitlin flung open the car door. Heat and smoke blasted her lungs and flesh as she ran up the steps into the foyer. The smoke stung her eyes, seared her lungs. "Alex!"

"Get out of here." Alex's voice from the back of the house. "I'm coming."

She stood in the hall, watching the flames march down the staircase from the second floor, devouring the Aubusson runner step by step with monstrous ferocity.

Alex ran down the hall from the kitchen. The smoke was denser and Caitlin could only dimly see Alex's strained face. Then she noticed Katrine's slim body in his arms and she felt a profound rush of relief. Her mother must be unconscious from the smoke, but at least the flames hadn't touched her.

"Get in the car and head for the village," Alex said hoarsely as he carried Katrine down the steps. "I'll carry her across the lawn down to the road."

Caitlin shook her head as she stood on tiptoe to look over his shoulder to see her mother's face. Alex was holding Katrine at an angle, half hiding her in the curve of his arms. "We'll take her in the car. We have to get her to the doctor. The smoke..." Caitlin took a step closer. "We don't have time to—" She stopped as she saw what Alex had been trying to hide from her.

A small, bloody hole the width of her index finger punctured Katrine's delicate temple.

Caitlin's gaze lifted to Alex's pale face. "Alex."

"She's dead," Alex said.

"She can't be dead." Didn't he see that Katrine was just the same? Her lipstick was as fresh as if she had just put it on, and the nails of the hand hanging limp at her side were lacquered a frosted mocha shade. Caitlin took a step closer and touched Katrine's beautifully coiffed hair. Not one hair out of place. Just the same as always. "Mother?"

"Caitlin." Alex's voice was raw with agony.

"Mother?"

"We have to get out of here," Alex said. "The fire . . ."

Fire. Death. Katrine. Vasaro.

Alex. But Alex wasn't there in the fire. Alex wasn't dead. She had to get him away from Vasaro before death took him too.

She instinctively stumbled toward the Lamborghini in the driveway. Burning branches from the trees lining the driveway had fallen on the roof, and the white paint had melted into ugly splotches wherever they touched. What a pity, she thought numbly, Katrine would be upset. She loved the Lamborghini and took such pleasure in driving it.

Caitlin opened the passenger door and collapsed on the passenger seat.

"No." Alex was beside her, his face contorted. "You'll have to drive. I'll carry her down to the road."

Then she understood what he was saying. This car was a two-seater, and so was the sports car they had rented at the airport to get them to Vasaro with all possible speed. There was no room for Katrine.

No room anywhere in the world for Katrine any longer.

She held out her arms. "I'll hold her. She doesn't weigh much."

Alex hesitated.

"Give her to me." Caitlin's tone was suddenly fierce. "I'm strong. I can hold her."

Alex's eyes were bright in his soot-stained face. "Yes, I know you're strong." Alex carefully laid Katrine's small body across Caitlin's lap, slammed the door shut, and ran around to the driver's seat.

Pain tore through Caitlin, blood bright, piercing to

the depths of her as she saw the ragged bullet hole at close range.

She reached out with a shaking hand and covered the ugly hole in Katrine's temple with a silky strand of hair. Katrine would hate that ugliness to show.

"All right?" Alex asked as he started the car.

She didn't hear him. Mother and child. When she was a baby, Katrine must have cradled Caitlin in just this protective way before her father had lured her away from Caitlin and Vasaro. Now the roles were reversed and she must hold and protect her mother on this last journey from her home.

She cradled Katrine lovingly in her arms as Alex raced beneath the gauntlet of burning trees toward the road leading to the village.

Fire!

The flames were licking at her, devouring her. She couldn't breathe.

Katrine!

Caitlin sat bolt upright, struggling to get away, struggling to get Katrine away before—

"Easy." Alex was sitting beside the bed, and his hand grabbed her own as he tried to keep her from throwing off the covers. He smelled of smoke, dark circles imprinted the flesh beneath his eyes, and he looked more haggard than she had ever seen him. "You're safe. You're at Renée's house in the village."

She looked around dazedly, realizing she knew the room. The big double bed, the pale pink flowered wallpaper. She had given Renée the ivory and gold crucifix that hung on the wall across the room for a wedding present when she had married her Pierre.

Memories flooded back to her, and she closed her eyes to shut them out. Safe. Perhaps she was safe, but nothing else in the world was either safe or sure any longer.

"My mother..."

"Don't you remember? They've taken her to Grasse. I didn't think you knew what was happening after we got here."

She had a vague memory of arriving at Renée's house, of Marisa gently washing her and putting her to bed, but nothing else.

She opened her eyes. "This is Renée and Pierre's bed. I shouldn't be here."

"They don't need it. They're out in the fields with the rest of the workers. Jacques is trying to salvage slips and cuttings from all the fields."

She doubted if anything could be saved. She shuddered as she remembered the blazing inferno of those fields. "Why did it happen? My mother never hurt anyone. Vasaro..."

"I—don't know." Alex spoke haltingly. "They came by helicopter. Jacques said it was like a commando attack. They knew exactly where they were going and what they were going to do. Jacques saw one of the transient workers jump into the helicopter just before it took off, and the police think he cut the telephone lines and set it up."

"Who was he?"

"An Italian. Ferrazo." He paused. "He killed Peter Maskovel too. Marisa was shot twice, but they think she'll make it."

"My God." Horror upon horror. She was silent a moment, trying to take it all in. "It was just to show us they could hurt me, wasn't it? All of this, just to hurt me."

Alex's hand tightened on hers. "Go back to sleep."

She shook her head. "Dreams . . ."

"I know."

He did understand, she realized dimly. She could see it in his expression. He knew the fear of closing his eyes and seeing horrors of the past.

"Okay, don't sleep. Just rest." He scooped her up in his arms and leaned back in the chair, cradling her.

His white shirt had a three-cornered tear at the shoulder, and the scent of smoke was stronger now that she was nearer him. "Your clothes . . . smoke."

He went still. "I haven't gotten cleaned up yet. I didn't want to leave you. I forgot it might remind you of—"

"It doesn't bother me. I can't hide from it." On a subliminal plane it even brought her solace to know what Alex had risked to help her. She nestled her cheek deeper into the hollow of his shoulder. "If I'm too heavy, tell me. I know I'm no lightweight."

"You're not heavy," Alex said thickly.

She felt heavy inside, so weighed down and full of tears, she could scarcely breathe. "I loved her. I always loved her."

Alex was silent. He began to stroke her hair.

"But I didn't know her. Not really. I was always too busy to talk to her. . . ." Her slim hand nervously gripped a fold of his shirt. "I wish I'd taken the time. I'll never get the chance now."

"Everyone always feels like that when a loved one dies. We all make mistakes. We just have to accept it."

"Yes." She didn't speak for a moment. "Why did they shoot her, Alex? Is it my fault?"

"No."

Her voice shook with anguish. "It doesn't make sense. None of it makes sense."

"No, it doesn't." His voice broke on the last word, and his arms tightened around her. "We'll talk about it later. Don't think about it now."

"Thank you for being so nice to me."

His laugh held a hint of harsh desperation. "Nice? My God!"

She closed her eyes. "You're kinder than you think you are."

"Tell me that later."

"I will. Kindness is important. You said that once, didn't you?"

"Yes."

"Your voice sounds funny."

"Because you're killing me."

It was odd, but at that moment of tragedy all the hurt and bitterness she had felt toward Alex had come crashing down. They were united in pain, bound together by a common guilt and sorrow. All that was important was the comfort he was giving her and the knowledge that he, too, had been fond of Katrine. Her arms tightened instinctively around him, trying to offer him the same comfort he was bringing to her. "I'm sorry."

He buried his face in her hair. "Don't talk anymore. Just try to rest."

She lay silent, letting his warm strength flow through her, until gradually it brought a peaceful numbness in its wake. "Alex?"

"Yes."

"Do you know, at times I actually thought I loved you."

He stiffened against her. "No, don't say that. You'll regret it later."

"I couldn't think of any other reason that I was hurting so." It was easy to admit to herself what she had fought so long to ignore, to speak the unspeakable now, when she was wrapped in this blanket of numbness and it didn't matter any longer. "I'm sorry. I didn't mean to embarrass you."

"You're not embarrassing me," he said thickly.

"That's good. I was probably wrong anyway. We both know it doesn't really exist...." She kept her eyes tightly closed, shutting out the world, but she could still smell the smoke clinging to Alex, clinging to everything around her.

Was Vasaro still burning?

14

"How do you feel?" Chelsea gently touched Caitlin's arm as they turned away from the grave. "Is there anything I can do to help?"

"No." Caitlin looked back at the coffin that had been lowered into the grave. "There's nothing anyone can do. She's gone. It's all gone." Her gaze wandered around the familiar faces gathered around the grave site; Jacques, Pierre, Renée, most of the other workers, a few of Katrine's friends from Nice. Jonathan Andreas had not been able to attend the funeral, as he had accompanied Peter Maskovel's body home to West Virginia for burial. Alex had been there earlier, but she didn't see him now. She quickly suppressed the remote pang of loneliness assaulting her at his absence.

Alex had taken care of all the funeral arrangements, fended off the reporters, police, Interpol, and government officials. He had held her when she woke screaming those first nights and kept the pain at bay until she went back to sleep. Thank God this blessed numbness had formed around her emotions after that initial nightmare period. Now she needed nothing and no one to help her. "Thank you for sending me this dress and for keeping those television cameras out of the cemetery."

"I'll take credit for the dress, but Alex handled the newsmen." Chelsea paused. "And Dalpré. I don't know how he managed to keep the ice man off you. He's certainly been plaguing the rest of us."

Alex again. Caring for her needs, making the way smooth for her. She knew she should feel gratitude, but nothing could get through this numb, icy wall that had formed around her.

"He thinks it's Krakow who's Ledford's partner, not Dalpré."

"I know. He told Jonathan. It's a pretty wild guess, and he could be wrong." Chelsea grimaced. "I hope he is. I could enjoy hating Dalpré's guts." She linked her arm through Caitlin's, pushing her gently away from the grave toward the ornamental gates at the entrance of the cemetery. "I have to get back to the hospital. Are you going to be all right?"

Caitlin nodded.

Chelsea frowned. "No, really. As soon as Marisa can leave the hospital, I'm going to send her back to Los Angeles. My place there has top-notch security. Why don't you go with her and stay until time for the launch?"

The launch. Chelsea was speaking of the perfume launch as if nothing had changed. Caitlin would have to talk to them about the perfume, but she couldn't face it now. "That's kind of you." It *was* kind, and for a moment she wished she could feel something besides this icy hollowness. "But it won't work. I have to—have to go back to Vasaro."

Chelsea shook her head. "For God's sake, Caitlin, you're almost in shock. You're in no shape to face—"

"I'm going. Will you drive me there before you go to the hospital?"

Chelsea hesitated and then shrugged. "Sure. Why not? This day can't get much worse."

Caitlin stood on the hill, her back to the ruin of the manor house, looking out over the blackened fields.

The trees of the olive and orange groves were only scorched, twisted skeletons. She had seen it all before in the last few days, but then she had hastily averted her eyes to keep the waves of sickness at bay.

She stood with her back straight, facing it, drinking it in, absorbing the pain, letting it fuel her cold rage and determination.

"You shouldn't be here." Alex came to her side. "Haven't you had enough? You've been to one funeral today."

"I needed to see it." Caitlin didn't take her eyes off the dark fields. "You're right, it's like the death of my child. No one has the right to do this...this... ugliness."

"It can be an ugly world."

"I didn't think so." Caitlin shook her head. "I always thought there were things we could do to keep bad things from happening. I was wrong."

Alex took a step closer, reaching out in comfort. "Caitlin, it's not the end of—"

"Don't touch me."

His hand fell to his side. "Okay. I understand."

"No, you don't." He thought she blamed him for this atrocity, but she had no blame for anyone but herself. The reason she could not let him touch her was the danger he held for her. In the past he had possessed more power than anyone she had ever met to make her *feel*, and emotion was a threat to the barrier she had erected against the pain. She flung her hand out to encompass the ruin before them. "Do you understand how I feel about this? Before Ledford did this, all I wanted was to get the Wind Dancer back for Jonathan, but now I want him punished. I want them all punished."

"You told me once you didn't believe in revenge."

"And you said I hadn't been hurt enough. Tell me, Alex, have I been hurt enough now?"

"Yes." He waited. Finally, he asked, "What now?"

"We go back to Istanbul. Did you think I'd give up? What else is there for me now? I was always so bitter that my mother had let my father hurt Vasaro." She laughed, incredulous. "But I did it myself. I could have made one phone call to Jonathan and stopped this from happening. But I was so stupid I—" Her voice broke and she had to stop.

"It wasn't your fault. It was mine." Alex's light eyes glittered in his strained face. "It all went wrong. Don't do this. Christ, I don't want you hurt anymore."

"Should I just let it go? Should I just sit here and look out at those fields? My mother's dead, Vasaro's dead, and thirteen months from now my perfume will be dead."

"I can't do anything about Katrine's death, but we can work something out about the rest."

"What? Are you going to import blossoms from other farms? With all the research you did you should know that won't work. The flowers have to be grown here in Vasaro earth to retain the true integrity of the scent. Look at that earth, Alex. It looks as if it were struck by a hydrogen bomb."

"Jacques said he managed to collect slips and cuttings from most of the plants. Let me think about it. I tell you, we can—"

"No!" She couldn't bear to talk about it. She turned on her heel and strode across the scorched lawn toward the car parked in the driveway. She could vaguely sense his pain and frustration, but she refused to let it touch her. She couldn't let anything behind this icy wall or she might shatter. The wall must grow harder, taller, closing out the pain.

"Okay, you win, dammit." He grasped her arm and turned her around to face him. "I want to show you something. A roll of film was found with Peter's effects. Jonathan had it developed." He reached into the inside pocket of his jacket and drew out a photograph. "The small, squat man working in the field is Antonio Ferrazo. Look at him. Memorize his face. He killed your mother and Peter. He'll kill you if he gets the chance."

Caitlin looked down at the photograph. The man in the picture was smiling, and yet a day later he had helped bring down this devastation on Vasaro.

Alex thrust another picture at her. "And this is Ledford."

She stared down at the blunt, ruddy face in the creased, dog-eared snapshot for a long time. "They both look so . . . ordinary." She tucked the photographs in her purse. "Don't worry, I'll remember them."

"You'd better."

"What about Krakow?"

"I called Goldbaum and told him to double the surveillance on him." He fell into step with her. "I've made arrangements to leave Nice today. I didn't think I could persuade you to leave it alone." His expression grew suddenly intent, as it always did when he was shuffling problems and possibilities. How well she knew that expression. Now that the decision was made, it was clear every effort was to be focused on methods to solve the problems it produced. "I've hired a jet to take us to a private landing field outside Istanbul. We'll take a taxi to the covered bazaar and I'll leave you there with

Kemal while I scout around the cottage and make sure it's still safe."

She nodded agreement.

"We'll stop at the village on the way to Nice and talk to Jacques about handling the insurance people." He met her gaze as he opened the passenger door for her. "Jesus, I'm scared. Change your mind. I can send you to Port Andreas, where Jonathan can keep you safe. Don't go back, Caitlin."

She didn't answer as she got in the car.

He swore as he slammed the car door.

"This is Ferrazo. I'm at the Hotel Divan in Istanbul."

"I don't give a damn where you are. Where are Karazov and the Vasaro woman?" Ledford asked.

"I can't find them. I was at the airport all day and Karazov and the woman never showed."

"Do you think Karazov would be fool enough to get on a commercial jet so that you could just pick them off as they left the airport?"

"Well, I couldn't risk going back to Vasaro. Half of Interpol was churning around there after we torched the farm."

Brian sighed. "I'm becoming very disappointed in you, Ferrazo."

"He's good," Ferrazo said defensively. "You should have let me take them both out at Versailles."

"No! You're not to touch Karazov. The woman is the target, you idiot. If you think you can manage it."

"I managed that bit at Vasaro, didn't I?" Ferrazo's tone turned surly. "But I have to find them first."

"That may not be easy. The Gypsy says Karazov's gone underground, and even he hasn't been able to locate him since he came back to Istanbul. However,

Karazov may try to contact him again." Ledford paused, considering the problem. "Karazov knows about the house on the Street of Swords."

"Then I'll stake it out."

"I'll be arriving in Istanbul in three weeks." Ledford's voice was soft. "I want the woman out of the way when I get there, Ferrazo. I won't tolerate a second mistake."

Ledford didn't wait for an answer as he replaced the receiver back on the telephone. It hadn't surprised him that Alex had taken such pains to lose Ferrazo. The scope of the destruction Ledford had wreaked on Vasaro must have signaled his displeasure with the Vasaro woman in no uncertain terms. Oh, well, it was time Alex realized there must be no further betrayal of the integrity of their match.

"Why not kill Karazov if he knows about the house?"

Ledford stood up and turned to face Krakow, who sat in a chair across the room. "He won't go running to Interpol. Don't worry, I'll deal with him."

"Just be sure I'm not involved." Krakow rose to his feet. "I'm going to call the news conference to announce the invitation this afternoon, and this will be the last time we'll meet before Istanbul. I don't think we should communicate by phone either. When this is over I must be—"

"Pure as the mountain air," Ledford finished for him with a wide grin. "We'll keep your skirts clean."

"You know what to do?"

"I'll have the threat phoned in to the police tomorrow."

"And you'll handle the job in Istanbul exactly as I've outlined?"

"Of course, you're calling the shots." Ledford beamed at him genially. "It's actually a very good plan."

"You won't regret it. Once I've taken power, you'll be—"

"You'd better leave," Ledford interrupted. He couldn't stomach the pompous bastard anymore today. "We don't want to jeopardize everything when we're so close to success."

Krakow nodded. "I'm glad you realize the urgency of being discreet."

Ledford watched Krakow move toward the door with military precision. God, he thought, Krakow's back was as rigid as if he had a broomstick up his ass.

Krakow paused at the door. "Let me know when you've set up headquarters in Istanbul in case I have some last-minute instructions for you."

"I'll be sure to do that." Ledford's smile never wavered as he watched Krakow open the door. The bastard was going to give *him* instructions? All the adulation Krakow had been receiving lately was making his ego swell to the size of the Goodyear blimp. He suddenly had the impulse to deflate that ego. "I've been thinking it might be a good idea to take out your wife."

Krakow froze with shock. "What?"

"When we take out the other targets in Istanbul, it might be a good idea to—"

"Helga?"

That had shaken him. Ledford lowered his lids to veil the satisfaction in his eyes. "Why not? You could play the heartbroken widower and I'm sure it would allay suspicion."

"I'll . . . think about it."

"For the cause. After all, I gave up three good men at the Louvre. One wife isn't so much."

"I told you I'd think about it," Krakow said through clenched teeth. "I don't believe it's necessary."

"You could trade her in for two of those long-legged blondes your country is so famous for."

Krakow drew himself up with majestic dignity. "*If* I sanction Helga's death, it would not be for puerile reasons."

"Of course not." Krakow almost had himself convinced he was doing all this for patriotic reasons and not to become a god. It was always a mistake to lie to yourself, even if you lied to everyone else in the world. Brian crossed the room and opened the door for Krakow. "Just a thought."

"I'll let you know."

"Do that." Brian closed the door behind Krakow and moved toward the telephone again. He probably shouldn't have pulled the son of a bitch's string, but Krakow was such an uptight prick, he hadn't been able to resist. Krakow persisted in believing that Brian Ledford was a stupid hit man. He laughed. Krakow would be damn surprised when he found out he had been dealing with a man of enormous cunning.

It was time, Brian decided, to start the next step of his own plan. He picked up the phone and dialed the White Star Shipping Line.

"Hi, baby." Chelsea breezed into the hospital room and dropped a bouquet of roses on the bed and a kiss on Marisa's forehead. Marisa's left arm and shoulder had been shattered and were now in a cast. The second bullet that struck her had gone through Maskovel's body first and then glanced off her rib cage. Jesus, she looked pale. "The doctor said you had a good night. We're going to have you out of here in no time." She perched on a chair by the bed. "Those reporters haven't been bothering you, have they?"

Marisa shook her head. "The head nurse hasn't let them past the station."

"Great."

"How's Caitlin?"

"Not good. She's like a robot."

"I guess we couldn't expect anything else." Marisa swallowed. "You went to the funeral today?"

"I hoped you wouldn't remember it was today." Chelsea leaned over and clasped Marisa's hand. "I sent flowers in your name."

"And Peter?"

"He's being buried tomorrow in West Virginia."

Tears filled Marisa's eyes. "He saved my life, you know."

"I know. Renée saw the whole thing from the hill and told us."

"He was my friend, Mother." Two tears rolled down Marisa's cheeks. "He was gentle and kind and...I've never met anyone I felt so close to."

"Then keep him with you always. Never forget him." Chelsea's hand tightened on Marisa's. "I never will. He saved a big part of my life too."

"Did Jonathan go with him?"

Chelsea nodded.

Marisa's teeth sunk into her lower lip. "I didn't want him to be alone. His only living relative was a great-aunt and he didn't care much for her. He was such a lonely man."

"He had Jonathan for a friend. That was a big plus."

"Yes." Marisa wiped her damp cheeks on a corner of the sheet. "Are you going to marry him?"

Chelsea's eyes widened. "What?"

"Jonathan. He's a good guy and you love him. Are you going to marry him?"

"Christ, where do you hide your crystal ball? You know I'm not the marrying kind. It's still going to be just you and me."

"It's time it stopped being just you and me. Forget about me. Marry him, Mother."

"Are you trying to get rid of me?"

"I'm trying to untie the albatrosses you insist on wearing around your neck."

"What a disgusting thought." Chelsea wrinkled her nose with delicate distaste. "All those stinking feathers. I hope I have more fashion sense than that." She avoided Marisa's unrelenting stare. "You're not going to let me slip around this, are you?"

"No."

"God, you're stubborn." Her index finger began tracing patterns on the sheet. "He's going to be the next president, baby."

"So?"

"You know that I—"

"Dear God in heaven." Marisa's mouth had fallen open. "You've found someone else to protect."

"I don't want to talk about it."

"Okay." Marisa paused. "There are more important things to talk about now anyway."

Chelsea looked at her warily. "What things?"

"Leave it alone, Mother."

"What?"

"It's too dangerous. Let the authorities handle it. Stay out of it."

"I don't have much respect for the wheels of justice these days." Chelsea should have known Marisa, who knew her best, would guess her reaction to this atrocity. "You almost bled to death."

"I didn't die. I'm going to be fine."

Chelsea withdrew her hand and tried to keep the fierceness from her tone. "Ferrazo doesn't deserve to live, and neither does Ledford."

"I don't deserve to have to worry about you."

"Low blow." Chelsea met her gaze. "Listen, what if it was me lying in this bed? What would you want to do?"

Marisa smiled tremulously. "Low blow."

Chelsea leaned forward and kissed her. "Face it. It's in the genes, baby. You're a fighter, exactly like me." She stood and picked up the bouquet on the bed. "I have to put these in water."

"Mother, don't do—"

"Don't worry, I promise not to pull a Rambo, and I won't leave you until you're ready to be shipped home to California." She suddenly frowned. "I only hope Caitlin and Alex don't get the bastards before I get to Istanbul."

Marisa shook her head resignedly. "And I hope they do."

It was close to midnight when Kemal and Caitlin arrived at the cottage on the Bosporus.

Alex was in the kitchenette and looked up as the front door opened. "I made coffee. Would you like some?"

"No, thank you." Caitlin went through the living room toward her bedroom. "I'm very tired. Good night."

A moment later the door closed behind her.

"She is not the same." Kemal stared worriedly at the doorway through which Caitlin had disappeared. "I do not like it."

"Do you think I do?" Alex's tone was fierce as he poured coffee into the cup in front of him. "She doesn't talk, she doesn't smile. She's not *there*. She's been like this since that first day at Vasaro."

"Shock," Kemal said. "I saw it sometimes with the children in the Harem. They do not want to believe what has happened to them, so they close part of themselves away."

"And how long does it last?"

"Years, sometimes." Kemal shook his head. "But that was not so bad. At least that part of them was inviolate The situation with Caitlin is different. There is danger when you are too numb to fear." His gaze shifted to Alex's face. "While we were waiting for you to check out the cottage she asked me if it was possible to smuggle her into the Harem so that she could find out more about Adnan."

"Christ."

"I told her it would do no good. Adnan hasn't shown up again since you left for Vasaro."

"Where the hell could he be?"

"It's been only seven days," Kemal reminded him.

Seven days. Those days at Vasaro seemed to encompass a lifetime of guilt and pain. Caitlin's pain, his own guilt. Alex's hand tightened on the coffee cup. "She has to snap out of it. It's too dangerous for it to go on."

"She's full of hate for Ledford. Vengeance can be a great liberator."

"Not for Caitlin. She thinks she wants vengeance now, but it's against her basic beliefs."

Kemal smiled at Alex. "But not against ours."

"No. But Caitlin's not like us."

"So what do we do?"

"Make her stop thinking about death and think about life."

"The circumstances are not of the best for that to occur."

"There's always a way if you look at the problem in the right perspective."

Kemal raised his brows inquiringly.

"The Wind Dancer. She feels she's lost everything, but there's still the Wind Dancer."

"I do not understand. The Wind Dancer has also been lost."

"But not the puzzle. We can still try to solve the

puzzle." Alex drank the rest of the coffee in two swallows. "Try, hell. Dammit, we *will* solve the puzzle. I may not be able to help her in any other way, but I can do that." He set his cup back on the saucer. "Maskovel was supposed to have a package rushed to the American Express office the day before he died. I want you to pick it up tomorrow morning and bring it to Caitlin."

Kemal nodded. "I hope she is aware of what a great honor I do her to become a mere errand boy for her sake."

"I don't think she'll allow herself to become aware of a hell of a lot right now," Alex said wearily.

"But that will change. Patience, Alex."

Alex glanced at the closed door of Caitlin's room. "You supply the patience. I'm too scared to wait until she comes out of this on her own. I'm going to blast her out any way I can."

"I come bearing gifts," Kemal sang out as Caitlin opened the door for him the next morning. "Come and smile with delight and appreciation."

Caitlin stepped aside for him to enter and closed the door behind him. "What's that?"

Kemal set the large box down on the coffee table with a sigh of relief. "You're lucky I'm strong as a bull. A lesser man would have crumbled beneath this challenge."

Caitlin felt a distant flicker of amusement. "What is it?"

"I don't know." Kemal took out his pocketknife and began cutting the sealing tape around the box. "Something to do with the Wind Dancer. Alex said it came from Peter Maskovel."

"Peter." She felt a sharp pang and remembered the last conversation she had with gentle, sunny Peter Maskovel. She watched with stinging eyes as Kemal opened the box.

"Three projectors." Kemal rummaged further, pulled

out a nine-by-twelve padded envelope, and handed it to her. "This is almost as heavy as the projectors."

"The translation," she murmured. The information for which she had waited so long was now in her hands. Excitement stirred deep inside her, melting an infinitesimal bit of the ice enveloping her emotions.

Kemal delved still deeper into the box, brought out another large envelope, and handed that one to her. "All kinds of treasures."

She opened the envelope, looked inside, then closed it quickly. "Just photographs."

"May I?" Kemal held out his hand.

Caitlin hesitated, and then handed him the envelope.

Kemal took out the photographs and began leafing through them. "I like flowers. How beautiful was your Vasaro."

"Yes, it was."

He glanced up, his dark eyes suddenly glowing with sympathy. "You had this joy but now you have it no longer. Now you must open yourself to other joys. I do not mean to offend by being callous, but losses must be faced."

"I have faced it."

"I do not think you have." He glanced down at the pictures again. "But I will help to—who is this?"

He had stopped flipping through the photographs and was staring at one picture, his expression curiously arrested.

Caitlin glanced at the photograph. "That's Marisa Benedict."

"The young girl who was shot?" Kemal's expression hardened. "Sons of bitches."

"Yes."

Kemal continued to study the picture. "I believe her to be extraordinary." His eyes narrowed on Marisa's face. "But she doesn't laugh, does she?"

Caitlin looked at him, startled. "Laugh? I suppose she doesn't go around with a big grin on her face, but she's not—" Caitlin stopped as she realized she couldn't remember ever hearing Marisa laugh.

Kemal nodded. "She smiles but she does not laugh. This is not good. Someone should teach her to laugh."

"Everyone cares about Marisa. I'm sure..." Caitlin trailed off, staring at him in bemusement. "How did you know she doesn't laugh?"

"*Sien mien.*"

"What?"

"It's the ancient Chinese art of reading facial expressions. I studied it at one time."

"For a moment I thought it was your second sight." Caitlin smiled faintly. "And, of course, you've become an expert on the subject."

"Of course." He took the photograph and stuffed it in the pocket of his jeans. "I keep this. Okay?"

"If you wish."

"I wish very much." He lifted one of the projectors out of the box. "Now I take these into the study and set them up for you. Come along and show me where you want them." He strode quickly toward the study.

Caitlin looked down at the envelope containing the translation and felt that flutter of excitement start within her.

Clutching the envelope tightly, she followed Kemal into the study. "Put the projectors on a chair in the corner of the room. We'll use the desk as a pedestal and focus and situate the other two projectors at angles that will—"

"*Star Wars,*" Kemal murmured as he gazed enraptured at the hologram of the Wind Dancer. "In the movie the actors played a three-dimensional game. Is this the same?"

"I think the filmmakers used special effects, this i the real thing." Caitlin adjusted the projector closest t her. "I don't know exactly how the motion picture filn is made, but I've learned the basic principle of holo grams. It's all done with lasers. The light coming fron the laser is split to create two beams called an objec beam and a reference beam. The object beam is sprea by lenses and reflected by a mirror to the object yo want to film. Light waves from the object are in turn re flected toward photographic film."

Alex stood in the doorway of the study, listening t Caitlin, but neither she nor Kemal realized he wa there. The curtains at the window had been drawn bringing an early dusk to the study, and they were botl kneeling on the floor, looking up at the hologram of th Wind Dancer. Even in the dimness Alex could discer the eagerness, the openness, of Caitlin's expression an felt something hot and primitive twist inside him Kemal had made her look like this. Kemal had manage to break through to her when he could not.

"At the same time the reference beam is also sprea and directed toward the film but without striking th object. The beams merge, interfering with each other t create new patterns. The interference patterns strik the film plate and expose the photographic emulsion. Caitlin absently ruffled her short curls. "Light wave from every spot on the object interact with the refer ence beam and are recorded everywhere on the film Then, when the film is developed, the interference pat tern becomes permanent."

"Very interesting," Kemal said in a bored tone. "Don' go on. You really know how to destroy one's illusions."

Caitlin chuckled. "You're like Gaston. He didn't like log ical explanations either, but he was only six years old."

"A clever boy."

Alex felt alone, shut out, raw. He deliberately shifted where he stood to make them aware of his presence.

"Ah, there you are," Kemal said. "Come and see this wonder. It's truly magic."

Alex watched Caitlin stiffen and her smile fade as she looked at him. The knife twisted inside him. "Abracadabra."

Caitlin's gaze flew back to the hologram. "You've been gone a long time. Where have you been?"

"I went to see Moduhl at the museum."

She went still. "Why?"

"I thought he'd had enough time to remember where he had seen the inscription."

"And had he?"

"After a certain amount of judicious probing. That's what took so long." He smiled faintly. "You'd have been proud of me. I kept after him with the same persistence that's made you famous."

"*Notorious* is a better word. Where had he seen it?"

"He was at a dig in the Tarsus Mountains five years ago near a village called Tamkalo. The dig was abandoned for lack of funds and the most valuable finds were transported to the museum in Ankara. The villagers asked that some of the relics be left in the makeshift museum they created in hopes of drawing tourists from the coast." He paused. "But the piece of the tablet on which he saw that particular script wasn't found in the dig itself. The child of a worker brought it down from the mountain."

"Like Moses?" Kemal asked.

"Hardly," Alex said. "The boy found a broken piece of a tablet in a cave and brought it down to the archaeologists for cold, hard cash."

"Then the rest of the tablet could still be in the cave," Caitlin said.

"Possibly."

Kemal stood up, turned off the remote, and the Wind Dancer disappeared from the desk. "So we go to Tamkalo."

"Caitlin and I go to Tamkalo," Alex said. "You stay here in case you get word on Ledford or Irmak."

"It's just as well. I do not like to climb mountains." He grinned. "Instead, I shall desert my cockroaches and move in here to protect your property."

"How self-sacrificing of you."

"Yes, I have a great heart. When do you leave?"

"Tomorrow morning."

"You will need a jeep. I will rent one and outfit it with all manner of fine outdoor equipment."

"We can do without gold pegs for the tents."

"Pity. I know just where to find such treasures and was going to charge you an extra fee for them."

"I'm sure the fee will be high enough."

"Me too. The jeep will be outside the gate at six tomorrow morning." Kemal held out his hand. "I'll need to make myself a key if I am to properly safeguard your possessions."

Alex reached into his pocket and handed him the brass key that unlocked the gate and the front door. "You're sure this is no trouble?" he asked dryly. "I wouldn't want to inconvenience you."

"Trust me. All will be well." Kemal turned to Caitlin and smiled gently. "This will be good for you. Let go all the bad memories and let yourself heal." He didn't wait for an answer as he walked out of the study.

Alex followed Kemal across the living room to the front door. "I'll try to call you here at least once a day for a report. You might get off your duff and try to find Irmak."

"I am trying." The sharpness of Alex's tone caused Kemal to turn to look at him in surprise. Then his own expression lit with understanding and he added softly, "Do not be angry with me. I did not do it. It's the statue that is making her come alive."

On one level Alex realized what Kemal said was true. But, dammit, Caitlin didn't grow stiff and wary when she looked at Kemal. "I don't know what you mean. That's the purpose of the exercise."

"A painful exercise for you. Someday she will know." Kemal closed the door behind him.

"We're really going?" Caitlin stood in the doorway of the study.

"Of course." He took only a glancing look at her eager face and went to his bedroom.

Jealous. Christ, he was seething, burning with jealousy. He was jealous of Kemal, jealous of that damned translation, even jealous of the Wind Dancer. He had never felt this way before, and he didn't like it.

Yet he had wanted to reach out and shake her, *make* her look at him as she had those first few days in Paris, cling to him as she had at Vasaro before she had turned to ice. He wanted only to help her, and she was closing him out, dammit.

He was lying to himself. That wasn't all he wanted. His motives in trying to shake her out of this cocoon were not nearly as pure as he was trying to convince himself. His body didn't give a damn about Caitlin's emotional problems; it wanted only to assuage its own.

The jeep crested the rise and they looked down on the tiny village of Tamkalo. It lay in the valley surrounded by the majestic mountains they'd just driven through. Puffs of white steam spewed from at least twenty hot springs in and around the village. A large, flat-roofed sod hut squatted beside a great trough gouging through the earth at the far end of the village. The house stood out because the other gray-brown huts resembled sod tepees of uniform size marching one after the other across the white-gray sandy earth.

"*Dieu*, I've never seen anything like this," Caitlin said as she stuffed the pages of the translation back into the envelope and sat up straighter on her seat. "People actually live in those queer houses?"

"Presumably. However, I don't see anyone." Alex stopped the jeep and leaned his elbows on the steering wheel. "It looks deserted."

Caitlin could see no sign of life in the village below her. No people. No livestock. No vehicles. "A ghost town. Didn't Monsieur Moduhl mention—" She answered her own question. "But he couldn't have known if he hadn't been here for five years."

Alex nodded grimly. "So much for calling Kemal every day. The village must have died when the archeological team pulled out."

"Look at that earth. They couldn't have managed to eke out much of a living before the team came."

"It must be loaded with minerals brought to the surface by the springs."

"Instead of trying to attract tourists with a museum, they should have made this a health spa. I've never seen so many hot springs in one place." Caitlin shivered as she jumped out of the jeep and started down the street, her boots striking up puffs of dust with each step. "Or maybe we can locate that museum. That looks like the dig over there to the west. Didn't Monsieur Moduhl mention it was by the—"

A bullet whistled by Caitlin's head!

Caitlin instinctively fell to her knees. She could hear

he echo of the shot ricocheting around her from the sur-
ounding mountains. Where had the shot come from?
Her gaze frantically searched the strange dwellings lining
he street.

"Stay down," Alex yelled.

Merde, did he think she was going for a stroll with
people shooting at her? She began wriggling, propelling
herself forward with knees and elbows toward the shel-
er of one of the cone-shaped huts on the left side of
he street.

Another bullet kicked up the dust in front of her.

She froze. Should she try to make it back to the
eep? She glanced over her shoulder. Alex was gone
rom the jeep. Where had he—Sweet Mary, it was no
ime to wonder where he had gone while she was still
n the open. The hut was closer than the jeep. She drew
a deep breath and rolled sidewise toward the hut, every
moment expecting a bullet to tear through her flesh.

A scream of pain echoed shrilly over the valley, fol-
owed immediately by a frantic sputtering of Turkish in
a high male voice.

Caitlin got to her knees behind the hut and saw Alex
coming out of the doorway of the flat sod house by the
dig. He carried a rifle in one hand and a pistol in the
other. "Are you hurt?" he called.

"No."

"Then get the hell over here and inside. We don't
know who else may be in those huts." He turned and
went back into the hut.

Another spurt of vitriolic Turkish issued from the
hut Alex had entered as Caitlin stood up and moved
warily down the street. How had Alex gotten inside the
hut? He must have circled around behind the other
cone-shaped huts and come in the back door.

"Caitlin!"

"I'm coming." She quickened her pace and a moment later entered the flat-roofed hut. A hasty glance revealed a large room that looked like a herd of elephants had stampeded through it. Tables and chairs were overturned, curio cabinets together with their contents had been dashed to the floor. The only piece of furniture appearing to have remained intact was a long, crudely crafted table set against the far wall.

The tall, wiry man kneeling on the dirt floor looked as wild and desolate as his surroundings. He was dressed in a dirty maroon-striped robe and grimy white turban, and she judged he must be somewhere in his early sixties. It was difficult to determine his exact age through the liberal layer of dust and grease coating his shaggy black hair and long, gray-streaked beard. His burning eyes focused on her with a fanatic fervor that reminded her of pictures she had seen of the Ayatollah Khomeini. His mouth was bleeding, but it didn't prevent the words from spitting from it as he saw her. Caitlin took an involuntary step back. "Who is he? Why was he trying to shoot me?"

"That's what I'm trying to find out. I'm not going to have any trouble. I can't shut him up." Alex listened a moment before he turned to Caitlin, raising his voice to be heard above the man's continuing diatribe. "His name is Abdul Kasmina and he says he owns the entire village. When all the others left, he stayed, and the village is his by the right of possession. We trespassed and therefore must die."

Caitlin felt a surge of relief. For a moment she had thought by some outlandish chance Ledford had caused this new threat. "He's mad?"

"Excellent conclusion."

Caitlin shivered. "Why would he stay here by himself?"

"To be king of all he surveys? Who knows?" Alex

glanced around the hut. "Judging by those tables and curio cabinets over there, I'd say this used to be the museum before Abdul made it into his own private pigsty. Why don't you look around and see if you can find that portion of the tablet Moduhl mentioned while I take Abdul outside and ask him a few questions?"

Caitlin barely heard him as she moved toward the long table set against the wall. Pigsty was a good description. Several pottery bowls and crude knives lay scattered on the table. She made a face as she saw a dozen or more flies hovering over the remains of food in one of the shallow bowls. Antiquity clearly held no reverence for Abdul Kasmina.

The corner of the tablet was lying underneath a broken urn.

She forgot about the flies. She forgot everything but that piece of gray-brown wedge-shaped clay. Carefully, afraid to breathe, Caitlin moved the urn to one side.

"Dear God." She was scarcely conscious she had murmured the words as she stared down at the ancient script. It was the same.

"Alex! It's the same," she shouted. She jerked off the blue cotton bandanna from around her neck, spread it on the table, and placed the portion of the tablet in the center and tied the bandanna carefully around it. She couldn't believe her luck. The artifact could have been smashed when that child dug it from the earth, or that madman could have dashed it to the ground in a fit of rage. She took another look at the jumble of objects on the table to be certain there was no other tablet bearing similar markings before she turned and ran out of the museum. "Alex, did you hear me. It's—" She broke off as she saw Abdul Kasmina lying on the ground and Alex standing over him.

Alex had made use of the Turk's grimy turban to gag

him. Now Abdul's lips were not only split, but his left eye was rapidly blackening.

"You've hurt him."

"I hope so." Alex turned to face her, and she saw a bruise darkening his cheekbone. "He tried to kill us."

"He's not sane. You shouldn't have—perhaps he was only trying to warn us off."

Abdul sputtered a barrage of venom at her that caused Alex's expression to harden even more. "I don't think so."

"You still shouldn't beat a helpless man."

"He wasn't helpless. I'll carry this bruise for a week. And I wasn't beating him, I was questioning him." Alex nudged Abdul in the ribs with the toe of his boot. "He just got a little tired and decided to lie down and rest."

Her lips tightened with disapproval. "Is that how the KGB questions men?"

"Sometimes." Alex met her gaze. "You wanted to know where that tablet came from. I found out." He gestured to the mountain closest to the village. "There's a path leading to a cave halfway up the side of that one."

"We could have found out some other way. Let him go."

Alex shook his head. "We don't know whether or not he's stashed another rifle in one of those huts."

"Then tie him up and leave him alone."

Alex gazed at her a moment before he picked up the kicking and writhing Abdul and slung him over his shoulder in a fireman's lift. "I'll be right back." He disappeared into the museum.

Ten minutes later he came out of the hut minus his burden. "Trussed up very neatly."

"You were gone a long time."

"I didn't do him any permanent damage." He started down the street toward the jeep. "And I'm not going to apologize for taking the information I wanted from him. Crazy or not, he's a vicious son of a bitch who wanted to out us both down." He shot her a sidewise glance. "Would you like me to translate what he intends to do, when he gets free, to the infidel woman who dares to wear men's trousers?"

"No." They had reached the jeep and she tucked the envelope containing the translation she had left there into one of the pockets of the backpack on the backseat. "I don't want to hear it."

"No, you don't want to hear anything that would make you believe I wasn't—" He shrugged. "To hell with it. Grab your gear and let's set up camp."

"We could use one of those huts."

"Do what you like. I prefer the outdoors to the filth that must have accumulated in those dung holes in the past five years."

Caitlin remembered the dirt, flies, and scurrying insects in the museum and changed her mind. She turned away from the jeep. "You set up the camp. I'll find wood for a fire."

Caitlin turned another page and placed it on top of the other sheets on the blanket beside her.

"Get to sleep," Alex said from his bedroll across the fire. "You have a mountain to climb tomorrow."

"Half a mountain," she corrected him, her attention still on the translation. "Abdul said the cave was halfway up."

"Whatever." Alex's voice was edged with impatience. "I still don't want to have to drag you."

She lifted her eyes. "You won't have to drag me. I'll keep up." She suddenly realized the words had a familiar sound. "That's what Jacinthe said to Andros."

"What?"

"When they left Troy." She looked thoughtfully into

the fire. "She told him she would match his pace. You know, Andros was of the Shardana, and I think the inscription on the Wind Dancer could also be Shardana. I believe Andros had the inscription engraved on the base after he left Troy."

"Why do you say that?"

"Nowhere in the first legend is the inscription mentioned. There's a detailed description of the statue but not one word about the inscription."

"It could be an oversight."

"But it was Andros who had this story set down by an Egyptian scribe. Caterina states in the preface that it became tradition for members to set down their family history, starting with Andros." Caitlin frowned. "Andros... I don't understand it."

"Why not?"

"Andros was a warrior. He was pragmatic and clever but not the type of man who would want the story of his life set down for posterity. Why did he feel so strongly about having his story written and kept for future generations?"

"You can tell all that from reading the first legend?"

"Read it yourself and see if you don't agree with me."

"Maybe tomorrow. Who were the Shardana?"

"No one really knows much about them. They were very secretive and left no records of their own. The ancient Egyptians referred to the Shardana as the sea people. They were greatly feared as fighters and actually attacked the Egyptian coast at one time. Later, they became mercenaries under the pharaohs. No one knows why they changed from enemy to subject."

"Well, you're not going to find out tonight." Alex turned his back to her and zipped up his sleeping bag. "Go to sleep."

"In a minute."

"Now."

His tone carried so much ferocity, it startled her. While she had been reading Andros's story, she had been oblivious of Alex's building tension, but now it was obvious in every rigid tendon of the back he had turned to her. She was tempted to tell him to go to hell, but God knows they didn't need more conflict between them. Besides, he was probably right that she needed her rest for the challenges of the coming day.

The climb proved far more difficult than Caitlin had anticipated, and they did not reach the cave until late afternoon. The rutted path slanted steeply and sometimes disappeared entirely as they were forced to make their way over a landfall of rocks and boulders.

By the time the large opening of the limestone cave came into view, Caitlin felt as if she had been climbing days instead of hours, and the knapsack strapped to her back weighed a ton more than when they had started out.

Alex turned and held out his hand to pull her up the last few feet to the ledge. "All right?"

It was the first time he had spoken to her since they had started to climb.

She nodded breathlessly as she wiped the perspiration from her forehead and the nape of her neck with her scarf.

"Stay here. I'm going to take a look inside."

He disappeared inside the cave.

She waited a moment until her breathing steadied again and then followed him.

The only light poured in from the opening. The roof appeared to be some thirty feet above her, but it didn't feel cool or drafty. It was almost hot in there. She could see shadowy rocks and boulders back in the cave and the shifting glow of Alex's flashlight as he walked toward her.

"I see you're obeying instructions as usual."

"How far back does it go?"

"About four hundred yards. The reason it's so warm in here is that there's another hot spring at the end of the cave." He smiled crookedly. "And no, I didn't see any symbols or writing on the walls."

"I didn't expect you would." Caitlin unstrapped her knapsack and dropped it on the ground. "I didn't see any wood on the trail. I guess we'll have to use the camp stove. At least we won't need a fire for heat tonight. Let's make camp now and start searching at daybreak."

"I'm surprised you don't want to start looking now."

She ignored the caustic note in his voice. "If the cave is as small as you say, it's not going to be a monumental task. We should be able to search the entire cave thoroughly by tomorrow evening." She knelt on the ground and undid the fastening of the knapsack. "And I want to read the second legend in the journal while the light still holds." She could feel his gaze on her back, but she avoided looking at him as she continued. "I fixed our meal last night. It's your turn tonight."

She took the translation out of the knapsack and carried it toward the entrance to the cave. She settled down just outside the opening and leaned back against the craggy limestone wall.

The valley was spread out before her, stark, pale, eerie in the late afternoon sunlight.

She could hear Alex moving in the cave behind her, but she firmly closed him out as she removed the pages of the second legend and began to read them. She had read only three pages when Alex came out of the cave.

"Let me read the first legend."

She looked up to see Alex standing beside her. "Now?"

"You said I should read it." He sat down beside her and took the pages from her. "What else do I have to do?"

He settled himself back against the cliff and picked up the first page.

The typewritten pages flew through his fingers with incredible speed, and she remembered he had told her that night in the perfumery that he had taught himself speed-reading.

She tried to concentrate on the second legend concerning Andros and Jacinthe settling in Alexandria and starting their family but found it impossible to concentrate. She was too acutely conscious of Alex sitting next to her absorbing, drinking in, the story of Andros and Jacinthe meeting that last day in Troy. She had read it only twice herself, but she could see it before her as if projected on a movie screen, embellished by imagination until it came vividly alive.

Andros, Jacinthe, and Paradignes . . .

And the Wind Dancer.

15

The golden statue of Pegasus stood eighteen inches tall, every radiant inch commanding the eye and riveting the attention. Two perfectly matched almond-shaped emeralds served as the horse's eyes, and its lacy filigree wings folded back against its graceful body as if buffeted by a strong wind. Lustrous white pearls shimmered on the filigree clouds on which the Pegasus ran, and four hundred and forty-seven diamonds encrusted the base of the statue.

"What do you think, Andros?" Paradignes rubbed a soft cloth gently over the filigreed wings of the statue on the table. "Is the Wind Dancer a prize worth dying for?"

"What do I think? I think you're mad," Andros said bluntly. "The king ordered you to burn the statue until it was no more than a shapeless mass of metal. What if he finds you've disobeyed him?"

"Then he'll probably order me burned in its stead." Paradignes's gaze was still on the statue. "Pour yourself a cup of wine. I have a proposition to make to you."

Andros crossed the chamber to the table and picked up the graceful blue ewer on which was depicted a beautifully painted Apollo pulling the sun across the heavens. The ewer *was as exquisite as everything else in Paradignes's chamber, and Andros had often admired it. He poured wine into the cup.* "Then make your proposition. Needless to say, I'll listen. As a prisoner in your city, I have not been offered many choices of late."

"You've not been badly treated."

"Not by you." *Andros lifted the cup to his lips.* "I've often wondered why you interceded with your brother when he wished to lop my head off."

"I thought I might have need of you. You're a brave man and have a surprising sense of honor." *Paradignes stepped back, laid the cloth on the table beside the statue, and asked softly,* "By Zeus, is it not a thing of wondrous beauty?"

"Get rid of the statue," *Andros said gruffly.* "I agree it's too beautiful to destroy, but keep it hidden. I've heard your brother thinks it has some magical power from the gods that bewitched Traynor into betraying his people."

"My brother is not always reasonable. If he believed it was the statue, then why did he have Traynor hacked to ribbons?" *Paradignes shook his head.* "My brother was never very clever even when we were boys together and was ever ruled by passion and greed." *He grimaced.* "I should have been king, you know. I was the firstborn. Without these crooked shanks I would have taken my place in the great hall and perhaps we wouldn't now be sitting beyond these walls, waiting to die."

"Perhaps you will not die."

"You think to comfort me?" *Paradignes shook his head.* "The siege has gone on too long, the bitterness is too deep, the wound on both sides unhealed. When we are finally defeated, there will be no mercy. We would show none if we were the victors."

Andros absently sipped his wine, studying the statue. He wished the old man would cease meandering and tell him why he had been brought from his prison cell. It was not the first time the king's brother had sent for him and given him wine and conversation, yet such action seemed bizarre now that the city lay on the brink of destruction. "You're right. Everyone dies sooner or later. But there is no need to hurry it by angering your brother."

"You did not seem to worry about incurring his rage when he was questioning you under the lash." Paradignes smiled. "You could have told him what he wished to know and you could have ridden out of the city in freedom."

A sudden glint of humor appeared on Andros's face. "What would I have done with a horse? I do not come from horse people as you do. I am of the sea."

"We are all well aware of that," Paradignes said dryly. "Your ships have been raiding our city and exacting tribute since the time of my father's father."

Andros shrugged. "Every city-state raids and pillages wherever it can. The Shardana are just better at it than the rest of you."

"And consequently must have great storehouses of treasure in your kingdom." Paradignes hobbled over to the table and poured himself a bowl of wine. "It's only natural that my brother would want to know the location of your homeland in order to tap that treasure. As you say, we are all raiders. The enemies besieging us now may mouth vengeance, but they, too, want only slaves and treasure. It's unfortunate your ship was storm-wrecked off our shores just before the city was attacked."

Andros's grasp tightened on the cup in his hand. "I'm not involved in your war and I will not be sacrificed to it." He smiled, showing gleaming teeth. "Give me a sword and let me fight my way out of the city and I'll promise you that you'll have a great many less to battle next time they rush the gate."

"I don't doubt that's true." Paradignes's gaze was still fastened on the ewer from which he had poured the wine.

"Tell me, do you have many beautiful objects like this in the treasure chambers of your city?"

Andros smiled curiously. "We have treasures you could never imagine."

"Like this?"

"Of far greater value."

"Then why do you raid us?"

Andros was silent.

"You won't even answer such an innocent question?" Paradignes smiled and lifted his bowl to his lips. "What a secret lot you of the Shardana are. You sail out of nowhere, you raid and pillage and are gone again in the mists. I believe I feel a twinge of sympathy for my beloved brother."

"Feel sympathy for my men whom your brother sacrificed on the altar of Poseidon to save your city." Andros's jaw tightened. "They were brave men and true."

"But the enemy."

"I was the enemy," Andros said. "They only followed me." He finished his wine with one swallow. "He could have made them slaves instead of butchering them. May the gods put a curse on his soul." He set his cup on the table and turned to Paradignes. "But I have no quarrel with you, old man. I've enjoyed our hours together. What do you wish from me? A clean thrust through the heart so you avoid the shame of death by your enemy?"

"No." Paradignes nodded toward the statue. "What do you know of the Wind Dancer?"

"That you're a fool not to have obeyed the order to destroy it."

"Acknowledged. What else?"

"Only what the guards told me. That it was given by your enemy as a bribe to your kinsman, Traynor, to open the West Gate. That their soldiers poured through the gate, put it to the torch, and since then have almost captured the city on two occasions."

"The next time the city will fall."

Andros nodded. "You can't hold them at bay forever now that the gate has been destroyed."

"The fever sickness that ravages our city would have destroyed us if betrayal had not," Paradignes said wearily. "Traynor was not a brave man, but he loved beautiful things, as I do. Do you know what he asked as a boon before he died?"

Andros shook his head.

"To see the Wind Dancer." Paradignes shook his head. "Do you wonder why my brother is frightened? He understands only war and battle. He could never comprehend the power of beauty." He turned to look at Andros. "But you understand that power. I've seen you look at my lovely things with admiration, not greed."

"Oh, the greed is there too." Andros smiled crookedly. "I'm not so foolish as not to weigh their value."

"I cannot see the Wind Dancer destroyed, nor can I let it fall into the hands of my enemies." Paradignes paused. "So you will take it from the city tonight, before the next attack."

Andros became still, his heart leaping with hope. "I trust you know how mad you sound. The city is surrounded."

"This is an ancient city and has been destroyed and rebuilt many times." Paradignes hobbled toward the far wall and threw back the carpet to reveal a wooden trapdoor set in the stones. "This passage will lead you down into the earth under the present city and far beyond the enemy lines."

"Your brother knows the passage?"

The old man nodded. "But he will not use it. His head is full of glory and his heart full of hate. He would rather stay here and die than run away."

"Well, I'm not such a fool. I'll gladly take your Wind Dancer and leave this place." Andros moved toward the statue. "Come on, let's get out of here."

"I stay."

Andros looked at him in surprise.

"It's my city, my home." Paradignes's lips twisted. "Perhaps I'm as much a fool as my brother after all." He leaned down and grasped the iron ring to open the trapdoor. "But you will not go alone. I'm sending someone with you. She's already waiting in the passage with a sword, a lantern to light your way, and enough food to last you at least—" A sudden uproar in the courtyard caused him to break off.

"Attack! To the walls!"

"Make haste. They have broken through again." Paradignes motioned to the Wind Dancer on the table. "Put the statue into the chest and be gone."

Andros quickly did as he was told, picked up the chest, and ran toward the trapdoor. "Who is waiting in the passage?"

"Jacinthe."

Andros stopped in midstride and slowly shook his head. "You too, old man?"

"She's not what you think her." Paradignes shrugged. "And I could no more allow her to be destroyed than I could the Wind Dancer."

"I give you warning. I'll not cosset and pamper her." Andros tucked the chest beneath his left arm and began carefully descending the rope ladder into the waiting darkness. "She'll find she has to keep up with me or she'll be destroyed."

"She'll keep up." Paradignes smiled faintly. "You may even find you have trouble keeping up with her. And as I said, she's not what you think her."

Andros hesitated, looking up at the old man. "Come with us. There is nothing but death for you here."

Paradignes shook his head. "I'm a crippled old man, and the path you travel is not for me."

Andros was silent a moment and then said haltingly, "Come. There are . . . ways I can help you."

"Would you carry me on your back? I have a dislike for discomfort and would rather die here among my treasures than in some strange land. May the gods protect you both." He flinched as shrill screams pierced the night outside in the courtyard. "Hurry! You must be far beyond the walls when they torch the city, or the smoke may kill you in those tunnels." He didn't wait for a reply but quickly lowered the trapdoor and kicked the carpet back over it, leaving Andros in darkness.

Paradignes limped to his chair and dropped down on the cushions, leaning his head against the high back with a sigh of relief.

The Wind Dancer was safe. A fierce warrior like Andros would be a fit guardian for the statue and protect it from all who would destroy it. In this world, where ugliness, blood, and violence thrived and flourished, one treasure of infinite beauty had been allowed to survive.

The screams and clamor of swords in the courtyard were drawing nearer. A chill struck through him as he realized he would soon die. He could yet escape if he chose to do so. The rope ladder would be difficult to negotiate for a cripple, but he had always found he could accomplish most things more favored individuals could do.

No, he was weary of hobbling painfully in the darkness of this world. Surely beyond this earth a place existed where the spirits of men of good heart soared on wings as strong and golden as those of the Pegasus he'd entrusted to Andros.

The Wind Dancer.

What would it be like to dance on a cloud, free of the chains of earth? Suddenly, for an instant, he imagined he could actually feel the wind on his face. The buoyant exhil-

aration of flying giddily, swiftly, over mountains and rivers with the warm sunlight in his face. Was the vision sent by the gods to comfort him in his time of need, or was it born of his own desperation? No matter. It was the vision itself that was important, not from whence it came. Perhaps if he concentrated hard enough, he could bring back that most exquisite of sensations.

Paradignes eagerly closed his eyes and only a moment later a radiant smile curved his lips. He was still smiling when the enemy broke down the door and came for him.

The flames clawed at the night sky as if trying to bring down the stars and devour the heavens.

Andros stood on the rise of the hill, his gaze on the destruction sweeping the city below.

"He was a brave man," Jacinthe said quietly from beside him. "My heart grieves for him."

"Paradignes?"

"Who else?" She leaned back against a large triangular gray rock, her gaze never leaving the city. "No one else in that wretched city cared for me."

"Can you blame them?"

"You believe their lies?"

"I believe nothing but what I can see, hear, or taste. I trust no one until they prove themselves." He stooped and picked up the chest containing the Wind Dancer. "But you're comely enough and you didn't whine or weep at the pace I set you in the tunnel. I suppose we can travel together for a time."

"Where do we go from here?"

"South along the coast to Egypt. I'll take service with the pharaoh until I can earn the money to build a boat and return to Shardana."

"She lowered her lids to veil her eyes. "You could sell off the jewels of the Wind Dancer."

He shook his head. "Paradignes died to preserve his treasure. I'll not betray him in that fashion." His gaze narrowed on her face. "And I believe you knew that would be my answer."

"I only hoped it would be your answer." A smile lit her exquisite face with radiance, and suddenly Andros realized why Paradignes could not bear to have her destroyed. By all the gods, he was being as soft-headed as the rest of them about the woman. He quickly glanced away from her. "Well, do you come with me? The road will not be smooth and you will be treated only as a woman, not a goddess."

"That's all I ever wanted." Jacinthe turned and took one last look at the burning city below. "No one understood that but Paradignes."

She picked up the lantern and wrapped her cloak more closely about her. "Give me that bundle of food. You have the statue to carry."

He hesitated, gazing assessingly at the delicate grace of her slim body. "I can manage both, the chest is not heavy."

She snatched the satchel containing their food and strode ahead of him down the trail. "Stop arguing. We have a long way to go and I will do my part, Andros. You set the pace and I will match it."

Andros stared after Jacinthe in stunned surprise, and then found himself smiling as he set off after her. Paradignes had said he might have trouble keeping up with the woman.

In another moment he had overtaken Jacinthe, and they walked side by side in silence toward the distant land that lay far to the south.

Neither Andros nor Jacinthe cast another backward look at the burning walls of Troy.

16

Alex put down the last page of the first legend and gazed thoughtfully down at the dusk-shrouded valley.

"Well?" Caitlin asked.

"They traveled south, along the coast."

"Yes."

"Tamkalo isn't that far from the coast."

Caitlin's eyes widened. "You think it may have been Andros who left the tablet here on his way to Egypt?"

"I'm not saying that. It's only a possibility to consider. You said the Shardana were very secretive and left little evidence of their existence. Yet we have the script on the Wind Dancer you attribute to Andros and now we find a tablet on his alleged route from Troy. If there's no connection, it's a pretty big coincidence."

"Why would he have come this far inland?" She glanced down at the valley. "And why would he climb up here?"

"We don't have those pieces of the puzzle yet." He straightened the pages and handed them back to her. "But if this legend is accurate, then I agree with you that Andros was out of character when he ordered a scribe to put down his story."

She absently stuffed the pages back into the envelope. The idea that Andros and Jacinthe had been there on the mountain, even in this very cave, gave her an uneasy feeling. The place was eerie enough without the knowledge that it may have been haunted by one of her ancestors.

"It bothers you."

"Of course not." She got to her feet and moved the few yards to the entrance of the cave. "It's getting cold out here. We'd better go inside."

Alex glanced at the pewter-gray sky. "I don't like the look of those clouds." He frowned. "I think we'd better search tonight and then get the hell out. I'd hate to be stranded here in a snowstorm."

"Very well." She had no desire to be there with Alex any longer than she had to be to accomplish her purpose. "We'll search now and eat later. Get the lantern."

The tablet was lodged upright behind a boulder inside the bubbling hot spring at the back of the cave. They discovered it after only three hours of searching.

Caitlin's heart jumped and then started racing as she fell to her knees in front of it. The tablet was perhaps nine inches wide and twelve inches high, and the left corner had been broken away from it. She gazed at the tablet in disbelief. "It was too easy," she whispered. "It's almost in plain view."

"Why shouldn't it be easy? It's not as if it's the Holy Grail." Alex kneeled down beside her. "Maybe whoever wrote it didn't want to hide it."

"We had to climb a mountain to find it."

"An obstacle but not an insurmountable one." With utmost care Alex gripped the tablet and tugged experimentally. "It's stuck in the earth. That's probably why the corner broke off when the boy tried to get it out."

He took a knife from his pocket and began digging away the earth around the tablet. Five minutes later he carefully lifted the tablet and handed it to Caitlin. "The moisture from the spring must have kept it in such good condition. It could have crumbled away thou—" He broke off as he saw her face. "What is it?"

"There's more." Caitlin leaned forward, peering into the dark recess in the wall of the cave that the upright tablet had covered. She reached into the recess and drew out a tablet, another, and still another. Before the recess was empty, five tablets lay before them on the stony earth. She looked down at them dazedly. "The same script." She laughed shakily. "*Dieu*, and I thought all we'd have to decipher was the inscription on the Wind Dancer."

"It seems our scribe was prolific."

Caitlin nodded as her gaze flew from one tablet to the next, excitement building higher every second.

She inhaled sharply as she stared down at the last tablet she had taken from the recess. "Yes," she whispered. "He *did* want to make it easy for us. Greek."

He leaned closer, studying the tablet. "You're sure?"

"I'm sure." The tablet was divided in two with a line running from the top to the bottom. On one side was the script she believed was Shardana and on the other side of the line were Greek characters. "I think he laid it out for us. He gave us the tablets and then he gave us the key."

"Why not write the tablets in Greek to begin with?"

She laughed exultantly. "How do I know? Maybe he wanted to give us a challenge."

"But how could he know it would ever be deciphered? In his day it never would have been possible."

"I know. The Rosetta Stone was discovered in 1799 and it still took years to decipher the Egyptian hieroglyphics with the knowledge available at that time."

Caitlin frowned thoughtfully. "Obstacles. Suppose he wanted his words to be lost but not forever."

"You're guessing," Alex said.

She knew it was only guessing, but she kept on, feeling her way. "If it was Andros, it would explain why he started the tradition of having the family history recorded. It would be a clue to those following after."

"And how could he be certain that either the history or the family would survive?"

"The Wind Dancer. He made sure the family fortunes were irretrievably bound to the Wind Dancer. If the Wind Dancer survived, so would the family." She looked down at the tablets. "And so would the legend that led us here. It would be a circle that ended at the same point and—" She stopped, her gaze lifting to his face as she realized what Alex had been doing. He had been feeding her questions and arguments to make her stretch, reach down deeper. "Why are you letting me ramble on? You've probably figured all this out for yourself."

"Maybe." He began to gather the tablets carefully into a pile. "But you let me know up front the Wind Dancer was your exclusive property. I didn't think you'd appreciate any help."

But he had found a way to help her and still let her keep control of the situation. Warmth stirred within her as she looked at him in the lantern light. His expression was intent, his brow furrowed as he painstakingly placed the tablets on top of each other like a small boy stacking blocks. How strange, she had never thought of Alex in connection with boyhood. He had always been the totally adult male, projecting intelligence, humor, and sexuality.

She could sense that sexuality now.

She became acutely conscious of the strength of his

hands moving the delicate tablets with such exquisite care, the way the muscles of his thighs pushed against the soft denim of his jeans as he squatted, the bunching of his shoulders beneath his black shirt as he reached for the final tablet and put it on top of the pile. She suddenly wanted to reach out and touch him, run her hand down the inside of his thigh....

He stood up and took a step back. "I'll carry the tablets and you lead the way with the lantern. I'd hate like hell to stumble and drop—" He tensed, and she could see the muscles of his stomach contract.

She couldn't breathe. She couldn't look away from him. "Caitlin?"

He could see it. She felt the panic rise within her as she scrambled to her feet and grabbed the lantern. "You're right. I don't want any help." She swung past him, walking quickly toward the front of the cave.

She heard him say something, but she was already too far away to discern the words. Then he swiftly followed her, the pounding of his boots on the rocky ground echoing through the cave. On the wall of the cave, magnified to giant proportions, she could see his shadow behind her, stalking her, and it added to the panic flooding through her.

She was already on her knees, rummaging through her backpack, when he got to the front of the cave. Without looking at him she pulled out a blue shirt and threw it to him. "Wrap the tablets in this and then give them to me. I'll carry them in my backpack."

He picked up the shirt from the ground and wrapped it around the tablets. Then he carefully set the tablets down by the wall of the cave.

"I said, give them to me."

"Come here." That faintly Slavic intonation in his voice.

She knelt with shoulders hunched, staring blindly down into her open backpack. "I don't want to."

He crossed the cave to stand beside her. "The hell you don't."

He reached down and turned out the lantern.

Darkness. Heat. Alex.

Her heart was pounding so hard, she was sure he could hear it. "It was nothing. I was excited about the tablets."

"Which lowered your guard and let me in. I'm not one to quarrel with hows or whys. I'm going to stay in, dammit."

"Turn the lantern back on."

"I don't want you to see me. I just want you to *feel.*"

He touched her.

A light brush on her throat, but a primal shudder went through her. "No," she whispered desperately.

"You want it." He pulled her to her feet and began to unbutton her shirt. "Tell me you want it."

She could smell him in the darkness, lime and musk and maleness. He unfastened her bra and drew it and the shirt off her. Why was she standing there? Why wasn't she fighting him? "You're wrong. I didn't want this."

"You're not surrendering anything." His lips lowered to her breast and his mouth closed on her nipple. Heat flashed through her, the muscles of her stomach clenched.

"You want it. You're taking from me. Take me, feel me." His hand reached between them. "Here."

Her spine arched and she cried out. She was barely conscious of him unfastening her jeans, but in another moment both the jeans and panties beneath them were down at her ankles. "Step out of them." Alex fell to his knees on the ground, kneading her bare buttocks in his palms. "Do it."

His tongue . . .

She stepped out of the clothes, her fingers reached out, blindly digging into his hair, her spine curving backward. He widened her thighs and pushed her back against the wall of the cave. The stone was cool against her naked hips and back, and yet she was surrounded by heat—Alex's warm hands cupping her buttocks, the heat inside herself. She could hear the harsh sound of her breath echoing in the hot darkness. "I can't *stand* it."

"Yes, you can. It's what you want. Take it."

She felt like howling, screaming, as sensation after sensation burned through her.

He pulled her down and she felt the cool, silky polyester of her sleeping bag beneath her naked flesh. He was on top of her, parting her thighs. He wasn't taking off his clothes, she realized dimly.

Then he was deep inside her.

"Alex!"

"Forget who I am," he muttered. "Pretend I'm a stranger. Take what you want. Forget everything but this."

What was he saying? No stranger could make her feel like that.

He thrust shallow, then deep, not letting her get used to the rhythm.

She writhed on the sleeping bag, her breath coming in gasps.

"It's all right. Do you feel me?" He was drawing out and plunging deep. "Is it good?"

"It's not—"

He withdrew until he was barely within her. "Is it good, dammit? You don't have to care anything about me. Just care about this."

She lunged upward, trying to take more of him.

"That's right." He withdrew a little more. "Do you want me deeper?"

"Yes!" The affirmative was a savage explosion o
sound.

He didn't move. "More?"

"More."

He went wild inside her, thrusting, rotating, diggin
into her with a force as primal as the whimpering crie
she found herself uttering. It was like lightning striking
striking, striking. . . .

He pushed her legs up above her head to furthe
deepen the thrust. She was open, every muscle clench
ing, responding. Sensation streaked through her, build
ing, spiraling until she couldn't breathe, couldn't hea
anything but the sound of his harsh breathing abov
her in the darkness.

"Give it to me," Alex said thickly as he buried him
self in her. "*Now*."

She spasmed in an agony of climax and felt him flex
ing within her as he released.

He collapsed on top of her, his breathing harsh an
strained, his chest moving in and out as he took grea
quantities of air into his constricted lungs.

Then he was moving off her, leaving her. She coul
hear him in the darkness, but she couldn't arous
enough energy to be curious. The lantern flared in th
darkness, and he thrust it into her hand. "Hold this."

He was carrying her, she realized vaguely. Where
were they going?

"Sit here for a minute." He had set her on a rock bor
dering the warm spring. He took the lantern from he
and set it on the rock beside her. Wisps of steam floate
around him, the moisture curling his dark hair and bur
nishing the tan skin of his face and throat. Their twi
giant shadows on the wall of the cave looked odd, no
frightening as Alex's had appeared to her before, jus
strange. . . .

He tested the water with his hand and then slipped er into the warm, bubbling water. The pleasant, senual shock brought her out of the exhausted lethargy nd back to full awareness. Her gaze flew to his face.

"I was rough with you." He smiled crookedly. "An un-erstatement. I nearly ripped you apart. I don't want ou blaming me tomorrow for any soreness."

And she had helped him. She had gone crazy, be-aved like a wild animal copulating in the darkness. "It . . didn't mean anything," she said haltingly.

"It meant something." Alex sat down on the rock, vatching her in the water. "It means you're alive." He net her gaze directly. "It means though your mother is ead, and you think Vasaro is dead, you're not. You ave needs and desires, strengths and weaknesses, all he things you had before. It means life goes on."

Caitlin gazed at him, stunned. "You're saying you did his to help me?"

"Hell no." He smiled recklessly. "I did it because I vanted inside you so badly, it was killing me. I thought ou knew better than to expect noble motives from me."

"I don't expect them."

"No, you expect me to be the villain in the piece. I night just as well have burned down Vasaro with my wn hands."

"I don't blame you for—"

"The hell you don't." He shrugged wearily. "But no nore than I blame myself. Stand up." He was taking off is shirt. "Come on, stand up."

She stood up in the pool and found he was right. A ull aching throbbed between her thighs.

He lifted her from the pool and began drying her riskly and impersonally with his shirt. "Don't worry, I now I rushed it. Everything is back to the status quo ntil you change it." He handed her the lantern, lifted

her again, and carried her back to the front of the cave
He tucked her naked into her sleeping bag. "Or until
can't stand it again."

He picked up the lantern, crossed the cave to h
own sleeping bag, and Caitlin watched him settle into
before reaching over and turning out the lantern.

Caitlin lay for a long time before she went to slee
The lining of the sleeping bag was a sensual abrasio
against her naked flesh. Her body was still throbbin
and tingling. . . .

From the hot spring, she assured herself quickly. No
because she wanted him again.

She had made a terrible mistake. She should neve
have let this happen. The barricades were down and sh
didn't feel safe any longer.

She felt confused, lonely, vulnerable . . . and alive.

The woman was too nervous. She would have to di
Hans watched Jeanne Marie Neunier scurryin
around the room, carefully avoiding looking at him ly
ing on the bed as she carried the paper sack full of gro
ceries to the cabinets across the room. He could almo
taste the whore's fear, and for an instant it brought hir
a smug sense of satisfaction. Jeanne Marie had bee
afraid of him since that moment he had allowed her t
pick him up in a sidewalk café over six months earlie
Her fear had been a balm to his ego when he had com
to her after bending his head beneath Brian's yoke. "Di
you get the newspaper?"

"Yes." She grabbed the newspaper out of the sac
and hurried toward him. "Krakow's team is still lookin
for you."

And so was Ledford. Hans smiled as he thought ho
frantic Brian must be after three frustrating weeks c

searching futilely for him all over Paris. How lucky that he had kept Jeanne Marie's presence in his life a secret from Brian. There had been no doubt in his mind that Brian would have disapproved of Jeanne Marie. With her, Hans was the master.

"You'll have to leave here."

Hans glanced coldly at Jeanne Marie.

"I mean it. I can't have you here any longer. I have to earn a living, and I can't bring my customers to my pension with you in my bed."

"I'm not well enough to leave yet."

"What if they find out I've been hiding you? Krakow's men could burst in here and kill me."

"How can I leave?" Hans reached for the newspaper she was clutching. "I'll need false papers to leave the country, and I have no money."

"I'll get the money. I have a little set aside."

"Oh?" He paused in the act of opening the newspaper to look at her with fresh interest. "And I'll need plastique and timers. I'm planning a little surprise package for Ledford and Krakow."

"Just tell me where to buy them and I'll get them for you."

"You're so eager to see me go." He pouted mockingly. "Don't you love me anymore?"

"Of course I do. Didn't I take you in and get a doctor we could trust?" She swallowed. "I just think we'd both be safer if you left Paris."

"Perhaps you're right." Hans's tone was abstracted as he caught sight of the headline of the newspaper. The stupid slut hadn't told him about Krakow's announcement. She had thought Hans would be interested only in news pertaining to his own situation.

KRAKOW INVITES EUROPEAN OFFICIALS TO MEET ON THE CONSOLIDATION OF A UNITED EUROPE

This was the big one. The meeting Ledford had told Hans about. He scanned the newspaper article quickly. The meeting was not scheduled until November twenty-sixth, three weeks away—and in Istanbul. Though Krakow's current popularity was putting considerable pressure on Cartwright to make at least a token appearance, there was strong doubt she would accept the invitation.

The old lady would come. Krakow and Ledford would see that they all came like sheep to the slaughterhouse.

But Ledford wouldn't be the only butcher present. In three weeks' time Hans knew he would be well again. In three weeks he'd be ready for Ledford.

"When will you leave?" Jeanne Marie's voice was quivering with eagerness.

"Three weeks. If you can get me the papers."

"Three weeks?"

He could see the disappointment in her face, and it suddenly filled him with fury. Did she think he wanted to lie there helpless in her crummy pension? He muttered an obscenity and saw terror replace the dejection in her face. That was better. She had to realize who was in control. If he had learned one thing from Brian, it was the intoxicating feeling being in control of another human being could bring. He had seen the pleasure on Brian's face every time he had subjugated Hans. Now it was Hans who was doing the subjugating.

"First I'll need a passport, a visa for Turkey, and as much cash as you can scrape together. Then we'll talk about the plastique. You understand?"

She nodded quickly.

"Now bring me your hand mirror and my knife."

Her eyes widened nervously. "Your knife?"

"Hurry!"

She moved quickly across the room, grabbed her

makeup mirror, and brought it to him. "Your knife is in the drawer of the nightstand."

"Get it."

She took out the leather holster and gave it to him.

"Now hold the mirror for me."

She sat down on the side of the bed and held the mirror in front of his face. "What are you going to do?"

The mirror shook in Jeanne Marie's hands. How the hell did she expect him to see himself? "Just hold the mirror still," he said impatiently.

He looked at his face in the mirror. Only a faint golden fuzz stubbled his cheeks, but in three weeks it would be a full beard. He glared at the cloud of golden hair framing his face. He unsheathed the knife, grabbed a handful of hair, and whacked it off with the razor-sharp blade.

"No!" Jeanne Marie flinched as Hans turned his cold gaze on her. "I mean . . . it was so *jolie*."

He ignored her as he reached for another handful of hair and began sawing through the soft mass. *Jolie*. He wasn't pretty. He wasn't the weakling Brian had tried to make him. When he was through making himself look decent again, he would show the whore who was boss. He was still too ill to have her sexually, but there was no reason he couldn't tease her a bit and see those mournful eyes stare at him in the way that made him feel like a real man.

A sudden thought occurred to him that brought a smile to his lips. Perhaps after he finished his haircut he would give one to Jeanne Marie. A very thorough haircut. It would amuse him for a while, and she offered little enough in the way of entertainment. But he knew the very nervousness and timidity that had attracted him to her would be a disadvantage once she was out of his range of control.

Yes, as soon as he had wrung all he needed from h⟨
the woman would have to die.

Snow flurries began near dawn, and by the time Al⟨
and Caitlin got down from the mountain at noon, the⟨
was a light dusting of snow on the jeep.

Another jeep was parked next to theirs, and Kem⟨
was sitting on the hood, swinging his foot.

"Ah, you've come at last." He hoisted himself dov⟨
from the hood with a lithe spring. "I was wondering i⟨
was going to have to come after you. I'm glad y⟨
spared me."

"What are you doing here, Kemal?" Caitlin asked.

"You did not call." He grinned. "So I came to rescu⟨
you. Who is that raving maniac in the shack? I was afra⟨
he might have killed you and devoured your bodies."

"Did you let him out?"

"Am I a fool?"

"Why did you come?" Alex repeated as he unstrappe⟨
his backpack.

"You do not believe me? After I gave up the comfor⟨
of your house to travel thousands and thousands of mil⟨
on that dusty road, breathing pollen and fumes and the⟨
to face this horrendous snow?" He took a newspaper o⟨
of his back pocket and tossed it to Alex. "I thought y⟨
should see this. Yesterday Krakow came out for a unite⟨
Europe and invited all the powerful figures of the EE⟨
for a meeting at a house he's leased." He smiled as he fi⟨
ished softly, "In Istanbul on the Street of Swords."

"Then you were right, Alex." Caitlin looked over Alex⟨
shoulder as he opened the paper. "Is that what this say⟨
It's in Turkish. All I recognize is the name Krakow."

Kemal shook his head. "No, this is yesterday evening⟨

newspaper. It says the Black Medina has forbidden the meeting and threatens reprisals if it takes place."

"Very clever," Alex said. "I suppose the British lion is bristling?"

Kemal nodded. "And so are the rest of the heads of state."

"Ledford wanted to force all of them to come or run the risk of being charged with knuckling under to the terrorists?" Caitlin asked.

Alex nodded. "And by having the Black Medina threaten the conference, it supposedly shows the Black Medina fears a united Europe and looks upon it as a threat. Even if Cartwright has no intention of going along with Krakow's plans, she'll have to show up now."

"Ledford took a chance."

"Not much of one." Alex looked at Kemal. "I'd bet Krakow issued a statement to the effect that he and his followers would be at the meeting but he would understand if any of his illustrious guests chose not to attend."

Kemal nodded. "Exactly."

"Which means Krakow won't be held responsible if anything happens at the conference. After all, he did urge them to stay away."

"Then you think the Black Medina will attack the conference?" Kemal asked.

"What do you think?" Alex folded the paper and tossed it into the jeep. "A few selected deaths at the conference would throw Europe into a panic."

"And might be the final impetus to put Krakow into a position to seize power," Caitlin murmured.

Kemal made a face. "I guess this means I'll have to go to work. I'll take over the job of watching the palace tomorrow from Haman. But for this sacrifice you will

have to promise to invite me to dinner every evening t
save me from my cockroaches. I'll make my report ar
then sing you songs and—"

Alex interrupted. "When they open the house, try t
get in and look around."

"What am I supposed to be looking for?"

"Paintings. Statues. I don't think they'll be there, bt
we have to make sure."

"I'll make sure." Kemal's tone was surprisingly ser
ous. "And I'll call my friend at the airport and have hir
be on the alert for Ledford."

"And once you start watching the house, I don't war
you to come to the cottage again."

Kemal's face clouded with disappointment. "No?"

"Why can't he come?" Caitlin asked.

"I understand." Kemal grimaced. "He's afraid while th
cat watches the mouse hole, other mice will be watchir
the cat. He doesn't want me to lead them to you." H
shrugged and gestured airily. "He's right to be cautiou
What he doesn't realize is that I'm a tiger, not a mere ca
I can devour all the mice with one great gulp."

"It sounds a bit gory," Alex said dryly. "Not to mer
tion giving you a bellyache. Let's just confine your a
tivities to watching the mouse hole. We'll meet yo
every evening at sundown in the covered bazaar at th
Street of the Turban Makers."

"If you insist," Kemal sighed. "My cockroaches wer
getting lonely anyway." His gaze went to the mountai
and then to Caitlin's face. "Did you have success?"

Caitlin smiled eagerly. "More than I dreamed."

"That is good." He studied her face and then smilee
"Yes, very good. You are much more relaxed."

She flushed and lowered her eyes as she began to ur
strap her backpack. "*Sien mien?*"

"Second sight." He turned, walked to his own jeej

and got in the driver's seat. "I will meet you back at the cottage. You must pamper me tonight if I am to sacrifice myself to such pedestrian work as watching the palace." He started the ignition and backed up. "By the way, Alex, you know I must charge you for the rental of this jeep and my own inconvenience."

"I assumed I'd be receiving a bill."

"A steep one." He smiled with satisfaction. "After all, knight errantry does not come cheap." He turned the jeep and roared off in a cloud of powdery snow and gray-white dust.

Caitlin carefully placed her backpack containing the tablets on the floor of the back of the jeep. "I guess it's starting, isn't it?"

Alex slowly nodded. "I can still get you out of here."

"I don't have anywhere to go."

"Bull!" His tone was so violent, she looked up at him, startled. "What the hell's wrong with you? You still have roots. Cling to them, for God's sake. Look, you may not want to talk about Vasaro, and that's fine with me." Alex took a step forward. "But Vasaro is a part of you. It's broken and burnt, but it's still a part of you. You can't live without roots."

"You do."

"Because I've never had any. You're different. You need—" He broke off and slung his backpack into the jeep. "Let's get the hell back to Istanbul."

Caitlin got into the jeep. "What about Abdul Kasmina?"

"How could I forget your welfare case? You won't mind if we don't take him back with us and adopt him?" He backed the jeep and turned it around. "We'll stop in the next town and talk to the authorities about the bastard." He stepped on the accelerator. "I've thought of a way to speed up the process of deciphering the script. The National Security Agency has a new computer that deciphers symbols as well as letters. It's still classified but we could ask Jonathan to pull some strings and get them to send it to us. It might take years to make sense of those tablets otherwise."

"I wouldn't know how to work it."

"I've dealt with cryptograph computers before. I could teach you." He didn't look at her. "I'm not trying to take over. It's just a suggestion."

If the machine would help to speed up the translation of the tablets, she would be an idiot to refuse it. Although the tablets had no connection with the news Kemal had brought them, his words had given her the feeling time was running out. "Thank you," she said formally. "I'd appreciate your help in getting the computer."

"I'll call Jonathan as soon as we get back to the cottage. He may need time to twist a few arms."

Ferrazo had seen that man before.

He slowly straightened away from the brick wall of the shop across from the palace on the Street of Swords.

He watched the curly-haired young man toss a laughing remark over his shoulder to an older man standing on the bed of the truck before setting off across the courtyard. He looked to be more boy than man, and his stride held a youthful exuberance. His lips pursed, and he began whistling a Bruce Springsteen song Ferrazo vaguely recognized. "Glory Time" or "Glory Days" or something. He stopped by the fountain to balance the small, elegant table more securely on his wide shoulders and then strolled leisurely up to the front door of the palace.

Yes, Ferrazo knew he had seen the man before; that face was too memorable to forget.

Two days earlier he had seen the cocky bastard in the doorway of a coffeehouse down the street from the palace, and today he was delivering furniture from the warehouse where Ledford had ordered it stored when he had purchased the house over a year before.

Coincidence?

Ferrazo didn't believe in coincidence.

He leaned back against the wall again and crossed his arms across his chest.

He had been about to give up his surveillance for the day, but now he would wait for the man to come out of the palace.

"Why don't Turkish men wear those fez hats you see in the films?" Caitlin idly asked Alex as she watched the crowd of passersby streaming by the fabric stall. "I guess when I first came to Turkey I expected whirling dervishes and women in veils."

"The fez was outlawed in 1926 when Turkey began looking to the West instead of the East for role models. The convent in Konya where the religious ceremony of the whirling dervishes took place closed in 1925. I believe once a year they still perform in a gymnasium somewhere in Konya, but I doubt if it still has any mystique." Alex's tone was abstracted as his gaze searched the crowd for Kemal. "And Turkish women in the cities are some of the most liberated in the world. It's only in the rural areas you find women still veiled and subjugated."

"Which says a good deal for city life." She looked down at the richly embroidered velvet she had been fingering. "Kemal should have been here by now."

"He's only fifteen minutes late. He said he had to go back to the warehouse with the delivery crew."

"Why don't you think the artworks are in the palace?"

"It would have made sense to transport them out of Europe to Turkey, but Ledford would never have left them in an unguarded house."

"Then they could be somewhere else in Istanbul."

"We'll see when Ledford appears on the scene." He nodded to the length of burgundy velvet in her hands. "Do you like that?"

"It's very beautiful."

"Let me give it to you." He turned to the bearded merchant behind the stall.

Her hands immediately fell away from the velvet. "No, thank you."

"For God's sake, it's only a bit of cloth. I want to give you something."

"Why?"

"I *need* to give to you. Is that so strange? Heaven knows, I've taken enough from—"

"There's Kemal," she interrupted. "He looks very pleased with himself."

"What's unusual about that?" Alex asked sardonically. "What would be really uncommon is for Kemal to look shy and retiring."

"You know you like him."

"*He* knows I like him. The scamp thinks he can charm the birds from the trees."

"Well?"

Alex smiled reluctantly. "He's right."

"He's grinning from ear to—oh, my God!"

Alex stiffened as he saw her expression. "What's wrong?"

"Beyond him." Caitlin couldn't get the words out of her stiff lips. "In the crowd behind him."

Alex whirled around, his gaze searching the mass of people thronging the bazaar. "I don't see—"

"I'm sure I saw—he was there, I tell you. The picture ou showed me. I know—Ferrazo!"

The next few moments were a blur of sight, sound, nd touch.

The metal gleam of the barrel of a gun pointed diectly at her head.

"No!" Alex turned, pushing her down, hitting the tall as they fell to the ground.

The fabric vendor shouting as his bolts of satins and elvets tumbled from the cart.

The boom of the shot echoing through the bazaar.

The sickening thud of hard metal on soft flesh.

Alex's gasp of pain as he fell on top of her.

Screams of the people in the crowd as they scattered vildly in all directions.

Warm blood. Not her blood. Alex's blood!

Panic tore through her. Alex's blood . . . pouring from iis temple.

She couldn't see Ferrazo. But that didn't mean anyhing. With so many people milling in the street, he could e close, coming toward them, almost on top of them.

Caitlin frantically began dragging Alex's limp body round the corner of the fabric booth. The bearded endor was crouched on the ground and immediately egan to scream at her in Turkish.

"Shut up!" she said fiercely as she pushed the vendor side. "Can't you see—"

She stopped wasting her breath. The man clearly ouldn't understand her. She ignored him, cradling Alex's ead on her breast. Was he still alive? She had held Katrine like this on that nightmare drive to the village. Katrine with a bullet in her temple . . .

"Caitlin!" Kemal's voice.

"Here," she called. "Be careful, Kemal."

"He's gone. He ran away after he fired at you." Kem
was kneeling beside her, his gaze on Alex. "Is he dead?"

"I don't know," she whispered. She reached out an
grabbed a length of satin from the tumbled disaster
the cloth bolts on the ground and began to carefull
dab at Alex's temple. "There's so much blood. . . ."

The vendor began to berate her again, and Kem
turned and shouted something at him in Turkish tha
caused the man's eyes to widen with indignation. H
shut up, rose to his feet, and stalked away.

"McMillan . . . no police."

Caitlin's gaze flew to Alex's face. His eyes were ope
and his lips were forming words. She leaned closer to hin

"McMillan. Doctor . . . tell him . . . Ferrazo." Alex sh
his eyes and, unconscious, slumped on his side.

Unconscious but alive!

Relief took away her breath and made Caitlin fe
light-headed.

"The police will be here soon," Kemal said urgentl
"Should we move him?"

The bullet had grazed Alex's temple, but it sti
might be dangerous to move him. What did she know

Yet Alex had said no police.

"Can you carry him?"

Kemal nodded. "Of course. I am very strong." Fo
once the air of bravado was entirely gone from h
speech as he gathered Alex's limp body in his arm
"You lead the way and keep an eye out for the polic
Once we're out of the bazaar, I'll show you a few sid
streets that should be safe. Your house?"

Caitlin rose to her feet and watched as Kemal strug
gled to his feet with his burden. "Where else?"

•   •   •

It took Caitlin four phone calls to Langley, Virginia, before she was finally put through to Rod McMillan. Once she reached him, she didn't waste any time.

"Alex Karazov has been been shot."

A silence on the other end of the line. "Dead?"

"No, but he needs medical attention and he doesn't want the local police involved."

"He's still in Istanbul?"

"Yes." She told him briefly what had happened. "He said to tell you it was Ferrazo."

"Give me the address there."

She gave him both the address and directions.

"I'll have someone there in forty-five minutes." McMillan paused. "You're Caitlin Vasaro?"

"Yes."

"Get the hell away from him."

Her hand tightened on the phone. "What?"

"First that mess at Vasaro, and now this. You're a target. I don't want Karazov near you, dammit."

Caitlin hung up the receiver without replying.

"Someone is coming?" Kemal came out of Alex's bedroom carrying a basin of water. "He's still unconscious."

"McMillan said he'd have someone here in forty-five minutes."

"That's good. It was Ledford's man?"

"Yes, his name is Ferrazo. They . . . think he was the one who killed my mother and Peter Maskovel."

"And shot the pretty girl in the picture?"

Caitlin nodded.

"A bad man." Kemal carried the basin to the kitchenette and dumped the bloody water in the sink. "It is my fault. I led him to you."

"He might have found us anyway."

Kemal shook his head. "I wasn't careful enough. I didn't even realize I was being followed." He set the basin on the sink. "Maybe I'm not as wonderful as I always thought. What a sobering realization."

"Everyone is entitled to a mistake."

"Not one like this." His expression was uncharacteristically grave. "You could have died. Alex almost did. I am sorry, Caitlin."

"It's done. Now we have to get to work and set it right."

He smiled crookedly. "You're very forgiving."

She hadn't been forgiving to Alex, she realized suddenly. She had told him the blame was her own for what had happened at Vasaro. Yet in her heart she had not allowed herself to believe it because she had been unable to bear the sole guilt.

I need to give you something.

Alex's words just before she spotted Ferrazo came back to her. Well, he had given her something. He had almost given his life for her and still might die because he had tried to save her.

"No." She shook her head. "You're wrong. I'm not at all forgiving."

She turned and walked across the room into Alex's bedroom.

Alex didn't regain consciousness until after four o'clock the following morning. Caitlin was dozing in the chair beside his bed and suddenly came awake.

Alex was staring at her, his blue eyes glittering in the lamplight.

"Hello." She shook her head to clear it of the remaining remnants of sleep. "You're going to be fine. The bullet only grazed your temple, which was serious enough.

The doctor said it was the equivalent of a hammer blow. You have a concussion and should stay in bed for the next week."

"Ferrazo?"

"He disappeared into the crowd after he fired the shot."

"You told McMillan?"

She nodded. "He sent the doctor."

He smiled faintly. "With all possible speed."

"He told me to get away from you."

His smile disappeared. "The hell he did. Forget it. I couldn't let you leave now. It wouldn't be safe. You'll have to stay until it's over."

She was silent for a moment before asking, "How do you feel?"

"Like my head's going to explode."

She shivered. "It almost did. I kept thinking of my mother..."

"Katrine..." Alex didn't say anything for a moment. "In the morning I want you to call Jonathan. Don't say anything about this business tonight, but tell him I think the United Europe meeting may bring Ledford out in the open, where we can grab him. I may need his help on the spot." His eyes closed. "And stay close to the cottage until—" He stopped.

"Until what?"

"Give McMillan time to do Ferrazo."

Do Ferrazo? Ah, he meant give McMillan time to have Ferrazo killed. She shuddered at the stark brutality of the words.

Alex must have sensed her revulsion, for he opened his eyes again. "Necessary. He'll try again."

"I'm not arguing. I think the world may get along very well without Ferrazo."

A flicker of surprise crossed Alex's face before a weary

smile touched his lips. "Maybe you have a place in my world after all."

His eyes closed again, and in another moment he was sleeping soundly.

Caitlin leaned back in the chair and studied his face.

His world. Her world. The two seemed to be merging, becoming one. She didn't know anymore where she belonged. What had seemed clear and absolute in the desolation and anger following her mother's death now seemed to be fading in and out of focus. She was no longer the naive woman Alex had met when he first came to Vasaro, but she was also not the woman who had stood on the hill looking out over the ruins of Vasaro. She was changing, evolving, becoming...

Merde, she didn't know what she was becoming. She was a mass of bewildering and conflicting emotions and only God knew what alchemy those emotions would produce when they were resolved.

But she had found out one unequivocal truth when she saw Alex lying bleeding on the streets of that bazaar, a truth with which she must now face and come to grips.

17

"Ferrazo."

Ferrazo awoke with a start, his eyes unadapted to the darkness of the hotel room. He had double-locked the door, yet the whisper of sound seemed not to come from the hall but within the room.

He heard something, a sound, a rustle, a movement.
Something.

His hand slid beneath his pillow and closed on the butt of his pistol.

"Ferrazo."

Ferrazo rolled off the bed, hitting the floor hard, his eyes straining to pierce the darkness.

A shadow to the left of the drapes at the window.

He got to his knees and crawled around the foot of the bed.

"You used me, Ferrazo."

"Who the hell are you?"

"I hate to be used."

The words came not from the window but the opposite corner of the room. How had he gotten over there? Ferrazo swiveled to face the corner.

No one was there.

"I think a man should know why he's going to die."

The voice came from the direction of the window again, but there was nothing *there*, dammit.

"Die? No way, you son of a bitch."

"Alex Karazov is my friend."

Keep him talking. He'd get a fix on him soon. "I didn't mean to take out Karazov. It was a mistake. I was after the Vasaro woman."

"But you still used me to find them."

Christ, it was only that cocky kid who had led him to Karazov and the woman. Ferrazo felt a rush of relief as he cautiously rose to a half crouch. No danger. He could handle the boy with no problem. There was no way a smart-ass kid could—

A flashlight flicked on and out of nowhere the heel of Kemal's hand crashed upward under Ferrazo's nose with faultless precision, splintering the bones and pushing them backward into his brain.

He was dead in two seconds.

"You shouldn't be out of bed." Caitlin looked up with a frown from her magazine as she saw Alex standing fully clothed in the doorway of his bedroom. "You know the doctor said bed rest for a week. It's been only four days."

"I'm well enough. I couldn't stay in that damn bed for another minute." He wandered toward her across the living room. "What are you reading?"

"*Newsweek*. There's an article about Krakow."

"What about the journal?"

"I've already read it four times. I need time to think about it. Kemal brought me an armload of books and magazines from the international bookstore in town." She watched as Alex bent down to pick up a copy of

Paris-Match. The late afternoon sunlight pouring into the room burnished the top layer of his dark hair and revealed the stark white square bandage on his temple. "And you can't read. That's against doctor's orders too."

"Nonsense." He began to gather the magazines into a haphazard pile on the coffee table. "I can't lie there and vegetate. I'll just take these and look through them."

Caitlin felt a reminiscent pang when she recalled that night in the perfumery when he had looked at her holding an armful of books. It was the only time she had seen him as restless and moody as he obviously was now. "No." She stood up and took the magazines away from him. "Maybe tomorrow. The doctor will be back tomorrow morning and I'll ask him if you can do a little reading."

He scowled at her. "I have to call Jonathan. That damn machine should have arrived by now."

"It did arrive. Kemal brought it from the American Express office two days ago. I had him put it in the study."

"Why didn't you tell me?"

"Because I knew you'd be in there setting it up. Now, sit down and I'll make you a cup of tea." She moved toward the kitchenette. "And after you drink it, you can go back to bed."

"This wound is nothing. In the Spetznez it wouldn't have warranted more than a half day in bed."

"Then they all must have been incredibly stupid."

Alex still stood watching her.

"Will you sit down?" she asked, exasperated. "You're not playing macho games with your little soldier friends now. You're supposed to be an intelligent man with a modicum of good sense."

A flicker of surprise crossed his face before he smiled grudgingly and dropped down on the easy chair she had indicated.

"That's better." The teakettle began to whistle, and she took it off the flame and made the tea. "Why were you in the Spetznez?"

"My father wanted it."

"I would have thought he'd realize you'd be wasted in the military."

He didn't answer, and when she looked up it was to see him staring at her with narrowed eyes.

"You're different," he said slowly. "You've changed."

"Have I?" She carried the tea tray around the breakfast bar and to the coffee table. "Why did your father want you to be a soldier?"

"He had been a soldier all his life. He had no use for anyone in any other profession." His tone was abstracted as he watched her pour the tea into the two cups. "The edge is gone. You're not cutting at me."

She merely looked at him.

"Why?"

"I didn't realize I was blaming you for Vasaro."

"You should have blamed me."

She shook her head.

"A clean slate?"

"As clean as it can be with all that's been between us."

He picked up his cup, and a silence stretched between them as he sipped his tea. "We'll have to keep you too busy with the present to remember the past." He set the cup on the coffee table, leaned back in his chair, and stretched his legs out before him. Alex was suddenly vibrantly alive, his restlessness and moodiness gone and that innate overpowering confidence in full rein—a confidence that made Caitlin uneasy.

"If you've finished your tea," she said, "you should go back to bed."

"In a few minutes."

"It's starting to get dark. I'd better turn on the lights."

"Leave them off. It's not dark yet."

No, it was only twilight wrapping the room in intimacy. She leaned back in the shadow.

The golden light mellowed. "Why the Spetznez?" she asked suddenly.

"Are we back to that?" He shrugged. "Because it was the elite corps and I wanted my father to be proud of me."

"And was he?"

"Yes, for a while. It was a feather in his cap having a son in the Spetznez. It added to his luster. Then the KGB tapped me and I went to Moscow." His tone was totally without expression. "In my father's eyes there was no glory to be had from me any longer, so he severed our connection."

"Were you hurt?"

"I don't remember. I guess I was hurt and angry at the time. I should have known how it would end. He made it clear when he took me from school what he expected of me."

"School?"

"I was in a state school in Bucharest. My mother died when I was five, but by that time I had demonstrated unusual intellectual potential, so they kept me around to show off to the visiting party bureaucrats. Then, when I was sixteen, my father came back to Bucharest and they were forced to give me up to him. He took me back to Russia with him."

"Did you want to go with him?"

"Oh, yes. I had the usual illusions about home and family."

"Where did you meet Pavel?"

"In the Spetznez. We went through training together." He paused. "I'll answer all your other questions, but I'd rather not talk about Pavel."

"Why?"

"I cared about him. He was my friend. It's hard for me to talk about people I care about." He went on quickly. "I promise, anything else."

"You don't have to answer any of my questions."

"Yes, I do. You said I knew everything about you, and that made you vulnerable. I'm trying to be fair." He smiled faintly. "Now that I'm sure you're not going to use it to skewer me. What else do you want to know?"

She shook her head as she rose to her feet. "It's none of my business."

"You asked me once why I defected from Russia. I was tired of being used. I thought in America I'd be able to live my own life." He grimaced. "It didn't work out that way. I merely changed one master for another."

No wonder Alex believed everyone used everyone else in the real world. From childhood he had been used by parents, schools, governments—and with total ruthlessness. Even she had tried to use him, Caitlin realized. She had been angry with him for manipulating her for his own purpose, but hadn't she used both his money and intelligence to gain what she wanted for Vasaro?

She picked up the tray and carried it back to the kitchen. "Go to bed. You don't have to tell me any more."

Alex rose. "If you change your mind, let me know."

"I won't change my mind."

He bent and picked up two magazines from the coffee table.

"No." She glanced back over her shoulder. "Drop them."

He smiled and dropped the magazines. "Just testing."

"Kemal is going to come by later. He can play cards with you."

"You could play with me now."

"No." He was coming closer with every word, every gesture, and she had to distance herself. Hell, she didn't even know if what he felt for her wasn't just a mixture of lust and obligation. "You'll have to wait for Kemal."

He studied her, and she was glad the room was now edged with shadows and he couldn't see her expression. "I can wait." His voice was soft as he turned away.

And she knew he was not talking about waiting for the arrival of Kemal.

Kemal drew a card and smiled gleefully. "Ah, I'm going to slaughter you again. You might as well fold right now."

"I'll stick it out." Alex looked down at his hand. "I called McMillan this evening to make sure Ferrazo wouldn't be around to be a danger to Caitlin any longer."

Kemal discarded a deuce of spades. "And how is the charming Mr. McMillan?"

"Puzzled."

"That's the fate of men of little vision."

"The night I was shot, Ferrazo was killed in his hotel room."

"Isn't that what you wanted? Now Caitlin is safe."

"McMillan's man didn't do it."

"No?"

"I need to find out who did."

"What difference does it make?"

"I don't like the idea of a new element appearing on the scene."

Kemal chuckled and shook his head. "I did it."

Alex went still. "You killed Ferrazo?"

Kemal shrugged. "I was afraid McMillan's man wouldn't act quickly enough."

Alex studied him shrewdly. "But that wasn't all."

"He used me to get to you," Kemal said simply. "I hate to be used. I think you are much the same, are you not?"

Alex was silent a moment. "Yes." He looked down at his cards again. "You took a lot on yourself. McMillan could have been displeased. He likes to run the show."

"It was only an isolated case and will not happen again. I do not like to kill. I have a gentle soul." He spread out three kings. "Match that."

Alex threw in his hand. "Gentle as a tiger."

"Only when necessary." Kemal's expression was suddenly grave. "None of us are without a touch of the savage. That is why we were given a mind with which to choose. Every day we must make the choice whether to hate or to love, whether to be good or evil."

"And which choice do you make?"

"It depends on what the stakes are. Sometimes we want to be good, but we must compromise."

"And was Ferrazo a compromise?"

"No." Kemal smiled gently. "No compromise was necessary. He used me and he hurt my friend."

"Your friend?"

"You are my friend," Kemal said. "Do you not know that?"

Alex gazed at him without speaking.

Kemal said, "You don't have to answer. I know it is difficult for you."

"What's difficult for me?"

"Trusting anyone enough to call them friend. I have such a problem myself." Kemal's black eyes suddenly sparkled with mischief. "Of course, I have the comfort of knowing everyone in the world is eager to have a friend with such remarkable qualities as I possess."

"Remarkable isn't quite the word I'd use."

"Fascinating, brilliant, ingenious?"

"You're still not quite there."

"Handsome, talented, articu—"

"I can't stand any more. The air is getting thick in here."

"I'm merely being honest." Kemal sat back in his chair. "But are you being honest with me?"

"About your remarkable qualities?"

"No." Kemal gestured to the deck of cards on the counterpane of the bed. "I've won the last three hands. With a photographic memory you should be able to remember what cards have been played. Are you letting me win?"

"No." Alex's gaze slid away and back to the cards. "Memory used to be a wild talent, but I've learned to block it."

"Why would you want to?"

"It makes the game more interesting. I'm not that competitive."

Kemal sat looking at him, his lips curved in a knowing smile.

"And besides, it's the kind of adjustment one makes." Alex looked up and suddenly smiled as he added quietly, "With a friend."

"Wake up, Caitlin."

Caitlin sat up in bed, her heart pounding wildly. Lamplight revealed Alex as a solid silhouette in the doorway. "What is it? Ledford?"

"No. Nothing's wrong. I couldn't sleep and decided we need to talk. I want to show you something."

She glanced at the clock on the bedside table. "At four-thirty in the morning?"

"Will you get dressed and come with me?"

Caitlin wiped the sleep from her eyes. "Can't we wait? Is it important?"

"It is to me."

Caitlin hesitated for an instant and then tossed aside the covers. "Give me fifteen minutes."

Alex turned away from the doorway. "Wear a coat or jacket. It's not cold, but there's a nip in the air."

"Galatea Bridge? Alex, you got me up in the middle of the night to see the Galatea Bridge? Kemal has already shown it to me. It was one of the first places on his list."

"At dawn?"

"No, it was light."

"Most of the tourists come at night, but I think it's best at dawn." Alex took her arm and pushed her gently forward. "When the sun comes up, it's a new beginning... like dawn at Vasaro."

She stiffened. "I can't imagine anything less similar than Istanbul and Vasaro."

"Now, don't tense up on me. We're doing fine." Alex didn't look at her as they stopped at the black iron rail and looked out over the waters of the Golden Horn. "I need to talk to you about Vasaro."

"I don't want to talk about Vasaro."

"I know," Alex said quietly. "And that's why we have to do it. You're burying Vasaro before it's dead. I've been in contact with Jacques, and he has enough cuttings and slips from the original flowers to start again."

"It will never be the same."

"No, it will never be the same." Alex's hands reached out and grasped the railing. "But does it have to be? You know I've been confused as hell about your attitude about this. You're a fighter, and it puzzled me that you

ave up so easily on Vasaro." She started to protest, but
e forestalled her. "Oh, I know it was a shock, but why
idn't you dig in like Jacques and start again? Then last
ight I figured it out. It was your mind-set."

"Mind-set?"

He nodded. "I remembered you told me once that
ou'd known from childhood it was your duty to pre-
erve and guard Vasaro. You've always been the guardian
f Vasaro, only the caretaker of what past generations
ave developed and initiated. Through no fault of your
wn, you failed to guard what they created." He turned
o look at her. "But don't you see? Now you can become
iore than a guardian. You can mold Vasaro and shape it
o what *you* want it to be."

His tone vibrated with such intensity, Caitlin felt a
tirring of answering emotion. "That all sounds very
opeful."

"There is hope, Caitlin. We can make Vasaro live
gain."

"We?"

"I can help you. *Let* me help you."

Caitlin stared at the pencil-slim minarets in the dis-
ance. "You may be right about all this, but it's still too
oon for me to grasp it. It hurts too much to think
bout Vasaro right now."

"All right. Forget about Vasaro. Let's talk about the
erfume."

She laughed shakily. "My God, don't you ever give
p? The perfume is dead in the water."

"I can't give up," Alex said. "Not until I make it right."

"Alex, we have only a thirteen-month supply of per-
ume. You can't launch a perfume if you can't supply
he orders."

"The hell we can't. I've been thinking about it." Alex's
orehead wrinkled with concentration. "If we work it

right, we can make Vasaro the premier perfume in tl
world."

"And just how can we do that?"

"By relying on one of the most basic desires of h
man nature."

"Which is?"

Alex grinned. "The desire to possess something that
forbidden or out of reach. What do we regard as tl
most glamorous commodities in the world? Diamond
emeralds, gold... Anything that's rare and hard to fin
Why do works of art become instantly more valuab
when the artist dies? Because we know that the ca:
vases in existence are all there will ever be."

Caitlin felt a sudden quickening, caught up in his e:
thusiasm in spite of herself. "You're saying that becau
we have only a thirteen-month supply—"

"Ten years."

"What?"

"We're going to ration that perfume as if it were tl
only water left on a dehydrated planet." Alex leaned t
ward her, his expression alive with vitality. "We'll sell
through only a few chosen shops in the world. They
all be willing to cut throats to get a supply." He pause
"At a thousand dollars an ounce."

Caitlin's eyes widened in shock. "It will never work

"We have to up the price to maintain the mystique
Alex said. "Trust me. It will work. With all the publici
about the Black Medina's destruction of Vasaro, no or
is going to believe this is an artificial ploy to goug
money. The perfume *is* rare and will be irreplaceable fe
a number of years."

"Ten?"

"Jacques estimates seven for the new growth neede
for the ingredients, but I thought we'd give the publ
another three years to get the mystique of Vasaro firm

established in their minds before we lower the price to gain a larger market. By that time every woman in the world will feel that the most desired luxury in the world is owning a bottle of Vasaro."

Caitlin stared at him in amazement. "You've got it all planned."

He smiled. "You wouldn't let me do anything else while I was lying in bed." His brow knit in concentration. "We'll run the commercials with Chelsea extensively after the launch but shift the focus to the rarity of both the statue and the perfume. After the launch we'll show the commercials sparingly and only in the most prestigious time slots. I think it would be a good idea to arrange for an ounce of perfume to be given from one head of state to another. Perhaps from the highest-ranking woman in France to, say, Queen Elizabeth. Why are you laughing?"

"Because I suddenly find myself sorry for Queen Elizabeth." Caitlin's eyes twinkled. "What if the poor woman decides she doesn't want to be involved with my perfume in any way—even acknowledging its receipt as a gift?"

Alex grinned. "We'll just find out what she wants and give it to her."

"You really mean to go through with the launch?" she asked soberly.

"Of course. In fact, I've called the advertising agency and pushed it up to December the tenth. Since we're selling a concept instead of the actual perfume, there's no reason that we can't—"

"If Ledford accommodates you by appearing on cue."

"He'll be here. It will happen, Caitlin. The healing of Vasaro, the launch, everything. I'll make it happen. Do you believe me?"

She was beginning to believe him. Hope was growing, pushing down roots. "I think I'm afraid to believe you."

"You've got to believe me. You need Vasaro and you
need your perfume. They're both a part of you."

"You said that before."

"Because from almost the first moment we met I
thought of you and Vasaro and your perfume as one. I
remember I read something once that..." He looked
away from her and quoted:

Who is this that cometh up from the desert like a
    column of smoke,
breathing of myrrh and frankincense,
and of every perfume the merchant knows.
How delicious is your love, more delicious than wine!
How fragrant your perfumes,
more fragrant than all other spices!
The rarest essences are yours:
nard and saffron,
calamus and cinnamon,
with all the incense-bearing trees;
myrrh and aloes,
with all the sublest odors.
Fountain that makes the gardens fertile,
well of living water,
streams flowing down from Lebanon
Awake, north wind,
come, wind of the south!
Breathe over my garden,
to spread its sweet smell around.

Caitlin stared at him, stunned. What had he just said
to her? His expression was as guarded as usual, and yet
she had an idea a more personal meaning lay beneath
those beautiful words. "The Song of Solomon."

"It was underlined in the Bible I took from your perfumery that night."

She tore her gaze away from him and laughed shakily. "You said your head was crammed with trivia."

His reply came with an odd awkwardness after the eloquence of the biblical words that had gone before. "It's you and Vasaro. That's not trivia, Caitlin."

"No?" Whatever it was, the words had affected her too deeply. She had to think about them and what they might mean to her. She turned away from him and jammed her hands into the pockets of her coat. "All this walking has made me hungry. Let's see if we can find a café that's open early."

"In a moment. It's almost time..."

"Time for what? It's not—"

The song of the muezzin broke the stillness, high and sweet, calling the faithful to prayer. The rosy light of dawn shone through the mists wreathing the slender minarets and domes of the ancient city like the warm flush on the cheeks of a veiled odalisque.

Caitlin listened, entranced. Alex was right. She felt as she had when she heard the larks at home at Vasaro.

Home.

She had told herself she had no home.

But Alex said she herself was Vasaro.

The muezzin's song ended. Caitlin drew a deep breath and turned toward Alex. "Lovely. A perfect ending to—"

He shook his head. "Not an ending. A beginning." He took her arm and began to walk toward the other end of the bridge. "That's why I brought you here. To show you there are still beginnings."

Beginnings. She had always felt herself part of the enduring beauty patterned by the past. It felt strange to realize she might be forced to create a new future for Vasaro. Strange... and exciting.

They walked in silence for a while. "There's your café." He gestured to a small shop with a red and white awning on the quay. A stout, gray-haired woman in a man's tweed jacket was just propping open the front door. "It probably won't serve bacon and eggs or those croissants you like, but maybe they'll have—"

"It doesn't matter." She started down the steps of the quay. "I just hope they have tea. A little of that Turkish coffee goes a long way."

Alex's quiet voice followed her. "Will you let me help you?"

"With Vasaro? I don't know yet." She hesitated and then turned and smiled at him. "But I do need help right now."

He looked at her inquiringly.

"The tablets."

"I'll set up the computer today and show you how to use it."

"That's not good enough. I want you to work with me on them."

He went still. "You want to share them?"

"I want us to find the answers together." Did he know she couldn't give him a greater gift?

"I... thank you." He took her arm and propelled her toward the door of the café. His voice was slightly thick as he added, "Then let's get breakfast over with and get the hell to work."

"It's all set," Chelsea said as she came into Marisa's hospital room. "I've arranged for a whole gaggle of doctors and nurses to meet the plane in L.A. on Thursday." She sat down beside the bed. "They'll whisk you home and put you in your own bed."

"I don't feel well enough to travel."

"The hell you don't. You've been playing possum for the last four days." Chelsea made a face. "You had me scared silly that first day, you little devil. I thought you'd had a relapse."

Marisa smiled faintly. "Maybe I did."

Chelsea shook her head. "You were trying to stall me."

"You can never tell what difference a day will make."

"Well, the last four haven't brought any gifts from heaven."

"You won't change your mind?"

Chelsea reached out and clasped her hand. "Stop worrying. I told you I wasn't going to do anything stupid. I'll simply show up for that conference and do what I do best. Vamp a few diplomats, ask a few questions—"

"Get in big trouble."

Chelsea laughed. "Brat. I'll be careful. You just get well." She got to her feet. "Now get some rest while I go down to the nurses' station and see if I can lure that nurse you like away from *la belle* France to sunny California." She frowned. "What's her name again?"

"Desirée Larue."

"That's right. How could I forget a name like that? She sounds like a porn star." Chelsea left the room.

Marisa gazed thoughtfully at the door. She had played the only card she had while she was lying helpless in bed, and it was now time to call in reinforcements.

With her left hand she reached for the telephone on the nightstand and, cradling the receiver in the crook of her neck, she dialed the operator. "I need to place a call to Jonathan Andreas in Port Andreas, South Carolina, in the United States. I don't know the number."

Caitlin called from the doorway of the study. "Lunch."

"In a minute," Alex said, his head bent over the computer.

"Now. You've scarcely eaten or slept for two days. Let me do the next pattern."

"One more run."

She crossed the room and her hand closed firmly on his shoulder. "I'll do it. So much for you not taking over."

"Christ, have I been doing that?"

She laughed. "Don't look so horrified. I didn't expec anything else. It's the nature of the beast."

"You don't mind?"

"No." She frowned sternly. "But I will mind if I hav to nurse you again because you're overdoing it."

He looked up at her, puzzled. "Why don't you mind?"

She just smiled and shook her head. "Go eat."

"One more run. I think we're coming close." He type a command into the computer. "Check the printer."

She went over to the printer and checked the mes sage. "Still garbage."

"Damn." He began to type another command int the computer and then looked up guiltily. "Okay, yo take over. I'll be back in ten minutes."

Caitlin shook her head in amusement as she sa down in front of the computer.

Then her smile faded and she eagerly leaned forwar as she was drawn into the intricacies of the linear pat tern on the screen.

Jonathan stood waiting on the other side of the bar rier as Chelsea went through Istanbul customs. H smiled as he saw her, and Chelsea felt a melting tender ness she quickly hid beneath a frown. "What the hel are you doing here?" she asked as Jonathan took he overnight bag.

"You didn't expect me?" He indicated her other suit cases to the two porters he had in tow. "I thought yo and Marisa had a rapport."

"Marisa." Chelsea shook her head. "Dammit, even from sickbed she tries to keep me in line. She called you?"

"Two days ago." Jonathan took her elbow and started through the lobby toward the exit. "We had a nice chat. When I first met her I was conscious only of that air of serenity she exudes, but she's definitely her mother's daughter."

"Which means?"

Jonathan grinned. "She's stubborn as hell. She handled me with the diplomacy of an ambassador, but she let me know in no uncertain terms that I was to get my ass to Istanbul *tout de suite* and look after you."

"I don't need looking after."

Jonathan opened the door of the taxi waiting at the curb. "Then you look after me." He tipped the porters and got into the taxi after her. "Hilton," he told the driver.

"I was going to stay at the Sheraton."

"I've checked in at the Hilton."

"Which is why I should stay at the Sheraton."

Jonathan shook his head. "I want you to be with me."

"You shouldn't even be here. I told you—"

"I know what you told me. Things have changed."

"Not that."

"I'm not going to argue with you, Chelsea." He took her hand. "I'd have come to Istanbul whether you were here or not. Peter was my friend. He didn't deserve to be shot down like an animal. Ledford has to be stopped."

"Ledford should have his nuts cut off, his scummy body coated with gasoline, and thrown into a bonfire."

Jonathan smiled faintly. "That's what I said."

"More diplomatically. You always say things the right way."

"And you always speak the unvarnished truth. Which is better, truth or diplomacy?"

She smiled reluctantly. "See, you're doing it again."

Jonathan's hand tightened on her own. "No matter

how I say them, my words never get through to you
Chelsea."

"Yes, they do. I just can't listen to them. The media
will—"

"Istanbul isn't exactly a hotbed of paparazzi. No one
will even know we're here."

"Every reporter in Europe will be descending on
Istanbul next week for the united Europe conference."

"We can always make adjustments then."

"Alex and Caitlin are here in Istanbul. Perhaps I can
stay with them."

"I don't even know where they are. Alex is afraid for
Caitlin's safety and won't chance a leak. He said he'd
contact me at the Hilton."

Then she had no real excuse not to stay with him.
Chelsea felt such a surge of gladness, she was afraid to
look at him as she asked, "You've made reservations for
separate suites?"

Jonathan smiled. "On separate floors."

Chelsea leaned back on the leather seat. "I suppose it
would be safe for a little while." She added quickly, "But
only for a few days."

Jonathan leaned forward and kissed her cheek. "We'll
talk about it later."

It was three o'clock in the morning when the break
came.

"I've got it." Caitlin looked over her shoulder eagerly
at Alex in the chair across the study. "I think this is it."

He jumped up. "You're sure?"

"I'm too scared to be sure. Check the printer." She
typed in the command and then held her breath as the
computer read the command and then sent the order to
print.

Alex stood over the printer as it started to rattle out the message it was receiving.

"Alex?"

He read, "I, Andros of Shardana, salute you and give—"

Caitlin whooped and jumped up from the desk and ran toward the printer. "We did it!"

Alex grinned as he turned to catch her and whirl her in a circle. "You're damn right we did."

She wriggled away from him and bent over the printer to read the words spitting from the machine.

"I, Andros of Shardana, salute you and give thanks to the gods there is someone left to read my words. As I sit here I have wondered if the Barbarians would cause the world to perish before they would acquire the knowledge to read this tablet. Battle is an alluring temptress as I, who have yielded to her call, should know, and the Barbarians like it even better than the guardians of the Wind Dancer. They do not fight better, you understand, they merely enjoy it more. Perhaps the Grand Healers of Shardana have had more success than they claim in tempering the violence in our souls. I have often thought our vocation was encouraged more to protect their secrets than to expiate the violence within us.

"I will write no more at this time. I have given you enough words for your purpose. I am no scholar, and this means of writing is so crude as to drive me mad with frustration. Why have the Barbarians never invented saavzen?"

The printer was silent.

"Saavzen?" Caitlin whispered.

"Did you notice he spoke of the guardians of the Wind Dancer as plural? He was the sole guardian Paradignes entrusted the Wind Dancer to, yet he speaks as if..." Alex trailed off, his gaze narrowing on the paper. "He

seemed to regard the entire world but Shardana as bar
barian. Yet he knew the most civilized cultures on eartl
at the time, the Greeks, the Trojans, the Egyptians . . ." H
turned back to the computer. "Let's key in the nex
tablet."

"No!" As Alex turned to look at her, she shook her head
"It's more than I thought. I want to think about this."

"This is what you wanted."

"Tomorrow."

His gaze narrowed on her face. "What are you afraid of?

She wasn't sure herself, but something in Andros'
words were lifting red flags of alarm. "Tomorrow."

"Very well." He turned off the printer. "We'll do it i
the morning. Come to bed."

She turned off the computer and the lights and fol
lowed Alex from the study. At the door she couldn'
resist glancing longingly back at the printer, torn be
tween fear and curiosity.

Who were the Grand Healers of Shardana?

Two hours later Alex felt Caitlin inch carefully awa
from him and slide out of bed. He had been aware sh
was lying there awake and that in spite of her appre
hensions she had been too excited to sleep. Alex knev
how she felt; he had not been able to sleep either. Th
puzzle they were unraveling was too fascinating and hi
mind refused to shift into low gear.

Caitlin moved quietly toward the door. He knew sh
was going to the study to key in the tablets. He wa
tempted to throw aside the covers and follow.

But it was Caitlin's puzzle, the one puzzle she ha
wanted to solve since she was a small child. She shoul
be the one to read the answers first. If he was fortunat
she would want to share them with him later.

He forced himself to relax again, waiting for the hours to pass until daylight.

Morning light streamed through the panes and high-lighted Caitlin's tan curls with streaks of gold as she sat curled up in the big chair by the window. As Alex watched from the doorway, Caitlin finished another page and dropped it on top of the others on the floor beside the chair.

Alex smiled at her. "You couldn't wait."

"I tried to sleep but I couldn't." Her gaze lifted guiltily to his face. "I didn't mean to shut you out. I just had to *know*. It was like a compulsion."

"I don't feel shut out." He crossed the room and knelt beside her. "It's your puzzle. Did you key in all the tablets?"

"All but the first one. That one seemed to be more personal and less informative." Caitlin shook her head. "It's unbelievable, Alex."

"Shardana?"

"Yes, they had a culture like none I've ever heard or read about. Shardana was a volcanic island in the Mediterranean surrounded by high cliffs and no visible way to penetrate the interior. Their civilization grew to be totally isolationist and self-contained, and the citizens faced exile if they revealed anything about Shardana to outsiders. Eventually they forbade any trade or inter-course with the outside world except by a chosen few."

"If they had something going for them, you could hardly blame them. As Andros said, it was a world peo-pled by Barbarians at that time."

"They did have something going for them," Caitlin said. "They were healers. They believed the basis of all contentment was to be healthy in mind and body."

"And?"

"Their entire culture revolved around that philosophy. Every man and woman was taught healing, and the most gifted were given the title of Grand Healer and jurisdiction over all Shardana. To become a Grand Healer a Shardanan had either to find a cure for a disease or a way to extend life."

"Jesus." He could see the direction this was taking. "How old was this hierarchy in Andros's time?"

"Five hundred years." Caitlin met his gaze. "With every generation producing at least one Grand Healer."

"And, at least, one cure or discovery."

"More. The average life span was a hundred and fifty years in Shardana. The terms are different, but from what Andros says here they had found cures and preventions for heart attack, cancer, diabetes, smallpox, polio, leprosy . . ." Caitlin made a helpless motion with her left hand. "And illnesses I've never even heard of. Do you know what that means?" The significance was still overwhelming her. "They were medical supermen."

"It's believed the Egyptians performed delicate brain surgery centuries before the birth of Christ."

"But this is more. This is . . ." She trailed off, her hand closing on the arm of the chair. "It's millions of lives saved. It's an expanded life of seventy-five years."

He went still. "You're talking as if Shardana still exists."

"I don't think it could. The planet has shrunk too much to hide such a society. But their medical knowledge may still exist. Remember what Andros said about the Grand Healer's secrets?"

"Yes."

"Shardana sent special warriors out to raid and bring home treasure to further glorify their city-state. Warriors who had been judged mentally incapable of adjusting to the peaceful life of Shardana. Their leaders were known as the guardians." She looked down at the sheets on the floor. "And their primary duty was to guard the Wind Dancer."

"The Wind Dancer was created by the Shardanans?"

"It was their artisans' greatest effort, the repository of their culture. Their aim was to create an object so valuable, so beautiful, no one could bear to destroy it."

"Then how did the Greeks get hold of it?"

"Shardana was extremely volcanic and subject to earthquakes. After the Wind Dancer was created, they gave it into the custody of their warriors, whom they sent out into the world. That way, if any major catastrophe struck their city-state, the statue would escape harm. Andros said the Shardana ship carrying the Wind Dancer was pirated by one of the captains sailing under Agamemnon and its cargo stolen. When word came to Shardana, Andros was sent to get the Wind Dancer back. He was pursuing Agamemnon's fleet when his ship went aground in a storm and the Trojans captured him and his crew." She lifted her gaze to meet Alex's. "You know the rest."

"Not quite. You used the word *repository* in connection with the Wind Dancer."

"The inscription on the Wind Dancer translated as 'The fire burns within.' The Grand Healers placed all the knowledge they had acquired up to Andros's time inside the Wind Dancer."

Alex looked at her, stunned. "How?"

She shrugged. "I don't know. Andros didn't say. Perhaps it's engraved inside the statue, maybe this saavzen has something to do with it. They were obviously more advanced than we were in many ways.

Perhaps they had their own equivalent of microfilm. Whatever they did, I'm sure it still exists. The Shardanans obviously intended their secrets to be safeguarded against every threat." She shivered. "And Ledford has the Wind Dancer. *Merde*, I'm scared. Do you know how much any country would pay to get their hands on that information? He and Krakow could use it to become anything they want to be."

"But Ledford doesn't know what he has. We'll just have to get the Wind Dancer away from him before it occurs to him it might be anything more than an art object."

The transcription of the last tablet was very different from the others. It was rambling, written in stops and starts, as if at different times.

"The woman, Jacinthe, is ill with the disease that was ravaging Troy. How bitter if she escaped her fate at Troy only to die here on this mountain, where we took shelter from the Barbarians who roam the coast.

"She fell ill four days ago and, think what you will, I am not a weakling for staying with her. Even if she is a Barbarian, she was a good companion and true and pleasing in many ways. It is only sensible that I wish to continue traveling in her company.

"I think it is the disease of foul water. I could cure her if I wished.

"What am I thinking? She is only a woman. I would not break my vows for a woman. If she dies, she dies.

"She burns with fever. She cries out in the night. Why does it hurt me?

"She is dying. . . .

"I am a guardian. I cannot break my vow. What barbarian woman is worth the price of never returning to Shardana?

"She opened her eyes an hour ago and tried to smile at me."

And then one last entry written with a trembling hand: "I think I will die myself if the gods take her from me. . . ."

"She didn't die," Caitlin said softly. "And he never returned to Shardana. He helped her."

"So it would seem from the legends."

"But he never revealed his secrets. He protected Shardana and the Wind Dancer from the Barbarians."

"Until now. As he suspected, there are still barbarians in the world."

"Yes." She turned to face him. "But there are more guardians now."

"Don't look at me. I'm no idealistic watchdog."

"No?" She smiled at him. "Yet you said I'd chosen that role and you've certainly mounted guard over me. I think you may be more like Andros than you think."

He shifted his shoulders uneasily. "Nonsense."

"What do you suppose happened to Shardana?"

"You're a student of antiquity. Didn't the description of Shardana strike you as familiar?"

"Not with a culture centering on healing." Caitlin thought about it. "But perhaps . . . Avalon? The island of healing, where King Arthur was taken when he received a mortal wound."

"I was thinking about the volcanoes and earthquakes. Some scholars think Atlantis was destroyed by an earthquake followed by a tidal wave. That would explain why the Shardanans stopped raiding and became mercenaries in Egypt. They had no place to go home to." He shrugged. "Or maybe Shardana was neither of those places. Perhaps Shardana's legend was never told." He gathered the printout into a pile. "I think I'll read through these myself and then move the computer and printer out of the way."

"Why?"

"To set up the projectors again. We have to study that hologram of the Wind Dancer and see if we can find out how to get into the damn thing." He frowned. "If they loved beauty so much, I can't believe they would just seal it and make us break into it. Maybe there's a pattern in the way the jewels are set...."

If Caitlin had thought deciphering the tablets was difficult, the next hours revealed that trying to find a way to cause the statue to open was nearly impossible. It was clear that days of work still lay ahead of them.

Caitlin was so exhausted, she had thought she would go to sleep at once that night, but an hour after she had left Alex she was still lying wide awake.

Suddenly she threw back the covers and got out of bed. A moment later she was standing in the doorway of Alex's bedroom.

"Alex."

She could see the tensing of his body as he half sat up in bed. "Yes."

She moved toward him across the room. "I don't want to be alone anymore."

He held back the covers in silent invitation. "You were never alone."

She slipped into bed and lay beside him, not touching him. "No?"

He drew the covers gently up to her chin and then lay back down on his side of the bed. "I was always here for you."

"Because you were sorry for me?"

"No, not because of that."

"Lust?"

"Not that either. Though God knows that is certainly there."

"I feel very . . . uncertain."

"I don't."

"Everything around us is changing. What should we do?"

"Go to sleep, get inside that damn statue, find Ledford, go to Nice, launch your perfume, start the plant—"

She chuckled. "I should have known you'd have an answer."

"Answers are what I do best."

"There's something else you do better."

He stiffened. "You don't have to pay me to have me here for you, Caitlin. That's what friends are for."

Not lovers, friends. "Are we friends, Alex?"

"I want to be your friend. I respect you. I trust . . . you." The words were spoken haltingly, as if forced from him, and yet she felt warmth blossoming inside her. She had the same feeling she had experienced on the Galatea Bridge, that he was trying to say something else to her. Passion was easy for Alex Karazov, but after years of repression and betrayal, trust and friendship were great and rare gifts. He had given his friendship to Pavel, and after Pavel's death only Kemal had managed to insinuate himself in Alex's affections. "Tell me, did you ever tell Pavel you cared about him?"

"Why do you ask?"

"Did you?"

"No." He added quickly, "It wasn't necessary. He knew how I felt."

"I see." Caitlin was beginning at last to fathom Alex Karazov. How wary he was, she thought with sudden compassion, as wary as she had always been. She was using the past tense, she realized in surprise. When had her wariness toward Alex started to fade and trust begin? They had started out with lust and progressed through all the spectrums of passion, despair, and enmity, and only now were beginning to fully understand each other. "Touch me."

He stiffened. "I told you that you didn't have to pay me for—"

"Who's paying?" She rolled over into his arms and felt a shock of desire as flesh met flesh. Full circle. They had traveled full circle back to lust, and yet she suddenly knew it would be richer, deeper, for the journey. "I'm just taking advantage of what you do best."

"Alex," she whispered, almost on the edge of sleep.

"Yes."

"There's something you should know." She cuddled closer and kept her eyes closed.

His hand stroked her hair. "What?"

"I love you."

She felt him stiffen against her, but he said nothing. She hadn't expected a reply. She knew he might never say those words to her, but that was all right. She needed to say them to him. "We were wrong. It does exist. . . ."

"Does it?" he asked thickly.

"Yes. Good night, Alex."

She felt his warm lips brush her temple with exquisite tenderness. "Good night, Caitlin."

Kemal tossed the last printout aside. "This is very interesting."

"Interesting?" Caitlin raised her brows. "Kemal, this is world-shaking."

"No." His black eyes were twinkling though his expression remained solemn. "*I* am world-shaking, this is merely interesting. But neither you nor Alex can lay claim to that state at present. You do not amuse me when you work so hard. Alex has not been out of that study all day."

"He thinks there may be some pattern to the placement of the jewels on the base of the statue. He says it has to be the base because that's the only part of the statue that could open without destroying the symmet—"

"You see? Patterns, legends, miracle cures... You have no time for the important things."

"You?"

"I would hate to be so immodest as to agree with you." He opened the door. "I will leave you to it and see if I can scramble up something concerning Ledford of interest enough to distract you." He sighed. "Now, it would, indeed, be world-shaking if I failed in any endeavor."

Caitlin chuckled and then turned to hurry back to the study and Alex.

18

"Irmak's back," Kemal said two days later when Alex answered the phone.

"You're sure?"

"I saw him go into the Kafas myself last night."

"Where the hell has he been?"

"I told you that you frightened him." Kemal paused "Maybe for more reasons than we thought."

"What are you talking about?"

"I've been asking questions about Irmak. I assumed knew everything about him, but I found it odd he wa so terrified of you, so I decided to do a little probing. He paused again. "Our lives have been intertwined so long that it surprised me that I—"

"Kemal."

"I'm getting to it. Adnan has a Gypsy connection."

"What?"

"His father's first wife belonged to one of the tribes who come to the Eridne every year."

"You're saying that Irmak could be the Gypsy?"

"Well, his father took the blood oath or he could not have married Adnan's mother. I suppose that makes

Adnan a Gypsy. I don't know about him being *the* Gypsy. But it would explain why he disappeared from sight when he found out who you were looking for. He knew Ledford would not have been pleased you were searching so diligently for him. He was probably as much afraid of Ledford wasting him as he was of you."

"You said Irmak didn't have the connections to get false papers."

"As far as I know, he hasn't. I'm looking into it. There are some forgers in town who might have branched out to deal in passports."

"Meet me at the Kafas tonight."

"Sorry. You'll have to handle this yourself. I tried to get into the Harem last night after the show, but they stopped me at the door. Adnan gave orders that I'm not to be allowed anywhere near him." Mockery layered Kemal's voice. "I was truly cut to the heart. And we used to be so close."

"Can I get in?"

"Possibly. Adnan's guards don't know you. But you can't go wandering around the Harem, looking for him. Let me think...." There was a silence on the other end of the phone before Kemal said briskly, "Here's what you can do. I think I can get word to Melis to help. You'll have to bring Caitlin."

"I doubt if she'd let me leave her here."

"Go to the Kafas tonight and stay after the show. The two of you will go through to the Harem and rent one of the rooms like regular customers. I'll have Melis come to your room and take you to Adnan when the coast is clear."

"And how are we supposed to get out of the Harem once I've talked to Irmak?"

"The same way you came in, through the Kafas, like

any satisfied customers. You just have to make certai]
Irmak doesn't give the alarm."

"If I get to him, I can promise you that."

"I thought as much. I have the utmost confidence i]
you. I'll see you back at the cottage when it's over. I']
have coffee ready and you can tell me all about th
evening's entertainment."

"May I remind you I'm not paying you to mak
coffee?"

"How can you say that when I've masterminded th
entire plan? Now you must only execute it."

"Only?"

"Brains are always more valuable than brawn. It'
nice when an individual has both, as I do, but I'm sur
you can compensate for any lack by—"

"Good-bye, Kemal."

"Good-bye, Alex."

As Kemal predicted, Alex and Caitlin had no troubl
getting past the two men dressed as eunuchs standin
guard at the door separating the Kafas from the Harem
Once inside, scarlet-robed attendants took care of eac]
patron, determining his wishes and escorting him to th
carved door behind which was the pleasure of his choic

Alex and Caitlin were left in a spacious chambe
with mirrors on the ceiling and two of the walls. Thic]
white carpet covered turquoise tiles, and the bed was ;
masterpiece of turquoise and cushions that looked f
for a caliph. She tried to smile as she moved across th
room. "You said this place was a sultan's fantasy." Sh
sniffed. "Good heavens, incense. How long do you thin]
we'll have to stay here?"

"Until Melis can get to us. Kemal didn't say." Ale]
still stood by the door. "Are you nervous?"

"A little." She made a face. "This is my first time in a arem."

"Mine too." A crystal wine decanter gleamed on a rose-wood table. Alex poured the ruby-red wine into two lasses, handing one to her.

Caitlin tentatively sipped the wine. "Too sweet. It's ke everything in the room. A little overpowering."

"Well, what do you want to talk about?"

"What?"

"We've got to do something. There aren't many op-ions unless you'd like to put this room to the use it was atended."

She had a sudden vision of the men and women in he Kafas copulating, writhing, inciting. Tonight she had ot been moved at all by the performance. She had nly wanted it over. "No."

"Neither do I," Alex said.

"Will Irmak be able to tell us where Ledford is?"

"If he's the Gypsy, and not just a front man, he may now. We'll have to—"

A soft knock on the door stopped Alex in midsen-ence.

"Melis?" Caitlin put her wineglass down on the chest.

"Probably." He quickly went to open the door.

"I have come for you."

"Melis?"

"Yes." The tiny, fine-boned child who slipped into the oom seemed younger even than the eleven Kemal had old them was her actual age. Golden hair flowed past er shoulders in tight ringlets, and she was dressed in victorian clothing—a starched white dress with a each-colored satin sash, white stockings, and shiny lack patent-leather shoes. "We must wait for a mo-ent." Nervous color ebbed and flowed beneath her ine skin, and the words came breathlessly. "Kemal says it must be quite safe for you. The guards have gone int Simal's room, but we must wait until they begin."

"Begin?" Then Caitlin understood and felt her stom ach churn with sickness. She wondered if this Simal wa as young as Melis. When Caitlin had been Melis's ag she had run through fields of flowers, playing game with her friends. She said huskily, "We have to do some thing, Alex. I can't stand to see—"

"I know. We'll find a way," Alex said. "The first step i to get rid of Irmak."

"Kemal said you would help us if we helped you, Melis whispered, her small hands nervously smoothin her starched white skirts. "I do not like it here. I want t go away."

Aching sympathy tightened Caitlin's throat. "Yo will go away. I understand how you must feel."

Melis gravely studied Caitlin's face before she slowl shook her head. "No," she said. "You are kind, but yo do not understand." She turned and opened the door. " will go first. Follow me four paces behind."

They negotiated the deserted corridors. Melis stoppe before a carved door. "Adnan," she said softly. "I must g now. I will be missed." She flitted away down the corri dor like a tiny ghost from another age.

"I wonder who the hell is going to miss her." Caitli added fiercely, "I'd like to *kill* Irmak."

"Easy." Alex's expression was grim in spite of his ad monition as he opened the door. "All in good time. promise you we'll get her out. I'd like to murder hin myself, but this isn't the—"

Adnan Irmak was already dead.

Caitlin gazed in shock at the man slumped over th massive desk across the room. "Is that Irmak?"

"Yes." Alex moved quickly toward him. "Close th door."

Caitlin obeyed him, watching the pool of blood pouring from Irmak's throat and spreading on the blotter of he desk. "Murder?"

"It's hard to slit your own throat."

"Shouldn't we get out of here?"

"In a minute."

She looked in morbid fascination at the pool of blood and swallowed, fighting back nausea. "Who do you suppose did it? Ledford?"

"Possibly. He might have thought we were getting too close and wanted to silence Adnan." Alex shifted Irmak's body to get to the middle desk drawer. The dead man's head wobbled. "It could have been anyone. One of his whores or one of the customers he's been blackmailing." He closed the desk drawer. "According to Kemal, he wasn't the most popular man in Istanbul."

"What are you looking for?"

"Records. Information." Alex opened the right-hand drawer. "Jackpot."

Caitlin came forward, trying not to look at Irmak. "You found something?"

"A drawer full of passports." Alex flipped open the top one. "Excellent quality."

"Then Irmak was the Gypsy?"

"So it would appear." Alex opened the bottom drawer and drew out two long black ledgers. "Let's see what kind of records the bastard kept."

He opened the first ledger, glanced inside, and then closed it again. "The Harem account books." He opened the second ledger and flipped rapidly through the pages. Suddenly a smile lit his face. "B.L. Now, who do we know with the initials B.L.?"

"Brian Ledford."

"Right." He took out his handkerchief and carefully wiped off every surface he had touched before slipping

the ledger under his white robe. "Let's get the hell ou
of here"—he grabbed Caitlin's hand—"in case Ledfor
has left one of his thugs who might recognize us."

Kemal put aside his guitar and rose to his feet whe
Caitlin and Alex walked into the cottage. "Just in time
The coffee's ready. Sit down and I'll get the tray." H
looked at Alex and shook his head. "You should hav
gotten rid of the robe before you left the Kafas. I
doesn't suit you. It takes a certain flair to wear suc
robes that you obviously don't—"

"Get the coffee and save the fashion critique." Ale
took the long ledger from beneath his cloak and laid i
on the coffee table before shrugging out of the whit
robe and tossing it on the chair by the door. "Irmak"
ledgers were too bulky to hide beneath a suit coat."

Kemal went into the kitchenette and got the tray
"You must have been very persuasive to get him to par
with them. Did you squeeze any inform—"

"He's dead," Caitlin said. "Murdered."

Kemal stopped. "Really? Alex?" Then he strolled i
with the tray.

"Not me," Alex said. "He was dead when we go
there."

"Too bad. So you weren't able to question him.'
Kemal set the tray on the coffee table. "How?"

"Knife. His throat was cut."

"Messy. That must have been distressing for Caitlin.'
Kemal smiled gently at her. "Sit down. You look terri
ble." He pushed her down in the chair and handed he
one of the cups. "Drink it. It will make you feel better.'
He turned to Alex. "You think the ledger will tell yo
what you need?"

The hot liquid did warm Caitlin and banish a little of the cold nausea gripping her stomach. They were both so casual about it. Irmak had been a terrible man and undoubtedly had deserved to be murdered, but she couldn't stop thinking about that pool of blood.

"I don't know," Alex said. "I haven't had a chance to look at it."

Kemal curled up cross-legged on the floor by Caitlin's chair and reached for a cup of coffee. "Then look at it now. I'll be silent as a corpse." He pulled a face as he saw her flinch. "Sorry, Caitlin."

Alex was leafing through the ledger. "Christ, the man must have supplied half the mercenary units in Africa and Europe."

"I told you Irmak was rich." Kemal lifted his cup to his lips. "Addresses?"

"No. Only lists of merchandise and delivery dates."

"Then you're back to square one?"

"Maybe not." Alex's finger skimmed down the list of merchandise listed under B.L. "There are some odd entries here. I'll have to study them for a while."

"You won't mind if I leave you?" Kemal took a sip of coffee, put his cup back on the tray, and rose. "I have something to do."

"What?"

"It just occurred to me that when the guards find Irmak, the Harem is going to be in an uproar." He moved toward the door. "I might be able to take advantage of the confusion if I move quickly."

"To do what?"

"The children," Kemal said quietly. "Melis and the others. With luck, I can smuggle them out before someone else takes control."

Caitlin asked, "Could that happen?"

Kemal nodded. "And probably will. Irmak told me he seized power from the former owner of the Harem."

Alex stood up. "I'll go with you."

Kemal shook his head. "You were seen there tonight. It would be more dangerous for me with you along."

"What will you do with the children?"

"They can keep my cockroaches company for a day or two while I find a place—"

"Bring them here," Caitlin said. "We can call Jonathan and he'll find help for them."

Kemal stopped at the door. "There are six. They will be trouble for you."

"Bring them here."

Kemal said solemnly, "I knew when I first saw you that you had motherly instincts."

"Liar. All you noticed was my breasts."

"It's the same thing. I told you it was psychological."

He picked up the robe Alex had discarded on the chair, slipped it on, and turned toward him. He struck a pose with arms folded across his chest, his legs slightly astride. "Now, this is how you *should* have looked in this robe. Like a proud king of the desert, like a handsome caliph who—"

"Go get the children."

Kemal grinned and swept out of the cottage, the full white robe flowing regally behind him.

"That was Alex." Jonathan replaced the telephone receiver and turned to Chelsea. "He said Caitlin needs our help. It seems she acquired six children last night."

"I assume not in the usual manner." Chelsea straightened in her chair. "What the hell?"

"Don't ask me. Alex didn't explain. Two boys, four

girls, ages ranging from ten to fourteen. He did say the children had been sexually abused."

"By their parents?"

"You'll have to ask Caitlin."

"*I* will?"

"Well, you're the logical one to deal with the problem. You're the chairperson of an organization that helps abused children."

"You're right." She grinned as she stood up and smoothed the skirt of her dress. "I'm damn good at solving other people's problems. I was getting sick and tired of waiting around here for the conference to begin anyway. Let's go."

He shook his head. "You go. Alex asked me to meet him at the embassy and see if I could discover the security plans for this meeting."

"What's Alex's address?"

"Alex said by now an escort should be downstairs in the lobby waiting to take you to where Caitlin and Alex are staying. His name is Kemal Nemid."

"I'm not going another step. We're running around in circles." Chelsea fixed Kemal with a cold glare as she plopped down on the balustrade of a railing leading up to a crumbling apartment building. "I've seen that shop across the street twice. You've had me tramping around these back streets in circles for two hours."

"Walking is good exercise."

"Not when you're wearing four-inch heels."

"You should not wear such shoes. Caitlin is much more practical."

"Caitlin is a head taller than I am."

Kemal smiled. "Ah, yes, such presence. She is very

beautiful. You are also attractive, but personally, I'm fonder of big women."

"Then why are you trying to wear me down to Thumbelina size?"

Kemal's smile faded. "I'm not trying to exhaust you. I just want to lose anyone who might be following us, and keep Caitlin and Alex safe. I don't have an automobile, and taxis and rental cars can be traced. Walking is best."

Chelsea studied his grave expression for a moment and then got reluctantly to her feet. "Hell, lead on."

Kemal immediately set off down the street. "Though you should thank me for the opportunity to increase your stamina. Caitlin improved immensely once I showed her how healthy walking—"

"We're here." Kemal threw open the door of the cottage. "Andreas sent this lovely lady. I approve."

"Chelsea, I thought you'd never get here." Caitlin gave her an affectionate hug. "I didn't even know you were in Istanbul until Jonathan told Alex on the phone today."

Chelsea returned the embrace and then limped into the house. "If I'd known your friend Kemal lived here, I might never have come."

"She doesn't like to walk either." Kemal closed the door. "But she complains louder than you do. Where are the children?"

"Still sleeping in Alex's room." Caitlin frowned. "Except Melis. She won't eat and hasn't slept since you brought her here last night. She just sits in the garden"— she shrugged—"but the others seem happy enough."

"She's frightened. Changes always frighten children. She's used to her place. I'll go and talk to her." Kemal went out into the tiny garden.

Chelsea and Caitlin followed him and stood at the door, watching as he knelt beside the fair-haired child sitting on the stone bench and began to talk to her.

"What place?" Chelsea asked.

"A brothel."

"Christ!" Chelsea shook her head. "It makes you wonder what kind of world we live in."

"Yes."

"And the others?"

"The same. Kemal got them all out."

Kemal's expression was intent, a gentle smile on his lips as he reached out and touched Melis's cheek with one finger. The golden-haired child in her white Victorian dress and the strong, dark-haired young man in his blue sweatshirt and jeans made a strangely beautiful contrast of past and present.

Melis was smiling now, a tiny ghost of a smile, but a smile nonetheless.

"Maybe he's not as bad as I thought," Chelsea said grudgingly. "At least the little girl doesn't think so."

Melis stood up and put her hand in Kemal's.

"She's hungry," Kemal called out. "How can she sleep when you do not feed her?"

"I offered—" Caitlin broke off as Kemal shook his head warningly. "I'll fix a sandwich."

Melis smiled radiantly up at Kemal as they began to walk slowly back to the cottage.

"He seems to know the charm," Caitlin said.

Chelsea nodded thoughtfully. "She obviously responds to him." She moved toward the telephone on the table. "I'll call New York and talk to the director of my safe-house organization and see if he can give me the name of someone to contact here in Istanbul. They can't suffer a language barrier now too. The children will need to be housed and cared for by their own

countrymen and they should start therapy under a psy
chologist immediately." She lifted the receiver of th
phone. "A feeling of security is everything in a situatio
like this. The first few weeks after children are remove
from an unhealthy environment is a crucial period fo
them." Chelsea began to dial the phone. "What are yo
waiting for? Make the kid her sandwich."

Caitlin discovered she was smiling as she entered th
kitchen and opened the refrigerator door.

"Your friend knows how to get things done." Kema
watched Chelsea as she briskly shepherded the six chil
dren down the street. She had arranged to have the statio
wagon from the government welfare office pick up th
children over two blocks away to maintain the secrecy o
the cottage's location and insisted on delivering the chil
dren to the vehicle herself. "But will they be treated as wel
after the American movie star leaves Istanbul?"

"Chelsea will see that they're protected," Caitlin
said. "She has a daughter who was abused. Believe me
no one is better at guarding the helpless than Chelsea."

"Her daughter? The girl at Vasaro." Kemal's glanc
flew to her face. "Ah, that is why she does not laugh
Who did this?"

"Her father."

"The betrayal is always worse when it is someone
you trust." His expression hardened. "Where is he?"

"Dead." Caitlin smiled gently. "You can't protect th
whole world, Kemal."

"It's often too late to protect, but there are still many
ways to help—and avenge."

"Well, it's too late for you to avenge Marisa, and
Chelsea gives Marisa all the help she needs."

Kemal's gaze returned to Melis, who was hanging back, staring desperately, pleadingly, over her shoulder at Kemal. "Some people's problems are more complicated. Sometimes no one understands or can help who hasn't been there."

"What did you tell Melis in the garden?"

"I told her she would probably be hurt again, but that she would never again be helpless to fight it."

"Not very reassuring."

"Should I have promised her that she would never be hurt again?" Kemal shook his head. "She would not have believed me. Melis already knows life is full of pain and compromises. It's enough for people like us to have a chance to change our lives." He lifted his hand in farewell as the little group disappeared around the corner. "That's a great gift in itself."

"Kemal, I think you may be a success as a philosopher after all."

Kemal's soberness was gone in an instant. "I've decided I will never become rich by being a philosopher. There's much more money being a superstar. Why don't I play my guitar for Miss Benedict? Perhaps she will discover me, take me to Hollywood, and introduce me to the extraordinary Marisa."

"It's not likely. I don't think she's forgiven you for making her walk from the hotel."

"Oh." Kemal brightened. "She is small. I have my bicycle in the garden. I'll ride her back on the handlebars. Do you think she'd like that better?"

Caitlin smothered a smile as she thought of the long stretch limousines to which Chelsea was accustomed.

"Why don't you ask her?" Caitlin asked.

• • • •

Alex didn't arrive back at the cottage from his meet‑
ing with Jonathan until nine that evening.

Caitlin came out of the bedroom when she heard th
front door close. "You've been gone for a long time. Di
you find out anything?"

"It took hours to pry the schedule out of the embass
people."

"I can see why they wouldn't want to reveal it t
everyone who asks. What is the schedule?"

Alex shrugged. "Special escort from the airport t
the palace at ten in the morning. Lunch catered unde
the strict supervision of British security. The meeting
three until seven in the evening. Then the members wi
be whisked back to the airport at eight that evening
Nothing very original or innovative."

"Have you eaten? There's still a little of the stew
made for the children."

"I'm not hungry. Are they still here?"

Caitlin shook her head. "Chelsea blew in like a hurr,
cane and whisked them off to a welfare shelter." He
lips twitched as she remembered her last glimpse c
Chelsea's scowling face. "And then Kemal took her bac
to the hotel on his bicycle."

"That must have been an experience for both c
them." Alex picked up the receiver of the telephone. "
have to call Goldbaum. I want him to check on some c
the equipment Ledford bought. Where did you put th
ledger?"

"I'll get it." Caitlin crossed to the hall closet, slippe
the ledger from the shelf, and brought it to him. "Wi
he still be in his office?"

Alex nodded as he punched in the number.

Caitlin sat down on the couch and waited.

"Where the hell have you been?" Goldbaum de

nanded irritably. "First you nag me to death, and then, when I do have something, you disappear into—"

"I've been busy. What have you got?"

"Ledford."

"What!"

"Well, we don't have him, but we've linked him to Krakow. My man, Nesmith, followed Krakow to an apartment sublet by a Daniel Bledsworth in Paris. When Nesmith's report came in, I told him to check out Bledsworth." He paused. "Bledsworth's description matched Ledford's."

"Christ, is he still there?"

"He left the apartment two days after the meeting with Krakow, but we managed to get hold of the records of his telephone calls for the last three weeks. That's going to cost you."

"Never mind. Were there any calls to Istanbul?"

"Several. All to the same number. I haven't been able to trace it. You're going to have to check that one out on your own. That Istanbul phone company isn't at all amenable to bribes. I couldn't even get *your* number."

"Give it to me." Alex snatched a pen and paper and scrawled down the number Goldbaum gave him. "What else?"

"The number of a phone in the hallway of a pension in Paris. We're still checking on the tenants who live there. Another number in Le Havre." Goldbaum paused. "White Star Shipping Line. Their ships fly a Liberian flag and Daniel Bledsworth is listed as principal stockholder. A ship departed Le Havre the same day Ledford moved out of his apartment in Paris."

"So much for Kemal's man at the airport," Alex muttered. "What's the name of the ship?"

"*Argosy.*"

"A passenger ship?"

"Strictly cargo, until now."

"Have you got a description, size, registration num
ber, tonnage, and so forth?"

"I'll get it."

"Right away. If Ledford left Paris a week ago, h
could be here now."

"Depends on the route," Goldbaum said. "And h
may have taken time to put into port and have th
ship's name changed."

"Maybe." Alex flipped open the ledger and his finge
went down the column. "I have a couple of items I wan
you to run through your computer for me. I need t
know what they are and what the common usage is fo
both of them. In this ledger I have a 'black damp' liste
with a question mark after it. Directly underneath it is
Sodium V."

"V or C?"

"V."

"Spell *black damp*."

Alex spelled it, then flipped the ledger closed. "Ge
back to me as soon as you can."

"Do I get a telephone number this time, or do I us
telepathy?" Goldbaum asked caustically.

Alex gave him the number and hung up the phone.

"You're excited." Caitlin's gaze was on his face.

"We've got a break," Alex said. "I didn't think it wa
possible, but we've actually got a break. Ledford ma
be on his way here by ship."

"What ship?"

"The *Argosy*. A name that would suit Ledford's pas
sion for antiquities."

"So what do we do?"

"Get Kemal to check out dockings. Find a way to ge
the name and address of these Istanbul telephone call

edford placed so that we can be there waiting for him
when he walks in the door. We're going to *have* him,
Caitlin."

"Are we?"

Alex looked at her. "You should be as excited as I am.
What's wrong?"

"I don't know." She tried to smile. "I guess I've blown
Redford up into some kind of malevolent superman in
my mind."

"He's clever and malicious but he's human. We can
bring him down."

She shivered. "Can we? What makes a man like
Redford become what he is?"

He could see she needed him to make sense of
Redford for her and tried to think of something that
would help her. "I don't know. As far as I can tell, he
had a normal childhood. He's the son of a minister in a
small town in Iowa. I remember him calling his mother
on her birthday back when we were both in the CIA."

"Somehow that makes him worse. What did you ever
do to him that he should want to hurt us so badly?"

"He wanted to be in the same position as McMillan
with all the opportunities for perks. When I bolted
from the agency, he lost his job. He wasn't supposed to
let me find out what happened in Afghanistan."

She looked at him inquiringly.

"They posed a location problem to me out of con-
text. Just figures and variables and a geographic terrain.
They wanted to know where and when a certain army
unit would pass. It was an easy puzzle. I had no problem solving it for them." He smiled bitterly. "McMillan
sold the information to the KGB. The supposed army
unit was a rebel leader escorting a village of innocent
civilians out of the war zone over the Pakistani border.
They were butchered."

"It wasn't your fault. You didn't know."

"That didn't make me sleep any better when Pave told me what had happened. I was the one who solve the puzzle." He stood up and pulled her to her feet. "It been a hell of a day. Why don't we go to bed?"

"Not yet. I'd just as soon not go to sleep thinkin about Ledford. I'm going to run the hologram one mor time before I go to bed. Coming?"

God knows, she must have been as tired as he was a ter the twenty-four hours they had gone through, bu she was still forging on. This was how she had been Vasaro when he first met her, enduring the hardship and still reaching for life. Alex experienced a rush o tenderness so intense, it came close to pain.

He slipped his arm about her waist. "Coming."

It all came together that night.

"You've actually done it?"

Alex looked at the complex number combinatio just printed out and smiled. "I'd bet on it."

"The base would swing open?"

"Open sesame."

Caitlin laughed shakily. "That's Aladdin's cave."

"There's a correlation. As Andros told Paradigne 'Treasures greater than you can dream lie in Shardana.'

Caitlin stared at the emerald eyes of the hologran "But we won't know until we have the real thing. W need the Wind Dancer."

"Soon. We're getting closer."

"Yes, we're getting closer."

"What do I have to do to keep you in bed? It's dam chilly out here." Alex tightened the belt of his terry-clot obe as he walked down the garden path toward the bench where Caitlin was sitting. "Don't you know it's nearly three o'clock in the morning?"

"I'm not cold. I couldn't sleep."

"Ledford? The Wind Dancer?"

"No, I keep thinking about the children." Caitlin's white corduroy robe blurred to soft silver in the moonlight, and her slender body appeared fragile as the stalk of a tall lily. "I've been so lucky, Alex. All my life I've felt a little sorry for myself because things weren't exactly as I wanted them to be, but look what I've had."

"Vasaro."

"Yes." She added softly, "And the Wind Dancer. Vasaro was the reality and the Wind Dancer was the dream. No matter what happens in the future, I'll always have those memories. What memories will those children have?"

"They'll have to create new memories, better memories."

"It won't be the same." She looked thoughtfully down at the ground. "Do you suppose Chelsea could persuade those welfare people to let the children come to Vasaro to live for a while? There's something very healing about working with the flowers." She went on hurriedly. "Oh, not right away. Perhaps next year, after we've cleared away all the rubble and started planting again."

He went still. "And are we going to do that?"

"Of course." She slipped from the bench to her knees on the ground and scooped up a handful of earth. "Just look at all this sand content. It's a wonder any flowers at all grow here. Remind me to ask Kemal where I can get some good topsoil."

"I will." His hand reached down and gently stroked the curls back from her face. "Of course, it still won't be as good as Vasaro earth."

"No, nothing could be that good." She closed her eyes tightly. "I want to go *home*, Alex. I want this all to be over so that I can go home."

"You're ready to face it?"

"It's my home, it's Vasaro. I want to make it come alive again."

"We will."

"You were right about me thinking of Vasaro as some kind of trust. I guess I became so involved in Catherine's journal that I thought the past had to be richer, better." Her lids opened to reveal eyes shimmering with moist brilliance in the moonlight. "But maybe Catherine and Juliette thought that about Sanchia and Sanchia the same about Andros. It's like a chain that goes on forever and we all have to forge our own links."

"And they'll be bright, strong links." He cleared his throat to rid it of the sudden tightness. "But right now we have to get you inside before you freeze." He lifted her to her feet and kissed her lightly on the tip of her nose. "Why don't you call Jacques and talk to him tomorrow?"

"Not yet. Not until this is over. I want to keep Vasaro separate and apart from anything to do with Ledford."

"Very well, we'll wait. It will only be a little while anyway."

"No ship by that name or description has docked at Istanbul during the past week," Kemal said. "Are you sure of your information?"

Alex frowned. "Yes, Ledford's got to be here. The meeting is three days from now and Krakow arrived last night in Istanbul. Were you able to check those phone calls Ledford made to Istanbul?"

Kemal shook his head. "Goldbaum was right. The

hone company is very stubborn about giving out information on unlisted numbers. I'm still working on it."

"Damn!"

"Did Goldbaum call back with any information on
hat number Ledford called just before he left Paris?"

"No help there. The phone was in the hall of a small
ension in the Pigalle section. According to Goldbaum,
's frequented primarily by whores and their cus-
omers."

"You don't know who he was trying to reach?"

Alex shook his head. "Not for sure. A prostitute by
he name of Jeanne Marie Neunier was found stabbed
o death in her apartment two days ago, but we can't
nd any connection between her and Ledford."

Hans wriggled along the narrow ledge on knees and
ips, pushing the canvas bag containing the plastique
nd detonators before him.

He couldn't breathe.

The darkness was closing in on him. He stopped to
est a moment, fighting the strangling fear of the black-
ess. He had always been afraid of the dark, a weakness
e had confessed only to Brian. He remembered how
he bastard's eyes had filled with crocodile tears and he
ad stroked Hans's hair and told him he need never be
lone again. They would fight the fear together, like fa-
her and son.

Well, Hans was alone in the dark again.

Just a few more feet...

He got to the end of the ledge and taped the plas-
ique carefully beneath the support beam. He set the
imers and began wriggling back.

Even if Brian stumbled on the other two charges,
e'd never find this one, and any one of the charges had

the firepower to blow Brian and his precious treasure to kingdom come.

God, he wished he dared turn on the flashlight. Why not? The cache had seemed deserted when he had entered it. . . .

No, it wasn't safe. He couldn't risk failing now when he was so close to getting the son of a bitch. He had only to get out of the darkness and go up on the plateau and set a similar surprise package for Krakow. Then he could hide out in the trees and settle down to watch the show.

Five minutes later he jumped the six feet from the ledge and landed in a half-crouch.

He gasped as pain seared through the scabbed wound on his side. He stood there for a moment, fighting the pain, fighting the bile rising to his throat. The pain diminished and then faded into a dull ache. He moved at a trot through the darkness toward the band of moonlight in the distance.

He burst through the opening, the chill night air striking his cheeks. He filled his lungs, relief and triumph soaring through him until he was light-headed. He muttered exultantly, "You're going to *blow*, you son of a bitch."

Ten minutes later he began climbing the steep slope toward the plateau, struggling to keep his balance as his tennis shoes slid on the shale.

"Hans?"

Hans went rigid, his gaze lifting to the edge of the plateau.

Brian stood directly above him, his powerful body in silhouette but his face silvered and illuminated by the moonlight. His mouth was twisted as if he was in pain and his eyes were filled with sorrow. "What are you doing here, boy?"

Rage scalded through Hans. He instinctively lurched forward, his hand reaching for his knife.

Pain!

His head rocked as if the plastique he had set in the cache had exploded in his brain.

He fell to his knees, darkness closing around him.

"I told you not to hurt him," Brian said sharply to someone behind Hans. "The poor lad's been hurt enough." He started down the steep incline toward Hans. "Ah, Hans, what have we done to you?"

Blackness.

Brian was gently bathing Hans's temple with a damp cloth when he opened his lids. He was instantly aware that he was no longer outside but lying on the cot in the storage room in the cache. His gaze passed over the crates and canvases against the wall to the Wind Dancer on the table across the room.

He'd like to crash the statue against Brian's head.

His stare shifted back to Brian. "Bastard," he whispered.

Brian flinched. "I deserve that." His eyes glittered moistly in the lantern light. "I didn't want to do it. Krakow made me set you up. You knew too much. He was afraid it was too dangerous to have you around after the Smythe bit."

"I'm going to kill you."

"The first moment I saw you I knew you were on your way to set a charge to take out Krakow at the conference." Brian added sadly, "There wasn't enough plastique in your pack to blow both Krakow and me. How were you going to take me out? A knife in the back, Hans? I remember you're very good with a knife."

Brian didn't know he had already planted the charges

in the tunnel, Hans realized. Brian thought he had inter
cepted Hans before he had a chance to go to the cache
A fierce surge of joy shot through him. He was going to
die, but Brian would follow him. "Maybe a few bullets in
the gut like you gave to me."

"I told you that was unavoidable." Brian gently
smoothed back a golden lock from Hans's forehead
"You look like a sheared sheep. What happened to al
your beautiful hair?"

Hans jerked his head sidewise away from Brian's
touch and glared silently at him.

Brian's hand fell away from him. "You hate me. And
how can I blame you? But it was Krakow, I tell you
God, I hate him for what he made me do to you."

"Sure."

"It's true. How can I convince you? You're like a son
to me." Brian mournfully shook his head. "I held my
hand when I could have had you killed out there on the
plateau. Doesn't that count for something?"

"Why didn't you?"

"Because I care about you."

Hans snorted derisively.

"I searched all over Paris for you."

"To finish the job?"

"To make amends. And now I can do it. We'll get
away together. Remember all the plans we made? It wil
be just like it used to be."

Brian thought he could fool him again, Hans realized
with wonder. Even after all the bastard had done!

But Brian wanted something. If Hans played it right
there might be a way of saving his neck after all.

Hans lowered his lids to veil his eyes. "What about
Krakow?"

"You know I never believed that pompous ass could

eally pull the entire game off. We'll take the loot and sail off to South America." Brian was silent a moment. "Krakow would object, of course. I may need your help with him. It should be a pleasure for you. After all, the bastard is to blame for all your troubles. You can still use your plastique, but I think we must refine your plan a bit. Let me guide you in this."

Now Hans got the picture. Brian wanted Krakow put down too, and he wanted Hans to do his dirty work for him.

"You've got to let me prove how much I regret hurting you," Brian said softly. "All I ask is a chance."

A chance to use him and then stab him in the back again. Hans could feel the rage and hatred rise and fought it down. He would be the one to use Brian this time. He would let Brian set up the hit on Krakow and then watch Ledford and his precious paintings and statues shatter into a million bloody pieces.

Brian's expression held only gentleness and affection as he reached out and touched Hans's arm. "*Will* you let me make it up to you?"

This time Hans forced himself not to draw away from Brian's touch. "I don't know if I can."

"But you'll try?"

Hans's lids opened, and he stared directly into Brian's eyes. He gave him an angelic smile. "Oh, yes, I'll try, Brian."

19

Goldbaum called Alex at ten o'clock the next morning.

"Black damp isn't a chemical product, it's a gaseous state. That's probably why there was a question mark behind it."

"Sodium V?"

"The solution to the question mark. Black damp is an atmosphere in which a flame won't burn because of an excess of carbon dioxide. V probably stands for vapor. Specially sealed sodium vapor lamps are sometimes used by miners to provide extra-brilliant light and prevent combustion with the gas underground."

"Miners." Alex sat upright in his chair. "My God!"

"Strike a bell?"

"Big Ben." Alex hung up the phone and turned to Caitlin. "I'm an idiot. I was so damn obsessed with that house of Ledford's that I let it slide right by me."

"What?"

"I couldn't understand why something kept nagging at me when Goldbaum told me about Ledford's trip to Turkey. He said he visited a few towns on the Dardanelles coast and went to Istanbul and bought the house on the

Street of Swords. I jumped on the house. I should have realized—Truve. Where it all began. Troy."

After they left the seaport town of Canakkale, Alex drove parallel to the coast through beautiful fertile countryside, passing small hotels, beaches, and campsites. About twenty-five kilometers from the main road was the turnoff and the sign that read TRUVE 5 KM.

"Do you think Ledford hid his loot in Troy itself?" Caitlin asked.

Alex shook his head. "The tunnel."

Caitlin's eyes widened. "Andros's tunnel?"

"I remember Ledford used to talk continuously about Lily Andreas's book and the legends of the Wind Dancer. The book didn't go into any detail on the legend itself, but it did mention how Andros escaped from Troy by way of the tunnel that led beneath the city to a hill some distance away."

"And you think Ledford found the tunnel?"

Alex nodded. "It fits together. One, he had an obsession about the Wind Dancer and its origin, and two, he ordered special lanterns to be used underground. I think he came here, discovered the tunnel, and thought it would be a perfect hiding place for the stolen art treasures. I believe Ledford persuaded Krakow that the final play should be in Turkey. Then, instead of Istanbul, Ledford set up headquarters here on the coast. It's only an hour and a half from Istanbul, and Troy's near a smaller seaport, Canakkale. That was another plus, since they were probably able to move the art treasures more easily by sea than air from Europe."

"Then the *Argosy* may be docked along this coast and not in Istanbul."

"I'd bet on it. That must be Troy just ahead."

A rush of excitement surged through Caitlin, and she sat up straighter on her seat. Her courses at the Sorbonne had included a study of the actual archaeological ruins of Troy. Nine separate cities were layered on these ruins, but little was known about any of them. The first settlement was judged to have been between 3000 and 2500 B.C. Troy VIIA, dated somewhere in the 1200 B.C.'s, was supposed to be Homer's palatial city, but this was only conjecture. Troy was as mysterious and shrouded in legend now as it had been when Alexander the Great had visited on his way to conquer the world.

She was disappointed.

The mound of Hisarlik on which Troy was situated consisted of little more than piles of earth and stone and gouged trenches overlooking the flat plain leading to the turquoise waters of the Aegean. Two tour busses were parked at the front entrance, and several school children were clambering up the steps toward the belly of a giant wooden reconstruction of the fabled Trojan horse. From this distance the roofed structure on the horse's back looked like a child's playhouse, and the huge horse appeared pitiful rather than impressive. Little trace of Homer's great city existed in these ruins.

Caitlin turned to Alex. "Have you been here before?"

Alex shook his head. "I heard it was a disappointment. Sometimes it's better to keep the vision and avoid the reality." He pointed to the hills in the distance. "Do you want to flip a coin to decide which haystack has the needle?"

"Or where on the haystack it's located," Caitlin added. "I guess we just search and hope to get lucky. A triangular red rock was supposed to have been somewhere near the entrance."

"Which may have crumbled to dust through the centuries. Was the rock mentioned in Lily Andreas's book?"

Caitlin nodded.

"Then that's the landmark we look for. If Ledford managed to find the tunnel, he had to have used something as a guideline."

"*If* being the operative word."

Alex started the jeep and headed past Troy toward the hills to the south.

They didn't get lucky.

They plowed the jeep through thick shrubbery and bounced over roughly rutted back roads for the remainder of the day but saw nothing of the triangular rock or anything else that gave any clue to a tunnel opening. Finally, when it grew too dark to see, they gave up the search and drove back to Istanbul.

Kemal was lounging on the couch as they entered the cottage. He carelessly tossed aside the pile of computer sheets he had been reading. "You think this sequence will really open the statue, Alex?"

"Possibly."

"Interesting. Not world-shaking, but definitely interesting." His grin faded as he glanced at Caitlin. "You look weary. Find anything?"

"Pine trees, mud, rocks, and flies," Caitlin enumerated.

"Too bad."

"I knew it was a long shot," Alex said. "Canakkale is the nearest seaport town. We'll go back tomorrow and scout around to see if we can find any sign of the *Argosy* and ask some questions at the hotels. Ledford likes his comfort. I don't think he'd set up permanent living quarters underground." The phone rang on the table be-

side him. "That must be Goldbaum. I hope to hell he
has something. Nothing else has gone right today." He
picked up the receiver. "Goldbaum?"

"Who is Goldbaum?"

Alex's heart jumped to his throat. "Ledford."

Kemal murmured something beneath his breath.
Caitlin moved a step closer to the phone.

"It's been a long time, Alex. Well, not really, but it
seems like a long time. It's always like that when good
friends are parted, isn't it? I hear the Vasaro bitch is still
with you. That's a mistake, Alex," he chided. "I thought
you realized how irritated I was with her."

"How do you know she's still here?"

"Why, you were seen together today. Truve is such a
pleasant area, isn't it? So much history..." Ledford
trailed off and then said briskly, "I really didn't think
you'd zero in on my little cache until I was ready for
you, but then you always did manage to surprise me.
No matter, you didn't find anything and you don't have
time now to be a danger to me. The clock's running out,
Alex."

Alex ignored the question. "Where are you?"

"I understand you almost stumbled on me today
while you were bouncing around in that jeep. You'll be
glad to know I've decided to reward your cleverness
with another snippet of information." He paused. "The
business isn't going to happen at the palace."

"What business?"

"Don't play dumb, Alex. It annoys me. I'm sure
you've figured out that the British delegation has to be
removed from the scene."

"From what scene are they supposed to be removed?"

"Now, that's asking too much. Figure it out for yourself." He chuckled. "If you do, I'll give you a reward."

"What kind of reward?"

"I'll kill the Vasaro bitch quickly instead of taking my time. And there's a very good reason to kill her." His voice lowered to velvet softness. "You see, we're going into the countdown now, Alex. You're going to have a decision to make, and I believe you'll think more clearly if she's not in the picture." He paused. "It's all very exciting, isn't it?"

"I don't find it any more exciting than hunting for game. You're just something to bag and then be disposed of, Ledford."

"You're lying to yourself as well as to me. You're looking forward to our coming together as much as I am. Do you know why?"

"I'm sure you're going to tell me."

"Because I'm like you. I told you once that you were a combination of medieval knight and Renaissance man. Ask yourself who dominated the Renaissance, Alex. The dark princes, Borgia and Medici." His tone was almost caressing as he continued. "I knew the first time I met you that you were a prince of darkness. That was why I found you so interesting. It's only that other deplorable streak of chivalry that's holding you back. Give it up, Alex."

"Screw you."

Ledford sighed. "Not yet? Oh, well, I've waited quite a while for this moment, Alex. I can wait a little longer."

Ledford hung up.

Alex slammed down the phone.

Kemal gazed at him inquiringly.

"It's not going to happen at the palace. We have to get in touch with Jonathan."

"How can you believe Ledford?" Caitlin asked.

"Because he wanted me to be sure and know about Krakow's plan. He was disturbed that we were messing around Troy, but he doesn't care that we know about the assassination attempt."

"Why not?" Kemal asked.

Alex's brow creased in a thoughtful frown. "Double cross?"

"Could be." Kemal nodded. "But before or after the assassination attempt?"

"I don't know. It wouldn't matter either way to Ledford." He turned to Caitlin. "We're moving to the Hilton right away. Pack a bag."

"In a minute." Caitlin's glance was still fastened on the telephone. "Alex ... how did he know the telephone number?"

"That's why we're moving. The telephone's still listed under the cottage owner's name. Goldbaum couldn't even find out the telephone number, but Ledford knew it." Alex turned to Kemal. "I want two guards on Caitlin until this conference is over. Can you arrange it?"

"No problem. I have many acquaintances who are both skillful and unpleasant." Kemal's expression was sober as he added, "I won't fail you again, Alex. I promise nothing will happen to Caitlin."

The next morning Alex left Caitlin still asleep in their suite at the Hilton and went to Jonathan's room on the third floor.

"Dammit, Jonathan, the embassy lied to you," Alex said as he strode into the room. "If the assassination attempt isn't to take place at the palace, then all their preparations and security measures are a fraud."

"Or Ledford lied to you. He did it before." Jonathan dropped down in an easy chair and stretched his legs out before him. "And you said yourself the man is unbalanced."

"He didn't lie to me this time. I know him. And God knows it's cost us all enough for me to find out how he thinks."

"All right, let's concede that Ledford told you the truth. Then the embassy either doesn't know or can't be persuaded to tell us where the meeting is to be held."

"Or when."

"When?" Jonathan said. "It's set for three o'clock day after tomorrow."

"No, that's when every newspaper in the world says it's going to take place," Alex said. "But if the meeting place has been changed, why should the time be accurate? Why wouldn't Krakow suggest a secret meeting at an entirely different time and place to protect the members of the conference?" He shook his head. "We can't be sure of anything."

Jonathan rose. "So we go and talk to the embassy again and see if we can twist a few arms?"

Alex moved toward the door. "It seems the logical initial move."

"You're not going to take Caitlin to the embassy?"

"No."

"She's not going to be pleased."

"Too bad." As Jonathan continued to gaze at him with no comment, Alex added with sudden fierceness, "Dammit, McMillan told her she was a target and he was right. She's safer here at the hotel under guard. Am I supposed to drag her all around Istanbul and get her—" He stopped, his eyes widening at a sudden thought. "Christ!"

Jonathan raised his brows inquiringly.

Alex shook his head. "It may be nothing. It doesn'
make any sense. I'll have to think about it." Alex's ton
was abstracted. "Let's go."

"Who are those sinister characters lurking in th
hall?" Chelsea asked as soon as Caitlin opened the doo
of her room.

"Kemal's choice of bodyguards. The one with the sca
is Ali, and the one who looks like a warmed-over cadave
is Hamad. Or maybe it's the other way around." Caitli
made a face. "I think I'd rather face Ledford than one o
them in a dark alley."

"After what happened at Vasaro, I somehow doub
that." Chelsea entered the suite and closed the doo
"Jonathan called me and told me you were here. H
said to tell you that he and Alex have gone to the em
bassy and Alex would call you later."

Caitlin frowned. "Why the devil didn't Alex stop b
and get me?"

"Alex thought you'd be pissed." Chelsea chuckled
"But he said to tell you it was a fact-finding mission, no
a foray, and for you to sit tight." Chelsea moved towar
the telephone on the desk across the room. "I just cam
back from the welfare home and I haven't had break
fast yet. Do you want anything?"

"Coffee." Caitlin dropped into the cane chair by th
telephone. "How are the children?"

"Pretty good." Chelsea frowned. "Melis is really th
only one who's traumatized. She's all eyes and raw
nerves this morning. I think we'd better get Kemal t
visit her again."

"Again?"

"The matron told me he visited her late last night af
ter the children were all settled in the home."

Caitlin felt a warm glow of affection when she remembered Kemal's expression of concern as he had watched Chelsea take Melis from the cottage. "It doesn't surprise me. He was worried about her when she left."

Chelsea punched the buttons for room service. "Well, the matron said it made all the difference in the world. Melis seemed contented and went right off to sleep after Kemal left."

"That's good."

"Where is Kemal?"

Caitlin shook her head. "I have no idea. He left after introducing those guards in the hall. He said he'd check back periodically."

"I tell you, they don't know anything," Jonathan said as he came out of the undersecretary's office into the foyer of the embassy where Alex waited. "Simons nearly had a stroke when I broached the possibility of a secret meeting." He grimaced. "If there *is* a secret meeting."

"Someone has to know about it." Alex frowned. "Do you know anyone on Cartwright's staff?"

Jonathan thought about it. "No, but I know Phillip Peabody, the head of Scotland Yard. He may be able to put me in touch with someone." Jonathan moved toward the small reception room adjoining the foyer. "I'll place the call from here. They'll probably have to call us back at the hotel later anyway, but at least we'll get things rolling."

"Then let's get to it." Alex followed Jonathan into the reception room. "For God's sake, let's do something right." As he saw Jonathan's glance of surprise, he said tersely, "Sorry, I guess I'm on edge."

And that edginess had started when the possibility
of that bizarre connection had occurred to him, Alex
suddenly realized. Since they had left the hotel he had
shied away from looking squarely at that possibility
tried to ignore it entirely. Why?

He slowly sat down in the brass-studded leather
chair across the reception room, watching absently a
Jonathan picked up the receiver and started to place hi
call. Then he deliberately closed out the sound o
Jonathan's voice talking to Scotland Yard, tried t
empty himself of his terror for Caitlin, his hatred fo
Ledford, and the odd reluctance to put this portion o
the puzzle together. Emotion always interfered with
solving the puzzle, and he couldn't afford it now. He
closed his eyes and began to examine the pieces befor
him clearly and coldly.

"We have to leave!"

Chelsea and Caitlin looked up, startled, as Kema
burst into the suite. His thick, dark curls were tousle
and his lips set in a grim line. "It is no longer safe fo
you here, Caitlin."

Caitlin felt a thrill of fear. "What's happened
Ledford?"

"Yes, Ali recognized one of Ledford's men dressed as
hotel waiter." Kemal pulled Caitlin to her feet. "Where'
Alex?"

"He went to the embassy."

"Damn." Kemal shrugged. "You'll have to leave him
note. Tell him we're going to my place on the Street o
the Turban Makers."

"I'll do it." Chelsea moved across the sitting room t
the desk and pulled a sheet of hotel stationery from th

lesk drawer. She quickly scrawled a few lines. "What's he address?"

"He knows where it is. We stopped there once to pick up my guitar. We don't want to leave any information lying about." Kemal grabbed Caitlin's wrist and pulled her toward the door. "Go back to your own suite, Miss Benedict. It's not safe for you here either."

"And how are you going to get her to your place?" Chelsea asked caustically. "You don't have a car. Are you going to ride her on your bicycle or hire a taxi that can be traced?"

Kemal frowned. "I will rent a car."

"Good idea." Chelsea picked up the telephone receiver. "I'll call down to the desk and tell them to have a rental car waiting for us out front."

"Us?" Caitlin shook her head. "This isn't your concern, Chelsea."

"She's right," Kemal agreed quickly. "You should not run the risk."

Chelsea's lips tightened. "Ledford and his goons are very much my concern. They almost killed my daughter. I've been waiting for a chance at that bastard."

"I don't like it," Kemal said flatly.

"I didn't like having the handlebars of your damn bicycle imprinted on my ass for the last twenty-four hours," Chelsea said. "Sometimes we have to accept things we don't like."

Alex's eyes flicked open, and he sat upright in his chair. "Jesus!"

"What?" Jonathan asked.

"Hang up." Alex jumped to his feet and strode across the room. "I've got to call McMillan."

Jonathan pressed the disconnect hook and hande Alex the receiver. "What about Peabody?"

Alex quickly dialed the number of McMillan's offic at Langley. "We may not need him."

Charles Barney answered the phone when Ale reached CIA headquarters and immediately put hir through to McMillan.

"What now, Karazov? I'm beginning to feel—"

Alex cut through McMillan's sentence. "I have som questions to ask. Confidential questions. Is Barney stil there in the office with you?"

"Alex, what the—"

"Is he?"

"Yes."

"Send him away on an errand."

"I don't like taking—"

"Do it!"

"You can't order—" He broke off and Alex hear McMillan's muffled voice as he turned his head awa from the receiver. Then McMillan said into the phone "I'll give you two minutes, Karazov."

"Where's the Krakow meeting to take place?"

Silence. "How should I know? No U.S. dignitarie were invited."

"But you do know, don't you? Twelve different coun tries with their corresponding security people descend ing on Istanbul. What a hell of a headache. How mucl better if they had a neutral party to handle it. Tell m didn't your office offer to act as a liaison to coordinat all their security measures?"

Another silence. "Yes."

"Why?"

"Barney thou—I thought it would be a diplomati gesture and chalk up a few favors."

"Where and when?"

"None of your goddamn business."

"No? It will be your business when Ledford makes corpses of half the members of the conference."

"It's not going to happen. The security measures are foolproof."

Alex switched the subject. "Who else knew where I was in Paris?"

"The man I had tailing you."

"And who else knew where I was in Istanbul?"

"The doctor I sent to treat you."

"No one else?"

"No."

"You're wrong. Ledford knew. I find that curious when only your office knew where I was in Paris and Istanbul. In Paris there could have been a slip, but not in Istanbul. Yet suddenly Ledford knew my telephone number here too, even though it was under another name."

"Ledford was fired from the Company years ago."

"He told me he had his sources for information. What would be more reasonable than for him to maintain a valuable contact with the Company?"

"You think it was me?" McMillan laughed, incredulous. "As much as I'd like to hang you out to dry, we both know I can't do it."

"No, I don't think it was you." Alex paused. "I think it was Barney."

McMillan said flatly, "You're crazy."

"Did Barney handle the arrangements for the Krakow meeting?"

McMillan hesitated. "I handled them myself."

"For God's sake, tell me the truth. You haven't done any donkey work since the day I met you. Barney handles everything."

"Okay, Barney handled it. But you can't think—"

"Where?"

McMillan hesitated and then muttered, "Troy Krakow thought Cartwright would appreciate it if th meeting was held in a historical setting. He wanted t show her he respected antiquity even if he wants t form a new—"

"When?" Alex interrupted.

"Three o'clock today. The representatives are meet ing in Canakkale. Krakow arranged for a bulletproof bu to take them all from Canakkale to Troy and then re turn them to the city after the meeting. It will arrive a two forty-five."

"Have you checked out the bus?"

"Our people haven't, but British security has gon over it with a fine-tooth comb. It's as tight as a drun and strong as a tank. They'll check it again before any one is allowed to board. No problem."

"And the ruins?"

"The road was corded off at midnight last night. Th entire area is crawling with soldiers and security men No one can get in or out without special papers."

"What if they're already in?"

"Couldn't be. A ten-mile area around the ruins wa searched before the roadblock was set up. I tell you, it' foolproof."

"And I tell you it's a setup. Barney is Ledford's man.'

"Barney?" He laughed incredulously. "I thin you're—what was that?"

Alex had heard it too. The soft click of a receiver be ing hung up on another extension.

Alex spoke sharply. "Get the hell out of there McMillan. Then call British security and tell—"

A soft pop on the other end of the line.

The clatter of McMillan's receiver as it fell from hi hand onto the desk.

"McMillan!"

The receiver was carefully returned to the cradle and he connection broken.

The last time Alex had heard that soft pop was when e was in the Spetznez. Once heard, the sound was un-orgettable; the discharge of a pistol with a silencer.

McMillan would not be calling British security or nyone else.

Alex hung up the phone and turned to Jonathan. McMillan's out of it. The meeting is at Troy. Barney nows we're on to Ledford, so he'll alert security to top us if we try to get near the place." It was already ine forty-five. Less than six hours until the meeting nd he didn't know how they were going to get past the rst checkpoint. "Jonathan, I need you to get the under-ecretary to do one more thing for me." He reached into is jacket pocket and pulled out the slip of paper with he number Ledford had called in Istanbul. "I need to now whose telephone number this is."

Jonathan took one glance at Alex's set expression, urned, and left the room.

Alex tried to keep his mind blank. He could be vrong. It was a variable. God, he hoped he was wrong.

Jonathan came back in the room. "The number is isted to Kemal Nemid, 423 Street of the Turban Makers."

And Alex knew why he had been so reluctant to olve the puzzle. "My God."

"You didn't expect it?"

"I expected it. I hoped I was wrong. I asked McMillan o provide me with the name of an agent in Istanbul. Ie had Barney check on it for him." He smiled bitterly. It was easy for Barney to substitute Kemal's name for he agent. Kemal is Ledford's man in Istanbul." Kemal,

who was now supposedly protecting Caitlin from
Ledford. Alex's hand was shaking as he punched in the
number for the Hilton. "Room 546." He waited as the
phone rang ten times. No one answered.

Alex had a chilling sense of déjà vu. Five months before, he had stood like this, listening as a phone rang the
night Ledford's men had murdered Pavel.

He slammed the phone down. "Come on, we've got
to get back to the hotel."

"You can park here," Kemal said. "It's difficult getting
an automobile up the street."

Chelsea looked up the narrow, twisting, cobbled
street and nodded. "I can see why you ride a bicycle."

Kemal got out of the passenger seat of the Ford,
opened the back door for Caitlin to get out of the car,
and then came around to the driver's door. "You will
not change your mind and go back to the hotel?"

Chelsea shook her head as she reached for the handle of the door. "No way."

Kemal looked at her thoughtfully. "That is too bad."
Kemal stepped forward, opened the door, and put his
hand on Chelsea's shoulder. "But I thank you for—"

Chelsea slumped forward onto the steering wheel,
her hair a bright banner against the gray plastic.

Caitlin rushed forward. "Chelsea, what's wrong?" She
glanced frantically at Kemal. "What's—"

"I don't think it's serious," Kemal said softly. He
grasped Caitlin's arm and gently pushed her forward toward Chelsea. "See, her color's good."

"She's unconscious." She scarcely felt the sharp pin
prick as Kemal's palm tightened on her forearm. "How
can you say—"

"Ah, how sorry I am, Caitlin," Kemal murmured.

He caught her with gentle hands as her knees bucked and she fell toward the ground.

"Alex, my lad, it's time for us to play the last act,"
Ledford said as soon as Alex picked up the phone in his
suite an hour later.

"Where are they?" Alex asked.

"You sound a bit tense. The ladies are both alive and
will remain so if you obey instructions."

"They're not at Kemal's place. We've already been
here."

"No, of course not. I'm surprised you even bothered
to pay any attention to that note. As a matter of fact,
they're on their way here."

"Troy?"

"Yes." Ledford added briskly, "Kemal will meet you at
the turnoff for Truve and bring you to me. Come at
once." He hung up the phone.

Alex turned jerkily to face Jonathan. "He says they're
live. I have to go to Troy."

"I'll go with you."

"It may be a one-way ticket. I don't have much to
bargain with."

"I'm going with you," Jonathan repeated. "How do
we get there?"

"We rent a jeep and meet Kemal at the turnoff for
Troy."

Ledford strolled to the ramp where Hans was waiting. "It's time for you to go, my boy," he said gently.
"You've chosen a good spot?"

"Good enough." Hans shrugged. "On the next hill.
Plenty of ground cover."

"In range?"

"I know my job."

"Of course you do." Ledford smiled benignly. "Afte
you rid us of Krakow, you come back to the tunnel an
we hide out until the soldiers are gone and the coast
clear. Understand?"

"I'm not stupid." Hans tightened the straps of h
black canvas backpack. "I take out Krakow and the ex
plosion takes out the old lady and the delegation." H
glanced back at the room from which Ledford ha
come. "When are you going to start moving those pain
ings and stuff?"

"Don't you worry. Kemal is going to smuggle ther
out past the checkpoint in a military truck. You just d
your part and trust me to take care of the rest."

When Caitlin woke, it was to see the emerald eyes
the Wind Dancer gazing enigmatically at her fro
across the room.

A dream . . .

Her heavy lids began to close again.

"Wake up!" Someone was shaking her shoulder wit
more determination than gentleness.

Caitlin opened her eyes again to see Chelsea gazin
down at her.

"Chelsea?"

"Who else?" Chelsea said. "Snap out of it. We don
have time for this."

It was just like Chelsea to ignore the fact that uncor
sciousness wasn't something that could always be cor
trolled. Caitlin shook her head to clear it as memor
flooded back to her. "Kemal—"

"Is a rat," Chelsea said. "A king rat."

"There must be some mistake." Kemal wouldn't do is to them.

"No mistake. He drugged us."

Caitlin looked around the small, dim chamber lit by single lantern set on the dirt floor beside the table. he was lying on bare earth and the walls were paneled rough boards. No windows. A cot was situated beside door on the far side of the room, and a table and chair ere located beside another door a few yards away. And n that table . . . the Wind Dancer.

It hadn't been a dream. The statue of the Wind Dancer ominated this small room with the same power as it had e mirrored hall at Versailles.

Caitlin sat up, wrapping her arms across her chest to ard off the chill of the room. "It's cold in here. Do you ave any idea where we are?"

"I just came to myself." Chelsea shrugged. "I tried oth doors, but they were locked."

Caitlin was beginning to think again. "Ledford. It has be Ledford. He had the Wind Dancer."

"That's what I figured. King rat Kemal must work for im."

"I can't believe Kemal would do a thing like this," aitlin said. "Chelsea, I know him. He wouldn't—" She opped as she heard a key turn in the lock of the door cross the room.

A heavyset man came in. "Good afternoon, ladies. ermit me to introduce myself. I'm Brian Ledford."

He looked as ordinary in person as he had in the hotograph Alex had given Caitlin—solid, robust, heerful, not a monster at all.

"I hope you're not feeling groggy. Kemal assured me ou'd have few aftereffects." He checked his wrist- atch. "You woke up exactly when he said you would.

But then, I can always count on Kemal. In a world ‹
bunglers, he positively shines with efficiency."

Caitlin suddenly felt colder as disappointment er
veloped her. Betrayal. "Where are we?"

"Haven't you guessed? You're in the tunnel fι
which you and Alex searched so diligently yesterda
Kemal tucked you neatly in the trunk of the rental cε
Ms. Benedict so kindly provided and got you here wit
no problem whatsoever."

"I suppose it's foolish to ask why we're here."

"Very." Ledford smiled. "How else could I bring Ale
into the fold without the danger of hurting him?" Η
turned to Chelsea. "Though you were an unexpecte
bonus. I should have known my friend Kemal woul
give me a dividend."

"And where is the little dividend maker?" Chelse
asked. "I'd like to split his stock."

Ledford's laughter boomed out. "I knew you'd prov
amusing. I sent Kemal to the crossroad to bring Ale
through the checkpoint. British security is being mo
unwelcome to anyone without papers." He turned ι
Caitlin. "Naturally, Alex will expect to trade for yoι
but I expect you'll probably be gone by that time."

Caitlin tried to keep her expression unrevealin
"You're going to kill us?"

A flicker of grudging admiration crossed Ledford
face as he studied her. "I was hoping you'd be moι
afraid. I should have known Alex wouldn't be drawn b
sex alone."

She was so afraid, she was sick to her stomach, bι
she couldn't let him know it. "But you won't kill Alex"

Ledford's smile faded. "Not if he proves reasonable.
don't want that to be the end of the game. You're th
one who's been endangering him with your interfer
ence."

Chelsea asked, "Wouldn't you do better to use us to
bargain with? I'm worth a bundle."

"I'll soon have all the money I could possibly want,"
Ledford said. "But I'm a fair man. I'm not going to kill
you without giving you a sporting chance." His gaze
turned to Caitlin. "I'm sure Alex must have told you
how much I love games."

"He told me you were a murderer."

Ledford flinched. "And you, of course, fueled his
anger against me."

"No fuel was needed. Why did you kill my mother?"

"A great sorrow." He smiled. "But you really
shouldn't have entered the match if you didn't want to
bet everything on the outcome." He waved dismissively.
"But that's all in the past. We have a new set to play."
He casually drew a pistol from his jacket and pointed it
at them. "I've prepared a little obstacle course for you
to run." He moved to the door beside the table. "Come
here."

Neither woman moved.

"Now, don't be stubborn. I'm sure you'd both prefer
a challenge to a sure thing." He took a key from his
pocket, unlocked the door, and pushed it open.

Caitlin and Chelsea reluctantly moved forward to
stand beside him. A blast of cold mold-laden air washed
over Caitlin. Darkness. No, not complete darkness. She
could barely discern a pinpoint of light far in the distance.

"Daylight," Ledford said softly, his gaze following her
own. "I was happy to find those ancient Trojans were
very farseeing. The underground network is cata-
combed with offshoots from the original tunnel. This is
by far the most interesting one. It greatly relieved me to
know there was an emergency exit. You never know
when you're going to need an escape route."

"You're offering us an escape route?" Chelsea aske skeptically.

"You doubt me? Actually, you're quite right to do s You may never make it to the end of the tunnel. I'v arranged a few surprises for you en route."

"And what if we choose to stay here?"

"Then I shoot you." Ledford beamed at them. "Tal the tunnel and you have a chance to not only save you lives but that of the British delegation and becon world-class heroines. Isn't that exciting?"

"Thrilling," Chelsea said.

"You see, the tunnel exits right below the Hisarl plateau, where Krakow's meeting is to take place." F nodded as he saw Caitlin's eyes widen. "Alex didn have a chance to tell you? The meeting is to take plac in a bit under an hour. The members of the conferenc should be arriving by special bus quite soon, an Krakow will greet them very warmly and escort the on a tour of the ruins." He paused. "Including that lud crous counterfeit Trojan horse." He grimaced. "What a abomination when you think that the Wind Dancer the real Trojan horse. Guess what will be waiting fc them when they climb the steps to the belly of th monstrosity?" He looked at both of them in anticipa tion.

"Greeks bearing gifts?" Chelsea asked.

Ledford's laugh boomed out. "Wonderful. Actually, German bearing gifts. Last night, before the soldiers a rived, I had my old friend Hans plant a charge in th head of the horse. It's set to go off as soon as they're i the belly of the statue." He gestured expansively wit wide-flung arms. "Boom!"

"Including Krakow?" Caitlin asked.

"No, he has no head for heights and won't be goir into the horse. I've planned something special fc

akow." Ledford nodded. "I've known all along my
end Krakow was intending to eliminate me and the
st of my team as soon as the foul deed was done. It's
ly sensible for me to act first. I paid off my other men
d sent them on their way yesterday. Now there's only
e, Hans, and Kemal, and a very tidy cleanup plan."

"And you're willing to let us interfere with your
eanup?"

"There's no torture more painful than losing when
ctory is on the horizon. You see, I don't think you'll
ake it to the end of the tunnel, much less to the ruins.
by some improbable chance you do reach the ruins,
u'll have to cope with Turkish soldiers, British secu-
y, and Krakow's antiterrorist group." He reached into
e pocket of his jacket and pulled out a stainless steel
shlight. Before handing it to Caitlin he flicked it on
d off a few times. "You'll notice the batteries are very
eak. What a pity. They may go out at any minute. On
e other hand, they might last until you reach the end
the tunnel. You won't know, will you?"

Caitlin's hand tightened on the flashlight. "Chelsea
as nothing to do with this. If you're so sure you're go-
g to escape anyway, you could let her go."

"And leave you without a companion to ease you in
our last moments? Alex would never forgive me." He
iled. "Now, run along. You have a great adventure
vaiting you." He snapped his fingers. "I almost forgot.
ease remove your shoes and stockings." His smile van-
ied as both women stood there, staring at him in
ewilderment. "Quickly. There's nothing like wander-
g barefoot in the darkness to make one feel vul-
erable, and I do want you to feel very vulnerable, Miss
asaro."

Caitlin and Chelsea removed their shoes and stock-
gs and dropped them on the floor.

"Very good." Ledford nodded approvingly. "And no
I bid you good-bye." He pushed them out into th
clammy darkness of the tunnel and slammed the do
behind them.

An instant later they heard the key turn in the lock

20

"Christ, the whole countryside is swarming with soldiers." Jonathan looked back over his shoulder at the truck filled with Turkish soldiers that had just roared past them. "How the hell does Ledford think he's going to pull this off?"

"He loves it." Alex turned at the Truve signpost and sped down the road. "It's a challenge. The greater the challenge, the better he likes it. It proves how clever he is."

"To you?" Jonathan asked.

"Yes." Alex's gaze searched the shrubbery at the side of the road for a sign of Kemal. "And to himself. What time is it?"

"Two twenty-five. The conference bus should be right behind us if it's supposed to arrive at the ruins at two forty-five. How are we going to get through the barricade?"

"That's up to Kemal." Alex's lips tightened grimly. "I'm sure a clever lad like Nemid will have an answer. He's thought of—"

He broke off as Kemal stepped into the road ahead of them and held up his hand to stop the car. Dressed

in a red cable-knit sweater and worn brown cordur⟨
trousers, he looked almost as young as he did on t⟨
day Alex had first seen him.

Alex jammed on the brake and the jeep screeched ⟨
a stop.

"You made good time." Kemal moved quickly arour⟨
to the passenger seat, where Jonathan was sittin⟨
"You're Andreas?"

Jonathan nodded.

"I thought so. I recognize you from your newspaper ph⟨
tographs. You're almost as famous as Bruce Springstee⟨

"Thank you," Jonathan said dryly. "I gather you're t⟨
Kemal I've heard so much about."

Kemal opened the car door and told Jonathan, "G⟨
in the back and let me sit up front. They'll be checki⟨
papers at the roadblock up ahead."

Jonathan got out of the car. "And you have papers?⟨

"Of course, Krakow supplied Ledford with speci⟨
entry and exit papers for all his men."

Jonathan settled in the backseat and slammed t⟨
door. "And who are we supposed to be?"

"Members of Krakow's antiterrorist team. It allov⟨
us to go anywhere without being stopped," Kemal sai⟨
"Let me handle everything."

Alex put the jeep in gear. "Why not? You're good ⟨
that."

Kemal glanced at Alex's set face. "You're very ang⟨
with me."

"I'm very angry at myself. My God, I *believed* you."

"You mustn't be hard on yourself. I'm very good ⟨
what I do."

"And just what do you do, Kemal?"

"What I have to do. I told you I was going to be ⟨
very rich man."

"By earning blood money from Ledford?"

"Ledford is a means to an end." Kemal made a face.
nd I seldom enjoy spilling blood. It's not my spe-
alty."

"What is?" Jonathan asked.

"I think Alex has probably figured that out."

"Supply and demand," Alex said. "The Gypsy."

Kemal nodded.

"Irmak?"

"Oh, he was a Gypsy too. As a matter of fact, he was
y uncle. When I ran away from my tribe, I felt very
mfortable coming to Istanbul to Adnan." Kemal's
ice deepened with bitterness. "After all, wasn't he my
other's brother?"

"You killed him."

"He *used* me. He almost destroyed me as he de-
royed many others. No one deserved more to die."

"I won't argue that point, but why didn't you kill
m before?"

"It wasn't the right time. Adnan had many powerful
ends in the city who would have been delighted to slit
y throat as I did his," Kemal said. "Do you think I act
impulse? I did only one impulsive thing in my life,
d that landed me in my dear uncle's house of pleasure.
nce then I take my time and plan every step. I knew I
ould soon be leaving Istanbul and it would be safe to
ke Adnan out. His death would serve a triple purpose.
would divert your attention from searching for me, it
ould free the children." He smiled tiger bright as he
ded, "And it would give me great pleasure."

"And you planted the ledger and passports in his desk."

Kemal nodded. "The idea of Adnan as the Gypsy was
bit thin, but I hoped you'd become too involved with
e supply lists to question it too closely."

"And I was. God, I was stupid."

"No," Kemal said softly. "You trusted me."

"Which proves I was stupid. You even risked sho
ing me the ledger with the supply lists."

"A mistake. I didn't think you'd have time to p
everything together. I've had to move very delicate
Ledford's known where you were since the nig
Ferrazo tried to kill Caitlin, but he didn't know I was
contact with you before that. I'd told him I hadn't be
able to find you after you came back from France. F
after you contacted McMillan I knew Barney would t
him, so I got there first."

"If Ledford knew where we were, why didn't
make another attempt on Caitlin?"

"Ferrazo's death threw him off balance. Barney h
told him McMillan hadn't done it, and you were out
the picture too." He grimaced. "I persuaded him tl
perhaps you might have made a deal with Krakow
protect you in return for helping him remove Ledfo
from the scene. He decided to wait and watch for
while. It was what I hoped would happen." As Al
continued to look at him skeptically, Kemal shook
head. "You don't understand. I have been protecti
Caitlin. I *like* you. I don't want anything to happen
you or Caitlin."

"So you served up Caitlin and Chelsea on a silv
platter," Jonathan said.

Kemal glanced at Jonathan's grim face over
shoulder. "Ms. Benedict insisted on going along. I tri
to talk her out of it." He turned back to Alex. "I tr
hoped to keep Caitlin out of this. I'm sorry I found
necessary to involve you both."

Alex's hand tightened on the steering wheel. "He
kill her."

"I won't let that happen."

"You son of a bitch, you won't be able to keep him from it." He could feel the helpless rage rising within him. "And all to make you the richest man in the damned hemisphere."

Kemal's lips tightened with pain. "You don't understand. When I ran away from the Harem I had to protect myself in the only way I knew how. How many opportunities do you think a street child has in Istanbul? No one was waiting out there in the world to hand me an education or a security blanket." Kemal smiled sadly. "You always thought I was joking, but I *will* succeed, Alex. I'll have my great house and fine life. I'll be so rich, no one will ever be able to use me again." He sat up straighter in the seat. "Slow down. The checkpoint is up ahead."

"Well, do we turn on the flashlight?" Caitlin asked.

"Maybe for a quick look," Chelsea said. "I doubt if the little surprises that bastard has planned for us will be in the first ten steps. He'll want us good and panicky first."

"I'm well on my way." Caitlin turned on the flashlight and extended her arm full-length. The weakened batteries cast a pale yellow glow and pierced the darkness for only a few yards. She had a quick impression of rounded stone and earth walls supported at intervals by crisscrossed lumber. Caitlin turned off the flashlight. "Did I ever tell you how I hate to be closed in?"

"It's a piece of cake," Chelsea said. "One step at a time." She began to move slowly forward. "Are there snakes in tunnels?"

"Sometimes. But it's very cold in here. Snakes don't

like the cold." Caitlin added, "I hope." The rocky ground chilled the soles of her bare feet, but at least it was hard and firm. Heaven knows, she didn't want to touch anything slick and slithering in this blackness. It was bad enough to—she stopped in midstride, her eyes straining to pierce the darkness. "What was that?"

"What?"

"Listen."

It came again. A low, deep hissing sound issuing from the darkness up ahead.

"Wind?"

Or things that go bump in the night. Anything seemed possible in this preternatural nothingness, Caitlin thought desperately. "I don't know, but I don't like it."

"The flashlight?"

"Whatever it is, it's too far away." Caitlin started forward again. "We'll have to wait until we're closer."

The hissing came again, low, deep, menacing.

The wind, she prayed. Oh, God, she hoped it was the wind.

Alex started to park the jeep beside a blue four-door Ford with rental car license plates.

"No, not there." Kemal gestured toward a little thicket of pine trees across the clearing. "Draw in there behind the shrubbery."

Alex obeyed. "Your friend Ledford doesn't appear to be so nervous about being seen."

"He thinks nothing can touch him and enjoys taking chances. I'm a more cautious man."

The triangular red rock towered over six feet high, but the trapdoor behind it had been artfully camouflaged with canvas, mud, and brush. Kemal lifted the door by the iron ring of the trapdoor. "Be careful, the ramp is pretty steep and there's no railing."

The wide wooden ramp he spoke about led down fifty feet into the earth. Once they had all entered the tunnel, Kemal closed the door and moved past them, leading them down to the bottom of the shaft. A door was positioned at either side of the thirty-foot clearing at the bottom of the shaft. The entire area was brilliantly lit by twelve sodium vapor lanterns affixed to the stone walls.

"Very efficient," Alex said dryly. "A home away from home."

"Ledford had to move the paintings and statues safely from the surface down here," Kemal said. "Originally there was only a rope ladder. The original ladder had rotted away centuries ago and we—"

"Ah, you've brought our guests."

Ledford!

Savage satisfaction tore through Alex as his gaze flew downward to see Brian Ledford strolling across the clearing toward them. He reached the bottom of the ramp at the same time they did and handed Kemal the Uzi he was carrying. "Keep an eye on them. I want to enjoy this."

Kemal nodded and cradled the Uzi comfortably in the crook of his right arm.

"At last!" Ledford's gaze fixed eagerly on Alex's face. "How well you're looking. There's nothing like tension to hone down the edges and make a diamond shine brighter."

"Where's Caitlin?"

"Alive. Both ladies were alive and well when I last saw them." Ledford looked at Jonathan. "You really shouldn't have come, Andreas. I heard you had a great career ahead of you." He turned to Alex. "I admit I'm disappointed you decided to bring help, Alex. I thought you'd realize this confrontation was strictly between us."

Alex glanced at Kemal. "You appear to have a crony of your own on hand."

"Nemid?" Ledford shook his head. "Kemal is his own man. He's rather like you. He takes assignments but he doesn't belong to me. A brilliant lad."

"So I've noticed."

"I have great plans for Kemal. But how rude of me to keep you standing there." He turned and led them across the clearing in the direction from which he had come. "I'm afraid there are only two barely habitable chambers down here. It was very difficult making even this clearing and shoring up the tunnel itself." He opened a door to the left. "Come in, gentlemen, and make yourselves comfortable."

"Shit!" Chelsea screamed the word. "Stop! Don't go any farther." Her hand reached out, her nails digging into Caitlin's forearm. She began cursing beneath her breath.

Caitlin froze. "What happened?"

"My feet. Nails or broken glass or something. Glass, I think. We've stumbled onto one of Ledford's surprises. For God's sake, don't move." Chelsea released Caitlin's arm and moved back a pace. Caitlin heard her give another gasp of pain. "Hell!"

"I'm going to light the flashlight."

"No, not yet. We can't waste the batteries. I'm going to sit down and you can dig the bigger pieces out."

"Bigger?" Caitlin knelt on the ground beside Chelsea and ran her hand down Chelsea's left leg to her foot. "How many pieces of glass . . . *merde!*"

Several large, jagged splinters were sticking out of Chelsea's foot. Caitlin could feel the warm blood flowing over her fingers from a multitude of wounds. "I need light."

"No," Chelsea said sharply. "Feel your way. Just get the worst of them out and let's get on our way."

"Will you be able to walk?" Caitlin pulled a half-inch piece of glass from Chelsea's instep.

"You're damn right I will. If I can't walk, I'll crawl before I let that bastard stop us." She gasped as Caitlin pulled out another bit of glass. "Hurry."

"I am hurrying. There must be dozen of bits and—are you *laughing?*"

"I just thought about Pauley and his damn foot fetish. I may never be an object of lust to him again. What a depressing—" She broke off as Caitlin jerked out another shard. "I never thought I'd think dancing on grapes as pleasant, but it's looming among my favorite things in contrast to—"

"Shut up, Chelsea." Caitlin tried to keep her voice steady. "You don't have to be onstage with me. I know it hurts."

Chelsea was silent a moment. "I hate this darkness. It's like being in a coffin. You know, I never really thought about dying. It was always something that happened to somebody else."

"We still have a chance." Caitlin ran her hand over Chelsea's foot. She doubted if she had gotten out all the shards, but she couldn't feel any protruding glass. "Give me your other foot."

"Are you scared too?"

"Good God, of course I'm scared." Caitlin pulled out a thin glass sliver. "This foot isn't so bad." She finally sat back on her heels. "I've gotten out all I can."

"Then help me up."

Caitlin stood up and helped Chelsea to her feet. "All right?"

"Moderately." Chelsea drew a deep breath. "Okay, now turn on the flashlight and we'll see if we can get around Ledford's little booby trap."

Caitlin lifted the flashlight and prepared to flick it on.

A hiss.

Louder.

Echoing in the darkness.

A shiver went through Caitlin, and she braced herself against the impulse to turn around and run. One booby trap at a time.

She pressed the button on the flashlight. The carpet of broken, jagged glass extended only five or six feet ahead of them. The beam weakened, flickered, and Caitlin quickly turned off the flashlight. "To the left. If we press against the wall and stand on our tiptoes..."

Chelsea was already limping past Caitlin. She pressed against the wall and edged slowly forward.

Caitlin followed her, clutching the metal flashlight tightly.

A hiss.

Closer.

It wasn't the wind.

"Are those boxes what I think they are?" Jonathan asked, looking at the stack of pine boxes and crated canvases around the small room.

Ledford smiled. "I'm sorry for the heat in here, but it was necessary to keep it warm and dry to protect the paintings."

"Where's the Wind Dancer?" Jonathan's alarmed gaze searched the room. "Is it in one of those boxes?"

Ledford answered. "No, the Wind Dancer's in the other room, where I spend the majority of my time. I like to have it where I can see and touch it. I have great plans for the Wind Dancer."

Kemal had not only known what the Wind Dancer

contained but also how that information could be broached. Had he told Ledford? "What plans?"

Ledford laughed and turned toward Kemal. "Tell them what I'm going to do with the statue, Kemal."

Kemal met Alex's stare and then moved his head in an almost imperceptible gesture of negation. "He has a more modest initial aim than Krakow," Kemal said lightly. "He doesn't want to be king of Europe, only emperor of South America."

"Actually, mine is a much more manageable plan. The art treasures could never have been used as a backup for a united European treasury, but South America is a different proposition." Ledford sat down and leaned back in the chair. "I got the idea from the Salazar fiasco that set you up so nicely, Alex. Once I've solidified my position in a small Latin American country, I can go on from there. Who knows where I'll end up? I have a much better chance at success than Krakow."

"My God," Jonathan whispered.

"You don't approve?" Ledford asked. "My friend Kemal thinks it's a wonderful idea, but then, he sees a prominent spot for himself in the scheme. I'm going to make him a very rich man." He turned to Alex, his voice becoming softly urgent. "Are you with us, Alex? I've proved I'm your equal, perhaps even your superior. There's nothing for you here. You need the stimulus I can give you. You need *me*."

"Where's Caitlin?"

An angry flush touched Ledford's face. "Are you trying to humiliate me?"

"Where is she?"

"I sent her and the Benedict woman down one of the offshoot tunnels to the ruins. Unfortunately, I don't believe they'll make it."

Alex stiffened. "Why?"

"You couldn't expect me to make it easy for them. However, I regard myself as being very generous. I did give them a flashlight and warned them they'd have a very bad time reaching the plateau."

Kemal frowned. "You said you were going to keep them both as hostages until Karazov came."

"I don't tell you quite everything, Kemal." Ledford smiled. "For instance, I didn't tell you about the plastique."

Kemal went still. "Plastique?"

Ledford nodded. "My old friend Hans planted it in the tunnels a few nights ago as a little surprise for me. I checked the timers and the charges should go off"—he checked his watch—"in twenty-five minutes, at precisely seven minutes past three. That's four minutes after the charge in the wooden horse takes out the members of the conference. The devastation will cause chaos and everyone will rush to the ruins. If there are any guards left at the checkpoint, they'll be easy for us to take out."

"You expect us to believe you'd destroy all these priceless paintings?" Jonathan asked, glancing at the pile of boxed canvases set against the far wall.

"One painting. A Rembrandt. The other paintings and statues are all aboard the *Argosy*. I kept the Wind Dancer, the Rembrandt, and those empty crates here only as window dressing to convince Hans that setting the plastique would be worthwhile. Naturally, the Rembrandt and the Wind Dancer will accompany me when I leave."

"You *want* the tunnel blown?" Jonathan asked.

"Oh, yes, it's imperative. That's why I've gone to all this trouble. After Hans does his work, Barney has arranged that he'll be apprehended by British security.

ontrary to popular opinion, the British can be quite
avage when their sentiments are aroused, and they're
ery fond of Cartwright. Under coercion, I'm sure Hans
ill confess he planted the bombs and blew up both
ae and these magnificent works of art. Naturally, since
ae confession will be made under extreme duress, they
ill believe him." He shook his head mournfully. "What
tragic loss for the world."

"And they'll no longer look for you or the artworks,"
lex said.

"That's right." Ledford smiled at Alex. "You see, Alex,
ometimes it's more difficult constructing a puzzle than
olving it. You have no idea how I had to nurture and
aanipulate Hans to bring him to this emotional point.
irst I had to make sure he had the appropriate mixture
f stupidity, stubbornness, and viciousness, and then it
ook months of psychological conditioning to bring him
o the point where I could use him. His wound had to be
onvincingly painful but not life-threatening, and I had
o set him up with just the right whore to provide him
vith a bolt-hole to run to and provide me with informa-
ion when he—" He broke off and shook his head. "But
here's time for me to tell you about that later. We
hould really be packing up so that we can get to the
heckpoint on schedule." He turned to Kemal. "Take Mr.
Andreas out of the room. I wish to speak to Alex alone."

Kemal nodded and gestured with his Uzi to the door.
If you please, Mr. Andreas."

"Alex?" Jonathan asked.

"Go on," Alex said.

After the two men had left the room, Alex said,
Show me the tunnel."

"You don't want to go after her," Ledford said. "You'd
lever make it."

"Show me the tunnel."

"Stay with me," Ledford said. "Come with me." H
flushed, his words stumbling out awkwardly. "It's no
really physical. I can understand how you—I simpl
want to be with you."

"Go to hell."

The color drained from Ledford's face. "I didn't war
it to come to this. I truly thought if I showed you I wa
your match, you'd realized how much better we coul
be together." A sudden flare of anger darkened his ex
pression. "You're a great disappointment to me."

"The tunnel."

"You want your cow of a woman?" Ledford's lip
twisted with fury. "Then *have* her." He turned towar
the door. "Kemal!"

Kemal appeared in the doorway.

"We're going to take the gentlemen to the tunnel t
join the ladies." His gaze narrowed on Kemal's face
"Unless you have an objection?"

Kemal shrugged. "Why should I have an objection?"

"You seemed so concerned about the ladies. Lead th
way."

A few moments later they entered a small room
"The women have a fifteen-minute head start on you
but I doubt if they've gotten far," Ledford said, the
took the lantern from the table and handed it to Alex
"I wouldn't want you not to be able to see the minute
ticking away on your watch. Last chance. This is on
puzzle you're not going to be able to solve, Alex."

"I won't know until I try."

"You'll die. She means that much to you? She'
death, I tell you."

Alex knew he might not be able to help Caitlin an
Chelsea. If he stayed with Ledford, he would have

ance to lull him into false confidence and then kill
e son of a bitch. God, how he wanted to do that. He
uld feel the frustration and hatred sear through him
ronger than ever before.

But if he stayed with Ledford, he would be helpless
• try to save Caitlin.

There was no contest.

He said quietly, "You're wrong, Ledford."

He turned and entered the tunnel with Jonathan.

"An interesting choice," Kemal murmured.

"You'll be sorry," Ledford shrilled after him. "You're
aking a mistake."

Alex looked over his shoulder. Ledford and Kemal
ere only dark silhouettes against the dim light of the
om, but he thought he could see a faint smile on
emal's shadowy face. He felt a sudden leap of hope. A
ariable? Kemal had never been predictable, but now
lex realized he was the most enigmatic man with
hom he had ever dealt. He deliberately repeated
emal's words to him the day Kemal had called himself
lex's friend. "We all have to make choices every day."

Ledford said, "You've made the wrong one today."

The heavy door slammed and left the two men in
arkness.

The hiss had become a roar.

"My God, what the hell *is* it?" Chelsea stopped, her
and clutched Caitlin's arm. "I feel like David going
rth to fight Goliath."

"Goliath didn't hiss. He probably pounded his chest
ke Tarzan of the Apes." Caitlin moistened her lips. "Is
he path inclining downward?"

"I don't think so. It seems pretty level to me."

"Then I think we'd better turn on the flashlight."

"Why?"

"That hissing is coming from somewhere...down
Caitlin aimed the flashlight at the floor ahead an
pressed the button.

"That son of a bitch," Chelsea breathed, taking a ste
forward.

They stood on the edge of a crevasse plunging over
hundred feet, the stone sides as cleanly cut as if carved l
a butcher's cleaver. Caitlin could glimpse something gli
tering, moving, writhing at the bottom of the crevasse.

"Water," Chelsea said. "A spring?"

Caitlin shook her head. "I think the hissing noise
the sea rushing and receding through those rocks."

"The sea is miles away."

"But the sea level is very low here." She clicked o
the flashlight. "And this is earthquake country. I re
member reading that one of the cities built on the Tro
site was destroyed by an earthquake. Maybe the earth
quake caused a fissure that let the sea run this far in
land."

The waters glittered, writhed, hissing up at them.

"You'll have to turn on the flashlight again," Chelse
said. "We'll have to see if there's a way across it."

"There isn't, unless you can jump thirty feet."

"We were looking down at the water. It's either fin
a way across it or stay here and rot. Turn it on."

Caitlin switched on the flashlight and played it ove
the surface of the crevasse. "I told you there isn't—" Sh
broke off as she saw the rope.

To their extreme right a strong mountaineer's rop
was anchored to one of the beams supporting the tur
nel on this side of the crevasse. It stretched taut ove
the abyss and was wound several times around a ma
sive rock on the other side.

Two thirds across the rope a wide red satin ribbon
with an enormous shimmering bow bounced merrily in
the beam of light.

"A present from Ledford," Chelsea murmured. "Gift-
wrapped."

"The rope looks strong enough."

"It's a trap."

"Probably. But what if it's not? Suppose Ledford set
this up as one of his sick jokes because he thought we'd
be too afraid to save ourselves." Caitlin stepped closer
and tested the rope. It held firm. "What else can we do?"

They both knew there was no choice.

"I'll go first," Chelsea said. "I'm lighter."

"And I'm stronger. I'm a farm girl, remember? It's
thirty feet across, Chelsea. We've got a better chance if
I go." Caitlin handed the flashlight to Chelsea and
tested the rope again as she sat down and dangled her
feet over the edge of the crevasse. She gripped the rope
with both hands. "Once I reach the other side, you can
undo the rope on this side and tie it around your waist
so I can pull you across."

"Like a sack of potatoes. How damaging to my image." Chelsea knelt on the ground beside Caitlin and
eyed the rope doubtfully. "It looks all right."

"Hold on to the rope on this side in case it won't
bear my weight." Caitlin closed her eyes, tightened her
grip on the rope, took a deep breath, and slipped off the
edge into nothingness.

Her arms snapped with strain in their sockets.

Her palms burned.

The water hissed below like a dragon hungry for a feast.

But the rope held fast.

"I'll have to go quickly." She gasped. "I can't stand—"
She stopped talking and started moving, propelling
herself hand over hand across the crevasse. The red bow

bobbed across the yawning emptiness. If she could kee
her eyes and concentration on the bow instead of c
the pain in her hands and arms...

She was a third of the way across.

The water hissed as it plunged through the fissure.

Almost halfway across.

The scarlet bow shone like a beacon, its wide, shimme
ing length in frivolous contrast to the rough hemp rope.

More than halfway. A few more feet and she woul
be within reach of the bow.

A few more feet...

She felt a jerk in the rope beneath her hands.

Panic screamed through her. The rope! Dammit, b
it had looked so strong. Her gaze flew to the rop
ahead. No weakness. Tough hemp.

Chelsea called, "Caitlin, what's wrong?"

"The rope—it's breaking." She hung frozen, afraid t
move.

The rope hadn't begun to break until she had almo
reached the two-thirds mark. Until she had almo
reached the red satin bow.

The bow.

Merde, it was that goddamned bow! Ledford ha
partially severed the rope and then covered the cu
with a wide band of ribbon. "It's the bow. He cut—
Caitlin felt the rope give again under her weight as an
other cord in the braided rope gave way. She couldn
go back. There wasn't time before the rope would snap
She could only take a wild chance.

Fast. She had to move fast. She swung forward wit
frantic speed, hand over hand, toward the scarlet bow. Th
rope gave, snapped, broke entirely. She released her grip
dove forward past the bow, grabbed the shredded dar
gling end of the rope with both hands, and held on tight

Chelsea screamed.

Caitlin's body weight propelled her forward toward e sheared wall of the crevasse. She felt a hot blinding ain in her left cheekbone as she crashed against the all.

A woman's scream echoed through the tunnel!

Sheer terror tore through Alex. He broke into a run.

"That was Chelsea," Jonathan muttered, pounding ehind him. Alex felt a twinge of guilt because he was relieved. He was vaguely aware of a crackling under e soles of his shoes. Shells? No, glass.

He rounded a curve in the tunnel to see Chelsea neeling, staring down into the darkness.

Alex felt a cold chill. What the hell was she staring at?

And then he saw Caitlin hanging from the rope cross the abyss.

He made a sound low in his throat and took a step orward.

"No!" Jonathan grabbed his arm. "Don't speak. Don't istract her. She may make it if—"

"If?" Alex felt the muscles of his stomach knot with anic. He had never felt more helpless. He could do othing but stand and watch Caitlin clinging desper-tely to the rope.

Caitlin's hands began to slip down the rope. One nch. Two inches.

"Caitlin, don't you *dare* give up," Chelsea shouted.

Caitlin hung there, trying to fight the dizziness and ain. If she let go now, Ledford would win. He had illed her mother and now he was killing her. Her head

fell back as she looked up at where the rope curv
onto the floor of the tunnel. Safety. It was too far. T
feet at least. But if she died, Ledford would wi
Dammit, it wasn't right for Ledford to win after .
they had gone through to defeat him. She braced h
bare feet against the stone wall of the crevasse and b
gan to half walk, half pull herself up the side.

Her hands were bleeding, she noticed vaguely, lea
ing marks as bright red as the scarlet bow on the rope

Six feet.

Her arms and shoulders were without feeling. Th
pain was gone but she was numb with weariness.

Four feet.

Her eyes stung with tears and sweat. She couldr
see the edge of the crevasse any longer. She climbe
blindly, automatically.

She was dimly aware of Chelsea encouraging, plea
ing, cursing at her.

She reached the edge of the crevasse and pulled he
self over the top.

She collapsed on the ground, panting, tremblin
burying her face in her arms. "I made it!" Her tee
were chattering. "Give me a minute. . . ."

"Thank God," Chelsea said quietly. "I thought you–

"Me too." Caitlin could feel the tears of profour
thankfulness running down her cheeks. She was goir
to *live*. He wasn't going to win. She wouldn't let hi
win. There might still be other unpleasant surprises
store, but nothing Ledford could throw at them cou
ever be as bad as what she had just gone through. "No
what?" Caitlin asked shakily. "We seem to be out
rope. How do I get you across?"

"You don't, Caitlin."

"Alex?" Caitlin stiffened in shock, her head lifting

stare across the crevasse. Alex stood beside Chelsea, his
face pale and grim in the light of the lantern he held in
his hand. Jonathan Andreas was behind him.

"Listen, there's no time," he said urgently. "Don't
worry about us. You have to get out of the tunnel and
get to the ruins to warn them."

"What about you?"

"We'll find a way across."

"You shouldn't have come. I don't want to leave—"

"Get going, dammit," Chelsea said. "The sooner you
get out of here, the sooner you can bring us help."

Chelsea was right. If Caitlin could get out of there
and reach the soldiers at the ruins... Caitlin stumbled
to her knees, flinching as her raw, bleeding hands braced
against the stone, aching in every muscle of her body.
"Yes... I'll get help. I'll be right back." She struggled to
her feet and started to run down the tunnel toward the
pinpoint of daylight. "I'll bring help...."

Jonathan knelt beside Chelsea. He touched her
cheek. "We heard you scream."

"Caitlin. I was scared to death...." Chelsea shook her
head and her tone turned fierce. "You had to come,
didn't you? What good is it going to do for you to be
smashed under Ledford's thumb too? You should have
stayed where you were safe. Why the hell don't you
ever do—"

"Hush." His fingers touched her lips, silencing her.
"You're being completely idiotic. I couldn't stay away.
You're always telling me what I should do, what I should
be. Don't you know I can't be any of those things without you? Don't you know how much I *need* you?"

"Need?" She looked at him, startled. She had never

connected that word with Jonathan. Everyone els
needed Jonathan. He was the shelter and the rock. "No
I guess—"

"We may be able to do something with two of thes
posts." Alex was studying the crisscrossed beams tha
supported the roof of the tunnel. He went over to the
post that still had the rope dangling from around it and
knelt to examine the ground in which it was implanted
"They're on loose, sandy ground. There's a chance w
could rope two of them together to form a bridg
across the crevasse."

"And risk the roof coming down on our heads?"
Jonathan asked.

"In twelve minutes it's going to come down on u
anyway. What have we got to lose?"

"Not a damn thing," Jonathan said grimly.

"What are you talking about?" Chelsea said. "We car
wait for Caitlin to bring help."

Jonathan shook his head. "Ledford said there's a plas
tique charge set in the tunnels."

"No wonder the bastard wasn't afraid we'd get out o
here alive. He had all the aces."

Jonathan rose to his feet and walked over to examin
the beam.

Alex tugged experimentally at the post. "I think it'
giving a little. If we use the rope to pull—"

"Really, Alex, I'd think you would have learned to
rely on your brain, not your brute strength." Kema
strode around the curve of the tunnel. "How ofter
must I tell you that?"

Alex stepped back away from the beam, staring a
the Uzi cradled in Kemal's right arm. "Are you sup
posed to finish us off?"

"Where are your instincts?" Kemal asked mockingly

Isn't it obvious I have the soul of a hero even if fate has been fit to cast me as a villain? It took me a few minutes to properly set up your escape and slip away from Bedford, but here I am to the rescue." His smile vanished as his gaze went to the crevasse. "Where is Caitlin?"

"Isn't it a little late to ask that?" Alex asked. "What if I told you she'd fallen?"

"Then I would not be able to forgive myself," Kemal said simply. "Did it happen?"

"She managed to get across," Chelsea said. "By now she should be almost out of the tunnel. No help from you, bastard."

Kemal expelled his breath in a sigh of relief. "Then you must join her immediately. You don't have much time." He turned and started back the way he had come. "Come along."

"Wait," Alex said.

"No time." Kemal didn't stop. "Hurry."

"I'm supposed to trust you?"

"Have you any choice?" Kemal's tone became softly urgent. "Believe me, I did not mean to put Caitlin in danger. He told me he was keeping them both as hostages."

Alex hesitated and then started after Kemal.

"I can't believe this. You're going to do as he asks?" Chelsea asked incredulously as she scrambled to her feet and followed them. "He's a louse."

"He's also our best bet," Alex said.

"I certainly am." Kemal stopped before a large boulder lodged against the right wall. He rolled it aside to reveal a four-foot cavity hacked out of the wall. He gestured to Chelsea. "Ladies first."

Chelsea looked at the opening suspiciously. "Where does it lead?"

"To the main tunnel," Kemal replied. "Since o‹ friend Ledford is such an abominable person, I though‹ it wise to make sure I had a way of escape if needed. S‹ while Ledford was off spreading chaos through Europ‹ I was exploring the countryside and tunnels and diggir‹ bolt-holes." He checked his watch. "Ten minutes. Yo‹ should have no problem. The main tunnel is a straigh‹ shot."

"No little surprises?" Chelsea asked dryly.

Kemal shook his head. "After you're through th‹ opening, turn left and keep going. It ends about a hal‹ mile from where this offshoot tunnel exists. Four mir‹ utes and you'll be out of the tunnel. I've parked you‹ jeep in the shrubbery about a hundred yards from th‹ exit. Take it and make a run for the ruins to warn th‹ delegation."

Chelsea dropped to her knees and began crawlin‹ through the opening and Jonathan followed.

"Why?" Alex asked Kemal bluntly.

"Go," Kemal said.

Alex fell to his knees and began to crawl through th‹ opening. Kemal followed, and when he rose to his fee‹ he gestured to the left. "Four minutes. I promise." H‹ gave Alex the Uzi he was carrying. "You may need thi‹ Krakow's team may not welcome your interferenc‹ Good luck, my friend." He turned right and strod‹ down the corridor in the direction from which he ha‹ come.

"Where the hell are you going?" Alex called.

"To make myself a rich man," Kemal called. "You for‹ get the Wind Dancer is still here."

"You idiot, the place is going to blow."

"Some prizes are worth a little risk."

Alex hesitated and Kemal smiled understanding‹ over his shoulder. "Another choice. You want to go wit‹

he and kill Ledford but you know Caitlin and the dele-
ation are still in danger. I think you know what your
hoice must be." He shrugged. "Will it help if I tell you
edford will not survive? It was my plan from the be-
inning of our association that he would die. In fact, it
vas why our association began."

Alex's gaze narrowed on Kemal's face. "It wasn't only
he money?"

"Adnan only managed the Harem, Ledford owned it."

"What!"

"He bought the controlling interest at the same
ime he came to Istanbul and arranged the purchase
f the house on the Street of Swords. It was a purely
ersonal extravagance on his part. He even acquired
hree of the children for Adnan." He shrugged. "I really
on't believe Ledford deserves to be emperor of South
America."

"But you do?"

Kemal glanced over his shoulder, his face illuminated
y a mischievous grin. "What do you think?"

In another moment he had disappeared from view.

"Do we trust him?" Chelsea asked.

"Yes," Alex said slowly. "Yes, we trust him." He turned
eft and started down the tunnel at a fast trot.

"Don't wait for us," Jonathan said as he slipped his
rm around Chelsea's waist to support her. "We'll be a
ittle slower."

"I can walk by myself," Chelsea protested.

"I'm sure you could walk on water if you chose,"
onathan said. "But it's quicker this way, so be quiet."

In four minutes Alex emerged at the tunnel opening
nd stood waiting for the others to join him. He stared
ut over the plateau and suddenly stiffened. Caitlin!

Caitlin, barefoot, clothes torn, was running down the
ncline to the plain that led to the Hisarlik plateau.

"Caitlin!"

She glanced back over her shoulder. "Alex?"

"Come back, there's a jeep."

She turned and streaked back up the incline. "Where?"

"In the underbrush," Jonathan said as he came out of the cave and started toward the place where the jeep was hidden. "Let's get going. We don't have much time. Stay here, Chelsea."

"No way."

"Look, those soldiers are going to come at us like bats out of hell when they catch sight of us."

She limped toward the jeep. "Don't argue with me. You never know. Maybe one of those soldiers is a fan. could save your neck. I'm going."

Caitlin started to follow her and then stopped, looking back at the cave opening.

Alex froze. "No, Caitlin."

"What if that bastard gets away?"

"Don't you think I feel the same way? Kemal promised me he'd take care of him. I trust him."

"I don't know why you're trusting Kemal's word, but I don't give a damn about his promises. Ledford killed my mother. He burned Vasaro. I have to make sure he' punished." She held up her hand as he started to protest. "I'm not idiot enough to go back in that cave. Do you have any idea where the main entrance is?"

"Are you coming?" Jonathan was backing the jeep out of the underbrush.

Caitlin met his gaze. "Where is it, Alex?"

"This entire hill could explode."

"Where is it?"

She wasn't going to be persuaded. And God forgive him, he was glad he was going to get his chance at Ledford.

"A triangular red rock, top of the hill." He waved onathan to go ahead without them before turning and abbing Caitlin's arm. "Move fast. Run. We'll skirt ound this cave opening and up the hill and hope we in get up there before it blows."

21

"Hello, Kemal, I've been expecting you." Ledford stood with his right hand resting caressingly on the filigreed wing of the Wind Dancer sitting on the table and his left hand gripping a .42 Magnum revolver. "Did you think I didn't suspect you? I found it singularly strange an efficient fellow like yourself wouldn't be able to locate Alex during those weeks after we destroyed Vasaro and then, too, you were a little too concerned about the fate of my hostages." He raised his brows. "But I do admit I'm disappointed. I thought you'd bring Alex back with you or I wouldn't have let you go after them."

"You've lost him," Kemal said. "You've lost everything, Ledford."

"Nonsense. Nothing has changed. My plan is proceeding quite nicely. The Rembrandt's loaded in the car and I have six minutes to get to the checkpoint before Hans blows the wooden statue." He lifted the gun. "And I have a weapon with which to blow out your brains."

"A gun loaded with dummies." Kemal walked slowly toward him. "An efficient fellow like me wouldn't overlook a minor detail like that."

Ledford aimed at the center of Kemal's forehead.
ou're bluffing."

"Am I?"

Ledford pulled the trigger.

It was almost time.

Hans blew on his hands to warm them, and sighted
wn the Springfield rifle at the path directly before
e wooden Trojan horse. Then he settled himself more
mfortably against the rock to wait.

From this hill he judged the distance to be a little un-
r a thousand yards, and the Springfield carried only
e shot. You didn't need more than one shot when
u were the best, he mused. He smiled as he watched
e scene below him. That big scarlet tent they'd set up
ade the plateau look like a bloody circus. The com-
rison amused him. Yeah, and Krakow's antiterrorist
ys and all those British soldiers strutting around were
e clowns.

Krakow helped the old woman from the bus and
niled ingratiatingly. He could see the bastard's lips
ove as he spoke and turned to walk beside Cartwright
the rest of the party followed them from the bus to-
ard the wooden horse.

Brian had told him to hold his hand until all the con-
rence members were inside that stupid wooden horse,
it he was done with orders. He would do as he
eased.

He smiled with pleasure as he thought of Brian's sur-
ise in that last moment before he sent him to hell.

Yes, it was almost time.

• • • •

"How much time?" Chelsea shouted.

"Five minutes." Jonathan pressed harder on the acc
erator and the jeep leapt forward.

"Can we make it?"

"How the hell do I know?" The jeep tore across t
plain toward the ruins on the plateau.

The jeep careened over the plain like a drunken rl
noceros toward the ruins.

Hans's gaze narrowed on the oncoming vehic
Another unexpected disruption of Brian's plans?

He lifted his binoculars to get a closer look. A m
and a woman. Should he take the driver out?

He decided against it. He was too far away to u
anything but the Springfield, and that one bullet w
reserved exclusively for Krakow. Besides, the soldiers
the perimeter had already seen them and might do l
job for him. He glanced at his watch. Five minutes b
fore the statue was due to blow.

Still, this new disturbance might upset the delica
balance of his own plan. He'd better consider the o
tion of escalating the action.

He reached into his pocket and drew out the tv
tiny black switch boxes that could override the time
on the plastique in both the Trojan statue and the tu
nel and set off the explosion. He had gone back in
both the tunnel and wooden horse the night before a
very carefully hidden the second radio-controlled det
nator beneath the plastique. A blue button for tl
Trojan horse, red button for the tunnel.

He held Brian's fate in the palm of his hand. Ha
had the power now. He was the one in control.

He didn't really have to wait another five minutes.

• • •

"They're actually going to shoot at us," Chelsea said
in disbelief as she saw one of the British soldiers in the
jeep approaching them raise his automatic rifle. "Don't
they know we're trying to save them?"

"I told you not to come, dammit. For all they know,
the jeep could be packed with dynamite on a suicide
mission. Get down on the floorboards."

"So they can shoot at you instead?" Chelsea held on
to the seat bar.

"Is it going to help me if you get shot?" Jonathan
swerved across the plain in a zigzag path to spoil the
soldier's aim.

"Can't we stop and try to explain?"

Jonathan shook his head as he glanced down at the
watch on his wrist. "Four minutes." He barreled down
the road toward the huge wooden horse.

Hans frowned, sitting up straight against the rock.

The jeep was going to get through. In another
minute Krakow would become aware of the jeep and
take alarm.

Hans sighted down the telescopic lens.

Krakow was standing beside Cartwright on the path
leading to the Trojan horse. He was smiling, his white-
gold hair lifting in the strong breeze.

Slowly, steadily, Hans's finger pressed the trigger of
the rifle.

A bright red blossom appeared on Krakow's forehead. His ingratiating smile was captured forever as his
brain functions ceased.

One down.

Now for the diversion and the signal to tell Bria
who was really in control.

Hans's thumb pressed down on the blue button.

The wooden horse of Troy blew into a cloud of flam

A flying spear of wood broke the windshield of tl
jeep as the wooden horse exploded.

Jonathan jammed on the brake and pulled Chelse
to the floor as the blast lifted the jeep three feet in tl
air and then slammed it down again.

"Something's wrong. We had another four minute:
Chelsea gasped. She clung to Jonathan, burrowing h
face in his shoulder. "Something went wrong. . . ."

"It appears Ledford's friend, Hans, changed tl
rules." Jonathan cautiously lifted his head and peere
over the dashboard. The scene was a madhouse
movement, shouts, and screams. Members of the co
ference were running back toward the bus. Soldie
milled helplessly, staring in bewilderment at the roarii
fireball where the giant wooden horse had stood. Tl
tops of the pines surrounding the statue had caught fi
and burned like giant torches at a funeral pyre.

Krakow lay crumpled, unmoving, on the groun
Jonathan's gaze went anxiously toward Cartwright an
saw her picking herself up, dazedly brushing the dirt an
leaves from her neat blue suit. "Cartwright's all right."

"Krakow?"

"I don't know. He's not moving. Everyone's rushii
toward the bus."

Chelsea sat up on the floor of the jeep. "But they'
all safe? I can't believe that—"

"Get out of the jeep." The order came with crisp an
deadly British incisiveness. "Keep your hands in fu
view or we'll blow your asses away."

Jonathan glanced sidewise to see that the jeep coi
taining the British soldiers that had been chasing ther

as now parked a few yards away. Three soldiers stood
eside the jeep, and a tall man with a hooked nose,
wearing the uniform of a British colonel, gazed at them
with flintlike grimness. "Do it. It would be a pleasure to
low your head off, scum."

"Cartwright may be safe," Jonathan said dryly as he
azed at the muzzles of the three M16s pointed at their
eads. "But I'm not at all sure about us."

The hammer of Ledford's Magnum clicked on an
mpty chamber.

Kemal smiled as he pulled the bullets out of the
ocket of his corduroy pants and held them up to show
edford. He threw them aside and reached for the .38
evolver in his jacket pocket.

A flicker of admiration crossed Ledford's face as he
owered his gun. "Ah, you could have gone far, Kemal. I
on't believe I've ever met—"

The earth shook and dirt suddenly rained down on
he table.

Shock froze Ledford's expression. "Hans! Goddam-
nit, it's too soon!" He snatched up the Wind Dancer
nd held it before him. "That son of a bitch!"

"Give me the Wind Dancer," Kemal said.

"Take it! I don't think you're going to risk putting a
ullet through a statue this valuable." Ledford's eyes
littered in his pale face. "I'm getting out of here. I
hecked that timer myself. The bastard must have gone
ack and set a double switch. He can blow us anytime
e wants to push that goddamn button." He unexpect-
dly hurled his gun at Kemal's head. The butt of the
weapon struck him on the temple.

Pain. Darkness. Kemal fell to his knees, fighting to
tay conscious.

When his dizziness cleared a little, he saw tha Ledford had dashed across the clearing and was o the ramp. The Wind Dancer gleamed in the lanter light. . . .

He raised the gun and aimed at the back of Ledford head. Get him. Ignore this damn dizziness. Steady you hand. Kill the bastard.

He pressed the trigger. Blood darkened the materia of the shirt high on Ledford's shoulder. He had missec Kemal realized in frustration. He had failed.

No, maybe not entirely. The impact of the bullet ha caused Ledford to drop the Wind Dancer. It was fallin through the air and hit the ground several yards fror where Kemal knelt.

Ledford muttered a curse as he stopped on the ram and stared down at the statue.

Kemal raised his gun again.

But Ledford was gone before he could fire off th second shot.

Go after him.

The Wind Dancer . . . get the Wind Dancer first.

God, he was dizzy. . . .

Emerald eyes gleaming . . . there it was. Now get t the surface. The ramp seemed to stretch upward int eternity, he thought dazedly. He smiled wryly at th thought. Eternity was just where he would be headin unless he managed to move.

He clutched the Wind Dancer and crawled slowl toward the ramp, gritting his teeth as hot, sickenin pain shot through his head. He reached the ramp an started to crawl up it. Too slow. Much too slow. He ha to get to his feet and make better time.

Hans could decide to blow the tunnel any minute. . .

•   •   •

The huge red rock beckoned.

Caitlin's breath came in harsh pants as she climbed toward it.

Katrine... Vasaro...

"Okay?" Alex didn't look back at her, his stride lengthening with eagerness as the target came into view.

She didn't have the breath to answer.

Ugliness. Blood. Evil.

Ledford.

"Son of a bitch." Alex had stopped short, his gaze on something ahead. "It looks like we're not going to have to dig the rat out of his hole. There he goes."

Her gaze followed his. A man was running toward a Mercedes parked in the trees. "Ledford?"

Alex nodded.

Ledford was now in the car and careening down the road.

He was getting away!

"No!" She darted to the left, through the trees toward the road. "We can cut him off at the bottom of the hill."

Alex was pounding after her. "Caitlin."

"Give me that gun."

"Not yet. We're not close enough."

"Then let's get in range." She had reached the road and could see the Mercedes barreling down the hill. "He's coming toward us."

She could see Ledford's face behind the wheel. His expression was twisted with anger.

Her mother. Vasaro.

"Give me that gun, Alex."

"Have you ever fired a Uzi?"

"No. Show me."

"This is no time for lessons. Allow me." He lifted the Uzi and the bullets exploded from the weapon.

The windshield of the Mercedes shattered.

And so did Ledford's skull.

Those stupid soldiers were running around the ruin like chickens with a fox let loose among them, Han thought gleefully.

And he was the fox.

He leaned back against the rock, watching them for moment, and then looked down at the second switc box. By then Brian knew he was no longer the man the helm. He was probably scrambling desperately get himself and his pretty statue out of the tunnel.

Hans hesitated, enjoying the moment, savoring th heady, godlike power.

"Good-bye, Brian," he said softly.

He pressed the red button to detonate the plastiqu in the tunnel.

The first charge didn't sound like an explosion at al more like a loud *whump* that whispered through th hill. Ten seconds later the second and third charg went off and the top of the hill blew off like an erup ing volcano.

Chelsea and Jonathan whirled around to see tree rocks, and earth catapulting high into the air.

"Dear God!" Chelsea whispered in horror. "Wh could live through that?"

"No survivors," Colonel Severn said in his cris British accent as he looked down at the gaping hol that once had been the trapdoor leading to the tunne

e turned to face Jonathan and Alex. "We'll conduct a
arch, of course, but no one could possibly have lived
rough that blast. We picked up Hans Brucker an hour
o, and he told us he set three charges with enough
epower to blow up half of London." He shrugged. "If
e explosion didn't blow Kemal Nemid to bits, he
ould still have been crushed by the falling rock. The
ound is so unstable here, it may take years to dig out
e remains."

"Did you check with the guards at the checkpoints?"
ex asked.

"It's been over five hours and no cars have passed in
out after the first explosion. Accept it, he's dead."
evern went on briskly, "We'll need statements from all
you."

"The ladies have been through a great deal,"
nathan said. "Can't you send them back to the hotel
rest and let Alex and me fill you in? You can get a
atement from them later."

"After all, I'm the one who actually shot Ledford,"
ex added.

Severn hesitated, glanced back at the yawning hole in
e earth, and then shrugged and nodded. "Tomorrow
ill do as well. I'll assign someone to drive Ms. Benedict
d Ms. Vasaro back to Istanbul. Tell them they're
ot to leave the city. We'll start with your statement,
ndreas."

"Let's get this over with." Jonathan turned away from
evern and said to Alex, "Tell Chelsea I'll see her at the
otel."

Alex didn't reply, and Jonathan noticed he was star-
g thoughtfully at the thicket of pines a hundred yards
way. "Alex?"

Alex glanced away from the thicket. "Oh, yes, sure."

He started for the jeep where Chelsea and Caitlin we
sitting.

The jaw of the doorman at the Hilton dropped
shock as he opened the door for Chelsea and Caitlin.

Who could blame him, Caitlin thought wearily. Th
were so dirty and bloodstained, they looked as if th
had been through a war.

And so they had.

"You should have those feet looked after by a do
tor," Caitlin said dully as they were going up in the el
vator. "I know I didn't get all the glass out."

"I'll call down to the desk and get them to ser
someone." The door slid open as the elevator stoppe
on Chelsea's floor and Chelsea straightened away fro
against the wall. "I'll phone you later."

She left the elevator and limped down the corridor

The telephone was ringing when Caitlin unlocke
the door of her own room a few minutes later.

As soon as Caitlin picked up the receiver, Chelse
said, "Melis is gone. There was a message from the m
tron of the welfare home when I got to my room. The
think she ran away."

"Oh, no, have they called the police?"

"An hour ago. Christ, what a hell of a day."

And when they did find Melis, they would have
tell her the only anchor she had in the world had bee
blown to bits. Chelsea was right. What a hell of a day.

"Is the matron going to call you when they find her

"Yeah, cross your fingers." Chelsea hung up the phon

Caitlin walked slowly into the bathroom and turne
on the shower. As she undressed she caught a glimps
of her reflection in the mirror over the washbasin an

nched. She looked even worse than she had thought
ossible. A huge bruise discolored her swollen left
week, and the purple shadows under her eyes looked
most as livid.

She stepped into the shower stall and let the hot water
n over her, taking away some of the ache of her mus-
es, if not of her spirit. She should be feeling satisfied.
edford was dead. Justice had been done. Yet the satisfac-
on was bitter, for Kemal Nemid had died with him.

Kemal. Strange, funny, complex Kemal, who had
uched her and healed her . . . and betrayed her. Yet Alex
d told her he had saved them all in the end. She could
el the warm tears run down her cheeks, and she didn't
now if they were just a release from the tension of the
ay or for that wicked, undeserving scamp Kemal.

It was after midnight when Alex came back to the
otel. He looked as exhausted and disheveled as Caitlin
ad been earlier.

"Any news?" When he walked into the bedroom
aitlin sat up in bed and pressed the off switch on the
emote control for the television set. "I mean besides
s? Evidently the British delegation has been talking to
he press. What happened at Troy is all over the net-
orks."

"It's front-page stuff." Alex shook his head wearily.
They're scouring the coastline but they haven't discov-
red where the *Argosy* is docked, and Severn is still con-
inced that no one could have survived the blast.
evern's men tried to do some digging to retrieve possi-
le remains, but they had to stop when the ground gave
way beneath them. As far as they're concerned, the
atter is closed."

"And the Wind Dancer?"

"Severn said it had to have been destroyed in t
blast."

Sadness swept through Caitlin. She felt as if she h
lost an old friend, an integral part of her life. "All th
knowledge and beauty gone."

Alex nodded and then was silent a moment. "Sor
about Ledford. I had to take the shot. I didn't mean
cheat you."

"You didn't cheat me. It didn't matter who pull
the trigger as long as he was destroyed. You had det
to settle too." She smiled. "We did it together."

"Yeah, together." Alex turned and moved toward tl
bathroom. "I'll be with you in a few minutes. I have
shower."

She nodded. "You'll feel better."

"I couldn't feel much worse."

"I'm afraid you can. Melis is gone."

Alex stopped in midstride. "What?"

"Melis ran away from the home this afternoon. The p
lice are searching the city, but they haven't found her ye

"Oh."

Caitlin frowned. "You don't seem very upset."

Alex nodded. "Oh, I'm upset, but maybe..." H
trailed off as he entered the bathroom and shut the doc
The phone rang a moment after Caitlin heard the show
start and she reached out for it on the nightstand.

Caitlin was just hanging up the phone when Ale
came back into the bedroom ten minutes later. H
looked at her inquiringly. "About Melis?"

"That was Chelsea to say they still haven't found he

Alex came toward the bed. "Istanbul is a big city."

"For God's sake, I know it's a big—" Caitlin broke o
as she realized how sharp she sounded. "Sorry. I'r
upset."

"About Melis?"

"About everything," she said. "But yes, about Melis. I can't do anything about the rest of this hellishness, but Melis...I want..." She looked up at him, trying to blink back the tears that had been hovering. "I want her to be safe. She's just a child. I don't want her to be hurt anymore. There's been too much pain for all of us. I want it to be over."

"Yes." He reached out and gently touched her hair. "Caitlin—" He hesitated. "I don't think they're going to find Melis."

"You can't know that."

"No." He sat down beside her on the bed and pulled her into his arms. "It's all variables."

"Variables?" She pulled back to look up at him. "What are you talking about?"

He didn't answer for a moment. "What if Kemal's alive?"

Her eyes widened in shock. "Severn said there was no chance."

"Severn doesn't realize how resourceful Kemal can be."

"You think he got out?"

"I don't know."

"No one passed the checkpoints." Caitlin's gaze searched his face. "But that's not all, is it?"

"I found bicycle tracks in the pine thicket. I caught a glimpse of them when Jonathan and I were wandering around, waiting to talk to Severn, and I went back to get a closer look after you left."

Excitement stirred within her. "A bicycle!"

"It's only a chance." He held up his hand to stop the eager flow of words. "The ground was so ripped up by the explosion, I couldn't tell if the tracks were fresh or not." He frowned. "But it set me to thinking. We know Kemal never intended to go to South America with

Ledford and that he meant from the beginning to ste
the art treasures for himself. Kemal knew if he put
spoke in Ledford's works, he'd have to have a safe wa
out. He told us no one knew those tunnels like he di
and it seems odd he didn't know about the charge
Hans Brucker had set. The Kemal we know would hav
made it his business to know everything about bot
Ledford and Brucker's plans."

"So you think he knew about the plastique?"

"It's a possibility. But Kemal has no taste for killing
He told me so himself. He'd want the diversion of th
explosion at the ruins, but he'd need to bring in anothe
element to foil the assassination attempt."

"Us," Caitlin said. "And he planned to use parts o
Ledford's scheme to disappear from sight with th
paintings as his own."

"We all knew there were only two cars in the thicke
and Kemal moved the jeep down to the tunnel opening
But suppose Kemal *did* hide a bicycle in the under
brush. Remember how he was dressed? Brown cor
duroy trousers, heavy shoes, jacket, that red woo
sweater, he could have been taken for any farm boy i
the area. I mistook him for a young boy myself when
first met him. He could hide in the hills until the sol
diers left the ruins and then cut over the plain towar
one of the farms that borders the Aegean."

"With a speedboat waiting on the shore," Caitlin said
"To take him—" She paused. "Where?"

"Wherever the *Argosy* is docked," Alex said. "H
wouldn't overlook distributing generous bribes to th
ship officers to allow him to be accepted in Ledford'
stead as master of the ship."

"So he sails away with no ties and a cargo of the mos
priceless art treasures in the world."

"Perhaps one tie."

"Melis?" Caitlin tried to remember what Chelsea had told her about Melis that morning. It seemed a thousand years since Chelsea had breezed into the room to tell her Alex had gone to the embassy without her. "The matron told Chelsea that Melis was very upset last night, but after Kemal paid her a visit she settled down and seemed content. But Chelsea said Melis was having a problem with nerves again this morning."

"Nerves... or anticipation?"

"Kemal told Melis last night he was going to take her with him?"

"He could have had her picked up by one of his cohorts and driven to wherever the *Argosy* was docked." Alex lifted the coverlet, slid into bed beside her, and leaned wearily back on the pillow. "Jesus, how do I know? Turn out the light."

She reached over and switched off the light before lying down again. "Did you tell Colonel Severn?"

"What could I tell him? It's all supposition."

She was silent. "If he did escape, he might have the Wind Dancer."

"If he chose to risk being caught with it. How can you hide a statue on a bicycle? It would have been smarter for him to leave it." He stirred restlessly. "But I don't have any pieces to put together. All I have is some damn bicycle tracks. It's all variables and guesswork."

"But you want it to be true?"

He was silent for so long, she thought he wasn't going to answer, and when he finally did speak, the words were nearly inaudible. "Yes, I do want it to be true."

That admission had not been easy for Alex. Neither of them trusted easily, and he had felt the same sense of betrayal as she had regarding Kemal. No doubt existed

Kemal was lethal, brilliant, and manipulative, but he was many other things as well. She had a sudden memory of his dark face lit with tenderness as he had spoken to Melis in the garden.

Caitlin moved into Alex's arms and nestled her cheek in the hollow of his shoulder. She whispered, "So do I."

Alex was gone when Caitlin woke up near noon the next day.

At first she thought he was merely in the bathroom until she saw the note on the nightstand.

> *Caitlin,*
>   *I've left for Nice. After you went to sleep I started thinking and it suddenly occurred to me we could use all this hoopla with the press as a tool to introduce the perfume. But we'll have to move fast with the arrangements if we're to take maximum advantage of the situation. Refuse all interviews regarding what happened at Troy and tell Chelsea and Jonathan to do the same. Tell the press, if they want a statement or interview, to be at the Negresco Hotel in Nice on December tenth for the introduction of Vasaro.*
>   *When Severn releases you, come to Nice. I'll need you.*
>
> *Alex*

Caitlin read the letter again, stunned. The past night Alex had been weary, dispirited, and vulnerable, yet sometime during the night the metamorphosis had occurred. He was moving again, thinking, shaping events to suit himself.

Give them what they want.

But it seemed the press was going to have to wait two weeks, until December 10, to be given what they wanted.

And in return Vasaro was going to be given news coverage never before seen in the world of perfume.

22

Chelsea caught sight of Caitlin waiting by the elevator and gave her a wave over the heads of the mob of journalists in the lobby of the Negresco. Then she turned and smiled brilliantly while cameras whirred and clicked and questions were fired at her.

"Is it true you were kidnapped by the Black Medina?"

"What have you been doing in Paris for the last week?"

"Have you signed to do a docudrama of the—"

"No questions." Chelsea held up her hand to stop the verbal barrage. "You know the deal. You show up at the presentation tonight with cameras rolling and we have a joint press conference directly afterward and talk about whatever you like." She started pushing her way through the crowd. "Now I need to get upstairs and kick off my shoes. I'll see you all tonight."

The assistant manager of the hotel, whose startling good looks rivaled those of Tom Cruise, quickly inserted himself between Chelsea and the reporters, clearing a path toward the elevators.

"Quite a show."

Chelsea turned at the familiar voice to see an equally

amiliar face among the crowd of reporters. "Fancy seeing ou here, Tyndale. I thought you'd have more social conciousness than to show up for a philistine extravaganza ke this. Aren't you afraid of being contaminated?"

"Why shouldn't I be here?" Tyndale's big-jowled face emained expressionless. "The bait was irresistible. No one an say you're not good at what you do, Ms. Benedict."

He turned and slipped away into the crowd.

Chelsea felt a flicker of annoyance mixed with grudgng respect for the newsman as she continued toward he elevator. The assistant manager whisked Chelsea and Caitlin into the elevator and closed the glass door, standng guard before it as Caitlin pressed the button.

Chelsea gave Caitlin a quick hug. "How are you?"

"Fine. Run off my feet, but fine."

"Christ, crystal chandeliers in the elevator?" Chelsea ilted her head to stare up at the ceiling. "Your Negresco Hotel sure knows how to put on the dog." Her glance raveled to the plush red-velvet-padded walls. "And all hose sexy Latin bellboys running around in eighteenthentury knee pants hugging those fantastic asses. Pure lecadence." She sighed contentedly. "I love it."

A smile tugged at Caitlin's lips. "The eighteenthentury livery isn't intended to stir your libido. The hotel opened in 1912, and it's supposed to provide a historic atmosphere."

"Then I was right the first time," Chelsea said. "If hey wanted to be historically authentic, why dress in eighteenth-century clothes when the hotel was built in he twentieth century?" She shook her head. "Sex nakes the world go round. Men's dress was much sexer in the eighteenth century, and that's why those bellboys' world-class buns are encased in knee pants."

Caitlin chuckled. "Have it your own way."

"I make a habit of it." She turned to look at Caitlin "Everything set for tonight?"

"No, but it's getting that way." Caitlin made a face "I've got only a few minutes before I have to go bac down and check on the audio people."

Two bellboys surrounded by luggage waited at th double doors of the suite when the glass door of the el evator slid open and Chelsea and Caitlin stepped int the spacious hall. Chelsea watched with amusement a Caitlin's gaze immediately strayed to the portion o their anatomy which had so enthralled Chelsea.

"See?" Chelsea murmured.

Caitlin's gaze jerked guiltily away from the bellboys buttocks to face Chelsea's mischievous smile. She nod ded gravely. "Remarkable."

Chelsea unlocked the door and the bellboys swep into the suite with her four suitcases and two trunks.

Chelsea received an immediate impression o eighteenth-century elegance combined with twentieth century comfort. She glimpsed a Louis XVI desk agains the far wall, two paintings that looked like originals, casement window overlooking the Mediterranean.

"Put Ms. Benedict's bags in that room." Caitlin ges tured to a door to the left of the sitting room. "Don' bother showing her where everything is. She'll find it."

"I should be able to manage." Chelsea grimaced. " practically live in hotels."

A moment later Chelsea had tipped the bellboys and sent them on their way. She turned back to Caitlin "Barbara Walters met me at the airport and tried to ge me to give her an exclusive before the presentatio tonight." She kicked off her high heels and prowle restlessly around the sitting room. "You have them sali vating."

"We've worked hard. The Versailles party was noth-
ng compared to this."

"How is Alex?"

"I scarcely see him except at night, and then we both
:ollapse into unconsciousness before we can say more
han two sentences." Caitlin paused. "Marisa's here."

Chelsea whirled to face her. "What?"

"She wanted to come, and Jonathan flew her in on
he Andreas company jet."

"Dammit, she was allowed out of bed only two days
ago. Where is she?"

Caitlin nodded at the door across the sitting room.
'She arrived late last night. I think she's still sleeping. I
hought you'd want her here in the suite, where you
:ould keep an eye on her."

"Damn right I do. Those idiot doctors shouldn't have
et her on that plane."

"She seems very well," Caitlin said. "I don't think
Jonathan would have let her come if—"

"He shouldn't have done it." Chelsea's hands
:lenched into fists at her sides. "What the hell good
does it do me to hop all over Europe to avoid seeing
him if he makes gestures like this? How do we know
someone won't find out he brought Marisa—"

"I think you're fighting a losing battle, Chelsea," Caitlin
said gently.

"The hell I am." Chelsea drew a deep breath and
slowly unclenched her hands. "Come into the bedroom.
I picked up a present for you while I was in Paris."

"You did?" Caitlin followed her into the bedroom,
watching curiously as Chelsea opened the trunk the
bellboy had set by the armoire. "What is it?"

"It's not really from me, it's from Jean Perdot. He
:alled me at the hotel and summoned me into his august

presence." Chelsea carefully withdrew a silk garment bag. "'A rose of deepest crimson, strongly rooted,'" she quoted as she took out a tissue-wrapped object from a pocket in the trunk. "With thorns."

"I'm honored."

"You should be." Chelsea took a gown of a crimson shade so dark it was almost burgundy out of the garment bag and held it up. The style was utterly simple; the gown would fall straight to the floor, baring one shoulder in the Grecian fashion. The magic was all in the fabric and draping, the subtle pleating over the bodice, the fluid fall of the silk.

"It's ... wonderful," Caitlin breathed.

"And you'll look boffo in it." Chelsea unwrapped the object in her hand. "This is to be worn on the upper right arm like a slave bracelet."

The shimmering gold bracelet was as simple as the gown; a vine of thorns sparkling with diamond dewdrops that would wind twice around her arm. "I don't know what to say."

"Thank Jean the next time you see him. I'm only playing messenger girl." She handed the bracelet to Caitlin. "You may not be so grateful when you get his bill."

"What are you going to wear?"

"We won't clash. I have that amber lamé I picked up at Chanel." She swung the trunk shut. "I promise I'll be everything a spokesperson should be."

"You'd be that no matter what you wore. I thought the first time I met you that you *were* Vasaro."

Chelsea felt inexpressibly touched. She knew Caitlin could give her no greater compliment. Caitlin had lost much since that day, and yet she had also gained in many ways. She was stronger, surer, at peace with herself. "Have you been back to Vasaro?"

"Not yet. There hasn't been time." Caitlin's face lit with a luminous smile. "Tomorrow."

"Do you think you can take it?"

Caitlin nodded. "It's time to start again. As Alex said, life goes on." She put the gown carefully back in the garment bag and draped it over her arm as she turned and moved toward the door. "I have to get back to work. The hotel hairdresser will be up at four to do your hair and nails, and the launch presentation is at eight. I've arranged to have a light supper served to you and Marisa here in the suite at six."

"You sound as if you have everything under control."

"Not yet. But I'm working on it." Caitlin lifted her hand in farewell as she left the bedroom.

Chelsea took off her suit jacket and tossed it on the bed.

"Mother?"

"Here." Chelsea moved quickly into the sitting room to see Marisa coming toward her dressed in the bottoms of her tailored blue pajamas with the matching robe draped over her shoulders. "You should have stayed in bed. I was coming to you." She studied Marisa critically. "You look much better. Almost well."

She spoke the truth. Marisa's color was good and, except for the cast on her upper arm and shoulder, she looked entirely normal.

"I'm fine." Marisa bent down to brush her lips across her mother's cheek. "I'm going back to school next week."

"That's too soon. What if—"

"I'll be okay." Marisa's tone was gently firm. "Chill out."

Chelsea found herself chuckling. It always amused her when Marisa used the slang of her peer group. It sounded completely alien coming from her daughter's

lips. Then her smile faded. "You shouldn't have com‹
Jonathan shouldn't have—"

"Jonathan did exactly what we both wanted." Maris‹
met Chelsea's gaze. "Jonathan is why I came here."

Chelsea stiffened warily even as she joked. "Not t‹
see me do my stuff?"

Marisa shook her head. "I'll watch it on televisio‹
from my room." She paused. "It can't go on, Mothe‹
You're cheating us both."

"*Cheating* you?"

Marisa nodded. "You're cheating me of a friend an‹
father and you're cheating Jonathan of a wife an‹
daughter." Marisa stared gravely at Chelsea. "I learne‹
something when Peter died. One of the last things h‹
told me was to *live*. Life is too precious to waste whe‹
you never know when it's going to end. We have to liv‹
it to the fullest. You're not letting us do that."

Chelsea was stricken. "I only want you to be happy."

"Then stop trying to run our lives."

Chelsea shook her head, dazed with pain. "You don‹
understand."

"Sweet heaven, you're stubborn." Marisa hesitate‹
"Let's look at it another way. What if Jonathan i‹
elected president? Presidents are sometimes target‹
Look at Kennedy and Lincoln and Reagan."

"No! I wouldn't let that happen."

"You wouldn't be there. He would be alone."

"The president is never alone."

"But he wouldn't have someone who really care‹
about him. He needs you, Mother."

I need you, Jonathan had said in the tunnel.

"He'll be all right."

"How do you know?" Marisa looked at her mother'‹
confused face and then decided to bring out the bi‹
guns. "We've decided we can't let you do this to us any‹

ore. If you won't marry Jonathan, I'm moving in with
m." She lifted her hand as Chelsea started to speak.
'ery publicly. How much chance do you think he'd
ive for the presidency living with a sixteen-year-old?"

"You're bluffing. Jonathan would never put you in
at position."

"You're right, Jonathan *is* bluffing." Marisa smiled.
But I'm not. You know I don't bluff. I'll find a way to
ake it happen."

"You don't know what you're saying. The press
ould tear you to ribbons."

"I've always told you that you were more afraid of
y being hurt by them than I was." Marisa added gent-
, "My pain was over a long time ago. You're the one
ho is still hurting."

"You'd destroy Jonathan."

"No, Jonathan's too strong to be destroyed by either
f us."

"The presidency is—"

"I like Jonathan. I love you. If I had to sacrifice one to
ake the other happy, which would I choose?" Marisa
et Chelsea's gaze. "Look at me. Do I mean it?"

Chelsea stared at her and then sighed shakily. "Yes,
ou mean it."

"I'm glad I've made myself clear." Marisa leaned for-
ard and kissed her mother's cheek. "Think about it. I'll
ve you until next week before I go to Port Andreas."

"Thank you," Chelsea said ironically.

"It will be easier once you accept it." Marisa turned
nd moved toward her room. "On most subjects you're
ot this muddle-headed."

As the door closed behind Marisa, Chelsea shook her
ead dazedly.

Jesus, she was being railroaded.

She moved slowly to an overstuffed brocade chair

and collapsed onto it. She would have to consider wh
to do. This was ridiculous. Marisa was only an inexpe
enced girl and she was a grown woman. There had to
a way to deflect Marisa from this course, if she cou
just think clearly.

But Marisa had said Chelsea wasn't thinking clea
in this instance. Was it so bad to want to protect t
people you loved?

Yet what if that protection protected them from li
ing to the fullest, as Marisa claimed?

She just didn't know.

She leaned back, resting her head on the chair. Sl
might be muddle-headed, but one fact was becomi
very obvious.

She had to come to some conclusions fast.

At seven-thirty that evening Chelsea knocked firm
on the door of Caitlin's room.

Caitlin opened the door. "Chelsea, you're not ev
dressed."

"Don't worry. It will take only a few minutes." Chels
came into the room. Her gaze went over Caitlin's sta
uesque form from head to toe. "I told you that you'd loc
great in that gown."

"Thank you." Caitlin made a face. "It's a wonder
don't have it on inside out. I just tore up here to show
and change twenty minutes ago and I have to get ba
downstairs and make sure security is checking those ir
vitations that—"

"I won't keep you long." Chelsea closed the door b
hind her. "There's something I have to tell you."

• • •

At four minutes to eight Caitlin hurried into the
and ballroom and down the long, cordoned-off aisle
ward the flower-festooned stage.

"All right?" Alex asked as Caitlin slipped onto the
at beside him on the stage.

"Breathless," Caitlin murmured. "I've just had it
ocked out of me."

Alex frowned. "Is something wrong? I thought every-
ing was going pretty well. Where's Chelsea?"

"She'll be here soon." Caitlin looked out over the
ated crowd and lifted her hand in greeting as she saw
nathan sitting in the back of the huge high-ceilinged
cular room.

The first ten rows had been reserved for journalists,
otographers, and TV crews, and as Caitlin glanced at
e podium she saw at least thirty microphones set up
d waiting for Chelsea's launch speech. "I'd say we got
ough coverage."

"We're broadcasting live by satellite to seventy-two
untries." The string quartet in the back of the room
gan to play, and Alex checked his watch. "Where is
e? We're due to start."

"Don't worry. Chelsea never misses a cue."

He must have caught the hint of suppressed excite-
ent in her voice, because he turned to look at her.
aitlin, what the devil are—"

Her hand grasping his arm stopped him. "Here she
mes."

The music rose, and a whisper rustled through the
om as Chelsea Benedict started down the aisle to-
ard the stage.

She wore the silver-sequined thigh-length tunic Jean
rdot had created for her that made her look like a
ung knight in chain mail. She wore no jewelry, but

her long, gorgeous legs gleamed with every step and
wildly curly hair shimmered torch-bright beneath
lights. She looked neither left nor right, her eyes g
tered sapphire excitement, her face luminous with
tality, every step exuding a crackling energy that
like a crash of symbols.

She was electrifying.

Caitlin heard the stir that went through the audien
even though she couldn't take her eyes off Chelsea. "
show time," she murmured as she rose to her feet. S
felt a sudden pang as she said the phrase she had he
Chelsea use so many times before. She had learned
much from Chelsea. Six months earlier she would h
been terrified to face an audience of this caliber. N
she found herself perfectly at ease.

She went to the podium and spoke into the micr
phones. "Ladies and gentlemen, I'm Caitlin Vasaro an
thank you for coming tonight. We're here to introdu
a perfume that we believe will become unique in t
history of fragrance." Chelsea had almost reached t
stage and Caitlin met Chelsea's gaze as she started
the stairs. "To introduce you to our perfume we've ch
sen a woman as unique as the fragrance itself. So uniq
we've decided to designate her as sole spokespers
forever for our perfume." She saw Chelsea stop in sho
on the steps but continued. "We believe our perfu
will endure through the ages, but there will never
another spokesperson for it. As Vasaro is irreplaceab
so is Chelsea Benedict."

She stepped back and sat down again beside Alex.

"What the hell is happening?"

"You'll see."

As Chelsea reached the podium the applause rose.
Chelsea stood, back straight, head high, before t

dium and waited for the applause to die down. She
eared her throat, but her voice was still a little husky
hen she spoke. "You have no idea what an honor
aitlin Vasaro has just done me, but you will soon." Her
nds gripped the sides of the podium as she gazed out
the audience. "First things first." She took LeClerc's
ystal bottle from the podium before her and held it
. "Vasaro perfume. Quite simply, it's the most won-
rful perfume in the world. I will never wear anything
se as long as I live." She grimaced. "If I can get hold of
I should have insisted on a clause in my contract
aranteeing my own personal supply. You all know
hat happened at Vasaro, and we may not be seeing it
r a while." She paused. "And now I'd like to announce
y retirement as spokesperson for Vasaro."

Caitlin heard Alex's sharp intake of breath.

"I've told Caitlin Vasaro I'll return all fees paid and
ill no longer represent any company's product." A
urmur went through the room and Chelsea smiled.
urprised? You ain't seen nothin' yet." She squared her
oulders and flung out, "It's my privilege to announce
at the man I am to marry, Jonathan Andreas, will be
nning for the office of the president of the United
ates of America."

The audience exploded into an uproar, and Chelsea
aited for a moment before holding up her hand to
iiet them. "I know this isn't how things are supposed
be done." She grinned. "But what the hell? Why
eak my record?" As laughter swept through the room
er smile faded. "Quiet down now. I have something
se to say."

Silence.

"Jonathan Andreas is the finest, most honorable man
ve ever known." Her voice reverberated with sincerity.

"Being president is a pretty thankless job, and I do
know why he wants it." She paused. "No, that's not tr
I guess I do know why. He wants to help, he wants
mend, he wants to create something better out of t
chaos. He's that kind of a man. After the mess we'
made, I don't know if we deserve him, but he's going
be there for us." She paused. "If you don't blow it b
cause you think I'm not the kind of wife a preside
should have.

"Jonathan has been told by some very savvy poli
cians that marrying me will deep-six any chance he h
for the presidency. They've told him that you ca
count on the public to embrace a woman of my noto
ety, that you have to appeal to the lowest common (
nominator." She smiled crookedly. "I told him the sar
thing, but he won't listen to us. He loves me." S
leaned forward and her voice vibrated with urgen
"And he respects you. He respects your intelligence a
your judgment. He says the world has changed a
people want honesty more than pristine images. I gu
we'll have to see if he's right."

Chelsea's hands tightened on the edge of the podiu
"I'm a fairly well-known actress and I haven't had to a
dition for a role for a long time, but that's what I'm d
ing tonight. You have to know that what you see is wh
you'll get. I won't be a Nancy Reagan or Jackie Kenne
and I'm a world away from Barbara Bush. I can play t
lady of the manor, but I won't always be the perfect fi
lady. I have a temper and I'll make mistakes. I'll be t
frank and call a spade a spade when protocol will d
mand I call it a diamond in the rough."

She smiled. "But there's a plus side. You'll alwa
know where you are with me. I'm not stupid. I'm loy
I do my job." She stopped and tossed back her head.

.ve one other quality that's been under fire lately from
·ople for whom I care a great deal. It's been claimed
at I'm overprotective. Well, maybe I am, but that's
·t all bad. We can make it work for us. Because it
eans that once I consider you all my family, I'll pro-
·ct you too."

Chelsea's cheeks were flushed, and her eyes glowed
·illiantly as she looked challengingly out over the audi-
·ce. "That's all. Now it's up to you. Don't be stupid
·d blow your chance like I almost did. You may not
·er get another one like Jonathan Andreas."

She turned and walked away from the podium and
·wn the stairs.

The audience was on its feet and the noise level deaf-
·ing as she walked up the aisle toward Jonathan.

"My God!" Alex whispered.

"Yes." Caitlin's eyes were stinging with tears as she
·se to her feet, applauding with the crowd. "Will they
·ow it, Alex?"

Alex took her arm. "I have no idea." He started to
·ad her from the stage. "But no one can say it wasn't
·e hell of a campaign kickoff."

"I know it took a little emphasis off the perfume, but
·ouldn't refuse to let her do it."

"It doesn't matter." Alex grinned. "If they do make it
· the White House, Chelsea's speech will be broadcast
·r at least the next eight years. You can't buy this kind
· publicity."

Chelsea stopped before Jonathan and lifted her chin.
·suppose I should have told you I was going to do this.
·hope you haven't changed your mind about marrying
·e. It's too late now."

"Then I guess I'm caught."

"Do you think Jennings will be angry?"

"Furious."

"Do you care?"

"Hell, no. Why should I? I have you to protect me."

"That's right, you do. How lucky can you get?" S took his hand and pulled him toward the entran "Come on, we have a news conference with Alex a Caitlin and I want to check on Marisa first." She caug sight of Tyndale standing behind the barricade a stopped in midstride, lifting her chin defiantly. "I ho the show suited you, Tyndale. Are you going to vote my husband for president?"

"Undecided." The corners of Tyndale's lips indent with what might have been the faintest smile. "Bu might vote for you if you decide to run."

She blinked and then grinned at him. "Didn't y notice? I threw my hat in the ring. It's a team oper tion." She sailed past him, her arm slipping throu Jonathan's. She whispered, "You know, I believe I li him. How do you think he'd do as press secretary?"

He laughed. "You're already making appointments?"

But she had forgotten Tyndale and was frownin thoughtfully. "I think I'll phone my publicist and fi out if he can get us a spot on Carson and *Nightline* t morrow night. That way we'll have both the entertai ment and the news audience cornered. I figure if we c ignite enough interest and popularity to make us zoo up in the polls, the party will have to give you the nor ination." He was laughing and she tried to look at hi sternly. "I'm serious. We have to make this work for Twenty years from now I'm not going to have yo blaming me for robbing you of the presidency. They' not going to take away a job you want. We're going fight them."

"I'm sure we are." Jonathan leaned forward and kissed
r cheek. "And I can hardly wait."

There is no love like that snatched from beneath the
adow of the sword....
The words came back to Caitlin as she stood on the
l, looking down at the rose field below her.
The sword had fallen, devastating Vasaro, but through
it devastation she had found another love and other
endships that would endure through the years.
As Vasaro had endured.
Somehow she had still expected to smell smoke, but
ere was only the clean scent of earth. The land had
en cleared, the earth turned, and below her she could
: Jacques and the workers planting the cuttings they
d salvaged from the original bushes. In another row
her workers were planting two-foot bushes pur-
ased from nurseries.
Then she saw Alex kneeling in the dirt, frowning
th concentration as he planted a cutting. His appear-
ce reminded her of those first weeks at Vasaro. He
ore a blue chambray work shirt and faded jeans, his
rk hair held off his forehead by a blue and white ban-
nna.
He looked up and smiled as she started down the
l. Her pace quickened until she was almost running.
"You didn't leave a note," she said breathlessly as she
me to stand, looking down at him. "I woke up and you
ere gone. That's getting to be a bad habit with you."
"I thought you'd know where I was." He finished pat-
ig the earth around the cutting. "We'd done all we could
th the promotion. It was time to get to work here."
She fell to her knees, facing him. "Jonathan, Chelsea,
d Marisa are leaving for New York this afternoon."

"I know. I phoned Jonathan and Chelsea before I l
the hotel to say good-bye." Alex sat back on his he
and looked at her. "We may not see them for a while.

"Interpol called Jonathan just before I left the hot
The 'Mona Lisa' has been recovered."

He went still. "What?"

"The insurance people were contacted and a finde
fee negotiated two days ago. An exchange of cash t
the painting took place on one of the islands in t
Azores yesterday afternoon."

"What kind of finder's fee?"

"Five million dollars."

Alex gave a low whistle. "I suppose it was an anor
mous transaction."

"Yes, I guess they would have bargained with t
devil himself to get it back." Caitlin looked down, ni
bling at her lower lip. "I . . . I thought it might have be
Kemal."

His reply was noncommittal. "Negotiating with t
insurance companies is a lot cleaner and smarter th
trying to fence art objects that famous."

"But do you think it was Kemal?"

"I don't know." He reached out and lifted her chin
the arc of his fingers. "Accept it. We may never kno
The man who made that deal could have been the ca
tain of the Argosy."

She nodded. "But if the Wind Dancer shows up,
Jonathan is contacted about a deal . . . We'd know the
wouldn't we?"

Alex nodded. "I don't see how anyone else b
Kemal could have the Wind Dancer." He paused. "B
he also knew about the contents and he could par
those cures into an empire if he chose."

"If he's alive."

"Yes." His hand fell away from her face. "If he's alive."
"I asked Jonathan to let us know as soon as he heard
thing from the insurance company about the Wind
ncer."

"Good." He reached into his pocket. "I have some-
ng for you. I ordered it when I first got back to Nice,
t we were so busy, I didn't have time to give it to
1." He held up a pendant by its delicate gold chain
1 dangled it in front of her eyes. "I know it's not the
nd Dancer, but it's the best I could do."

An exquisite golden Pegasus with emerald eyes.

Memories rushed back to Caitlin of that twilight
1e long ago. "Jacques told you?"

He nodded. "I couldn't locate the one your father
ve you, so I had this one made. I know it won't mean
e same—"

"No, it's not the same." Sunlight glittered on the gold
she held it up to look at it. "It's more beautiful."

His gaze met hers. "And I'll never let anyone take it
ay from you. I'll never let anyone take anything from
u again."

"Then it means more too, doesn't it?" The Pegasus
mmered through a veil of tears as she lowered
r arm. "You didn't need to do this. I can't help hoping
e Wind Dancer isn't lost, but I don't need it any longer.
eeded the dream and we fulfilled that dream. Now
saro, a *new* Vasaro, is the dream." She sat back on her
els. "What's that big truck parked in the driveway?"

"Trees." Alex grinned. "Twenty-year-old orange trees.
gured we'd get a head start. I still want to be around
1en they become useful to us. Another truck comes
s afternoon with the rest of the rosebushes, and an
chitect will be here tomorrow for a consultation
out the new manor house. You can have any style you

like as long as I have my say about my study. I like sp
to move around."

"You're certainly looking ahead. I assume you
footing the bill? I can't afford all this."

He looked away from her and didn't speak for a m
ment. When he did, the words came awkwardly. "I
treat." Another silence. "I thought perhaps we co
come to an arrangement."

"An arrangement?"

"We could make a deal. I'd restore Vasaro for y
and maybe you'd let me stay around awhile."

She held her breath. "How long?"

"I don't know." He moved down the row and beg
overturning the earth with the spade. "What ab
starting off with forty or fifty years? After that w
renegotiate."

She let her breath out in a rush. "I thought y
didn't want roots."

"I told you once that everything changes. Is it a dea

" 'Give them what they want and they'll give y
what—' " She stopped as he swiftly lifted his head a
she saw his expression.

"Name anything in the world you want and I'll g
it," he said thickly. "If you'll just let me stay with you

"You will?" A luminous smile lit her face. "Then
be an idiot to refuse you, wouldn't I?"

"Yes."

She chuckled as she reached out and took his han
She laced her fingers through his own and the gold
Pegasus was caught between them. "Fifty years, y
say?"

"At least."

"Marriage?"

"If you don't mind."

"I don't mind." She paused, suddenly tense. "Do you
e me, Alex Karazov?"

"Of course," he said, surprised. "What else is this all
out?"

Her joyous laughter rang out over the rose field.

*There is no love like that snatched from beneath the
adow of the sword....*

Epilogue

The Wind Dancer was not returned to Jonath
Andreas.

During the next five years all the other works of
stolen by the Black Medina were redeemed by their
spective countries in exchange for staggeringly la
amounts of money in finder's fees.

Charles Barney was never apprehended for the m
der of Rod McMillan.

As far as could be determined, the *Argosy* and
crew had vanished from the seas.

Vasaro

Jack Kilon parked his gray Renault rental car on t
driveway at Vasaro, jumped out, and walked toward t
limousine that had drawn up ahead of him before the ste
of the brick manor house.

The chauffeur was helping Marisa Benedict from t
car as he reached the limousine, and she smiled at Ja
"You're going to like it here. It was once one of my f
vorite places in the whole world."

He already liked it here. He had grown up on a farm
North Carolina and he missed the sight and smell of
w growth. Being a Secret Serviceman for the presi-
ntial family had its perks, but he'd never liked living
big cities. Therefore when he had been assigned to
ard Marisa Benedict after her stepfather had won the
esidency he had found it a painless assignment. Her
b as a marine biologist in San Diego usually took him
away from Washington's political hotbeds, and be-
es, he genuinely liked the woman. She was always
easant, even chummy, and reminded him a little of
sister back in Bostic. "It's a beautiful place, Miss
nedict."

A faint shadow knitted Marisa's forehead as her gaze
ndered past the flowering lime trees lining the drive-
y to the road leading to the village. "It looks different
m the last time I was here."

Jack had been briefed about the attack on Vasaro
en he had been assigned to protect her. "No need to
rry this time, Miss Benedict. Nothing is going to hap-
n. When the president and your mother arrive to-
rrow, there will be enough security to stop an army."

"I know, Jack." She smiled again, that grave, sweet
ile she always gave him. "It just brings back memo-
s."

"Ah, you must be Marisa." A dark-haired young man
essed in a dazzling white suit had come out of the
use and was strolling down the steps toward them. "I
ve been expecting you. Caitlin and Alex have gone
o Grasse to arrange additional security and asked me
welcome you if you came before they got back. I am
is Delgado."

Jack stiffened and automatically took a step back and
the side to enable him to move quickly should it be-
me necessary. He had been briefed on everyone who

was supposed to be at Vasaro, and there was no I
Delgado on the list. "Just who are you, Mr. Delgado?"

"Secret Service?" Luis Delgado nodded approvin
"And very alert. You're quite right to question
Caitlin and Alex purposely didn't give you my na
when they furnished your organization with the l
I'm a surprise for the president."

"We don't like surprises."

"I assure you that the president will like this one
must get very dull in the White House at times."

"Why would additional security be needed?
manage pretty well on our own."

"Ah, I'm sure you do, but I'm very finicky about
luggage, and Alex indulged me by arranging it be pr
erly protected." He turned to the chauffeur. "Take
Benedict's bags into the house. The housekeeper
show you which room." He turned back to Marisa
chose it for you myself. I saw you in a yellow room,
diant with sunshine."

"Why, how kind of you."

He nodded. "I can be kind." His smile suddenly flash
in his olive-dark face. "I will always be kind to you."

Jack saw the arrested expression appear on Maris
face and felt a flutter of apprehension. Cripes, if no
ing worse, this bozo could be some kind of gigolo
confidence man and Chelsea Andreas would have
head if he let him near her daughter. He stepped f
ward. "I think we'd better check out the house bef
you go in, Ms. Benedict."

"By all means. And I'm sure you'll want to cont
your superiors and Alex and Caitlin about me. It wo
be remiss of you if you didn't." Luis Delgado to
Marisa's arm. "In the meantime, I will show
Benedict the rose field. It's in bloom now and the si
is breathtaking. I'll be sure to keep within your sight.

Before Jack could protest, they were strolling across the lush green front lawn toward the field in the distance. He muttered a curse and hurried to his car phone to patch through a call to Nice to Sam Gesler, his superior, who was handling the arrangements for the president's arrival the next day.

"A surprise package," he told Gesler grimly as he kept his eyes on Marisa and Delgado. "A man called Luis Delgado met us at Vasaro. Do we have anything on him?"

He heard Gesler rustling through papers. "No mention. What kind of profile?"

"Good-looking, dark, about thirty, two-thousand-dollar suit, smooth. Knows his way around the place. Doesn't seem to be evasive."

"It's possible he could be okay."

"Do you want to tell that to Chelsea Andreas?"

Gesler sighed. "You know better than that. We have to make sure damn quick. I'll see if I can check him out. I hate these hurry-up trips. The president gets one telephone call and he drops everything to run to France. What the hell could be that important?"

Jack had been wondering that himself. "Maybe a family emergency. Why else send his daughter here?"

"Damned if I know. Stay on Delgado. I'll get back to you."

Jack hung up the phone and hurried after Marisa and Luis Delgado.

Luis Delgado threw out his hand to indicate the crimson glory of the carpet of roses below them. "Is it not magnificent? Can you not *feel* the strength of renewal? Caitlin and Alex have done well."

"Yes." Her gaze wandered back to the road leading to the village.

"You are thinking about the man who died for you."

She stiffened and turned to face him. "You kno
about Peter?"

He smiled gently. "It was not your fault. A ma
chooses himself what is important enough for him t
die for."

How had he known? Even her mother had neve
guessed the guilt that had haunted her over the years.

He said, "I thought when Caitlin told me the stor
that there are few women extraordinary enough t
arouse that response in a man."

Marisa glanced at him curiously. "Alex and Caitli
wouldn't confide that story to just anyone. You must b
a very good friend, Mr. Delgado."

"Luis. Yes, very good, though we have not seen eac
other for a long time. I live on an island off the coast o
Chile and I don't get to Europe often."

"An island?"

He nodded. "You would be very interested in my is
land. I understand you're a marine biologist. I hav
funded a research laboratory on the north shore t
study dolphins. My group has been coming up wit
some amazing research lately. Perhaps you've heard o
the Delgado Institute?"

"You're *that* Delgado? I've read papers from some o
your people." Her face was alight with enthusiasm. "Yo
also funded the last Save the Dolphin campaign?"

He nodded. "My niece is very interested in the dol
phins as well. She would like to meet you."

"Did you bring her with you?"

"Not this trip. Melisande was involved in an experi
ment and I have personal business to conduct." H
stopped on the hill and looked out over the rose field
"It is time I married. I have brought a marriage settle
ment to buy a bride."

"Buy?" Marisa smiled. "Here? Surely, even in Sout

America, arranged marriages and settlements have gone out of fashion."

He shook his head. "The old ways still linger. Marriage settlements are important. They show good faith and a promise of fine treatment for a bride. The bigger the settlement, the stronger the promise." His gaze shifted from the field back to her face. "And I have brought her father a bride price richer than any man has ever given for any woman."

"Is that why you're so finicky about your luggage?" She frowned. "Good heavens, you didn't carry cash with you?"

"No."

She breathed a sigh of relief. "That's good. It's very dangerous to—"

"Not cash. A very special treasure."

"Jewels?"

"Oh, yes, there are jewels." He grinned. "Gold, emeralds, diamonds, pearls... and sixty or so pages of very interesting documents I've been working on for the last few years." His smile faded. "You do not ask me why it is necessary for me to give such a high settlement."

"It isn't my—" The devil with politeness. She wanted to know. "Why?"

"I will need it if her parents are to trust me. In the past I have not always been a good man." His next words were softly intense, as if he were trying to convince her. "But I have always tried to give good for good."

His forcefulness gave Marisa a strange sense of being swept away. What the devil was happening to her? She made herself ask lightly, "And have you chosen your bride?"

"Long ago. But it was necessary I wait to claim her. Circumstances were not of the best." He reached out

and tucked a strand of hair behind her ear. "Do you be
lieve in fate, Marisa?"

"I'm not sure."

"I believe in it." He made a face. "Though a man lik
me can twist it a bit to serve himself."

She smiled. "Then it's hardly fate if it can be twisted.

"You have a lovely smile." His gaze fastened on he
face, and she again felt that strange tingle of response
"But you should laugh more."

"I beg your pardon?"

"Do not worry. I will teach you. I will teach yo
many wonderful things."

She found herself staring with fascination into hi
glowing dark eyes. She whispered, "You will?"

"Oh, yes, I tell you the truth. It will happen. Trus
me." A gentle smile that still held a hint of mischief li
his face. "I have second sight."

Dear Reader,

If you've only read any of my recent suspense novel you'd probably be surprised to learn that I actually be gan my career writing historical romances. About te years ago I began thinking of writing a book centered o a magnificent ancient statue with mystical powers calle the Wind Dancer. But the more I thought about th book, the more complex the concept grew, and I realize it could not be contained in one book. It was soon clea this was to be a trilogy—the story of a family whose fat was intertwined with the Wind Dancer through the cen turies—and although they were love stories, they wer also filled with suspense and adventure. Each boo stands alone, but the Wind Dancer is central to th thread of suspense that runs through each of them.

You've just read the third book, *Reap the Wind*, whic as you know is a contemporary suspense novel.

The first book, entitled *The Wind Dancer*, is set i Renaissance Italy during the reign of the Borgias. It's story of ambition and revenge and the statue that sent th mighty Borgias spiraling downward. Interestingly enough Lorenzo, the Assassin, is probably my favorite of all th secondary characters I've ever created.

The second book, *Storm Winds*, takes place during th turbulence of the French Revolution and concerns th role played by the Wind Dancer in the rescue of a mem ber of the royal family. It's also a love story and follow the lifelong friendship between two women.

The characters came alive for me and the enthusiasm

or writing these books became obsession. I've always believed that some books are written with the mind and others with the heart. The Wind Dancer books involved both my mind and my heart, and the characters and mystique stayed with me long after I finished writing the trilogy. Even though a decade has passed since I finished *Reap the Wind*, I couldn't resist bringing the statue back to ignite the swirl of violence and intrigue in *Final Target*, one of my most recent thrillers.

After *Final Target* came out, I found myself inundated with mail from my readers asking about the history of the Wind Dancer, and I was delighted to be given the opportunity to explain this link to my earlier titles. I got to do what most authors never have a chance to do—go back and do a little reworking. What author can resist tweaking a bit when given the chance?

The books in the Wind Dancer trilogy are a little different from my more recent thrillers, because they're a bit more sensual. But if you want to find out more about the Wind Dancer, there's no better place to go. You can read more about the Wind Dancer's history in *The Wind Dancer* and *Storm Winds*. I think you'll like them. I'm very proud of these books. You can read an extract from each of them—just turn the page.

I guess it's obvious that I'm one of the lucky people who truly love their work. I'd like to thank you for reading my stories and making that work possible. I'll try never to disappoint you.

Iris Johansen

From *The Wind Dancer*...

Florence, Italy
March 3, 1503

"Stop, thief! Stop her! I've been robbed!"

Sanchia tore across the Mercato Vecchio, raced past the church and on down the street, jumping over an emaciated brown-and-white mongrel that devoured garbage scattered over the flagstones. She ducked under the outstretched arm of a leather-aproned cobbler, but his large hand caught the coarse woolen shawl covering her head. She jerked it from his grasp and kept running.

The merchant chasing her was plump, but still he was closing the distance between them, and Sanchia's heart slammed against her ribcage in a delirium of panic.

She was going to be caught.

Her hands would be chopped off at the wrists.

She would be thrown in the Stinche to be eaten by the rats.

Hot, agonizing pain shot through her left side. A stitch. She had to keep running.

What would Piero do? she wondered wildly. The others were older; they could find a way to survive. But Piero was only six. So many things could happen to so young a child....

"Grab her, you fools. The slut stole my purse!"

Dio, Sanchia thought, he sounded close. How could he

n so fast with all those rolls of fat hanging around his
iddle? She dodged around a wheelbarrow filled with
sh, turned the corner of the Canto di Vacchereccia, then
olted down an alley yawning between a goldsmith's
op and an apothecary.

Darkness. Twilight lay over the city but full darkness
igned in the alley.

Bright eyes glittered in the deep shadows at the base
f the small buildings.

Rats. Dozens of them!

She stopped short, involuntarily recoiling.

The stones beneath the thin soles of her shoes were
easy from the garbage thrown out there by shopkeep-
s. She need have no fear of the rats, though, while they
ere feasting on the garbage.

The smell of rotting food in the closeness of the alley
as overpowering. She swallowed, trying to fight down
e nausea caused as much from terror as the stench.

"Which way did she go?"

The merchant's voice was wheezing and sounded a
ttle farther away. Had she lost him when she darted
to the alley? She shrank back into the densely clotted
adows of the goldsmith's shop, her palms pressed flat
gainst the stone wall. Her breath was coming in harsh,
ainful gasps. Could he hear her? She tried to hold her
reath, but there was no breath to hold. *Cristo*, what if
e had heard her?

The cold, wet slime-covered wall chilled her back as it
enetrated the wool of her gown. Her muscles felt
aden, the blood frozen in her veins. She was suddenly
cutely conscious of the sharp, rough texture of the stone
all against her palms, but the sensation was almost
leasurable. Touch. What would she do without her
ands? How could she live? How would all of them live?

"This way, you stupid blunderer."

She stiffened. The voice was not that of the fat me
chant but one with which she was bitterly familiar. H
heart gave a wild leap of hope. The alley door of t
apothecary shop had opened, and even in the darkness s
recognized Caprino's slight, foppishly dressed silhouette

She darted the few yards separating them and almo
fell through the doorway into the shop. Her gaze flew
the front of the store, but the apprentice behind the sm
counter was scrupulously avoiding looking in her directio

"He's safe," Caprino said. "He does work for me."

Poison, Sanchia thought with a shiver, or perhaps t
strange white powders Caprino gave his whores.

Caprino slammed the door and held out his han
"The purse."

She fumbled beneath her shawl for the soft leath
pouch and then dropped it into his palm. She leane
back against the door, her knees shaking so badly sh
could barely stand upright.

"You were clumsy," Caprino said harshly. "I shou
have let that fat fool catch you. Next time I will."

She had to wait until she could speak without pantin
"There won't be a next time. I'm never going to do it agai

"You will," Caprino said coolly. "You're frightene
now, but it will pass. You'll forget the fear and rememb
only the money that buys bread. You're not usually th
clumsy. You may not come this close to being caught f
the next ten lifts."

"I'll find another way." Sanchia's hands clenched
her sides. "There has to be another way."

"You didn't think so when you came to me." Caprin
opened the door. "I have no more time for you. I hav
important business at Giulia's. Stay here for another fe
minutes before you go back to Giovanni's." The do
swung shut behind him.

He hadn't given Sanchia her share of the purse, she r

...zed dully. Trust Caprino to try to steal even the smallest ...urse, if given the opportunity. She would have to seek ...m out tomorrow and demand her portion. She had ...ouths to feed and Caprino was right about hunger being ...harp dagger that might goad even a saint into thieving.

But was hunger worth the risk of having her hands ...opped off?

Fresh panic clutched at her as a chilling memory re-...rned. Two months before she had seen a thief thrown ...t of Stinche Prison into the streets, his arms ending in ...eeding stumps. Since then the fear of that punishment ...d lived with her during the day and invaded her ...eams at night. She had tried and tried to think of an-...her way to earn money to feed them, all the while ...aring her frantic scheming would come to nought. ...here was no other way.

As there would be no other way the next time or the ...me after that. She would have to steal again just as ...aprino had predicted. But he was wrong about the ter-...r holding her in helpless thrall; it wasn't a thing of the ...oment.

She knew the fear would never go away again.

"Good evening, noble messeres, I have the honor to ...resent to you my greetings. I am Guido Caprino." ...aprino stood in the doorway and smiled ingratiatingly ... the two men sitting at the polished table across the ...amber. "The enchanting Madonna Giulia assured me I ...uld be of some slight service to you."

He carefully kept a bland expression on his face as he ...praised the two men. The older had to be Lorenzo ...asaro, he decided. His high cheekbones and deepset eyes ...atched the description Giulia had given him of the ...an—and besides, Caprino's own instincts responded to ...e shadowy aura of menace surrounding him. The man

was lean, faultlessly elegant in his fashionably slashed bla
doublet, and clearly more dangerous than his companic
He gazed at the other man and felt a ripple of distaste. F
was so *male*. Lionello Andreas might stand well over
feet, Caprino surmised, and he was too big-boned to h
claim to elegance no matter how richly he was garbe
Now, dressed only in gray hose and a loose white shirt,
appeared to be exactly what Caprino had expected: a b
barian warrior with more brawn than brains; he was n
wearing a weapon, not even a dagger. Andreas might be t
lord of Mandara, but Caprino would wager it was Vasa
who was the shrewd power behind the scenes there.

"Come in, Messer Caprino." Andreas picked up tl
silver goblet on the table in front of him and waved it
a cushioned chair beside the window before raising it
his lips. "Be seated."

The arrogant bastard hadn't bothered to stand up
greet him properly, Caprino thought as he smiled p
litely and crossed the room to take the seat indicate
No doubt Andreas did not think him worthy of respec
He would soon learn differently.

Lorenzo Vasaro rose and moved with silent grace
lean against the wall to the left of the window. He fold
his arms across his chest and gazed blandly at Caprino

A good move. Caprino's respect for Vasaro rose ev
higher. His action had placed Caprino between Vasa
and Andreas. Caprino was tempted to address Vasaro
the worthier of the two but turned instead to Andreas.
am overjoyed to accommodate any friends of Madon
Giulia. What is your pleasure?"

"I need a thief." Andreas leaned back in his chair a
studied Caprino with narrowed eyes.

Caprino met his eyes and continued to smile politely. '
will be my pleasure to provide you with the finest thief
all of Florence, Your Magnificence. Only a thief, or must l

ossess other talents? An assassin, perhaps? I have a few as-
ciates who have talents in that direction, but no one
ith the extraordinary skills of Messer Vasaro."

Andreas stiffened. "You know of Vasaro?"

"How could I not?" Caprino remained sitting forward
his chair, one graceful hand resting with seeming ca-
ualness on the jeweled hilt of his dagger. "He shines in
e firmament like a bright star, dazzling all who see
m. Is it any wonder I should recognize him?"

"Not at all." Andreas cast an amused glance at Vasaro,
ho was still gazing at Caprino with no expression. "Do
ou hear that, Lorenzo? A star, by all that's holy. Aren't
ou going to thank the kind gentleman?"

Lorenzo inclined his head in acknowledgment.

"No thanks are needed," Caprino said quickly. "I merely
ve homage where homage was due. It was foolish of me
suggest you might need an assassin when Messer
asaro is in your service. Why should you need any—"

"As you say, I need no assassin," Andreas interrupted
ith sudden impatience. "I need a thief with hands as
vift and sure as an arrow drawn by a master bowman
d a touch as delicate as the kiss of a butterfly."

"There are many thieves in Florence," Caprino said
oughtfully. "I myself have trained an honored few."

"So I've been informed." Andreas's lips twisted in a
ynical smile. "No doubt you've also tutored many indi-
iduals in my friend Lorenzo's former profession."

Caprino shrugged. "One or two. But to be an assassin re-
uires a certain fortitude not found in every man. A thief
different. Easier. Not as profitable but . . ." He trailed off.
How long would you need this thief, my lord Andreas?"

Andreas went still. "You know me also?" His voice was
angerously soft. "Does my name, too, shine in the firma-
ent?"

Caprino's hand tightened on the hilt of his dagger. He

could feel a bead of moisture dampen his temple as
realized his mistake. He had judged Vasaro to be t
threat. A stupid error. In his experience most soldiers, ev
condottieri, had none of the skill and subtlety Caprino a
mired. But he shouldn't have let his contempt for the pr
fession overshadow his judgment of the man. No, that w
not entirely true, Caprino admitted reluctantly. His i
stinctive revulsion at Andreas's overpowering virility h
also contributed to the blunder by keeping him from a s
rious study of the man. Now he discerned the intelligen
as well as cynicism, in Andreas's brilliant dark eyes whi
were fully as merciless as those of Vasaro. Caprino mo
tened his lower lip with his tongue. "Your fame has spre
over all Italy, my lord. An illustrious condottiere such
yourself must expect to be recognized and—" Capri
broke off. "I had no idea your visit to our city was in secre
If you wish to go unrecognized, then it goes without sa
ing that I never have seen your face, never heard the sou
of your voice, never even heard your name pronounced.

"And who did pronounce my name to you?" Andre
asked silkily. "And on what subject? I asked Giulia to te
no one I was in Florence."

"You know how careless women can be, *Magnific*
When Madonna Giulia summoned me here, she me
tioned your name but nothing else. I swear this, my lo
Andreas. Would the Madonna have sent for me if
wasn't a man of discretion and honor?"

"Lorenzo?" Andreas's gaze never left Caprino's face

Vasaro's voice was hoarse and scratchy as a woode
coffin pulled over flagstones. "He will betray you for
price high enough. Shall I dispose of him?" Loren
asked as casually as if he'd inquired about throwing o
the dregs of the wine in Andreas's cup.

Caprino leaned forward in his chair, prepared
spring, his dagger at the ready for a—

"I think not," Andreas said. "He doesn't know enough hurt me, and I'd find it inconvenient to search out an-her procurer."

"A wise decision." Caprino's grasp on his dagger re-xed. "A man should always keep the long view in mind. ow about this thief?"

"Just this moment I have thought of a quality he must ossess," Andreas said, looking down at his heavy leather untlets on the table. "I must own him."

"Own?"

Andreas's long, broad index finger rubbed at the brass eting of the gauntlet. "He must be mine body and ul. I'll not have him running back to you with tales u can sell to the highest bidder." Andreas smiled. "Of urse, I could have him removed after he finishes his sk, but I dislike rewarding good work in that fashion. ot an intelligent way to proceed."

"I can see that." Caprino's uneasy gaze darted to asaro. Rumor had it that Vasaro had accepted service ith Andreas when the condottiere was a boy of seven-en. How had Andreas managed to hold such a skilled sassin all these years? Did he own *him* body and soul as wished to own the thief? It was something to ponder, r who but Satan was capable of possessing a demon? uch men aren't easy to find. How could I—"

"You must know ways." Andreas pulled a purse from s belt and tossed it on the table to Caprino. "Greed, re-nge, a woman. We both know the weapons to bind a an. Use them."

Caprino opened the pouch and counted the ducats. fair price."

"A princely sum for one insignificant thief, as well you now, but a small price for the soul of a human being."

Caprino smiled. "I'm sure you'll discover shortly hether or not that is so."

From *Storm Winds*...

Ile du Lion, France
June 10, 1787

Jean Marc Andreas strode around the pedestal, stud
ing the statue from every angle. The jewel-encrust
Pegasus was superb.

From its flying mane to the exquisite detail of the go
filigree clouds on which the horse danced, it was a ma
terful piece of work.

"You've done well, Desedero." Andreas said. "It's perfec

The sculptor whom some called a mere goldsmi
shook his head. "You're wrong, Monsieur. I've failed."

"Nonsense. This copy is identical to the Wind Dancer
it not?"

"It is as close a copy as could be made, even to the p
culiar cut of the facets of the jewels," Desedero said. "I h
to journey to India to locate emeralds large and perfe
enough to use as the eyes of the Wind Dancer and spe
over a year crafting the body of the statue."

"And the inscription engraved on the base?"

Desedero shrugged. "I reproduced the markings wi
great precision, but since the script is indecipherable th
is a minor point, I believe."

"Nothing is minor. My father knows the Wind Danc
in its every detail," Andreas said dryly. "I paid you four m

ion livres to duplicate the Wind Dancer—and I always get my money's worth."

Desedero knew those words to be true. Jean Marc Andreas was a young man, no more than twenty and five, but he had established himself as a formidable force in the world of finance since taking over the reins of the Andreas shipping and banking empire three years before from his ailing father. He was reputed to be both brilliant and ruthless. Desedero had found him exceptionally demanding, yet he did not resent Andreas. Perhaps it was because the young man's commission challenged the artist in him. Certainly Andreas's desperation to please his father was touching. Desedero had loved his own father very much and understood such deep and profound affection. He was much impressed by Jean Marc Andreas's wholehearted zeal for replicating the Wind Dancer to please his ill and aging father.

"I regret to say I do not believe you have gotten your money's worth this time, Monsieur Andreas."

"Don't say such a thing, sir." A muscle jerked in Andreas's jaw. "You have succeeded. *We've* succeeded. My father will never know the difference between this Wind Dancer and the one at Versailles."

Desedero shook his head. "Tell me, have you ever seen the real Wind Dancer?"

"No, I've never visited Versailles."

Desedero's gaze returned to the statue on the pedestal. "I remember vividly the first time I saw it some forty-two years ago. I was only a lad of ten and my father took me to Versailles to see the treasures that were dazzling the world. I saw the Hall of Mirrors." He paused. "And I saw the Wind Dancer. What an experience. When you walked into my studio some year and a half ago with your offer of a commission to create a copy of the Wind Dancer, I could not pass it by. To replicate the Wind Dancer would have been sublime."

"And you've done it."

"You don't understand. Had you ever seen the origina you would know the difference instantly. The Win Dancer has..." He searched for a word. "Presence. On cannot look away from it. It captures, it holds"—he smile crookedly—"as it's held me for these forty-two years."

"And my father," Andreas whispered. "He saw it once a a young man and has wanted it ever since." He turne away. "And by God, he'll have it. She took everything fror him, but he *shall* have the Wind Dancer."

Desedero discreetly ignored the last remark, though h was well aware of the lady to whom Andreas referre Charlotte, Denis Andreas's wife, Jean Marc's stepmothe had been dead over five years. Still the stories of her gree and treachery were much passed about.

Sighing, Desedero shook his head. "You have only *copy* of the Wind Dancer to give to your father."

"There's no difference." A hint of desperation colore Andreas's voice. "My father will never see the two statue side by side. He'll think he has the Wind Dancer until th day he—" He broke off, his lips suddenly pinched.

"Your father is worse?" Desedero asked gently.

"Yes, the physicians think he has no more than si months to live. He's begun to cough blood." He tried t smile. "So it's fortunate you have finished the statue an could bring it now to the Ile du Lion. Yes?"

Desedero had an impulse to reach out and touch hin in comfort, but he knew Andreas was not a man who coul accept such a gesture, so he merely said, "Very fortunate."

"Sit down." Andreas picked up the statue and started towar the door of the salon. "I'll take this to my father in his stud That's where he keeps all the things he treasures most. Then I' return and tell you how wrong you were about your work

"I hope I'm wrong," Desedero said with a shrug "Perhaps only the eye of an artist can perceive the differ ence." He sat down in the straight chair his patron had in icated and stretched out his short legs. "Don't hurry, Monsieur. You have many beautiful objects here for me to study. Is that a Botticelli on the far wall?"

"Yes. My father purchased it several years ago. He much admires the Italian masters." Andreas moved toward the door, carefully cradling the statue in his arms. "I'll send a servant with wine, Signor Desedero."

The door closed behind him and Desedero leaned back in his chair, gazing blindly at the Botticelli. Perhaps the old man was too ill to detect the fraud being thrust upon him. Whole and well, he would have seen it instantly, Desedero realized, because everything in this house revealed Denis Andreas's exquisite sensitivity and love of beauty. Such a man would have been as helplessly entranced with the Wind Dancer as Desedero always had been. Sometimes his own memories of his first visit to Versailles were bathed in mist from which only the Wind Dancer emerged clearly.

He hoped for Jean Marc Andreas's sake that his father's memories had dimmed along with his sight.

Jean Marc opened the door of the library, and beauty and serenity flowed over him. This room was both haven and treasure house for his father. A fine Savonnerie carpet in delicate shades of rose, ivory, and beige stretched across the highly polished parquet floor, and a Gobelin tapestry depicting the four seasons covered one wall. Splendid furniture crafted by Jacobs and Boulard was placed for beauty—and comfort—in the room. A fragile crystal swan rested on a cupboard of rosewood and Chinese lacquer marquetry. The desk, wrought in mahogany, ebony, and gilded bronze with mother-of-pearl inserts, might have been the focal point of the room if it had not been for the portrait of Charlotte Andreas. It was dramatically framed and placed over a fireplace whose mantel of Pyrenees marble drew the eye.

Denis Andreas always complained of the cold these days

and, although it was the end of June, a fire burned in the hearth. He sat in a huge crimson brocade-cushioned arm chair, reading before the fire, his slippered feet resting on matching footstool.

Jean Marc braced himself, then stepped into the room and closed the door. "I've brought you a gift."

His father looked up with a smile that froze on his lips as he looked at the statue in Jean Marc's arms. "I see you have."

Jean Marc strode over to the table beside his father's chair and set the statue carefully on the malachite surface. He could feel tension coiling painfully in his every muscle as his father gazed at the Pegasus. He forced a smile. "Well do say something, sir. Aren't you pleased with me? It was far from easy to persuade King Louis to part with the statue. Bardot has virtually lived at court this past year waiting for the opportunity to pounce."

"You must have paid a good deal for it." Denis Andreas reached out and touched a filigree wing with a gentle finger.

His father's hands had always been delicate-looking, the hands of an artist, Jean Marc thought. But now they were nearly transparent, the protruding veins poignantly emphasizing their frailty. He quickly looked from those scrawny hands to his father's face. His face was also thin, the cheeks hollowed, but his eyes still held the gentleness and wonder they always had.

"I paid no more than we could afford." Jean Marc sat down on the chair across from his father. "And Louis needed the livres to pay the American war debt." At least that was true enough. Louis's aid to the American revolutionaries along with his other extravagant expenditures had set France tottering on the edge of bankruptcy. "Where should we put it? I thought a white Carrara marble pedestal by the window. The sunlight shining on the gold and emeralds would make it come alive."

"The Wind Dancer *is* alive," his father said gently. "All eauty lives, Jean Marc."

"By the window then?"

"No."

"Where?"

His father's gaze shifted to Jean Marc's face. "You dn't have to do this." He smiled. "But it fills me with joy at you did."

"What's a few million livres?" Jean Marc asked lightly. ou wanted it."

"No, I have it." Denis Andreas tapped the center of his rehead with his index finger. "Here. I didn't need this lendid imitation, my son."

Jean Marc went still. "Imitation?"

His father looked again at the statue. "A glorious imita-on. Who did it? Balzar?"

Jean Marc was silent a moment before he said hoarsely, Desedero."

"Ah, a magnificent sculptor when working in gold. I'm rprised he accepted the commission."

Frustration and despair rose in Jean Marc until he could arcely bear it. "He was afraid you would recognize the ifference but I felt I had no choice. I offered the king nough to buy a thousand statues, but Bardot reported aat Louis wouldn't consider selling the Wind Dancer at ny price. According to His Majesty, the queen has a par-cular fondness for it." His hands closed tightly on the rms of the chair. "But, dammit, it's the *same*."

Denis Andreas shook his head. "It's a very good copy. ut, my son, the Wind Dancer is . . ." He shrugged. "I think has a soul."

"Mother of God, it's only a statue!"

"I can't explain. The Wind Dancer has seen so many enturies pass, seen so many members of our family born nto the world, live out their lives . . . and die. Perhaps it has come to be much more than an object, Jean Marc. Perhaps it has become . . . a dream."

"I failed you."

"No." His father shook his head. "It was a splendid gesture, a loving gesture."

"I failed you. It hurt me to know you couldn't have the one thing you so wished—" Jean Marc broke off and attempted to steady his voice. "I wanted to give something to you, something that you'd always wanted."

"You *have* given me something. Don't you see?"

"I've given you disappointment and chicanery and God knows you've had enough of both in your life." Denis flinched and Jean Marc's lips twisted. "You see, even I hurt you."

"You've always demanded too much of yourself. You've been a good and loyal son." He looked Jean Marc in the eye. "And I've had a good life. I've been fortunate enough to have the means to surround myself with treasures, and I have a son who loves me enough to try to deceive me ever so sweetly." He nodded at the statue. "And now why don't you take that lovely thing out to the salon and find a place to show it to advantage."

"You don't want it in here?"

Denis shook his head. "Looking at it would disturb the fine and fragile fabric of the dream." His gaze drifted to the portrait of Charlotte Andreas over the fireplace. "You never understood why I did it, did you? You never understood about dreams."

Looking intently at his father, Jean Marc felt pain and sorrow roll over him in a relentless tide. "No, I suppose I didn't."

"That hurt you. It shouldn't." He once again opened the leather-bound volume he had closed when Jean Marc came into the study. "There must always be a balance between the dreamers and the realists. In this world strength may serve a man far better than dreams."

Jean Marc stood up and moved toward the table on which he had set the statue. "I'll just get this out of your

ay. It's almost time for your medicine. You'll be sure to
remember to take it?"

Denis nodded, his gaze on the page of his book. "You
must do something about Catherine, Jean Marc."

"Catherine?"

"She's been a joy to me, but she's only a child of three
and ten. She shouldn't be here when it happens."

Jean Marc opened his mouth to speak, then closed it
abruptly. It was the first time his father had indicated he
knew the end was near.

"Please do something about our Catherine, Jean Marc."

"I will. I promise you," Jean Marc said thickly.

"Good." Denis looked up. "I'm reading Sanchia's journal, about old Lorenzo Vasaro and his Caterina."

"Again?" Jean Marc picked up the statue and carried it
toward the door. "You must have read those old family
journals a hundred times."

"More. I never tire of them." His father paused and
smiled. "Ah, our ancestor believed in dreams, my son."

With effort Jean Marc smiled. "Like you." He opened
the door. "I don't have to return to Marseilles until evening.
Would you like to have dinner on the terrace? The fresh air
and sunshine will be good for you."

But Denis was once more deeply absorbed in the journal and didn't answer.

Jean Marc closed the door and stood a moment, fighting the agony he felt. His father's last remarks shouldn't
have hurt him, for they were true. He was no dreamer; he
was a man of action.

His hand clenched on the base of the statue. Then he
squared his shoulders. The pain was fading. Just as he had
known it would. Just as it had so many times before. He
strode across the wide foyer and threw open the door to
the salon.

Desedero's gaze was searching. "He knew?"

"Yes." Jean Marc set the statue back on the pedestal. "I
have my agent in Marseilles give you a letter of credit to o
bank in Venice for the remainder of the money I owe you

"I don't wish any more money," Desedero said. "
cheated you."

"Nonsense. You did what you were paid to do." Je
Marc's smile was filled with irony. "You were given n
livres to create a statue, not a dream."

"Ah, yes." Desedero nodded in understanding. "T
dream..."

"Well, I'm only a man of business who doesn't unde
stand these idealistic vagaries. It appears a duplicate wor
do, so I will have to get the Wind Dancer for him."

"What will you do?"

"What I should have done in the beginning. Go
Versailles myself and find a way to persuade the queen
sell the Wind Dancer. I didn't want to leave my fath
when—" He broke off, his hands again slowly clenching.
knew he didn't have much time left."

"But how can you expect to succeed when she's clear
so determined to keep it?" Desedero asked gently.

"Information." Jean Marc's lips twisted in a cynical smi
"I'll find out what she most desires and give it to her in e
change for the statue. I'll take lodgings in an inn near th
palace and before two weeks are gone I'll know more abo
the court and Her Majesty than King Louis does himse
even if I have to bribe every groom and maid in the palace

Desedero gestured to the statue on the pedestal. "A
this?"

Jean Marc avoided looking at the Pegasus as he stroc
to the door. "I never want to see it again. You may sell o
the jewels and melt it down." He jerked open the doc
"God knows, I may need the additional gold to temp
Louis into selling the Wind Dancer."

The door slammed behind him.